PATH ⚙ OF THE
TITANS

BOOK 2 SYSTEM EXPANSION

A LITRPG EPIC FANTASY
TIMOTHY MCGOWEN

PATH OF THE TITANS - SYSTEM EXPANSION

A LITRPG EPIC FANTASY

PATH OF THE TITANS
BOOK 2

TIMOTHY MCGOWEN

ILLUSTRATED BY
CHRISTINA P. MYRVOLD

EDITED BY
CANDACE MORRIS

RISING TOWER BOOKS

Fantasy / LitRPG / Gamelit

OTHER BOOKS BY THE AUTHOR

Haven Chronicles

Haven Chronicles: Eldritch Knight

Short Stories/Novellas

Dead Man's Bounty

Exiled Jahk

Last Born of Ki'darth

Reincarnation: A Litrpg/Gamelit Trilogy

Rebellion: A Litrpg/Gamelit Trilogy

Retribution: A Litrpg/Gamelit Trilogy

Order & Chaos

Arcane Knight Book 1: An Epic LITRPG Fantasy

Arcane Knight Book 2: An Epic LITRPG Fantasy

Arcane Knight Book 3: An Epic LITRPG Fantasy

Arcane Knight Book 4: An Epic LITRPG Fantasy

Arcane Knight Book 5: An Epic LITRPG Fantasy

The Elemental Realms

Nexus Guardian Book 1: A Fantasy LitRPG Adventure

Nexus Guardian Book 2: A Fantasy LitRPG Adventure

System Expansion, Book 2

Path of the Titans

Ebook ISBN: 978-1-956179-39-2

Paperback ISBN: 978-1-956179-40-8

Hardback ISBN: 978-1-956179-41-5

First Edition: March 2024

Published By: Rising Tower Books

Publisher Website: www.RisingTowerBooks.com

Author Site: AuthorTimothyMcGowen.com

REVIEWS ARE IMPORTANT

Every review matters, get your voice heard. Follow me on Amazon to get informed when my next book is released!

https://www.amazon.com/stores/Timothy-McGowen/author/B087QTTRJK

Join my Patreon for early Chapters!

https://www.patreon.com/TimothyMcGowen

Join my Facebook group and discuss the books

https://www.facebook.com/groups/234653175151521/

SPECIAL THANKS

I wanted to give a special thanks to those that helped bring this book to its current state.

Candace Morris - Editor and Super Hero.

Dantas Neto, Sean Hall, Hugo Morais. (Elandar) - Proofer

I dedicate this book to my fans. Without your loyalty and dedication I'd never be able to craft so many wonderful stories.

CONTENTS

CHAPTER 1
LOST

-Starting Knox Stats-
-Personal Status-
-Name: Knox-
-Level: 19 (E Rank, Tier 9)-
-Essence To Next Level: 3,201/4,700-
-Health: Fair Tier 9-
-Mana: Fair Tier 9-
-Stamina: Fair Tier 9-
-Mind: 87-
-Body: 87-
-Spirit: 87-

"I'm not lost," Knox repeated for the fifth time. "I just don't know exactly where we are, but I can sense our destination."

Night rolled in hard, filled with cold rain and the promise of snow if the temperature continued to drop, but Knox wasn't worried about that just yet. No, right now he was more worried about the distant yet faint feeling of the Titan Complex. Why was it that he could only barely feel it? Why wasn't it a blazing beacon as it had been before?

His thoughts immediately turned to the three pirate golems he'd left with Mic and wondered if perhaps that was a mistake. His footsteps sloshed water about as he walked, his thoughts as dreary as the current weather.

"What are the chances they've messed something up without me being there to keep them in line?" He questioned the air around him in a muttering tone. Dernal seemed to hear him well enough and grunted in response.

"Hhrmm," he said with his usual verbal affinity.

Dernal was the type of man who had few words to say, but when he spoke you listened. Knox could tell that Dernal was working himself up to speak, a chore he didn't much enjoy, so he fell into silence and let the old Adventurer get his words together.

After a time, Dernal put a hand on Knox's shoulder and spoke.

"How much further?" Dernal asked. Knox's connection with the Titan Complex was something visceral and hard to define, but he knew one thing for certain, they were getting closer. But would it be fast enough?

Understanding the implied question within the question, Knox chose to answer the unspoken question first.

Letting out a deep sigh and feeling thoroughly soaked through, Knox said, "If the rain continues, I think we will lose the Serpent Dragon's scent before we reach the Titan Complex. If that happens, we will have a fight on our hands and we will lose lives."

"Hhrmm," Dernal said in response to their dire situation.

Then, conjuring up more words than he typically liked to say in a day, Dernal continued to share his thoughts with Knox.

"And will this Titan Complex truly be a safe haven for these people? Don't just nod—convince me." Dernal's usually composed manner of speaking grew hot, surprising Knox. "You are certain that it will be safe; we have women and children that who can't defend themselves."

Knox leveled his gaze on Dernal and looked him straight in the eyes, not wavering in the slightest as he spoke with confidence.

"It is a safe haven away from the dangers of the world," Knox said. Upon further reflection, he added, "Our people are strong and resilient. You don't live this far out without growing some bark on your skin. There will be dangers, and some people might even die, but trust me when I say this is the safest place within a hundred miles."

Knox's thoughts turned to the Guild Charterhouse and the strange activity that had occurred there during his last visit. He wondered if Garrick was well and pondered the mysteries awaiting at the Guild Charterhouse. Then his mind shifted to the Mire Gloom Dungeon Town and its slow rebuilding. Surely, they were safe now that he had taken care of the A Ranked Serpent Dragon with the help of Dernal and the mysterious Aetex.

The thought of Aetex had him wondering about the whereabouts of the mysterious B Ranked hero. He'd met the man when saving a group from captivity, but since their meeting, he'd acted as if he knew Knox all along and was sent to aid him on some grand mission. Everything about the man spoke of heroism and grandiose heroic moments. Even the way he'd left at their last meeting, flying off into the distance, was over the top.

Sighing, Knox nodded, reassuring Dernal and himself at the same time. Yes, The Titan Complex—he'd need to figure out a proper name for it eventually—would be the safest place for his friends, family, and the townspeople.

Dernal let the conversation slide back into silence as dark thoughts weighed on Knox when contemplating his family. As far as he knew, he had only one living family member left: his father, Askar Trelling. The man was the living embodiment of sloth and wrath. But something he'd said during their last conversation echoed in his mind.

"Just like your mother," Askar had said, his words angry and stern.

What had he meant? Knox knew so precious little about his

mother, but it had been her influences that led him to where he was today. Her precious journals, a mix between research and random ramblings, gave Knox insight into the woman she might have been—keen and intelligent.

They continued to walk in silence through the rain and the muck, with no monsters yet daring to challenge the powerful scent of the Serpent Dragon that lay heavily on Dernal and Knox. However, thoughts of his mother wouldn't leave him be, and in time, he found himself walking closer to where his father trudged through the mud.

Knox found his father walking beside a wagon that slowly carved a path through the muddy terrain. He carried a heavy load, and once more, Knox was surprised to see him doing more than he'd ever seen him do since his injury. Since the woodcutting incident that deprived him of his arm, he'd always blamed others and stewed in his own misery.

But now, seeing him working hard to help, sweat glistening on his forehead as he pushed himself, Knox couldn't help but feel a small sense of pride in his father. Of course, it was all shattered the moment his father saw him, cursing and picking up his pace.

There was no pleasing this man. Knox had become a being of myth and legend, a Titan, or at least a Titan Born, and it still wasn't enough to impress his father.

Picking up his own pace and wiping sweat from his brow, Knox hurried after his father. He got another 'look' for his trouble, but he ignored it, choosing instead to just walk beside his father for a time.

In the heavy silence that lingered between them, filled with unspoken grief and anger, Knox chose to let it all slip away as they walked. After a time, Askar slowed to a more manageable pace—

they'd very nearly reached the front of the caravan by this point. Knox could see Murdoch leading the way on a once-majestic-looking horse that was now covered in mud and muck, same as everyone else.

For what it was worth, Murdoch had somehow managed to keep himself mostly clean, if not extremely wet. Knox slowed his pace to match his father's as he thought about his friend. As far as he'd been told, Murdoch's father had died in the attacks and now Murdoch took the position as head of the village.

He was a bit young still, but he had the talent for it, and a few speeches had been all it took to get the rest of the town in on the idea. It was fine with Knox as well, since he had no plans on being some great leader. It was enough that he was expected to be this Titan of Light and endure all the responsibility that came with it. He'd happily given over any sense of leadership to Murdoch when the chance came, much to Dernal's chagrin.

It was an odd sight, seeing Dernal express any emotion really, but the slight disappointment in his eyes was hard to miss when Knox passed over the buck to Murdoch. What had he expected of him anyways? He wanted to be an Adventurer and that was still his primary motivation.

Like his mother before him, he wanted to discover new things, study magic and its many mysteries, maybe even create new magic himself one day. It was while his thoughts traveled back to his mother that words finally escaped his lips to his father.

"Why don't you speak of her?" Knox asked, his words ringing out clear despite the rain and sound of travel all around them.

A long silence followed and for once in his life, he thought his father might actually be considering speaking about her. However, all it took was a single look at the angry face and heaving chest of his father to tell him that wasn't what was holding his tongue.

Despite only having one arm, his father was an imposing figure, much more than he had been months earlier. Most of his belly had gone away, likely due to shortening in rations and the daily experience of working all day long. His muscles on his one good arm bulged and Knox was sure that Askar was about to throw down his pack, ruining whatever rations were being stored in the thick burlap material.

But once more, he was surprised by his father's resilience. Eyes set forward and a scowl on his lips, Askar continued to walk in silence. This being the longest his father had gone without slinging an insult, Knox began to worry that perhaps something had gotten to him.

But there was no sign of the black goo or the dead eyes that came with possession, though it did remind him of how Garrick had looked back at the Guild Charterhouse. The sudden realization that the Guild Charterhouse might be in danger did nothing to hamper the frustration he was feeling with his father.

"Damnit, father!" Knox said, the words spilling out before he could stop himself.

"Don't call me that, you little runt!" Askar said, finally breaking the silence. There was pure malice in his voice, and the fury of it caught Knox off guard. But what surprised Knox most of all was what his father had said. What did he mean by that? Why shouldn't he call him father? Had he excused himself from that duty as well, or did he mean something else?

"What do you mean?" Knox asked, swallowing hard.

There was a weight in the air between them and it was as if someone had paused all of Knox's senses other than his ability to hear the words that came next.

"What I said," Askar replied, his voice low and rumbling. "I've lost it all because of her—my own son lost." As he spoke, he shook his head, and Knox noticed something unusual, thanks to his special sense, which remained vigilant over his surroundings at almost all times.

A sparkle of something radiated around Askar, almost as if he had an aura himself—but that was impossible. Only Adventurers had auras. There was even a hint of color in it, but it came and went so fast that he couldn't tell what it had been.

"You haven't lost me," Knox said, feeling a moment of weakness for his father and the burdens he carried. "Why won't you speak of her? Tell me stories of my mother, how you met, what she was like, *anything*."

Askar walked in silence, rain soaking him to the bone, a blank expression on his face. Knox could tell that Askar had noticed the slip-up as well, and as they continued to walk in silence, Knox became sure of something. Askar was not willing to say anything else lest he lose all control of himself and reveal more than he wished. There was more to his father than he knew, and somehow, he would find out what he was hiding.

The caravan was more than a day's journey away from the Titan Complex, that much Knox was sure of, but he wished he could gauge the distance more accurately. Many people were relying on him to get them to safety. They'd stopped for the night, planning to rest for four hours, just long enough for the most exhausted to get some sleep. Though, Knox wasn't among those seeking to rest.

His inner Strength and Stamina were now far above that of a normal human. Knox was confident that he could sprint the entire way to the complex and only be slightly winded. The idea tempted him, but he couldn't—no, he *wouldn't*—leave his people behind with no true protection. Despite Dernal's power, he wouldn't be a match for the beasts that would fall upon them once the scent finally left them.

Would I even be a match? Knox wondered, but he pushed those thoughts away as well, preferring his analytical mind. What-ifs were fine; in fact, he used them plenty of the time to work out mysteries of magic and life. However, some what-ifs could be dangerous, such as: what if they didn't make it?

So, say that we didn't make it, Knox thought, *then what?* He had unparalleled power at his disposal, but protecting those around him was difficult at best, impossible at worst—power, or no. But he wasn't alone. He had friends that, while not very powerful, were loyal and ready to lay down their lives to protect each other. He found his friends at a fire with Murdoch regaling them of a tale that was all too familiar.

"And then, I appeared with sword drawn and we ended that foul beast. I'd wager that if any of the creatures that stalk us are owlbears, they'd best think twice about challenging us," Murdoch said in his usual overconfident way of speaking.

Much had changed in the year Knox was away. Beth, for instance, seemed no longer interested in him as she had been before. Murdoch had all the same fire, but there was a certain restraint to it that hadn't been there before. Frederick looked livelier than Knox had seen him when he'd left—he spoke animatedly to Terrim, who nodded along to whatever was being said.

The group quieted down as Knox approached. Murdoch stood and moved over to give him a place to sit, and the gentle roar of conversation continued.

"Where was I? Right, there was a beast that needed hunting and..." Murdoch said, but Beth shot him a look. He cleared his throat, as if he wasn't just about to go over the whole story all over again.

"There are more than owlbears waiting for us out there," Knox said, gesturing toward the black void outside of the circle of wagons and campfires. He could sense the presence of dozens of creatures, if not more, all lurking just far enough away to be outside of sight.

Terrim looked up from his quiet conversation with Frederick and smiled in Knox's direction. "Thanks for the reassuring words. Next, will you be telling us who will die first and how?"

Knox tried to smile back, but it didn't feel real. Terrim had a way of joking that always got Knox laughing, but it was hard to see the humor in something so close to the truth. For Knox had thought about fighting alongside each of them, weighing their strengths and weaknesses against what they'd face and deciding who would need the most help.

Terrim was a heavy hitter with his massive axe, but he was far too slow to deal with these monsters on an even footing. Beth was quick, possibly quick enough to face off against some of the weaker monsters they might face, but she lacked the power behind her blows to do significant damage. Frederick was a mystery—as much of what Knox knew about his skills, it mostly had to do with his farming abilities.

He was strong, quick when he needed to be, and as sturdy as anyone that made a living farming the harsh lands that they called home. Then there was Murdoch, the fastest among them—save for Knox now—with a precision to his blade that meant he was a deadly foe to face off against. Duels for honor were a thing of the past out on the frontier, but Murdoch had studied and trained his entire life for that type of combat. He was the pinnacle of human speed, wiry strength, and accuracy, yet still, in Knox's eyes, he found him wanting.

"I'll die first," Knox said, breaking the awkward silence that was growing over the group as he pondered the very thing Terrim had been joking about. "Before I let any of you fall, I will gladly give my life."

"Stop that shit," Terrim said, reaching across the fire with his massive arms to nudge Knox hard enough to nearly dislodge him from his seat. "Between the five of us, we will be plenty to deal with whatever tries to get in our way. Plus, you said your complex place was safe. We will get there soon, and it won't matter how dangerous these monsters are, right?"

Terrim seemed to want some reassurance, but Knox had none to give. Instead, he only met Terrim's gaze, searching his friend for any signs of fear. He found none—just the same old Terrim with too few shits to give and more humor than sense.

"He's right," Beth said, suddenly breaking the silence and looking at Knox for the first time since he'd arrived in their midst. "Whatever comes, if we work together, we will overcome. If you'd only come back a little sooner—" Her voice broke off and her breathing increased. She stood suddenly and left, leaving a perplexed Knox looking after her.

Moving to stand, Murdoch laid a hand on his friend's leg, pushing him back down. "Leave her for now," he said, no mirth in his voice. "She's had a rough time of it lately, we all have, but her pain is freshest."

"Why were you gone for so long?" Frederick asked, his voice a rumbling low thing that Knox could swear had only gotten deeper with the passage of the last year.

Knox looked at each of the faces that awaited his answer but didn't really know what to say. He'd explained the basics to them when he first met up with them, so what was left to say?

"I came as soon as I was able," Knox said, deciding that was as close to the truth as he could get. If he were being honest with himself, he'd left sooner than he thought was safe. Which was why he was in the trouble he was now, facing off against a possibly overwhelming force of monsters.

"Leave Knox alone," Murdoch said, producing a flask from seemingly nowhere and handing it over to Knox. "Let's drink a bit and warm our bellies. For tomorrow we might be drinking with the Titans in the hereafter. To death!"

"To Death!" Everyone said as one, the group of friends comfortable with the more morbid humor that was prevalent in such an untamed land.

To Death... drinking with the Titans. How little Knox's friends understood the reality of the words which they spoke. For Knox *was* a Titan now and they very well might die soon. The future remained uncertain, and Knox was determined to sacrifice himself rather than let any harm befall his friends.

"To Death," Knox muttered the words once more as he took a warming swig from the flask.

CHAPTER 2
MONSTERS

Two days passed, and the monsters were becoming more daring, launching attacks with ranged abilities and such. Knox's sense of the Titan Complex had finally narrowed down to a stronger connection, and he was confident they were only a day or so away. Relief, soft and even, washed over him as he realized the Serpent Dragon's scent might endure long enough for them to reach safety.

It was with these thoughts in mind that Knox argued with Dernal and Murdoch.

"We just can't afford to stop, we are too close," Knox said, his hands moving emphatically along with his words.

"We haven't the strength to continue on for more than an hour or two, *tops*," Murdoch argued, stress lines on his face growing more visible with every passing day. "It isn't a matter of pushing ourselves, the young and sick just don't have it in them."

"Then we carry them, we must not stop," Knox said, looking to Dernal for support.

"Time's up," Dernal said, finally adding his weight into the conversation. "Monsters are coming, strongest ones first then the weaker. We need to circle the wagons and prepare for battle."

"We are so close," Knox pleaded, but neither Murdoch nor

Dernal seemed willing to budge. Focusing on the bond he had with the Titan Complex, Knox tried to communicate with it, but he wasn't sure if it was working.

Send help, desperate for help, send help! he repeated over and over again in his head as he nodded to his two companions.

"We could have really used John and Leo right now," Knox said, looking to Dernal.

However, his only response was his usual, "Hhrmm."

"They said they'd return before winter, any chance they did?" Murdoch asked Dernal, hoping for any chance of salvation.

"Wouldn't matter if they did, they aren't strong enough to make it through the swamps. We are on our own," Dernal said. There was a finality to his words that really hit Knox as he considered how true they were.

"Can you call your friend back, that Aetex fellow?" Murdoch asked, suddenly more worried about the battle ahead than the need for rest. "Or what about the trick you did to beat the dragon, you said something about rings?"

Knox visibly shuddered at the thought of removing any of the restraining rings that kept his power in check. Taking off two when he'd been in the lower to mid-Level 20s had unleashed enough power to almost rip his entire body apart. He had used some spare Cores over the past few days to bring himself back to the lower Level 20s again, so the idea of taking off even one ring scared him.

Seeing him shake, Murdoch sighed and put a hand on his friend's shoulder. "We will figure out a way. Maybe Mr. Tome has some gadget that will give us an edge. You should have seen him against the horde of undead that nearly overwhelmed us. He had crossbows that could reload and shoot by themselves. Then there were the flasks of fire he threw; they exploded on impact, taking several enemies down at once. He wouldn't give me any when I asked. He said I was too fickle to be trusted with such a weapon. Can you imagine? Describing *me* as fickle, *pfft*."

Dernal and Knox shared a look but said nothing to disparage

Murdoch. Instead, Dernal spoke, breaking the growing silence, "Circle the wagons, the young and the sick in the middle. Build fires, arm anyone who can fight and be ready to defend yourselves."

Knox cut in, grabbing Murdoch's arm as he turned to leave. "Gather the team, we will be the spear that pierces the foes that dare threaten our kin."

Murdoch smiled a wicked grin at that and nodded his head.

"To Death," he muttered as he turned to run. Knox repeated the phrase, it beginning to feel like their motto.

"To Death..."

The wagons began to slowly circle, and Knox finally saw what Dernal was referring to. The larger of the predators, two B Ranked auras, were closing in on both sides. The only benefit from the seemingly disastrous situation was that the lower C Ranked Monsters were scattering in all directions, except toward the inner camp—likely attempting to avoid a confrontation with one of the more powerful B Ranked Monsters.

It was slightly confusing to Knox where most of these monsters had been when he fled the swamp or when he was at the Titan Complex. Where were all the lower-level Nolics and wolves that he'd trained himself up on? Maybe their large group was too tempting of a treat for the monsters to refuse. But this was one snack that wouldn't be consumed so easily.

"Eastern one will get here first. Come with me," Dernal said, his power no longer masked, rolling off him like waves.

The darkness of night had swiftly taken over, and only the glow of the Elemental moons lit up the sky. Each moon radiated with the color of its element, but the white moon of Light shone brightest. Knox felt a tingling sensation inside him and a surge of energy, as if he could feel his aura swelling under the Light—something he'd never felt before. Whether it was his imagination or a fact of the nature of the moons that he was unaware of, he felt much stronger than his Level 20 denoted.

He reached Dernal's side just as his team formed up around them.

"You are all a liability," Dernal grumbled to them, but Knox took strength in knowing they were by his side.

He knew that it would take more than physical or even magical strength to get through the night. Ultimately, it would come down to the trust he had in those standing beside him. If nothing else, Knox took a sort of morbid comfort in the idea of facing death alongside those he cared about most.

"How long do we have before the other B Ranked Monster shows up?" Knox asked Dernal while taking the time to try and gauge its approach with his special sense.

He could feel it, but it didn't seem to be drawing closer. Knox waited, seeing if Dernal came to the same conclusion. It seemed he did, as his eyes widened slightly, and he subtly turned his head toward the west, where the monster lurked in the shadows.

"It might be waiting for us to drop our guard, but for now, we have more pressing problems. Focus up, here it comes," Dernal said, lowering his gaze back to the line of trees that hid the incoming beast.

Knox could easily sense the creature as it approached and, whatever it was, it was big. It finally moved past the clearing of trees, but the swamp water hadn't drained from this area yet. Whatever it was, it was able to stay hidden in the shallow swampy water. The group stood on a raised area of the swamp, along with the entire caravan, so if it wanted to attack, it would have to show itself eventually.

Looking around, Knox saw his group, weapons ready, standing with heads held high and no sign of fear in their eyes. Beth had a bow out, an arrow already nocked and two more in her hands, ready to be loosed in quick succession. Frederick held a massive club with pieces of metal poking out in random directions, it was as close to a mace as one could find out here in the frontier and Knox applauded his ingenuity in creating it.

Terrim had his massive axe in hand, ready to strike down with it, and Murdoch kept his hand on his hilt, not yet pulling free his saber. Knox had taken a note from Leo and used some basic rune crafting to give each weapon a bonus to damage. Without such actions, and the dozens of others he'd done with the villager's tools, they'd have no chance in damaging anything above E Rank.

Even so, it would be hard for their weapons to do much against the thick hide of a B Ranked Monster. Knox knew by well-earned experience that his own weapon was powerful enough to be effective against B Ranked Monsters, but barely so against A Ranked Monsters.

Knox's hand fell to his axe, and he pulled it free as the monster stopped just short of the raised ground where they were making their stand. His mind went over his most effective spells, Luminous Surge being his bread and butter, but also spells like Void Grasp being just as effective in battle. As he went over his spells he realized he could cast a few helpful ones and began to do so.

First, he laid down Mystic Veil, one of his Mystic spells. It triggered and a veil fell over the group making them harder to target and reducing incoming damage. Next, he cast Mystic Armor, armor shimmering up and around his form. Then, he used Radiant Glyph to set barriers behind them, hopefully keeping an attack or two away from the most vulnerable of the caravan.

All the while, the monster inched closer, keeping to the shallow waters. There were a number of spells Knox had at his fingertips with his two Pathways he'd unlocked: Mystic and Titan-Born. As they waited, Knox could feel his Titan's Aura kick in, granting increased physical damage to all those around him. A part of him wished he'd taken the Lightforged Armor talents to supplement his Mystic Armor, which had a tendency to shatter after only an attack or two.

Ready with his Radiant Ground spell, Knox eyed the area and

made a decision when the B Ranked Monster didn't immediately attack. Focusing as best as he could, he grabbed hold of the many weaves of magic inside of himself and began the process of casting Arcane Pulse. It triggered and he felt the necessary Mana flow from him to feed it.

A sudden surge of power smashed free from his outstretched hand and into the water some thirty feet away, causing it to stir upon impact. A gut-wrenching roar echoed out of the water, and instinctually, Knox's hand went to his leg where his boomstick lay. He'd taken the time to inscribe each of the rounds with runes, making the weapon that much more deadly. Still, it wasn't time to use it yet, but it would be soon.

He had a plan, and it involved using Mr. Tome's invention to devastating effect if the chance presented itself. He wanted to get one clear shot into the monster's eye—hopefully, it had an eye or two to choose from. A shot right into an eye would penetrate into the brain, effectively ending the threat.

So, imagine Knox's surprise when three separate heads rose up out of the water, each with snapping maws matching that of an alligator but with long, snake-like necks lifting them out of the water. Still, no body could be seen, but the twisting, snake-like necks with their elongated heads took them in with a single look and made another ear-deafening roar.

At the edge of his sense, he felt the other B Ranked Monster move. However, instead of charging inward, it appeared to be running away, putting distance between itself and the roaring monster with three heads.

"Alligator Hydra, we have to kill all three heads; it'll keep its body hidden as to make it harder to kill. I'll take the one on the left, Knox, you take the middle one, and the rest of you take the one on the right. Good luck," Dernal said, his voice barely a hoarse whisper, but everyone heard him and readied their weapons.

Knox focused his sense on the monster and felt a buildup of power in the right most head. "Watch out!" Knox yelled, beginning the intricate work to cast Prism Ward. It ignited around them at the very last second as red-hot fire erupted out of the right most hydra's maw. Some of the heat made its way through, but surprisingly most of the damage was reflected.

Somewhere in the back of his mind, he knew it was a combination of Dernal throwing up his own barrier, his use of Prism Ward and Mystic Veil that kept them alive in that moment, but Knox couldn't directly think about that now.

He let his Ward fall and used Ethereal Step to put himself just close enough to strike out with his axe. He planned on surprising the hydra head and taking it off in one quick cut, but it was ready for him, and many times faster than he was, clamping down on his shoulder and picking him up.

He heard his name being called out from below as his world spun, and pain lanced up his shoulder. His Mystic Armor cracked and shattered, letting the teeth sink deep into him. What had he been thinking, taking on such a powerful foe without a true plan? Clearing his mind, he remembered that he did have a plan, and despite the pain, a smile appeared on Knox's face.

He was lucky that his free arm was the side where his boomstick was holstered. He grabbed it free and prayed to any gods or titans that were listening to bestow him a touch of their luck. Barely making out a single squinting eye, Knox reached around and placed his boomstick right against it, then pulled the trigger.

A roar, as loud as any monster went off, leaving his ears ringing. But the blast had done the trick; he was falling through the air, and the pain suddenly didn't seem so bad as he thought that he'd killed the monster, or at least one of the heads. But to his surprise, the head followed him down, maw wide, just as he splashed into the water.

Using Solar Wings, he swooped himself out of the way and activated Ethereal Step to put himself on the back line once more, bloodied and breathing hard. Struggling to focus his eyes, he looked at the battle as it ensued.

Frederick and Terrim were down but breathing. The hydra

head he had shot seemed confused; it whipped around at seemingly random directions, shooting off a spray of blue that must be some type of ice attack when concentrated. Instead of doing any damage, though, it was just sending a spray of frozen water or slushy snow all over.

Dernal wasn't fairing much better than Beth and Murdoch, each of them spending all their time dodging attacks and not a single one of them getting their own attacks through.

Focusing on Terrim and Frederick, Knox cast Luminous Surge, being sure the beam of light hit them before moving up to smash into the already confused hydra head. It did the trick, healing them a small amount and doing damage to the monster as well. Rushing forward while throwing up another Mystic Armor, Knox slammed his foot down at the base of the hydra, casting Radiant Ground.

All three heads screamed in pain and the sudden distraction allowed Knox's friends to strike a few glancing blows. The hydras barely seemed to care after a moment of taking the slow ticking damage and focused back up on their targets. However, the middle one, damaged by Knox's earlier attack, continued to thrash about wildly. Whatever instincts had allowed it to track him as he fell seemed lost now.

Knox cut deep with his axe and was rewarded by a large gash on the beast's neck. It wasn't enough though, and the pain of the attack snapped the middle head out of whatever was driving it wild. It looked down at Knox with one bloody ruined eye and roared as power began to amass within its maw.

Stepping back to give himself some room, Knox cast Lustrous Chains on the heads, hoping to entangle all of them. To his dismay, the chains shot out and instantly snapped against the terrible strength of the B Ranked foe. However, one of the effects of the chains had enough time to work, cancelling the buildup of the breath attack before it could go off.

That didn't prevent it from immediately beginning to channel another breath attack, but it bought them some time.

Just as the breath attack let loose, Knox cast Void Grasp, an attack that restrained and drained energy from an enemy caught within its grasp.

A sudden pulse in his mind left him staggering and confused. This gave the hydra the time it needed to hit him full in the face with a blast of ice. As he became suddenly too cold to do much else other than think, Knox wondered where his boomstick had gotten off to. It must have been knocked from his hands in the thick of battle. He knew it was useless until reloaded, but he didn't want to lose something so precious to him.

Another mental pulse hit him, and he nearly doubled over. It came with a message this time, but what it was trying to say was lost in the rush of pain that the pulse came with.

It was only when several figures appeared around the hydra, glinting in the bright light of the Light moon did Knox realize what was happening.

Reinforcements.

Edgar, Boris, and Vlad were easy to recognize, they wore some of their old pirate gear, including swords, but the other three golems must have been some of the new six. Wearing armor that Knox didn't recognize and wielding more power than he felt they should reasonably have, the six total golems leapt upon the hydra, turning the tide of battle in their favor.

Slamming his foot down hard, Knox activated another Radiant Ground and felt the slow healing begin to repair some of the tissue damage the cold had done. It reached out enough to hit both Terrim and Frederick, bringing them both to their feet. All three of them ran for the hydra heads, knowing full well this moment of the tide turning wouldn't last forever.

Even with the power he felt coming off of the golems, they weren't a match for the hydras and definitely not in the B Ranked range, which is to say between levels 41 through 50.

But Knox knew that his axe and his strength was a match for at least the middle hydra's head. He'd already cut into it, and where he had, it seemed to freeze over a bit, not bleeding as it should. The hydra snapped Frederick from beside the three of them as they charged, but Knox couldn't falter now. He swung his axe and hit the spot, chunks of frozen flesh giving way.

A moment after he hit, Terrim's axe fell, and then Knox's, followed again by Terrim's. The one-two-combo took care of the neck within two seconds, and it fell to the ground in a mighty thump. The other two heads couldn't help their brother and screamed in rage as they were reduced to just two.

One of the heads that hadn't yet shown its terrible breath weapon began to build up energy, the air crackled, and Knox bit his lip as he realized the type of attack it had. His Prism Ward came up first, followed by as many Radiant Glyphs of shielding that he could scribe into the air around them. He had no time to shout to the others, but it wasn't needed, the attack was headed right for him.

Pain erupted all around him as his body went stiff and he felt himself draw nearer to death's door. He fell to the side, only his many Wards, shielding Glyphs, and Mystic Armor saving him from instant death. Even so, Dernal appeared at his side as the fight waged around them and began to heal him with brutal efficiency.

When he could finally speak, his tongue no longer numb, he cursed and yelled at Dernal. "Help them, I'm alive. Go help them!"

Dernal laid Knox back gently and in a flash of speed was back in the battle. However strong this hydra had been, the separate heads were not up to B Ranked status by themselves. Without even looking, Knox could tell the tide of the battle was changing and it was only a matter of time.

It was a race between the cooldowns and ability to use their breath weapons and cutting their heads off. Because of that fact, Knox made it to his feet and limped over toward the battle. One of his golems had been cleaved into two and another was smashed badly, but the three tricky pirates were doing just fine, throwing attacks and keeping their distance.

"Must... help... them," Knox said, blood filling his mouth as he walked. Terrim began cutting into the lightning one, but it used its head like a hammer and smashed him away, leaving him in an unmoving slump some twenty feet away. "Stop hurting my friends!" Knox screamed, ripping free a ring and pocketing it.

If he thought he was in pain before, it was a world of unknown levels of pain now. But he clenched down hard and moved with the speed of a C Ranked Adventurer. One solid cut put him halfway through the neck. Before the hydra could turn, he cut again, taking its head off.

What happened next, he wasn't sure. He knew he dropped his axe and put the ring back on as if by instinct. Another level had been lost, and suddenly his body was weaker than it ought to be. He lay on the ground as the rest of the team fought and eventually took down the final head of the hydra, accomplishing the impossible.

In and out of consciousness, Dernal appeared over him, breathing hard and bleeding more than Knox felt was normal. The entire world spun, but a light from Dernal's hands and a steady chanting had much of his blood traveling back into his body.

Terrim leaned over him, even more bloody and breathing harder than Dernal.

"To Death," he said, collapsing beside Knox.

"To Death," Knox repeated as he lost consciousness.

CHAPTER 3
TITAN COMPLEX

KNOX AWOKE to someone shaking him. His groggy eyes, wanting nothing more than sleep, opened just the tiniest bit. Above him stood a metal man; for eyes, he had a visor that spread the length of his upper face. For a mouth, he had a small opening in a similar visor 'V' shape as its glowing blue eye.

For a brief moment, he recoiled from the alien sight, the oddity stripping away any sense of familiarity. However, as strange as it was, recognition dawned on him a moment later as the drape of sleep was pulled free.

"Eh there, boss, you ready to move?" Edgar asked, the scarf he wore around his neck and the way he spoke a dead giveaway to which golem Knox was speaking with.

"You heard my call for help," Knox said, not meaning it as a question but a statement of fact.

"Aye, we did," Edgar said, then looking around he leaned in to add, "Though we didn't expect you were bringing so many newcomers. We've been working on getting the facilities, as they are, to a more, how to say, livable for your kind."

"My kind?" Knox asked, standing and noticing that Terrim was no longer lying beside him. Scanning the horizon, he saw the barest trickle of light over the horizon and a trail of wagons leading off into the distance toward the Titan Complex. It seemed he was the last one to be moved. Dernal stood nearby, looking like —well, like Dernal—sporting a mix of smug and pissed-off expressions all jumbled together.

"You know, flesh bags," Edgar said, elbowing Knox in the ribs as he laughed. The blow was meant to be friendly, but Knox groaned as it hit one of his many bruises on his body.

The sudden harsh reality of events came crashing down on Knox as he remembered how he had ended up in such a state. Throwing his sense wide, he searched for predators but found none close. Looking to Dernal, he received a quiet nod.

"We should hurry, I doubt the scent of the hydra will mask us for long," Knox said, jogging after the caravan with Dernal and Edgar a step behind him.

Without his connection to the Titan Complex, Knox wasn't sure he'd have found it as easily as his golems seemed to. They reached the area with a sinkhole, and five of Knox's golems—one had been destroyed, but its scraps were being carried along—jumped in ahead of the group.

Knox ran his eyes over the area, then opened his sense as wide as he could. Just as he'd thought, the stronger monsters kept their distance, but several Nolics, as well as wolves and even a few monsters he didn't recognize, patrolled the area. For several miles leading up to the Titan Complex, the terrain had gone through drastic changes.

The watery swamps that were so iconic to the Shadowfall Swamp gave way to dry, healthy soil with trees that couldn't be as young as they were, considering how tall they stood above every-one's heads. Yet it was true that this area had been changed by the Titan Engine in more ways than Knox could understand. The type of monsters, the terrain, and even the general feeling of the air and sky all spoke of an area budding with life and power, but a young power, not the age-old power that it had once been.

The newness of it all was something that Knox was keenly aware of, and he wondered if Dernal felt it too now that they neared the area. Looking over to him, he saw the usual constipated look on his friend's face give way to something resembling awe, but as quickly as it appeared, it was gone.

"Pretty amazing, isn't it?" Knox said, thinking that perhaps Dernal was feeling the same waves of power he was. But something else flickered over Dernal's expression as he looked at Knox and then at the large caravan of people. Suddenly, Knox had the presence of mind to look around and realized that everyone had an odd expression on their face. What were they seeing?

"I'm being told that we are now part of the Titan System. A window of information is explaining that the Age of Chaos has ended, and we have once more entered an Age of Order. Now it is asking my name—the name is Dernal Dorntooth, damnit. Oh, it worked. Whoa, now it is laying out... well, I don't know what to call this." Dernal was giving a blow by blow as his eyes glazed over and he interacted with the Titan System.

Knox hadn't expected this to happen, in fact, he thought he was going to have to have everyone touch the Titan Engine for them to become part of it. This presented a disturbing challenge now that he thought about it. How far out was this aura of change going and did the pirates also have access to the system, despite not being friendly to them?

This brought with it so many conflicting thoughts. First, he wasn't sure he was against having the system spread out, but was that his own thoughts or the influence of the Titan Born nature that he now had as part of himself? He wasn't sure, nor could he be sure that his worries were even justified. It wasn't until they'd moved right up to the Titan Complex that these messages had overtaken everyone's sight.

Looking around, he saw his father with a similar glazed over expression and he couldn't help but wonder what his attribute layout and level would look like. There was a tug in his consciousness when he had the thought, but whatever it was, it wasn't concrete enough to latch onto, so he let it pass. There was so much he didn't yet know about the Titan System and his ability to interface with it.

"Dernal," Knox said, touching his friend on the shoulder. He started and looked at Knox confused, as if waking from a daydream.

"It gave me a quest to collect three low level monster cores and deposit them into something called a 'Titan Engine'," Dernal said, looking perplexed as he reached into a pouch at his waist. "I've got the cores, take me to this Titan Engine."

"Whoa, slow down," Knox said, putting a hand on his friend's shoulder. "If your experience is anything like mine, you'll be given a choice of a 'Path' to walk. Are you sure you want that?"

"Not sure I have much of a choice," Dernal said, rolling his shoulders as he tried to expel some of the stiffness there. "I can feel this system already mucking around in my body and changing things. I'm not sure my way of accessing magic and healing will ever be the same."

"Let's get everyone into the complex and then I will take you to the Titan Engine," Knox said, now feeling a bit guilty that he'd led his friend to the Titan System. What if it made him weaker than he'd already been? But no, he pushed that thought away. The Titan System and his Paths had risen him to new levels of power, and he was sure it would do the same for his friends.

The thought of his other friends prompted him to look around, and he noticed them approaching as a group. Their expressions varied from excitement to frustration. Terrim appeared to be the most excited of the bunch, while Beth looked as if someone had just told her that there wouldn't be any more violence for the next month. Beth loved some good violence.

"Hey there guys," Knox said, smiling at his friends as they surrounded him. "Ready to join the Titan System?"

There were several floors in the Titan Complex, but Mic met greeted them on the first level just under the throne where the skeletal armored figure had once sat. Hundreds of people spread out in the wide area, with only Dernal and Knox's friends—Frederick, Murdoch, Beth, and Terrim—at his side.

"Welcome home, Master Knox," Mic said, his voice the usual proper stern tone.

"I've brought some guests; can you see to it that food is prepared from the supplies I've scavenged and see about fixing the water system within the complex?" Knox asked, then seeing Mic eye the destroyed golem that one of the other new golems carried, he added, "They saved our lives, without them we wouldn't have made it."

"I sent them straight away when your message was received by the Titan Engine. In fact, it issued me my first quest in memory. A shame that Sextor didn't make it. No matter, his parts can be used for repairs and upgrades, he will not go to waste."

"Sextor," Knox said, remembering the name as one of the Physical golems that had been created. "That means the other two are Prime and Sek?"

"That is correct, sir." Mic said, nodding.

Leaning in close Knox asked, "Do you think we have enough food to care for these people?"

Following Knox's lead, Mic leaned in as well. "Without a doubt. The combat golems have been collecting meat from the local monster pools while growing stronger, and all that meat has been prepped and smoked. I've a memory bank filled with countless ways to prepare meat and make it last. The gardens have also begun to produce fruit and vegetables. It is on a lower floor that needed much repair, but I've had the maintenance golems working nonstop. However, perhaps I should call them back to help with the young and sick." Mic pressed his hand on his head and his glowing eye pulsed for a moment, then went back to the steady blue color it had always been. "There, they are on their way."

"Let's move everyone to the housing level and get them settled in as best we can," Knox said, turning to his friends as he did. "There will be time to explore and have everything explained in more detail later, but for now, I think it is best that we get people resting and those wagons taken apart above."

"Why do we need to take the wagons apart?" Terrim asked, scratching at the stubble that was beginning to grow thick on his face.

"This area has pirates, and I don't want to give away our location," Knox said, then turning back to Mic as the golem put a hand on his shoulder, he asked, "What is it?"

"I believe you have the means to complete a quest that will make our required anonymity a thing of the past," Mic said. "However, I will have the maintenance golems begin work on the outer wall structures immediately, after we've gotten your people to a safe resting place."

"What quest and what do you mean?" Knox asked, he'd started out only half listening, but now Mic had his full attention.

Mic made a noise that sounded like he was clearing his throat, despite not having one. "I can sense that you have several C Ranked Cores with you, enough to complete the Tier 2 of the Titan Engine, and besides that, you have an A Ranked Core that will bring you all the way up to Tier 4 by itself. Once you've reached Tier 4, the Titan Complex will reach enough power for the automated process to begin once more. When that happens, the city will rise from the ground and only certain levels will remain below. However, fear not, there are defenses in place, and we've activated an additional ten golems while you were away—six maintenance and four combat oriented. We will prevail over any enemy that seeks to overcome us."

"Wait," Knox said, pinching the bridge of his nose. "What if I don't want the city to rise up and be visible to everyone?"

"But it must, the magic that is growing and building up is activating the old catacombs below the complex and we must allow them to expand as they once did or risk the destruction of the complex," Mic said, a worried tone filling his voice as he spoke.

"We need to discuss this further, but for now, send a couple maintenance golems above to take apart the wagons. I still think it's prudent not to give away our location," Knox said, feeling his plans for hiding in the ground and slowly building up his power falling to pieces at his feet.

Murdoch took charge after Knox explained to him how to get to the housing level, leading the people down. Beth caught his eye as the room began to empty out and he walked over to see what it was she wanted.

In all the excitement, Knox hadn't paid much attention to her or her boyfriend Richard, but now that he thought about it, he hadn't seen him for some time. Where had he gotten off to?

"I want to say sorry for being so cold to you," Beth said, biting her lip. "You'd think I'd be used to losing people by now, but I feel hollow inside."

Remembering that she'd lost someone important to her—a guy named Brian—to the black sickness, he felt bad for her. Knox had a hard time placing who Brian was, but apparently Beth and him had gotten really close. Though, what loss was she talking about now? Or perhaps did she mean someone else in the past? Knox knew surprisingly little about her past, as she'd always been close-lipped about it.

Not wanting to be rude, but having responsibilities, Knox asked, "Where is Richard?" Surely, she'd rather talk to her boyfriend about this stuff and not Knox.

Beth's lips went into a line and her brows furrowed. "You are so dense, aren't you?" She stomped away as if Knox had done something extremely wrong.

Looking around and feeling more confused than ever, he walked over to Terrim and nudged him on the shoulder.

"What's up?" Terrim asked, he was eyeing the line of people heading deeper into the vast Titan Complex.

"Where is that Richard guy?" Knox asked, looking into the crowd, and trying to remember the last time he'd seen him.

"Oh, you're just now noticing, huh?" Terrim said, chuckling at Knox's expense.

"He didn't..." Knox said, sudden realization hitting him.

"He left," Terrim said. "He went with the other group to try and be refugees, leaving Beth to choose between her friends and him, but she chose us. Is that why she's glaring at you now? You put your foot in your mouth, didn't you?"

"I may have," Knox said, finding Beth in the crowd, and she was unmistakably shooting him a disapproving glare now.

"You ought to be nicer to her, man. She's lost a lot and I swear she still has feelings for you, but what do I know," Terrim said, throwing his hands up.

"Did Danielle make it?" Knox asked, suddenly remembering he hadn't really talked with his friend much about the girl he was sweet on, all those months ago.

Terrim smiled, but it was a haunted smile. "She's with us, but she's sick. It took a lot of convincing for me to get Murdoch to bring her. He thinks it's the black sickness, but I couldn't just leave her behind."

"Why hasn't Dernal healed the sick?" Knox asked, confusion evident on his face. Even before all this happened, Dernal would regularly heal all manner of ailment when he visited town. A part of Knox was sure he did it to gain favor with the townsfolk, but still, they mistrusted him even when getting healed by him. Adventurers just didn't have a good reputation for helping without huge payments or obligations. Thinking about it, he couldn't help but wonder if Dernal asked for payment as well.

"Dernal tried, but many of the sick have ailments that his

magic can't fix," Terrim said, his head hanging a bit lower than normal.

Knox had heard of such sicknesses before, mostly diseases, failure of internal organs and the like. It made him wonder what the limitations of his own healing might be. But he had to try, didn't he?

"Take me to her and let me try," Knox said, his resolve firming as he saw the look of hope cross his friend's face.

"You really think you might be able to help?" Terrim asked.

Meeting his eyes, Knox sighed. "No promises, but I need to try. If not me, then when Dernal chooses a Path, he will gain access to many powerful magics that might also allow him to cure disease."

They fell into line and traveled down to the housing section of the complex. It was much more vast than the first floor and could house thousands by the looks of it. They found Danielle's housing unit, a larger rectangular house where all the sick were being placed on beds of stone with a padding made of harvested straw.

It wouldn't be the most comfortable, but it was better than what they'd been getting while traveling. Along with the sick, were several injured and bleeding folks. Whether new injuries or what, Knox wasn't surprised to find Dernal already in the room. He was speaking with an elderly lady, whose name Knox couldn't remember, about the care of the patients.

"Dernal," Knox called and Dernal finished up his conversation before walking over to greet them.

"Hhrmm," Dernal said, his eyebrows raised in expectation.

"I have several spells that have healing effects and I want to try them on the sick," Knox said, reading the threads of magic that would be required.

"Won't work," Dernal said. "Some things can't be healed."

"Why not?" Knox asked, a little heat coming into his voice to have his idea dismissed so quickly.

"Has to do with how the spirit and the body perceive damage

to itself. Very powerful healers can override the nature of the body to make changes, but it is outside of our ability," Dernal said, shaking his head as he spoke.

"I'm trying," Knox said, stepping up to Danielle's bed.

"Fine," Dernal said, returning to the elderly lady to speak with her.

Knox put his hands over Danielle and examined her. She had dark red hair, almost a dark brown in the dim light of the housing units. But her eyes were a gentle blue like the sky on a warm summer's day. She was far skinnier than Knox remembered, and there was a darkness around her eyes that looked similar to what they'd described about the black sickness. Then there were the black veins covering every bit of her visible skin. There was certainly something wrong with her.

"Here goes nothing," Knox said. Holding his hands out over her, he began casting Luminous Surge.

It would do damage to his foes but also healed friendly targets for a small amount, so in his mind, he focused on her being a friendly target and the sickness inside of her being an enemy. Honestly, he didn't know if such thoughts helped or how his magic knew what was considered friend or foe, but he had to try everything he could.

Unleashing his spell, Knox sensed and witnessed something odd. Danielle jolted upright in the bed, a scream escaping her lips, as if the power of Knox's spell was scorching her skin. Rough hands grabbed him from behind, throwing him off his feet and effectively ending the spell. Yet, the screaming didn't stop.

Knox saw Terrim standing over Danielle's convulsing body, and he looked back at Knox with a fury on his face he'd never known from him. The screams cut off suddenly and Dernal was at her side, his chanting filling the room, but no lights of magic followed. He cursed and ran over to me.

"What did you do? My magic doesn't work yet, I'm still jumbled up inside. Tell me what you did!" Dernal had hands on Knox's shoulders now and shook him roughly.

"I used a spell that damages my foes but heals my allies. She's my ally, she shouldn't have been hurt," Knox said, his words a quick scramble as he tried to get his thoughts in line. "I tried to imagine her sickness as an enemy, maybe I hurt her in doing so—I didn't know!"

The room grew suddenly still as Danielle stopped making any noises at all. A heavy feeling settled in Knox's gut as he considered what he'd done. Was she dead? He didn't know, but he had to find out, had to try and help her still. Getting to his feet, he walked up to Terrim, who leaned over Danielle, caressing her face. Tears streamed down his scruffy face as he did so.

"Is she..." Terrim said, but he couldn't finish the sentence, his words choked with grief.

"Not yet," Dernal said, then, turning to Knox he said, "Take me to this Titan Engine. I need a Path and I need it now."

Knox's eyes never left Danielle though, something was different about her. Sure, she was weaker, but the dark circles around her eyes and the ugly veins of black all over her body were gone as well. She was clearly sick still, that or injured to the point of near death, but the darkness was gone.

"Let me try again," Knox said, both Dernal and Terrim looked at him as if he had lost his mind, but Knox was working on a theory that he had to prove.

"Stay away from her!" Terrim said, and suddenly Dernal was there holding back the half giant of a man.

"I see it too," Dernal said, looking over his shoulder. "Try it again, but be careful, she is close to death."

Putting his hands over Danielle, Knox began weaving the spell together. There was doubt and plenty of fear in it this time, but he focused on the idea that Danielle was a friendly target and needed healing.

The light of his spell poured over her and this time, she didn't scream. In fact, the opposite happened. She let out a sigh of relief as the blood that had begun to come out of her eyes, mouth, and nose, all traveled back into her body and a measure of her color returned to her.

By the time Knox cut off his spell, holding it for as long as he could without losing control of it, she flicked her eyes open. Her sky-blue eyes flicked from Knox to Terrim, then to Dernal, who was still holding him back.

"The little girl, did you see her?" Danielle asked, breathing hard and sitting up.

CHAPTER 4
TITAN ENGINE

TERRIM SPOKE softly with a very confused, but healing, Danielle, while Dernal and Knox left to go visit the Titan Engine. It was down deep in the complex and he encountered Mic along the way.

"Question for you Mic," Knox said, before Mic could begin to ask him the myriad of questions he probably had or reports that needed Knox's attention.

"What is it?" Mic asked, keeping pace with them as they traveled further and further down the main stairwell.

"What was this place called before, do you remember anything now that it has been a while since you've awoken?" Knox asked, curious about what information the golem might have retained.

"Let me think," Mic said, stopping and pressing both hands to the side of his head. "Yes. I believe I do know of a name it was once called. Luminarion Hold, or Luminar for short."

"Luminar, sounds fine to me," Knox said, saying the word a few times in his head to really get the sound of it. "Welcome to Luminar."

"Hhrmm," Dernal said, his response as insightful into his mood as always.

"You remembered the name, perhaps other new information has come up, like the fate of the last Titan to rule here?" Knox asked, seeing just how far he could get Mic to go with his recall.

"I'm afraid much of what I knew and who I served is still a mystery to me, but I will endeavor to serve you as best I can," Mic said, reciting a similar line to when Knox had first met him.

"Very well," Knox said, but he noticed Dernal taking a long look at Mic, as if sizing him up.

Mic eyed Dernal right back. "Will he be accompanying us to the Titan Engine?" Mic asked.

"Yeah, we need to get him up to speed and using his Path spells as soon as possible. He is a healer and I'm hopeful that between the two of us, we can solve a small problem brewing in our makeshift healing hut," Knox said, as he mentally counted how many were still infected with the black sickness below.

He'd counted at least three, which was one more than Terrim said there had been when this entire trip started. Knox applauded their resolve to not just dispose of the infected after what they'd done to them, but this sickness was a bit different than they claimed. Instead of them returning with quiet words and odd behavior, they'd all been found passed out and barely responsive.

Two such individuals had died early on, but these remaining four—now three thanks to Knox—were the strongest of the batch that didn't turn immediately.

"Do you think they have some innate resistance to it?" Knox asked Dernal, trusting that Dernal was thinking on the same lines as he was.

Sure enough, Dernal answered without much pause. "That's my guess."

"Then once we get you back to healing, I'll kill off the sickness like before and you heal them. Problem solved," Knox said, biting his lip and hoping that it was that simple.

"Hhrmm," Dernal said.

They continued downward for another few minutes before reaching the complex where the Titan Engine sat.

Though it was a machine, it had smooth organic features, and none of the gears that were found on the golems, or the rest of the place were present. Almost as if it were of some different construction than the rest of the complex. But one thing was certain, this room—only about a hundred paces from end to end and circular in shape—was different than the rest.

For one thing, it was spotless. Not a speck of dust entered the room and even the dirt and grime on Knox and Dernal seemed to be pushed away and out of the room as they entered.

Turning to Mic, Knox was about to ask what the deal was with that dirt, but apparently, he knew Knox's mind on the matter and answered before he could even ask.

"Sterilization field, but don't worry, it specifically doesn't impede sexual organs. Or at least I don't think it does," Mic said, looking at Dernal strangely when he froze in place, a look of horror settling over him.

"I'm sure it's fine," Knox said, reassuring his friend, but secretly wanting to be in and out of this room as fast as possible now.

"Place your hand on the Titan Engine and the Path selection will begin, or you can just wait until Knox completes the next two Tiers and the field will be strengthened. Once that occurs, all within the field will be able to select their Paths," Mic said, happily as ever.

"Come again?" Knox asked, looking at Mic with raised eyebrows. "Are you saying once I finish the Titan Engine quests anyone within the area of influence will be able to pick a Path?"

"Well, yes," Mic said. "And they won't *be able to*, they will *have to*. It is the natural order of things, after all. The Titan System was meant to rule over this planet, and you are just assisting it in returning the natural order."

"What about our enemies? Anyone who wishes us harm will be granted powerful magics that can be used against us!" Knox said, looking toward Dernal but unable to read the stoic man's expression.

"They already can," Dernal said, shrugging. Before Knox could ask what he meant, he continued. "If what you've explained to me about them is true, then they are powerful already with access to powerful techniques. This will even the battlefield. We can study these Paths and know what to expect from almost any foe."

Dernal's words struck a chord deep within Knox. He understood that knowledge and strategy, not just pure strength, would be their most potent weapon against any invading force. If only the monsters they faced followed predictable Paths as well.

"Do monsters also have Paths?" Knox asked on a whim, and Mic nodded, surprising him.

"They do, but you haven't reached a high enough Tier with the Titan Engine to examine them. Once you reach Tier 10, all monster Paths will be viewable to you. However, I do not recommend picking one when you get stronger, as they are meant for the more chaotic Cores of beasts and not the chosen races."

"I've already chosen my Paths," Knox said, brushing off Mic's odd suggestion. Then a flash of realization hit him, and he turned to take Mic in his arms. "I don't get to pick a new Path eventually, do I?"

"What? No why would you get to walk new Paths?" Mic asked, tilting his head to the side as if confused by Knox's sudden interest.

"But you said," Knox began to say but Mic shook his head.

"You misheard me," Mic insisted, and when Knox looked at Dernal for support, he found his friend already touching the Titan Engine and his eyes glazed over.

"He is choosing his Path and learning his abilities," Mic commented, but Knox figured as much and walked up to the Engine to give it the Cores he'd collected.

First, he fed it enough to reach Tier 2. Then, getting a new quest, he saw he could give it an A Ranked Monster Core to get it to Tier 4.

. . .

-Quest Received-
   -Reach Higher Tiers of the Titan Engine (Ongoing)-
   -Feed the Titan Engine to increase the base range of its influence, increase its effectiveness and unlock additional bonuses.-
   -Objective: Add additional Monster Cores to increase the Tiers (Current Progress Tier 2/10)-
   -Rewards: 25,000 Essence Per Tier-

Knox read the quest twice. This one would be an ongoing one, which meant for each Tier he achieved, he'd get additional essence to use to level up. Slotting in the additional Monster Cores, including the A Ranked one, Knox watched as he shot up from Level 20 to Level 28. A moment after the realization, Knox dropped to his knees as the changes in his attributes took effect. He'd just gone from a 90 in Mind, Body, and Soul to 114. It was enough that he felt the changes and suddenly the world around him seemed clearer.

As he rose, he felt the power in his limbs and could imagine that he had the power of a C Ranker. Though, technically he was just deep into the D Ranks. It was an intoxicating feeling, the rush of power and knowing he was more capable of dealing with threats than he had been just moments before.

Of course, he still had C and B Ranked Monsters that needed dealing with out in the Shadowfall Swamp, but they could wait for now. Instead, Knox put his hand back on the Titan Engine and willed himself into the time dilation, as Mic called it, but it didn't work.

"Give it a moment," Mic said and suddenly Knox saw that Dernal had stopped using it as well. "Remote access is being unlocked and it takes some time."

"Remote access to learning abilities too?" Knox asked, his voice filled with exasperation.

"Only for a limited time, a year at most," Mic said, then

added, "There needs to be enough time for professionals to learn it so that Titan-System-specific abilities will spread properly."

"Of course, silly me for not knowing something you failed to tell me, yet again," Knox said, doing his best to keep his sarcastic tone under control.

"There we go. Now access it by saying the words: 'I need Training.' And picture in your mind using the Titan Engine," Mic said, his arms wide.

"Wait," Knox said, smiling. "You have to say those words and picture the Titan Engine?"

"For the first few weeks at least," Mic said. "It's all about the connection speeds and area of control that the Titan Engine controls. With time it can adapt, but for now, yes, be specific; otherwise, it might not work."

"Interesting," Knox said, smiling. If the access was limited by the phrase, what are the chances the pirates would figure that out or even know to ask it? He knew they definitely wouldn't be picturing the Titan Engine. Though, he wondered if that part was truly necessary or if Mic was adding his own qualifications.

Knox spoke the words while focusing on the image of the Titan Engine, and sure enough, he felt himself pulled into the time dilation as he had before. It was an odd sensation, a mixture of being pulled and feeling lightheaded, maybe even a bit more than the last time he used the Titan Engine.

Information hit Knox instantly and he automatically began reading it.

-Titan Engine engaged. Titan System Aura activated: Base 1, Tier 4. Current spread of aura: 16 cubic miles. All targets within aura

will be added to the collective Titan System... Current subjects within the Titan System Aura: 632 Souls.-

-You have 1 Unspent Trait Point. Before you can learn additional abilities, please assign your Level 25 Trait Point to Tier 2.-

Then, without a new thought from Knox, the newest Tier of traits appeared before him.

Unbound Mastery (0/1): Further hone your Unbound Sight, enhancing your ability to sense and perceive your surroundings. This expanded perception allows you to detect hidden threats and opportunities more effectively.

Ironclad Endurance (0/1): Your dedication to the Path of Iron has granted you even greater physical resilience and endurance. This newfound strength and vitality enable you to endure longer battles and recover more swiftly from injuries.

Essence Attunement (0/1): Develop a deeper connection to your Titan Born heritage, refining your essence manipulation skills. This heightened attunement results in faster essence gains and reduced essence costs per level.

Elemental Affinity (0/1): Delve further into your Mystic Resonance, specializing in a particular elemental energy. Choose one element (e.g., fire, water, earth, air), and gain increased control and power over it. This specialization allows you to harness and manipulate your chosen element more effectively.

Knox was being presented with not one, but several sound options, and he knew he had to take his time to make sure he made the right decision. On the one hand, Unbound Mastery seemed like the perfect choice, but he'd been in a battle or two and that had him leaning toward Ironclad Endurance. Essence Attunement and Elemental Affinity were 'nice-to-haves' but not when compared to the first two options.

Taking his time to really read through each of them, he found his answer after about ten minutes of inner debate. Ironclad Endurance would be amazing to have, but if he leaned further into his sense, he'd be able to do more than he could already do in combat.

Thinking back to the frenzy that was the hydra battle, he'd relied heavily on his sense to detect incoming attacks and stay a step ahead of his opponent, even though he hadn't realized he was doing so. With an increased sense, he'd be able to be that much faster in his reactions and detect threats that only trained rogue-types could detect. It just had too much utility and raw power to pass up.

His choice was made. He selected Unbound Mastery, a Tier 2 Titan Trait. At first, he didn't feel any different, then suddenly like flipping a switch, it hit him. The room all around swirled with potent magics, and at the very edge of his awareness he could sense Dernal in the same realm as him but separated by a thin veil.

What was more, he could feel a titanic presence nearby, lurking just out of range of his sense. But when he focused on it, the presence drew further away. Was this perhaps the Titan Gowlen he'd seen in his dreams?

As if in response to his thoughts, everything about his sense was cut off and he fell to his knees gasping. The very air he breathed seemed strained, but after a moment, he got ahold of himself and rose before the metallic figure he recognized from his dreams.

"Hello, Titan Gowlen," Knox said, and the titanic shape of a man nodded its head to him in turn.

"Which abilities do you wish to learn?" Gowlen, or at least the visual representation of Titan Gowlen, said. His voice rolled like a low rumble of thunder, weathered by endless time.

Knox pulled up his screens with a mere thought and checked

what he could learn. For his Path of the Titans, he had two new abilities—one passive and one active.

- Aeon Gaze: Focus the Titan's vision on a target, unveiling their vulnerabilities and rendering them susceptible to attacks.-
- Font of Wisdom: Over time, gradually restore energy faster, representing the Titan's endless reservoir of knowledge.-

This Aeon Gaze was an interesting ability and Knox was eager to try it out after he learned it. He wondered if it would give specific information or just a general sense of their vulnerabilities. He had no way to know before learning it, but he wanted to check his other Paths' possible skills before going forward. He had one active ability, Reality Ripple, and two passives: Magic Resilience and Celestial Alignment.

- Reality Ripple: Distort the fabric of reality in a specific area, slowing down enemies and their attacks.-
- Magic Resilience: Gain increased resistance to arcane and mystical damage sources.-
- Celestial Alignment: Periodically align with a celestial body, granting the Mystic a random buff depending on the alignment.-

This would take a while to learn five new abilities, but Knox hunkered down and began the process. He also had 21 new talent tree points to spend, so he pulled up his talent trees to study them while he waited.

His choices were not endless, but he had so many to choose from that he narrowed it down to just a few and studied them closer.

He disregarded the Celestial Adept tree because Dernal was

going to be taking on the major brunt of the healing, so he didn't see the point to add too much more into his healing abilities that already came naturally to him.

Then there was the Druid tree that offered some amazing utility, but he wasn't sure how he felt about turning into an animal during combat. Something about the idea rubbed him wrong, but he reminded himself that he'd also be able to transform into useful things like perhaps a mouse, but still he kept the idea at arm's length. Perhaps it would be right for someone else, but that wasn't the build he was looking for.

Then there was his chosen Path, the one he wanted to follow and learn the secrets of but hadn't used many talent points on, the Arcanum Scholar. So far, the abilities had been a bit lackluster when it came to discovery and new knowledge, though each talent promised things like 'increasing knowledge of ancient spells.' But really, he hadn't seen or learned much more than couldn't just as easily be used with his Titan ability, Radiant Glyph.

It allowed him to bypass much of the ritual-type magic or specialty crafted scrolls in favor of enacting the magic straightaways. Funnily enough, the skill had been meant for more simplistic means, but Knox's overuse of it had opened up its usefulness. He could do it fast enough and hold his concentration firm enough that he could do entire runic scripts in the air and activate it on will.

In the end, he decided that despite having a fair bit of success himself with translating and understanding the writings he'd found inside Luminar, he'd put five points into the Arcane Translator talent. He put five to give himself a total of 15% more effectiveness with scrolls. *Perhaps I ought to do a few scrolls, even if I personally don't need them,* he thought.

- The Arcanum Scholar gains the ability to decipher and understand ancient texts and runes, increasing the effectiveness of scrolls by 15% per point.-

. . .

Then, because he was in for a penny, he decided to be in for a pound. So, he placed three of his remaining points into Arcane Warding—a talent that increased wards and barriers he created by a whopping 5% per point. This gave him a total of 15% increased effectiveness. Next, he threw two points into Ancient Secrets, reducing the cooldown of his Mystic abilities by 10%. It wasn't much but the stronger he'd grown, the longer the wait between spells he'd noticed.

Having spent ten points so far and a total of fifteen points in the tree, he could now access the fourth Tier and see down to the sixth. In the fourth Tier, he eyed the two available: Sigil Mastery and Arcane Resonance. One was a defensive buff for his Mystic Veil and the other a flat boost of his sigils and runes, enhancing their effectiveness.

He couldn't see himself passing up the opportunity to spend five additional points for a 15% buff to the effectiveness of his runes. It would buff not only his ability to make more potent scrolls or do rituals, but also enhance his ability to scribe them into the air around him and enchant weapons and armor. There was no way he could pass that up, so he unlocked it and set his sights on the next Tier.

They were well worth looking at, with one called Enigmatic Aura, giving him an aura that increased spellcasting speed and damage by 2% per point up to five. The other was less effective for the group but potentially a huge game changer in general, called Timeless Knowledge.

It unlocked an ability to temporarily manipulate the flow of time, allowing him to rewind up to a second of time per point added up to three. However, there was a note that the time-rewind applied only to the caster and would not affect those around him. So, in that sense, it wasn't true time travel; more of a way to either double cast a spell or reposition oneself mid-combat.

Knox wanted to think about the party, but this new ability

was just too impressive to pass up. He put three points into Timeless Knowledge and then because he felt guilty about it, two points into Enigmatic Aura. That left him with 43 more talent points to spend. He had been neglecting to spend them because of how busy he'd been, but at three points per level and 28 levels, they'd gathered up a good bit. He then had a nagging annoyance that he ought to have looked at his Titan Path first, but knowing himself, he might have spent all the points there again and he wanted to keep his Paths balanced as best he could.

Sure enough, as soon as he saw and remembered what was available to him in the Path of the Titans, he wondered why he hadn't spent all his points in that tree. But he had plenty to spend, so he started the arduous task of reading over all available talents.

First, he looked at the Luminous Vanguard branch. It had been the sole place where he'd spent points thus far, and it held a good bit of promise. He noticed a talent he'd had his eye on for a while, Lightforged Armor, but again decided against it since his own Mystic Armor spell was working fairly well. Next to catch his eye were several talents that added Light damage to his basic attacks. Both Illuminated Strikes and Searing Strikes had promise, so he invested six points into them, three each. That left him with 37 points and a significant amount of talents left to study.

Because of a level requirement that his Mystic Path hadn't shown, Knox was unable to see past Tier 6 yet, so he looked over what he had still available. There was Blinding Resilience, reducing stuns, silences, and slows, then Aegis of Light that increased the percentage of health Knox gained while Prism Ward was active. And finally, Titan's Fortitude, increasing physical resilience and reducing stuns and roots by 5% per point up to five.

None of these screamed at Knox as game changers, so he went to the next branch of the Titan Born talent tree, Arcane Luminary.

Surprisingly, the first three Tiers of the branch seemed dedicated to increasing either his magic damage or mana spending efficiency. Not as much utility as he'd have hoped, but boosting his magical abilities and combat efficiency wasn't a bad thing. Before spending any points, he decided it would be best to check out the last branch, Illumined Sage.

The talents here were a bit better—increasing specific abilities and giving utility to some defensive spells. Since he had enough points to reach pretty deep into a single branch, he really wanted to focus on a single one. Deciding that the utility was nice, but the raw increases of his own power would be even nicer, Knox chose to dive into the Arcane Luminary branch of talents.

First, he took Radiant Surge to amplify his Light-based magic spells, which cost 5 points. Because he wanted to balance out all his capabilities, he sunk an additional 3 into Soul Infusion, reducing all spell casting by a sizable 15% of their mana cost. Looking to the next Tier, Knox's attention was instantly caught by Illuminated Recovery.

Though he was feeling selfish and wanting to focus on building himself up right now, he could take these talents that boosted the healing effects of his Titan abilities so that Dernal wouldn't be as hard-pressed being the only central healer. Despite the 15% boost that came with sinking 5 points though, he still wouldn't consider himself a straight healer, knowing Dernal would have far more potent spells at his beck and call.

In the next Tier, Knox spent an additional 5 points to Resplendent Burst. It allowed for a 25% chance that his spells would burst on impact with enemies, dealing additional damage to the target and nearby enemies. It was a sound investment and Knox looked to the next Tier with his remaining 22 points.

However, his eyes were drawn back to Soul Channeling, it increased the maximum mana pool by 4% per point up to three. Putting 3 points into it, he felt his mana pool expand and knew he'd be all the better for it. That led him right into his next choice, Radiant Infusion. It increased his max health by 4% per point up to three as well. That left him with 16 points and many more options to choose from.

In the end, he spent them on the following: 5 went into

Arcane Radiance, increasing Critical Strike chance; 5 in the Illu-minated Sage branch for Enhanced Luminosity, increasing the range, damage, and healing by 50%; another 5 points into Rune Mastery, allowing all his Radiant Glyphs and runes to stay for 100% longer than before; and with his final point, he stuck it into an ability called, Beacon's Call, which allowed him to summon a beacon that pulled enemies toward it for 2 seconds.

Having spent all his talent points and learned the abilities that he set out to do, he released his hold on the time dilation and fell to his knees as he adjusted to his new reality. He was stronger, keener of mind, and had several new abilities at his disposal. He had so many now that he hoped he'd remember to use the right abilities at the right time.

"Took you long enough," Mic said.

Knox turned to regard the golem and saw that Dernal stood not too far away, looking bored.

"What did you pick?" Knox asked him and Dernal smiled.

"Hhrmm," he said, but Knox didn't let his response slide; stepping forward, he narrowed his eyes on his friend and mentor.

"Fine. Listen up because I won't explain twice," Dernal said.

Before Dernal got another word out, the entire complex began to shake and move.

"Oh, looks like we are finally rising up," Mic said, not at all seeming surprised by the sudden shakes and movement.

CHAPTER 5
THE CITY RISES

DERNAL, unperturbed by the rumbling and moving all around them, explained to Knox that he'd chosen the Mystic Path. He went on to explain that he was level 38 and had invested heavily into the Celestial Adept branch of talents. He noted that it wasn't exactly like the healing he'd done before, but that it was the closest thing he could find. Then he mentioned that he might even go further into the Druid tree as he leveled, but he wasn't sure yet.

With his explanation finished, he lapsed back into silence and Knox went to Mic to see when the shaking would end. Asking as he approached, he was greeted with a sudden stillness.

"Right now, I believe," Mic said. If he could smile wide, Knox was sure he'd be doing so right now.

"I need to get above and talk to people about their Paths, make sure they know it'll be alright," Knox said, but Dernal put a hand on his shoulder.

"Let's find Murdoch," he suggested, and Knox nodded. Murdoch was better at delivering news, so he would let him do so.

There were a surprising number of golems walking around and Knox wanted to ask Mic exactly how many had been brought into functioning life, but he'd disappeared at some point and Knox didn't know where he'd gotten off to.

So instead, he followed along with Dernal until they reached the housing area—a remarkable sight, considering it had made its way to the surface. From there, it was a simple matter of finding Murdoch. He was inside a building, surrounded by a fairly large crowd, reassuring them that everything was going to be fine.

Seeing Knox and Dernal, he finished with the crowd and waved them over as he stepped to the side.

"It *is* going to be alright, isn't it?" Murdoch asked, his eyes following a hawk as it flew overhead.

Knox looked around and admired the surface of the sprawling complex—or Luminar, as he had begun to think of it in his head.

Luminar was a massive city of buildings with tall trees sprouted all around, making the inner city look more like a forest-city hybrid. The ground, cracked in many places, was built of cobblestone and much of it was already covered in moss, as if it had been this way all along and not just recently snapped together out of the ground.

In all, it was a sight to behold. The city spanned at least a mile wide if Knox's guess was any good, and the most internal part of it, where Dernal and Knox had climbed free from the ground, had a pyramid shaped structure lifted high into the clouds above.

"Just when I was getting the hang of everything's location," Knox muttered, turning his attention back to Murdoch. "Everything will be fine. Tell everyone that a Path to power will be available to all. Tell them that they must speak the words, 'I need training' while picturing... well, perhaps just have them say the phrase and see how it goes. If that doesn't work, then we will need to bring people, in small teams, to the Titan Engine to get an idea of what it looks like. Just make sure they focus on their need for training and—well, here, let me draw it."

Knox knelt down and found a patch of mostly loose dirt and drew out the Titan Engine. Murdoch sighed and disappeared into the building, returning a few short moments later with a quill and paper. He effortlessly sketched out Knox's crude drawing with a level of skill that surprised Knox.

"So, say 'I need training' while picturing this odd lumpy thing?" Murdoch asked. Suddenly, his eyes glazed over, and his body went limp. He stood like that for a solid ten seconds before returning, eyes going wide.

"I'm level 7 and I'm a Diplomat focusing on the Silver Orator branch," he exclaimed, then he started laughing rather hysterically. "Watch this," he added as he stepped before the crowd of people and began to speak.

It was odd, Knox always knew that Murdoch spoke mostly honeyed words to people to get what he wanted, but as he spoke, Knox found his mood shifting to excited encouragement. He even yelled out above the crowd with a glee-filled hoot of approval when Murdoch suggested that everyone pool their resources and gold together for the betterment of the new colony.

When Dernal also hooted for joy, Knox knew something was off and he strained his brain to focus on what it was. It took only that act of will for the charm to fade and he glared at Murdoch in his usual disdain for such manipulative tricks. However, this time felt different. It wasn't just him speaking words people wanted to hear; there was legitimate magic behind Murdoch's words. Thinking back to the Path that would allow Murdoch to do that, Knox knew that he'd likely used his Silver Tongue ability.

Just to be sure, he pulled up the menu with his mind and began to look through it, happy to find that he could still see the information on each Path.

Sure enough, there was a base ability listed; he couldn't see much more than his own level would allow him, but that was plenty more than even Murdoch had access to. Murdoch's abilities and even his talent tree options were all non-combat related, but that didn't make them any less potent.

Monster or not, if Murdoch could stop them in their tracks with a few words, even for a moment, Knox could think of a thousand ways he could deal deadly blows to such an opponent. Though Knox trusted Murdoch, he felt that he should be on guard and strengthen his ability to block such charms. Knowing

Murdoch as he did, that power of persuasion could become addictive enough for him to abuse it.

Dernal snapped out of it only moments after Knox and he did not look happy. Pushing through the crowd, he grabbed Murdoch by the collar, an impressive feat considering how much shorter he was than Murdoch. As Dernal began to drag him back toward Knox, whatever charm he'd been laying on the crowd quickly began to fade, leaving everyone looking confused.

"Easy, easy," Murdoch said as Dernal let go of him and stared daggers in his direction.

"That wasn't smart," Knox said, looking at the crowd, who now stared at Murdoch with anger in their eyes. However, Knox's attitude changed to one of awe when he realized that it wasn't Murdoch they were eyeing with violent anger in their minds, but rather at Dernal and Knox. *"Murdoch?"*

"Oh, dear me," Murdoch said, a wide grin on his face. "I've gotten them a bit riled up, haven't I? You see, I used both my Silver Tongue skill and with the extra effects of Crowd Charmer, it really laid it on thick. This is way more exciting than unsuccessfully trying to use my abilities on that Gowlen fellow. You know it felt like weeks, if not a month, to learn my abilities in there? All the while, I had only the company of that dull, metal man who refused to be as insightful as I was about myself. Oh, right."

Murdoch saw a few of the larger men step forward as if coming to his aid and he realized the danger he'd begun. "Easy there, all is fine."

Then, leaning toward Knox he added, "That is a bit of my Mass Pacification talent at work. Watch."

Sure enough, the crowd seemed soothed. Hell, even Knox felt its effects, and what little anger he'd had building up seemed to wash away without any recourse.

"You are going to be one dangerous man," Knox said, unable to suppress a smile as he considered Murdoch and the powerful abilities he'd unlocked. "Oh, better try to avoid messing with Dernal's emotions and such. He's level 38, and I'm not sure he is against the idea of killing you to stop you from messing with his mind."

"I'm not," Dernal said, his hand beginning to pulse with a spell Knox knew all too well—Arcane Pulse. "And don't think I can't be anywhere, anytime, to deal with you." The spell in his hand pulsed and then another ability triggered, one that Knox hadn't experienced before. A see-through, almost shiny, version of Dernal stepped out of himself and moved with deadly speed, stopping before Murdoch.

It whispered something to him that Knox didn't catch, but Murdoch went a few shades paler, and his hand instinctually went for the saber at his waist. But he didn't pull it free, instead, his hand trembled there until in a puff of magic, the other Dernal disappeared.

"What was that?" Knox asked, more interested, and amazed by Dernal's casual use of his spells—particularly the one he hadn't seen before—than the threats his friends were exchanging.

"I'm sorry," Murdoch said, his voice more genuine than Knox had ever heard it. "It won't happen again." Then he gave a little bow, turning to go speak with the crowd.

"What in the hells did you say to him?" Knox asked Dernal.

"Hhrmm," Dernal answered, leaving Knox biting his lip as he imagined what threat would so swiftly turn off the bravado that Murdoch normally showed.

With everyone slowly being told how to access the Titan System, Knox was left with little to do but help with the clean-up efforts. Supplies that had been left outside buildings were missing and were being found on different levels of the complex. Some had even been crushed, but so far, no injuries had occurred when Luminar rose to the surface.

However, the large area that made Luminar's surface had a few issues: monsters. Several Nolics, large spiders, and other monsters had made their way inside the surrounding area, but they were weak enough that they were almost not worth the effort to take them out. Mic was busy handing out quests to clear them out, as well as a general collection of Monster Cores that were necessary for the improvement of the Titan Engine.

Knox took such a quest, along with Terrim, Murdoch, and Beth. Frederick asked for time to look over the crops and go over how they grew so fast, with some of the maintenance golems assigned to the area. Knox was all but happy to allow it as they needed to understand the workings of Luminar if it was to be their long-term home. And the longer he spent on the surface in the fresh air that buzzed with power, the more he knew that he wanted to live here.

Sure, Knox still wanted to study, learn, and grow stronger, as well as discover hidden places, secrets, and more. But, having a place that felt like home, *truly* a home where he could feel comfortable, was a new experience for him, and he liked it.

"So, tell me again, what Paths did you all choose? So many people have told me theirs that I've lost track," Knox asked. They were narrowing in on a pack of lower-leveled Nolics, and he wanted to know what his team's capabilities were, even though he didn't plan on actively helping.

"Well, I'm obviously a Ranger, but I haven't spent my talent points as I'm not sure the specialty I want to do yet," Beth said. Her mood had improved ever since she unlocked the system, but she still refused to look directly at Knox.

He understood to an extent, and he hoped that bringing her along on this quest wasn't a bad idea. He had to trust those by his side during combat—but it wasn't like they were going to face anything difficult that he couldn't solo if things went bad. Still, he kept his gaze on Beth for several long moments, wishing that things could be how they'd been before. He'd never been a huge fan of how overtly sexual she'd been toward him, but he'd trade that for how she seemed to feel for him now any day.

Reaching into his pack, he pulled free his notebook and looked over the area where he'd made notes about the Ranger talent tree. Beth had three main focuses she could take, Beastmaster, Marksman—or in this case, Markswoman Knox supposed—or Warden. He had barely considered the Ranger Path, but if he did take it, he knew that he would walk the Path of the Warden. It mixed magic and force well enough that it was almost like being a Druidic Path without having shapeshifting. Knox kept his thoughts to himself, instead looking at Terrim.

"What, me next?" Terrim asked, swinging his axe in a half swing. "What do *you* think I picked?"

Knox shrugged. "Honestly, I don't know. Warrior would be my first guess with a focus in either Berserker or Guardian, but there are so many choices that I guess I could also see you as an Elementalist with how obsessed with Fire you were as a kid."

Terrim laughed and made a mock swing for Knox's head with his axe but missed deftly as Knox bent just out of reach.

"I almost went for a Magic Path, I even considered a Mind-based Path, but in the end, the Warrior Path was the only one that felt right," Terrim said, his hand going to rub behind his neck.

Knox let out a breath of air he'd been holding in. It was a relief to know the team had someone willing to be a more physical-focused Path. With his own abilities being mostly magical in nature, he'd really pushed into the Titan Born Luminous Vanguard branch to ensure that he wasn't outclassed by anything that might be more immune to magic. But he wouldn't be a match for someone going purely Physical.

Knox fit into a role that was more balanced between both magic and physical, leaving his weak link being his mind. There, he had Murdoch to cover his ass, at least he hoped. The young mayor-to-be was taking to his new role as a Silver-Tongued leader a bit too well. But Murdoch was good people, if he sometimes allowed himself to go too far, that was what friends were for. Knox and the rest of his friends would keep Murdoch straight, and if they failed, Dernal would probably chop off his dangly bits. At least that was what Knox had figured he must have threatened him with. What else would cause good ole Murdoch to go so pale?

"Have you placed any points or decided on which branch of your talent tree you'll go down?" Knox asked Terrim after staring at Murdoch for a few moments.

"I'm with Beth, I haven't picked. Figured we could all talk about it together and decide what would be best. We are going to team up and slay monsters together, right? What are the chances we can clear that dungeon you went to?" Terrim asked, shooting of question after question in rapid fire.

"I'm down to team up for a dungeon run, what level did you all make it to?"

Terrim and Beth answered at the same time, nearly overlapping their response.

"Level 6," Beth said.

"Made it to 6!" Terrim exclaimed.

"And everyone is down to group together? Because I would love to, but it might take you all awhile to get up to my level. But I bet we could clear the dungeon out by the time you all reach level 10," Knox said, watching Beth more than anyone else as he spoke.

"You know I'm ready to slay some hideous monsters," Murdoch said, swishing his thin blade through the air and lunging forward as if stabbing one through.

"Let's do it," Terrim said, pumping his fist in the air.

"I could be convinced," Beth said, shooting a quick glance at Knox. He barely noticed it, distracted by Terrim's huge hand pumping into the sky, but he smiled when he realized she finally looked at him.

"Good, we just have to get Dernal and Frederick onboard," Knox said, adding, "We have to have a Healer and Dernal is the best."

Flipping through his notebook to the Warrior talent tree he

looked at the available choices. Then flipping back to the Ranger tree, he considered which branch would be the best help for them.

"What Path did Frederick choose?" Knox asked.

Beth and Murdoch shrugged and Terrim started becoming very interested in looking at the ground. Knox walked a bit faster and put himself in front of his massive friend. Terrim easily stood two heads taller than Knox, and not for the first time, Knox wondered if maybe his friend had some kind of foreign giant blood in him.

Knox wasn't short by any means and was taller than most in general. He was as tall in comparison to Dernal, as Terrim was to Knox.

"What's wrong?" Knox asked Terrim, forcing himself into the giant man's view.

"Nothing," Terrim assured him, trying to deftly slip by him, but Knox's newest improvements to his sense made it possible to pick up on even the most subtle of movements and he easily moved in sync with Terrim, blocking his path.

"Just tell me what happened, is Frederick okay?" Knox asked, beginning to be concerned for his somber friend.

"He picked an odd Path is all," Terrim said, throwing up his hands in defeat and looking at the ground, avoiding Knox's eyes.

Flipping through his notes Knox found the Path Frederick had likely chosen and understood Terrim's hesitance.

"He picked Necromancy, didn't he?" Knox asked.

Terrim nodded and finally looked at him. "I told him it wasn't a good idea. I mean, *Necromancy*, messing with corpses and stuff... that can't be a good idea."

"It's a valid path," Knox said, letting out a breath. "If a bit morbid."

"Does that mean he can raise people who've died?" Beth asked, an odd look on her face, something between hope and anguish.

"Let me look," Knox said, pulling up his system menu and accessing the Necromancer Path. He'd taken notes on it, but at his new higher level, he'd be able to see more abilities and passive abilities than before.

"Well?" Terrim asked; he'd started biting at his nail, a nervous habit that Knox hadn't seen him do in years.

"He can raise the dead, but it looks like only for a short period of time and they act as minions, not free-thinking beings," Knox said, his eyes glazed over as he studied the list of abilities and the talent tree.

Necromancy had a good bit of cool, if morbid, abilities and the talent tree was very intriguing. Perhaps he ought to have given this class more thought after all, he thought as he looked at the Soulbinder branch. It allowed for souls to be infused into weapons, creating powerful artifacts. It even allowed for the creation of golems later down the line in Tier 3 of the talent tree.

An insight hit him like a ton of bricks suddenly, and he smiled. "I think the last Titan Born, maybe the one I found stabbed through the chest, was a Necromancer. It is the only Path that I've seen that allows for the creation of golems as part of its talent tree."

"Really?" Terrim asked, seeming to lighten a bit. "In that case, it must not be so bad. Yeah, see, I told you all you were worrying for nothing."

"You said no such thing," Beth said flatly.

"Yeah," Murdoch said, laughing. "You were practically pissing yourself. But don't worry, we don't judge you. So, relax."

Knox felt a magical aura around Murdoch pulse, and he turned, pointing a hand in Murdoch's face. "Stop that shit," Knox said in a flat tone. The aura disappeared and Terrim was left blinking as whatever charm Murdoch was about to use faded to nothing.

"Did you just hit me with your mojo?" Terrim asked, opening his mouth, and moving it around like he had a bad taste there. "That stuff hits hard."

"Any idea what path he took or plans on taking?" Knox asked Terrim, but he shook his head, signaling that he didn't know. So they lapsed back into a friendly quiet, moving ever closer to the group of Nolics in the distance. "Okay, focus up and watch out for their claws. Nolics are fast and vicious but go down easy. I'm going to stay out of the combat unless you really need me, that way you get a good bit of the essence yourselves. Ready?"

CHAPTER 6
PREPARATIONS

THE BATTLE BEGAN with Beth unleashing a carefully aimed shot into one of the greasy looking Nolic's face. It had the body of a naked rat, except for an occasional tuft of whiskers on its face and randomly throughout its body. The creature was as much saggy skin and bone as it was anything else, but the three fingered claws and wide eyes gave it an odd look.

Almost as if whoever created these creatures was going for cute but missed the mark severely. The Nolic screeched in a way only Nolics could and fell dead from Beth's shot a moment later. There were five left and Terrim showed great bravery running head long into them, axe raised to strike. His axe seemed to give off a reddish glow as he struck downward, and Knox was sure he'd just witnessed the skill Power Strike.

As if confirming that he was indeed using abilities, Terrim moved with astonishing speed as he activated Charge, slamming into the furthest Nolic. Knox readied his own spell to heal Terrim as lines of red appeared all over his arms when the Nolics attacked, but he held off after seeing Terrim begin to swing harder and faster.

Murdoch appeared with his sword out, spearing one through

the eye with it and turning to another, muttering some rhyme Knox couldn't hear from a distance. Whatever he said stopped two of the Nolics dead in their tracks, giving Terrim the opening he needed to slice through both of their midsections with ease.

The fight was over before it really had a chance to start, finished by a barrage of arrows from Beth, killing the very last Nolic.

"Now for the fun part," Knox said, examining his friends for serious injuries. "We have to cut into them and look for Monster Cores."

"Whoa, look at me heal," Terrim said, his eyes fixated on the fine, thin cuts he'd received. They were indeed healing, very slowly, but fast enough that you could see the shallow cuts begin to close.

"One of the many benefits of the system," Knox said, a bit amazed himself by the swiftness of his healing. That would come in handy if he was the main focus in the front lines, a job Knox had only seen Caleb do up to this point. "We should get you a shield," he added, remembering how effective it had been for him in the dungeon.

"Hey Knox," Terrim said, a wide smile on his face.

"What?" Knox asked, eyeing his friend suspiciously.

"To death!" Terrim exclaimed, then he smashed a wide-eyed Nolic head to nothing but wet gore.

"To death," Knox repeated back, but then going a bit closer to the now blood-covered Warrior, Knox added, "You probably just destroyed a core, that one comes out of your share."

"Aw shit," Terrim said, looking down at his feet with eyebrows raised and a downturned face.

They continued the hunt for several hours, killing everything from wolves, Nolics, and even an owlbear that found its way inside the complex of Luminar. Knox only had to step in once, with the owlbear. It was a bit stronger than the one they'd faced before. But there was no sign of black goo or infection on any of the creatures, so that was good.

"We need to organize teams, get patrols set up and begin clearing out the weaker of the monsters," Knox said to Murdoch, who nodded along agreeably. He had asked what the next steps would be, and Knox was outlining what he thought as best he could.

"And once we've cleared out all the weaker monsters?" Murdoch asked, looking around the massive city of buildings and unexplored complexes he added, "Perhaps we spend some time exploring and mapping the full extent of Luminar?"

They'd all picked up on calling it Luminar, seeing as 'Titan Complex' just didn't have the right ring to it. Knox nodded at the suggestion because it was a good idea. First, they could explore, then map it, and from there it would be easier to know how to defend it.

"We should also see about repairing the walls, there are holes big enough to let owlbears in all over the place," Terrim said, Beth nodded along with him but remained mostly quiet.

A thought occurred to Knox, and he turned back to Murdoch. "We should get a list of everyone's Path they chose and what talent tree focus they are planning on taking. Perhaps after we've got them into groups, so they will know what will best suit each other."

"Not everyone will want to fight and clear monsters, we need to set up a trade system using Monster Cores as a base to trade for other services. For instance, we all have much more strength and endurance than we once did, so manual labor will be easy enough," Murdoch said, a keen smile appearing on his lips.

"We have golems for that, speaking of which, I've got several dozen more souls captured inside my Soulstones, so we will have a legion of golems soon. Which is good because based on the number of people within the influence of the Titan System and how many we currently have in Luminar, we are outnumbered two to one," Knox said.

"You should speak with Frederick about the Soulstones and maybe spread them out so we can collect more faster," Beth suggested, breaking her silence. Still, she didn't meet Knox's eyes as she spoke, preferring to direct her comment to Murdoch.

"Brilliant idea!" Murdoch exclaimed as they turned and headed back for the most central area where the housing units were located.

Knox surveyed the area and his eyes locked on the sizable pyramid in the center of Luminar. That was where the throne room was located, the seat of power of Luminar. Knox had meant to explore it a bit more, perhaps order maintenance golems to fix it up even more, but he hadn't gotten around to it yet. No time like the present.

"I've some work to do, will you all be fine bringing your Monster Cores to either Mic or the Titan Engine for rewards?" Knox asked.

A round of 'yeahs' and 'sure thing' followed, and Knox jogged ahead toward the housing area and eventually to the pyramid. However, Terrim caught up with him before he'd gotten far away, a solemn look on his face.

"I never really got a chance to thank you," Terrim said, and Knox knew immediately what he meant.

"She is doing alright then?" Knox asked, Terrim met his eyes and tears glistened there.

"She lost her family during the black sickness, so her learning that was a bit of a shock. It's like all those weeks she spent under its affects she has no memory of it. I almost didn't come on this hunting trip, but Dernal said he'd watch over her and I want to get stronger for her," Terrim said.

"And for yourself," Knox added. "I'm glad to hear Danielle is doing better, but you are right to go out and hunt. The stronger we all grow, the better suited we will be to fight against whatever growing darkness is brewing out there."

"So much has changed," Terrim said, rubbing at the back of his neck and looming over Knox with how close he was.

"There are still trees to be cut," Knox said, smiling up at the big guy. "I know it's a lot, but we will adjust and overcome."

"We kind of have to, don't we?" Terrim asked.

Knox sighed. "Seems that way," he said, his thoughts going to the Titan Engine and knowing that it wouldn't stop spreading its influences anytime soon. "Might be that the System will take over the world. I think, at least based off all I've learned, that that was once the normal state of the world."

"I can't imagine a world where everyone walks a Path, from child to aged adult. It is going to change everything," Terrim said, patting Knox on the shoulder.

"I've got to get going but tell Dernal when you see him that I will be there for purifying the rest of the sick in a few hours. He wanted to strengthen them up a bit with his new healing spells before we killed off the sickness. The system healing he learned packs way more of a punch than his previous techniques."

"Will do," Terrim said, turning to jog off toward the makeshift healer's hut that had been set up to keep the sick separated from the rest of the population.

Knox stepped out from the building he'd been waylaid in, a few people had questions about Paths, and he couldn't help but give his own opinion to them on the best choices to make concerning the talent tree and whatnot. They'd been nice, though he could hardly say he knew them too well. First, he spoke with Darcy and Marcy, identical twins who had lost their parents to the black sickness.

They'd picked interesting paths, one going for Scholar and the other Mentalist. Checking through his notes, Knox had noted that each had much more straightforward offensive capabilities than the Diplomat path and wondered if perhaps Murdoch would have been better off taking one of those paths. But no,

Murdoch was Murdoch, and using his words and manipulating people was his strong suit.

Darcy, the Scholar, had been happy when Knox allowed her to borrow his notes on runes, and promising that he'd bring her by his book he had on it. He hadn't told her that there was an entire system-based library on runes because he wasn't sure sharing the Titan base language was something he could do without a person being on the Path of the Titans. He'd have to ask Mic about it later.

Regardless, she had two impressive starting abilities; she could cast a spell called Arcane Blast that dealt a great amount of arcane damage, but also took a great deal of Mana to do so. And then there was Rune Inscription, which allowed her to do what Knox had been doing all along, but with safeguards and help from the system itself. With her ability to inscribe runes, she showed off by doing a few she'd just saw on the ground, she was likely to be someone they'd lean on when it came to enchanting gear.

Gear, weapons, equipment, there was so much to do and so little time. They needed to prepare for battle, possibly even war. He had some supplies of armor and weapons in the vaults—which luckily stayed below the ground—but not enough to arm everyone. Another thing to discuss with Mic, getting the new golems to work on creating armor and possibly making quests to find ore.

It would be difficult to find any suitable ore out in this half-forest half-swamp area, but if they had any chance of surviving the coming months, they'd need a literal ton of it.

With all this on his mind, he told himself he would be waylaid until he found Mic and started to get reports on how things were going, giving his own reports in turn to the golem. Mic was really turning out to be a big help, he kept the pirate golems in check easily enough and kept the rest of the golem population busy and efficient.

Most of the people Knox had encountered were wary of the

golems still, keeping their distance and not communicating with them. That would have to change eventually if they were going to prosper. Sure, the golems were simple and weak, at least the newest batches based on the lower-leveled souls, but they would grow in strength as they completed their own quests and tasks.

The combat golems that he'd made before leaving were already stronger than most of the people here. Shoot, Edgar, Boris, and Vlad could probably take on a dozen or more citizens at their current strength. They still weren't a match for Knox, but the gap between them continued to slow as more Cores were brought in by their hunting trips.

Thinking back to the twins, Knox thought about Marcy and her new abilities. She had one called Mind Crush that dealt mental damage, something Knox was both excited to hear about and wary of having done to himself. Then there was a more straightforward ability called Telekinetic Push that allowed her to push objects with her mind and a measure of focus. She'd displayed this ability to Knox with a surprising measure of finesse, easily throwing over an apple to him without touching it.

It was like everyone, even the kids, had been given powerful Paths to follow, making the challenge now to get everyone up in level fast enough to prepare for any threats Luminar might face.

"Slow down, damn you," a familiar voice sounded behind Knox and it took all his control not to sprint away just by principle. Turning, he regarded Askar Trelling, his father, jogging over to him, an axe in his one good hand.

He wasn't left-handed, but after so long of only having one hand, he managed fine with it. But to see him holding a weapon, Knox's mind first went to the worst-case scenario, that he was under attack, but that faded quickly and was replaced by genuine curiosity.

Why had his father chosen to take up a weapon and more than that, why did he feel the need to talk to him right now?

"What?" Knox answered, his voice deadpan.

"I heard you were the one to talk to about getting assigned to a hunting party," Askar said, his words so casual and normal that Knox had to blink several times to make sure it was actually his father.

First off, he wanted to *help?* Secondly, he was talking to Knox in a way that he hadn't for countless years, casually and without insult. Knox wouldn't be so easily fooled by his father's words.

"Why do you want to be part of a hunting party?" Knox asked, unable to keep a little heat out of his voice.

Askar didn't look away, his face didn't twist in anger, he just stared at Knox with a look that he could only describe as pure confusion.

"I've chosen a Path. I have abilities that I can use again. I'm not worthless anymore," Askar said, a bit of heat coming into his own voice.

"What Path did you chose?" Knox asked, his voice going deadpan again. It was so unlike his father to come out and speak with him like this. Just the fact that he revealed he felt worthless before getting a Path or that he said he could use abilities again both caught Knox's attention.

"Ranger, level 19," Askar said, lifting his axe and twirling it skillfully.

"Ranger? Wait, did you say level 19?" Knox asked, his father's words confusing him utterly. How in the hells would Askar Trelling, the woodcutter, be level 19 already? That would mean that he would have to have been an E Ranked Adventurer, nearly a D Ranked.

"Who are you?" Knox asked, leveling his best glare at his father, the stranger of a man he apparently knew very little about.

"I have a past," Askar said, shaking his head. "Big surprise that I lived a little before settling down to raise your ungrateful ass." His voice was little more than a growl at this point and the Askar Trelling that Knox knew reared his head.

"Fine, whatever," Knox said, but Askar stepped forward and spoke before he could finish his thought.

"You want to know about your mother don't you? Well, trust me when I tell you that you are better off not knowing," Askar said, he was practically shouting the words. "Now assign me to a hunting party so I can be damned useful."

"Why won't you tell me about her?" Knox's hand went down to Scarlet, the name of his axe, his mother's name.

"That axe is a reminder of everything I hated about being an Adventurer. She enchanted it herself, she was always talented in that kind of magic hoo-hah," Askar's eyes seemed to glaze over as he spoke. "I was more skilled in tracking and killing things, but together we were an unstoppable team. But she abandoned me, she abandoned *us*! And after all I've done for you, you still hate me!"

"She didn't abandon us, you fool!" Knox returned with heat in his voice to match his father's. "She died!"

Askar looked like he wanted to say something, but he just stared daggers at Knox and let the quiet grow between them. Finally, having enough of it, Knox spoke again.

"I'll get you on a team but talk to Dernal next time and he can tell me. I don't want anything to do with you, so stay out of my way," Knox said, his words a calm steel compared to the heat he'd just had. He really thought he was making progress with his father, but the man was the same stubborn angry fool he always was, and he wouldn't change, Path or no Path.

Askar stayed standing where he was, axe fallen to the ground at his feet as Knox walked way. Knox's sense felt when he finally stirred, picking up his axe and walking in the opposite direction. Had he been too hard on him? Perhaps he should accept that his father had major flaws and just be happy he was willing to work for his keep now.

But knowing he'd once been an Adventurer, the very thing that Knox wanted more than anything else, just boiled his blood in a way he'd never felt before. How could his father, his freaking *father*, have been an Adventurer? It boggled the mind to consider the possibility of it, but he had to admit he knew very little about his father's past. And he had been a damn good woodcutter in his prime. Perhaps the increased power of being an Adventurer had lent him that strength?

CHAPTER 7
HUNTING

KNOX FOUND MIC, asked his questions, and relayed his concerns. Before the golem could tell him much himself, Knox excused himself, gathering Edgar, Boris, and Vlad to do some hunting. He had some steam he needed to work out, and there was no better way than collecting some Monster Cores.

"Where we going to hunt, boss?" Boris asked, as he began to travel outside the city gates. They were mostly intact, and the wall was buzzing with activity already, golems and people alike working to repair the damage.

Several large ballista were in various stages of being constructed, several mounted on the upper walls and a few down below in front of the walls. Knox knew little about siege warfare, but it seemed odd to have one where the enemy might take control of it and use it against them. Just another item to bring to Mic, on top of all he was handling, along with Murdoch, the settlements welfare.

If he wasn't so angry, he might have even been able to appreciate their hard work. As it was right now, he was fuming and wanted to attack something, so he ignored Boris and headed to where he knew he'd find powerful monsters to kill, toward the land that still functioned as a swamp.

They met their first C Ranked Monster within minutes of crossing over to the swamp land. Despite the spread of the Titan System, this particular area seemed resistant to the change. But Knox was sure it was just a matter of time. The changes around Luminar had taken a year, surely it would take just as long to affect the newest area that moved under the Titan Engine's influence.

"Flank it and bring it down," Knox said, eyeing the fierce looking owlbear as it slashed in the air around them, missing each strike as Knox focused on it with his sense.

It was like he could predict the very movements of it now, each muscle twitch and feathered movement plain to see as he wove through its attacks. It wasn't perfect and his Stamina would run out eventually, but for now, he was untouchable.

Vlad rushed in using his abilities, then a glow enveloped his fist as he delivered a mighty blow to the back of the owlbear's head. Using Ethereal Step, Knox put himself in position to slash down with his axe, Scarlet. She bit deep into its arm and blood splattered in an arc, barely missing him.

Just as Vlad and Knox backed off and gave the thrashing owlbear some room, Edgar called down a fireball on its head, the flames enveloping the owlbear for several seconds. However, Boris unwisely decided that it was time to attack with his elemental water attack, the surge of water smashing the Owlbear off balance but also putting it out.

Knox turned just in time to see Edgar blast Boris off his feet with a gust of air, before turning his gaze to Knox and shrugging.

"Damned pirates," Knox cursed under his breath as he rushed back in with Vlad coming at the exact opposite side.

In a show of power, Vlad stomped his feet as he reached the Owlbear, knocking it down. Knox followed up by using Radiant Ground, stomping his foot and causing fissures of golden light to appear.

He used Radiant Rush to create a path for Vlad to escape to his comrades. Then, triggering his Timeless Knowledge talent, he appeared back at the feet of the owlbear, ready to strike once more. The time shift was an odd feeling, but his sense warned him in time to miss a strike from the owlbear and he was back in the game.

He slashed upward—he was purposefully avoiding using too much magic as he wanted to purge himself of his built-up emotions, and physically expending his energy was the easiest way to do so. Back and forth he fought with the owlbear, his companions staying back as his close-up presence prevented them from doing much. Other than Vlad, who delivered a punch here and there as the fight went on.

Cut after shallow cut began to appear on his exposed flesh—he wore minimal armor and hadn't activated his Mystic Armor—but the pain did nothing but help burn away more of his frustration. It was a battle that looked like it would end with a thousand cuts being delivered by both sides.

After a time, and with his Stamina flagging, Knox used Ethereal Step and appeared twenty paces away. Raising his hand, he was determined to finish the fight so he could get to the next one. His opponent was slow and barely holding on at this point. Knox unleashed a Luminous Surge right into the face of the owlbear and once his sense caught the moment it died, he cut off the spell.

"Collect the Core and let's find our next target," Knox said, sitting down and leaning against a nearby tree in a patch of ground that stood above the ankle-deep water.

Closing his eyes, Knox couldn't help but think that his plan to blow off steam wasn't working. All he could think about was his father and how he'd lied to him his entire life. He'd been an Adventurer! Perhaps with his guidance and training, Knox could have been so much more than he was now, but no, his father had chosen to be a bitter old fool, hiding the truth of his past life and his mother from him.

If he lied about his past life, then what else had he lied about? A sudden thought occurred to Knox, and he cursed under his breath. Could his mother still be alive? Could she have truly abandoned them at some point and his father lied about it to save face? Surely, someone in the town would have known, but who was old enough to remember or know? Perhaps Mr. Tome, but wouldn't he have told him if he knew something of his past?

Then another thought occurred to him. Dernal had been visiting the town for as long as Knox could remember, was there a chance Dernal knew anything about his mother? No, Dernal was his friend, he would have told him, or would he have? More anger and frustration bubbled up around him. With only about half of his Stamina refilled and his health still below three quarters, Knox stood and began reaching out with his sense for monsters to fight.

They were skirting the edges of the changed area, and so far, there had only been C Ranked Monsters. But right then and there, Knox wanted to encounter a B Ranked Monster. He wanted danger and to prove he was better. He let the thoughts run through his head, growing in anger and frustration as they did.

"You feeling alright?" Edgar asked, coming over and offering the C Ranked Monster Core to Knox.

He took it and absorbed the energy there without a thought, pocketing the empty Core for later. The essence surged into him, and he felt himself advance another level. It was just barely enough, leaving him with only a few essence left over, but he didn't feel guilty about it.

Just one more step closer to reaching level 30, the same as if he'd reached C Rank. The fact that he was fighting and winning against C Ranked Monsters meant, to him at least, that if he got to C Rank he'd be able to tackle even B Ranked Monsters by himself. Of course, he wasn't a complete fool, even with so much anger and angst going through him. He brought his metallic companions and, despite the initial thoughts to do so, he would avoid B Ranked Monsters or groups of C Ranked Monsters... for now.

They killed three more before returning, Knox collected each of the Cores but decided against using them. His anger aside, the Titan Engine or his friends could use it much more than he could. Despite all that, he wanted to have a talk with Mic about a few items, so he set off to find him.

Before finding him, he came upon Frederick and decided he should have a chat with the man as well.

"Frederick, you busy?" Knox asked, Frederick was talking to a maintenance golem, but upon seeing Knox he smiled and walked toward him.

He looked different than what Knox remembered, perhaps a bit paler but happier than any time he could remember, except for when his family was still alive.

"Wonderful day today, isn't it?" Frederick asked, catching Knox off guard. Looking around, Knox shrugged.

The clouds were obscuring the sun, and the weather was getting bitter cold, but no snow had come yet and likely wouldn't if the pattern held for the Shadowfall Swamp area. It was one of the few areas where snow didn't seem like it ever touched. That didn't keep it from becoming bitter cold, but no snow was a welcomed expectation.

"I suppose," Knox said. "You feeling alright?"

"Did you hear about my Path?" Frederick asked, ignoring Knox's question. Before Knox could answer, he continued. "I'm going to tell him, just wait." He looked to the side as he spoke as if someone was there, but Knox checked with his sense, and there was no one.

"Frederick?" Knox asked, his voice filled with concern.

"It isn't what you think," he said, shaking his head. "I took the Necromancy Path and I've leveled up a fair bit, hit level ten already helping with maintenance quests and farming. There is a branch of the talent tree that is called Spiritcaller."

"I'm familiar with it," Knox said, his eyes flicking to the space where his friend had spoken and putting it together. "You are speaking to spirits?"

"My family, they've been with me the entire time," Frederick said, excitement clear on his face. "I've encountered a few other spirits, but they are faint. Something about them being my family has made them more solid, more real."

"I can't see them," Knox said flatly.

"No, but other Necromancers can," Frederick said, his smile widening.

"Interesting, we have more than one Necromancer?" Knox asked, he hadn't looked at the reports on Path choices yet, but now he knew he needed to.

"Several dozen, but I'm the strongest so far. Our Plague Bolt ability, our main offense ability, is tricky to cast, does very little damage at first, and so far, group spots have been hard to get," he said, his smile wavering as he explained how the Necromancers were being left out.

"I'll see that you are all given a spot, even if I have to force the issue," Knox said, trying hard to be comfortable with the idea of spirits around that he couldn't see. "Hey, Fred."

"Yeah?" he asked.

"Can you see any spirits around me?" Knox asked, his eyes darting back and forth.

"None," Frederick said, shaking his head.

"Okay," Knox said. "I've work to do, but I'll be sure to speak to Murdoch and Mic about getting your fellow Necromancers into groups."

"Thanks!" Frederick said, and Knox blinked several times, still processing the eager and happy Frederick. He'd always been so somber and quiet but connecting with the dead has really added a pep into his step.

Hurrying off, Knox found Mic in the throne room. It had

been cleared of broken stone and debris, looking like a proper throne room now. The chair had even shrunk to normal size, whether that was an automatic feature or something they'd done, Knox appreciated it. He went and sat on it just as Mic came up to him to speak.

"Before you start," Mic said, holding up his hands and preventing Knox from saying anything. "I need to inform you of a new development. The Door has been discovered; the Labyrinth can be opened!"

CHAPTER 8
PIRATES

"WHAT IN THE hells do you mean, labyrinth?" Knox asked, pinching at the bridge of his nose. If it wasn't one thing it was another. Knox just wanted to get through a day without one big surprise. However, his recent exertions took much of the fight out of him, so he waited to hear the golem's explanation.

"It is exactly what it sounds like," Mic said, tilting his head to the side. "I'd been struggling to remember anything I could about Luminar, and then I remembered about the Labyrinth. It is a place of challenge and a proving ground for the Titan Born. Your first step to truly unlocking your power and potential."

"So, there is a maze somewhere in the complex that will make me stronger, is that what you are saying?" Knox asked, following the ramblings of Mic as best he could.

"Yes, but there is more to it. The Labyrinth was created by one of the first Titan Born and the strongest to ever yield the power of Light. They spread parts of an emblem that contains great power within it, each one protected by a Guardian. Each Guardian, protected by minions," Mic said, his hands waving about as he spoke.

"How much power are we talking about?" Knox asked, suddenly very interested. If he could power himself up enough, not even the pirates would be able to stand in his way. *Hells, if I got strong enough, I might be able to work out what is happening with the black goo and the appearances of the dark child.*

"Power that will lift you far higher than you are now, enough power to truly make you and the Titan Engine, a force to be reckoned with," Mic said.

Knox shifted in his place on the throne and putting his hand down on the arm rest, he was surprised to see a screen appear, mapping out Luminar and its surrounding fields. What was most startling about this was the fact that there were two dozen red dots moving closer to the complex from outside.

"Mic?" Knox asked, gesturing to the screen and hoping his golem companion could see it.

"Oh, I see," Mic said, moving to stand closer to the throne. "Looks like we have incoming by an unknown force."

"We can discuss the Labyrinth later, send word to all battle golems to gather at the East Gate," Knox said, getting ready to lift himself out of the throne.

Mic held up a hand and forestalled him. "Send your will through the command chair and they will get the message. Do as you did before when you reached out to us, but it should be far easier with the help of the chair."

Knox began to protest, but thinking better of it he closed his eyes in concentration. Sending out a command for all available golems to gather at the gate, there were several impressions that hit him all at once. They were moving, and fast. Deciding he could do more, he focused on speaking to the maintenance golems and ordered them to gather up all civilians inside the walls, and to tell anyone able to fight to be ready at the East Gate.

It was the only gate that was mostly operational and also the direction that the red dots were approaching. Focusing back on the map, Knox saw that they were still a mile out at least, but something else hit him as he focused on the map.

The square mile area was so large that he could sense, if only barely, hundreds of other threats, likely a mix of monsters and pirates, but that wasn't what was getting his attention. It was the green dot surrounded by red dots at the very limit of his viewport. As he watched, one by one the red dots went out and the green moved with furious speed.

"Can I get more information on the dots?" Knox asked, he had his idea of who it was—Aetex. But he wanted to see if there was a way to confirm it.

Mic shook his head. "Not at this level of the Titan Engine, but as it grows stronger, so will your command chair and its features."

"Fine, back to the present threat," Knox said, finally getting free of the chair and feeling his connection to it fade.

"Are you sure you don't want to guide the fight from here?" Mic asked, his head tilting the way it does when he is confused.

Knox shook his head and stretched out his back muscles. He was sore from the exertion from earlier, but that wouldn't stop him from helping. "I'm the best chance we have to end threats as quickly as possible. I'm going."

"Very well, I will stay here and monitor the situation," Mic said, taking a seat on the throne and a screen appeared before him.

So, it would work for him, Knox thought, *interesting.*

He rushed out of the throne room and pushed himself hard to get to the East Gate. There were buildings nearby, though what their purpose was, he'd yet to figure out or even explore them. The wall had a giant hole that hadn't been patched but the gate at least stood closed and formidable looking.

It was a massive single door about twenty paces high and curving on the top. Two stone towers with stairs running up to them stood on each side of the door. The door itself had oversized gears on it and Knox wondered if it would open easily or if he'd need to find a switch.

The golems he'd called into service lined the top of the wall, nearly a dozen and a half. A few people were beginning to trickle over to the area, but no one was running or seemed to understand the approaching danger.

"Hhrmm?" Dernal asked as he appeared before Knox.

"We've got incoming, several dozen and I think it might be pirates. They've found us," Knox said, cracking his neck to the side as he cast Mystic Armor over himself and then laid down what buffs he could on his team as they approached.

They at least had put on some armor and Knox could sense the power of their weapons, enchanted beyond what little he'd done for them before. Questions on how they'd made their way into the vaults and workshops would have to wait, but Knox felt a little itch of annoyance.

"Metal face said we should come here?" Terrim asked, he wore some impressive heavy armor and had a new axe, plus a shield on his opposite arm. It appeared to be attached to his forearm leaving his hand free to grasp hold of something.

"Incoming threat. Pirates, and they are decently strong," Knox said as at that very moment the targets came close enough for his sense to get a read on them.

They were pirates alright, and they burned with enough power to be a match for Knox before he'd gotten his last boost of power, so around level 20. His friends would be vastly outmatched by them, as well as most of his golems.

"We will hold the wall, fight at the opening and rain hell down on them from above," Knox said, ready to get the show going already.

"Perhaps I should try to talk to them?" Murdoch said, a knowing smile appearing on his face.

"That isn't a bad idea," Beth said. She wore a mix of leather and chainmail, her bow different from the one she'd used to hunt the Nolics.

Murdoch was the only one not really armored up. Instead, he wore fancier clothes than he'd had on before, with a small little leather chest guard, but it seemed it was more fashionable than it was practical.

Knox began to give orders, putting golems as the first line of defense, then assigning any golem or people with ranged attacks to take shelter atop the stone towers that flanked the door and sat just beside the hole in the wall. The pirates moved close enough that they could be seen through the trees and Knox focused on the brightest amongst them. The dark-skinned pirate with massive muscles was easily as strong as Dernal, but Knox knew something they didn't.

Whatever techniques they'd used before would be useless to them now, unless they really forced it and even then, it wouldn't be as effective as using System abilities. And System abilities were something they shouldn't have access to yet, as they didn't know how to access the Titan Engine. They'd have a Path, but no way of getting abilities for it.

Murdoch stood to Knox's left and Dernal to his right. Behind them stood his golems and the rest of his team as well as a few others that were stronger than the rest, including his father. Knox tried to forget the last bit, he needed to be grateful that everyone one with a bit of power had come.

"Hail there, strangers!" Murdoch called out and the group of pirates, all wearing warm-looking long coats and hats Knox had only seen before in his previous interactions with the pirates.

"By the decree of Captain Dread, this uhh..." The strongest of the group looked around at the walls and chose his words carefully, "city is now under his purview." He was missing his left eye and had a black patch covering it, a ruby the size of an eyeball set into it. But none of that distracted from the power he was letting off in waves.

"Oh, I believe there has been a misunderstanding," Murdoch said, his smile never wavering. "You see, this is the settlement of Luminar and we are not beholden to your Captain Dread. In fact, how many of you are truly happy in his employ?" Murdoch looked over and winked at Knox before continuing. "Surely, you lot would enjoy the freedom of living life your way. Throw down the shackles of responsibility that this, *Captain Dread*, has set upon you. Join us and taste of the sweet freedoms that life has to offer."

Several of the pirates stirred, but not the lead one whose name Knox still hadn't gotten. About half of the pirates began to walk forward, not in a threating way, but almost as if they were transfixed by Murdoch and his words.

The lead pirate pulled his sword and ran the closest one through the belly as he stepped past him. This had the effect of getting the rest of their attention and the pirates quickly returned. Murdoch went pale and took a step back, clearing his throat for another attempt.

"They are just much stronger than you," Knox said, holding a hand up to forestall him.

"Wasn't even my best attempt. You sure I shouldn't try again?" Murdoch said, stepping forward once more and fixing some of his hair with his hand.

"Hhrmm," Dernal said, then turning to Knox he added, "Best to get this started before they can retreat and tell this Dread Captain of theirs where we are."

"Attack!" Knox yelled after considering Dernal's words. According to his display screen back at the throne, these were all that were coming and none had stayed behind to act as scouts.

The pirates stiffened at Knox's words, and swords, crossbows, and clubs were pulled free. The battle began as swiftly as they'd appeared.

Several balls of fire came down on the force of pirates, followed quickly by several balls of green ethereal fire from Frederick and his Necromancers. Next came the arrows, from both sides. Someone on Knox's side screamed out in pain as an arrow found its way into their gut.

Luminar's melee forces waited, taking cover behind the metallic golems who took arrow after arrow in stride, taking minimal damage. Then came a gale force wind from the pirates' side, throwing several people off the tops of the walls. This was followed directly by a charge from the enemy, forcing Luminar's ranged attackers to stop or risk hitting friendly targets.

All the while, Knox had held back for this very moment. Stepping ahead of Vlad, he led the ground troops of golems, Knox raised his hand and began the process of weaving the magic together. Chains of bright light appeared all around, tying up at least half of the charging pirates, while tripping several more. Next, he cast Void Grasp, and between the two spells, he had tied up all but the strongest of the pirates.

"Charge!" Knox screamed, unleashing a Luminous Surge before them, and taking the lead pirate off his feet in the process. Using Ethereal Step, he appeared right over the man and cut down with his axe. However, the pirate was faster than he looked, getting his weapon up to block the blow and kicking the side of Knox's knee.

Pain lanced up his leg and he went over in a heap, out of place and on the ground amidst the enemies. He closed his eyes and relied fully on his sense. Rolling, he dodged first one blow, then another, as pirates saw him within range. He made it to his feet, snapped his eyes open and slammed down his foot. Radiant Light damage spread out in a large circle around him, damaging foes and healing friendly targets as they entered it. Using Ethereal Step, he charged over a measure of the ground, knocking two pirates on their ass.

Turning with his axe raised, he ended one and turned to do the same to the other, when pain lanced up his side. Warm blood began to leak down his back as he turned to see a weaselly looking man with dark shadows around his eyes, flicking blood off a long, wicked-looking dagger that glowed with obvious power. Whatever it had done, it bypassed all his armor like it wasn't there.

These pirates had techniques and were still able to use them to a certain extent. The fight had just gotten a lot more dangerous.

Before Knox had a chance to react, an axe came down on the skinny man's head and a cry of triumph rung out behind him.

Askar Trelling stood there as the body fell, a hungry gleam in his eyes. He briefly looked up to his son, nodding once, before charging back into another fray.

It was so unlike anything he'd attributed to his father that

Knox had to stand still for a moment or two before his brain told him to get back into the fight.

All around him, chaos reigned and cries of pain from both sides could be heard as men fell and wounds were inflicted. Knox had never been in such a battle before, a clash of men versus men, where the numbers were so evenly matched.

Dernal faced off against the strongest of the pirates, Old Ruby-eyepatch, but his healing abilities had very little combat effectiveness and he was being fought to a standstill.

Time for this good for nothing pirate to learn what it's meant to be a Titan Born.

Using Ethereal Step, Knox appeared behind him and cast Arcane Pulse right into the back of his head. The pulse of arcane energy snapped the pirate's head forward and sent him sprawling. Dernal wasted no time in stabbing him with his dagger right in the neck, but Old Ruby-eyepatch just grunted and stood, even while Knox's axe connected into his leg.

The blows barely seemed to affect him, his very skin as hard as any armor Knox had come across. Suddenly, Knox thought perhaps his sense wasn't getting the full measure of power that this man had to offer. As if in answer to such a thought, his power surged and suddenly Knox could see that he was clearly a B-Ranked Adventurer.

A blow, solid and unyielding, sent Dernal flying backward, breaking a tree in half. Knox hadn't laid in wait though, finishing his cast of Aeon Gaze, hoping that his ability would truly give him some edge over the strong opponent.

Several small windows appeared, noting that his speed was already falling minute by minute, and that his blows, while powerful, weren't a match for Knox's. It also showed that he was already below half Health, he just wasn't showing it very well. Though his technique allowed his skin to be hard as armor, it was still taking severe damage. All this information hit Knox at once and caused a moment of distraction, as he hadn't been expecting it.

Sense or no sense, the blow that took him in the face wasn't expected. Warm blood washed down his neck as his cheek lay open from the slash that he'd only barely been able to dodge. If he hadn't gone backward, it would have been *his* neck laid open.

Knox ignored the pain as best he could and raised his axe to block another strike. Using Solar Wings, he attempted to put distance between them so he could attack from afar, but the pirate grabbed his foot and flung him to the ground like a rag doll.

Rolling over and over, using his sense to avoid strikes, Knox gained his footing once more and caught another blow meant for his head before slamming his foot down. Radiant energy lanced out around him, but the damage was so slight that the pirate didn't even flinch.

His Stamina was still good, but he needed healing badly, so he cast Prism Ward, setting a barrier around him that would return a portion of the damage back as healing. Two attacks came at the same time from behind, but Knox used his sense and reaction speed to avoid both, getting two chunks of healing as the attacks passed through the ward.

Then with a moment of inspiration, he cast Reality Ripple on the strongest pirate, so he'd have time to deal with the two behind him. But as he turned, a roar cut the air and Terrim appeared in their midst, a giant of a man.

"To death!" he roared, and Knox stood in stunned silence for a moment as dust billowed around his friend, his shield taking blow after blow from superior foes, but he didn't yield or give an inch. He was a true friend and Knox couldn't leave him to his fate. As he stepped forward to help, someone else appeared between them—Murdoch, all smiles.

"Allow me to aid you," he said, slashing with unreal speed and opening up one of the pirate's necks. Then an arrow took the same pirate in the eye, and he dropped. Beth was back on the wall and raining death down from above. She saw Knox look and gave him a small nod of her head in acknowledgement.

Next came Frederick with a very dead-looking pirate fighting beside him. He had his minion throw itself at the ruby-eyed pirate just as he escaped Knox's time slow.

Using Ethereal Step, Knox put himself right behind the powerful pirate, placing his hand on his back he let loose the most powerful Luminous Surge he could create. Then just as his opponent began to fly forward from the blow, he used his talent to jump back right before he cast his spell and hit him again.

The first blow knocked the pirate to the ground and the second slammed him deeper into it, his back a black, scorched mess of blood and burns. Not waiting to see if he was still alive, Knox took the axe to him until he was sure the pirate was finished. Sweating and with blood pouring down his leg, face, and back, Knox surveyed the battlefield.

They'd won, and according to his sense, no one had escaped to report their location. But rogue types, like the one that stabbed him, could be tricky, so he called out for the bodies to be gathered and counted.

Two were missing and nearly a dozen of Knox's own men and women were injured—three critically. Dernal began to work on the worst cases, but it would be close.

Knox saw his father, several bloody cuts on him but alive and standing. He met his gaze and despite his feelings, he nodded his appreciation to him. His father just looked away, busying himself with other business.

CHAPTER 9
LABYRINTH

"MAKE FIXING the walls a priority and I want you to stay on that throne monitoring for incoming threats around the clock; if not you, then another golem," Knox said, his words coming out harsher than he'd meant them to.

Mic just nodded as he sat on the chair, giving order after order to the other golems. Another came to relieve him, and Knox and him began to walk down to the location of the Labyrinth. Four days had passed, Knox had spent most of them out hunting for more pirates, but he'd never found the missing two. *That meant that more would be coming, and they'd not underestimate us this time*, Knox thought.

With that thought, Knox clung all the more tightly to this notion of the Labyrinth and the relief it might offer by collecting the prizes found within. Surely, the power there could be his answer, his way to overcome the pirates and deal with the most prudent threat.

But to do that, they had to get inside, and that meant solving some kind of puzzle, or so Mic said. Knox hadn't been around the last few days to worry about it. But now he was back and ready to figure out how to make his way through this puzzle.

They reached the entrance; it was in a room at the bottom of a long staircase. It wasn't a place you'd find by accident, as many of the floors between were now just rock, as the complex shifted to put a large section toward the top. What ancient and powerful magics were employed to do all that moving, Knox could only ponder at.

Like most of the complex, it was lit by a dim steady light, but down here it seemed dimmer and Knox had to squint his eyes to see what lay ahead. It was a circular door with carvings in it, many hundreds of pathways set into it but nothing that looked like any puzzle Knox had ever seen.

"How do I solve it?" Knox asked, eyeing Mic critically.

"I do not know," Mic said loudly and with a little more spunk in his voice than Knox thought necessary.

So, Knox took it upon himself and walked right up to the wall, placing a hand on it as he examined possible ways to open it. The first thing that became apparent to him was the lack of a doorknob and the fierce glow that emanated from it when he focused his sense.

If he could only figure out why certain points glowed more brightly than the rest, then he might be able to start figuring out the puzzle at large. He started by touching the brighter points and then tracing his finger down the paths open to them.

A thought occurred to him, and he suddenly wondered if this was meant to be a puzzle at all. Perhaps instead, it was a map of the routes he could take within the labyrinth. He relayed his idea to Mic, but the golem shook his head.

"I distinctly remember this being a puzzle or test that needed to be passed before you could enter the labyrinth," Mic said, arms crossed from where he watched from across the room.

"We need more minds on this than me. Let me get some people down here to help figure this out," Knox said, releasing his hold on the round barrier and turning to find some help.

Mr. Tome had on a pair of spectacles and another magnifying glass atop that, as he studied the door. He'd even brought along a ladder that he leaned against the door and used to walk up and down the area.

Mr. Tome was a short man; some had said that he was ridiculously so at times. He stood just a hair past four feet, but none of his diminutive stature meant he was less of a hard-working man. He wore his same old work clothes, a thick white shirt that had been stained many different colors over the years, and a heavy apron. Rarely had Knox seen him out of this uniform.

"It is an energy conduit of some sort," Mr. Tome declared after finishing a long and quiet observation of the door.

"What does that mean?" Knox asked, Mr. Tome often used words that made little sense to Knox or other villagers.

Curling his fingers at the edge of his mustache, Mr. Tome inspected Knox.

"It takes power and moves it," Mr. Tome said, saying each word carefully as if expecting that Knox didn't understand the language in which he spoke.

"So how do we open it?" Knox asked, ready to get down to business.

"Before we go any further, I have a request I need your permission for," Mr. Tome said, Knox nodded for him to continue and he did, "I have need for several warehouses and space separate from the rest of the common folk. Grant me that, and I will oversee the creation and repair of the doors and siege weapons. Those halfwit constructs of metal are doing a poor and slow job of it."

Knox looked at his mentor and friend, he'd taught him all he knew about tinkering and woodworking, surely, he could trust that he had his best interests at heart. But something inside told him not to just give him whatever he wished without haggling a bit first.

"One warehouse and you fix all the gates and siege weapons first, as we have a clear and present danger being posed by the pirates," Knox said, smiling at himself.

"Three warehouses minimum and permission to build an internal gate to keep riffraff out of the area," Mr. Tome said, his shrewd eyes narrowing.

"Two warehouses and a housing unit, you get the wall but you must enforce it well enough to be a fallback for when the main wall falls, so you'd have to have space to fit most of the villagers of Luminar. So, let's make it four warehouses if you'll agree to being a fallback," Knox said, a smile of his own twisting onto his face.

"Deal," Mr. Tome said, holding out a hand. "I'll have official documents drawn up and I suggest you do the same with all those residing in your territory, otherwise they'll take you for a ride."

Knox had already set Murdoch to task, getting everyone assigned locations and given official rights over that housing unit and surrounding area. He'd even had each household agree to a certain amount of hard labor in a weekly to monthly capacity to ensure a way of payment could be collected. Of course, they could always pay with Monster Cores if they wished not to do hard labor, a choice those of fighting age were happy to take.

Then of course there were the too young, too old, and lame. They were assigned to a family member or friend to watch over them and enough food would be provided, assuming meat could continuously be supplied. Fruits and vegetables were coming in each week, the complex providing incredible yields in several times faster and out of the normal season cycle.

"I've taken care of that, see Murdoch about the contract and tell him you've haggled directly with me over it, he'll understand," Knox said, then turning his attention back to the task at hand, he asked his question again. "So, how do we open it?"

"Should be simple enough, you just have to channel power

from one focus point to another, without ever faltering the amount and speed at which you do so. I take it you've got an easy enough time moving your internal energies around than the rest of us. Have a go at it," Mr. Tome said.

Knox nodded along and had a good idea of how to start now, but a thought occurred to him, and he had to ask. "What Path did you end up choosing?"

"Scholar, of course, it just had too many useful abilities and talents to pass up. Did you not choose the same?" Mr. Tome asked, lifting his spectacles, that were more like goggles than not, off his face.

Knox grimaced and cleared his throat. "I actually went the Mystic route with a focus on the Arcanum Scholar branch," Knox said.

"Aw, very similar to the Path I chose, but I didn't see as many options to branch into different types of study with that Path, so I selected Scholar," Mr. Tome said, beaming up at Knox. "I'm surprised to learn you didn't come to the same conclusion. But you've much to worry about and having powerful abilities is as important as learning I suppose."

"It also left me open to explore two branches that might offer more utility than a straight Scholar Path. I stand by my decision," Knox said, letting his own words act as a comfort for himself. It wasn't that he wasn't confident in his choice, but he *had* been having a few doubts after seeing other Paths in action.

The Necromancer Path, for instance, was already producing some interesting and powerful weapons, a fellow named Clide was focusing on the Soulbinder Path. He also had experience as a blacksmith's apprentice, so Knox had put him to work with the golems to create weapons and armor. He wanted badly to have a hand in it himself, but his time was stretched so thinly that he was forced to delegate.

"Give the puzzle a try," Mr. Tome prompted, and Knox turned his attention back to the doorway.

Reaching out a hand, he remembered the lessons he'd had

with Dernal about controlling the energy within him. It was difficult and much different than it had been before, but he used the lessons as a point of grounding and began moving the energy within himself around.

It moved sluggishly, having already been told by his body and the system how best to move and where to go, but Knox needed it to act differently if he was going to overcome this task. Little by little, he moved it around and toward his outstretched hand. He focused on the dimmest of the nodes on the puzzle, hoping to fill it easily enough and move to the next.

The work was slow but finally enough energy reached his hands and he pushed it outward. His palms burned and his focus wavered, the energy slapped back into place and his progress was lost. This was going to be difficult at best, impossible at worst.

Starting again he pushed the energy, slow and steady but with a firmer hand than before. It reached his hand and bled out toward the puzzle. Pain appeared once more, but Knox was ready this time and his focus didn't waver.

The glow of the node ignited under his own power and a path began to be formed moving toward the next closest node. It took more power than he'd expected to push it along and the pain never stopped. He made it halfway there before his concentration faltered and his progress was lost again.

"This is going to take some time," Knox declared. His stomach suddenly felt tight, and Knox felt hunger for the first time since becoming a Titan Born. "Let's grab a bite to eat and I'll try again after."

"We've got trouble," Murdoch said, sitting across from Knox at one of the many long tables that had been built for eating. They were still very much doing community meals and Knox had been lucky to find the lunch being served as he made it to the surface. Knox sat alone, Mr. Tome leaving to stake out his new property, and none of his friends had been sitting when he arrived.

"What kind?" Knox asked, taking a bite of the hearty meat stew he'd been served. They were low on any kind of wheat, so bread wasn't an option, but potatoes were in full supply and this stew was filled with them, along with a few carrots and some gamey meat that Knox hoped wasn't Nolic meat.

"After the attack from those pirates, we've got a large group of people wanting assurance of their safety. And if you won't give it, then they want to be taken to the nearby Guild Charterhouse," Murdoch said, shaking his head. "I even tried to give them a rousing speech, but it wasn't as effective as it could have been." With that, Murdoch gave Knox a look but Knox shook his head.

"I don't want you using your abilities on our own people, it isn't fair," Knox said. He'd told Murdoch as much while they were out hunting for more pirates and failing to find those that had escaped. "Besides, how do they even know there is a Guild Charterhouse close by?"

"Your father," Murdoch said, rolling his eyes. "He's been the main mouthpiece of this little micro rebellion."

"Of course, he is," Knox said, sighing. "I really thought he might be starting to change, but this behavior is just what I expect from him."

"Should I talk to him, lay the whammy down?" Murdoch asked, his dour expression turning to one of eager excitement.

"The *whammy?*" Knox asked, his turn to roll his eyes but he held back, instead leveling a critical stare at his companion.

"Yeah, you know," Murdoch said, laughing as he spoke. "Give him the old one-two of my abilities until he's submissive and ready to shut up."

"I already told you no, we've got to earn the trust of the people without magic," Knox said. "It's bad enough that we are cut off from other civilizations and trade isn't much of an option with winter coming. When full winter settles down, there will be no traveling outside the swamp, and they have to know that. Why don't you gather up the people, my father included, and I will speak with them."

"*You* will speak with them?" Murdoch asked, his lifted eyebrows suggesting that perhaps that wasn't the best course of action.

He knew his friend fancied himself the only one able to win the hearts of people with his words, but Knox had a plan. It was really simple, he would tell them the truth of the matter and really push how dangerous things would be, then invite them to leave if they weren't up for it. Sure, it seemed harsh, but they were just beginning a critical phase of living beyond civilization, and everyone needed to be onboard.

Murdoch left, coming back after twenty minutes to fetch Knox. He'd finished his stew and though he felt none the fuller from it, the meal was pleasant. There was a deeper hunger inside of him that only after much waiting was beginning to subside. It was like his body's use of his internal essence or energy had depleted something deep inside of him. Perhaps this 'puzzle' was more a 'test of power' than anything else.

Following Murdoch into the open, where the sky sent rain down to muddy the ground and turned an already difficult day into an even more annoying day, Knox saw his father entering a small hut along with a group of others, about ten strong. Knox knew those must be the ones that were malcontented, and he braced himself for what was to come.

He noted that half appeared to be elderly, while the other half were older, but more around the age of his father and still able to work. He recognized a couple as his father's sometimes drinking partners, and to his surprise the former foremen of the woodcutters, Bill.

"Good afternoon, everyone," Knox said as he made it to the door and entered. The quiet whispers died off and his father, standing in front of the entire group, spoke first.

"We've a list of demands you'll meet if you want to keep us

here. First, we want bigger housing. We've all been stuck in small places despite being the elders and important folk of the village. Second, we want better trade conditions for those Monster Cores and," Askar looked to the older folks that most certainly wouldn't be collecting any Monster Cores themselves anytime soon, "we want a payment of Monster Cores given to those that can't fight for themselves each week. With enough, they could get strong enough to be helpful again."

"Now listen here," Murdoch began to say, but Knox put a hand on his shoulder to stop him.

"That it?" Knox asked, raising an eyebrow at his father and his demands.

"We also want your assurance of our safety. You and a few others are strong enough that, given our circumstances, it would ease many a mind to hear you tell us we'll be safe from threats while in your care," Askar said. Knox couldn't believe his father and he had to take several steady breaths before speaking again.

"Alright," Knox said, finally finding words.

This put the room to a sudden quiet and Murdoch looked at him with wide eyes.

"Alright?" Murdoch hissed his question. "We can't show favoritism and there is no guarantee of their safety."

"I know," Knox said, raising his voice to be heard by all.

Knox looked to the eyes of each in the room and found the same thing lying in wait behind each—fear. They feared what was to come and his father had used that fear to leverage better living conditions for himself and those he'd found. In a way, he was proud of his father, but he couldn't bring himself to say as much.

"Everyone has the right to pick suitable housing and if you feel you've been assigned one too small, then Murdoch will look over it and make adjustments. As for the better trading rates, those are fixed and will improve as more Monster Cores and supplies are collected and created. The second to last request holds merit and I'm sad I didn't think of it earlier."

"All those who cannot, will be given a small supply of

Monster Cores to be used as trade material or for the advancement of their Path. Personally, I'd recommend advancing your Path, as you might find yourself more useful than you currently view yourself."

This garnered a few grumbles and more than one smile from the group.

"As to a guarantee of safety," Knox said, staring down Askar as he spoke and shaking his head. "Have we ever had such a guarantee living out here so far from anything resembling civilization? I won't lie to you and tell you everything will be alright. It won't. But I will tell you that if we work together as a community that we have a fair chance of making it. If, however, you wish to flee to the Guild Charterhouse, I have some vague sense of where it is, and I will see to it that you are well-informed as you go there."

"You won't escort us?" asked an elderly woman with keen eyes and a grimace on her face.

"I won't," Knox said, shaking his head. "To do so would leave us vulnerable here and I can't do that to everyone else that has chosen to stay and help with our cause. I'm sorry you feel the need to leave, and while I can't guarantee your safety, I can tell you this." Knox stepped forward and stood tall.

"I will do all within my power to see that you are safe and provided for. I do not take such a responsibility lightly."

Askar shook his head and spoke over Knox.

"What power do you have to save us? I remember having to save you during that conflict. Seems that we might be better off on our own, not targets to enemies you've made."

Knox glared at his father, then shook his head. "If you must go, then go. You've heard what I have to say, and I won't say more on the matter," Knox said, turning and leaving the way he'd come.

Murdoch followed him out, putting a friendly hand on his shoulder. "You've more a gift for speaking than I realized," Murdoch said, smiling across to him. "Perhaps you ought to have taken the Diplomat Path as well."

"There are lots of Paths I wished I'd considered more deeply,"

Knox said. "But for now, I've work to do. I'll be down below if I'm needed. But Murdoch."

"Yeah?" Murdoch asked, releasing Knox's shoulder.

"Make sure I'm not needed," Knox said, walking off toward the command chair and the stairs that led downward.

CHAPTER 10
INTO THE LIGHT

GETTING one node to another took several hours of lonesome focus, but when he did it, something in the door clicked and Knox knew without checking that he was one step closer to getting through the door. It was turning out to be a simple matter of force of will, not really a puzzle at all, but a test of strength. With a single lock undone, Knox left to rest.

His new body, enhanced and strengthened, recovered quickly from traditional uses of his abilities and spells, but this was different. It was like he was giving parts of himself to accomplish this task and in doing so, he found himself increasingly tired.

Weeks went by as he attempted to unlock each node on the door, each one more difficult than the last. He trained and killed monsters after expelling himself, which paid off well in leveling his friends, but he made no real progress. Instead, he acted more like a safeguard for the teams, ready to step in if needed. By the time the average level of the group had reached 20, nearly a month and a half had passed and only a single lock remained.

Weapons and armor were being created, but what supplies they had were quickly being depleted. If something new wasn't figured out soon, then they'd be out of ore and metals to make new arms and armor. Luckily there was a steady supply of leather and other needed materials, so much so that Mr. Tome had begun to buy up much of the supply using his Monster Cores as currency.

Mr. Tome had been assigned a group with an elderly man who said he was fit to fight and three younger kids, but despite that, they'd cleared out their sections and leveled up steadily. The area around Luminar had actually begun to be filled with stronger monsters, as the average level of the inhabitants rose. It was good too, otherwise their progress would have flatlined.

The pirates continued to be a nuisance, but they hadn't tried to attack in force again. Several times scouts encountered Luminar's hunting parties and they'd lost one person to the attacks, forcing Knox to make the hard decision that two hunting parties ought to be combined for each hunting expedition, unless accompanied by a higher-level person.

The walls had all been repaired and Mr. Tome worked hard to get the siege weapons in a functional state. Overall, everything was going well, if not for this final node on the door.

Knox focused up his will and pushed with all his might. It would truly take every last drop of his available power to make the final connection, but he was confident that he could do it, despite the pain. So, he pushed and then he pushed some more. Mic would often come down here with him, noting his progress, but he was alone this time, and he was sure he could manage it now.

It was so close, so much work, but so close.

The pain hit a new threshold and the sweat running down Knox's face increased. It hurt so bad, all he wanted to do was let it go and throw up in the corner. Nausea was the worst of it, inner mixed with the pain, that overpowering desire to wretch all his insides out.

But still, despite it all, he pushed and pushed. Nothing would stand in his way; he would get access to this 'Labyrinth' and claim the prizes within.

Suddenly the pain ceased, everything ceased, including the

flow of power. He fell to his knees and couldn't even summon up enough power to look with his sense. Instead, he watched as the door began to spin with many cogs and wheels, a final click sounding. The door began to swing open, and Knox had to hurriedly move himself from being in its path.

Knox wasn't sure what he expected inside, but what he found had him scratching his head. A smooth brick hallway led to a room, both the hallway and the room had enough light that you'd think it were noonday, but Knox saw no points of light. Then, finding enough strength to do so, he activated his sense and had to shield his eyes.

The room was lit by a haze of powerful essence, if he'd been as he was before the system, he'd had gobbled all of it up and been all the more powerful for it. With his sense as it was, it was hard to tell, but he was sure this essence was as pure as he'd ever encountered.

Taking a step into the hallway, he felt the soothing presence of the essence all around him like a warm blanket. Then a voice spoke out behind him, and he jumped, surprised that he wasn't alone after all.

"Master Knox," Mic said, his voice steady and calm. "Exit the Labyrinth at once. With its opening, more has been revealed to me. You will require a group before exploring, for many challenges await you inside."

Knox yearned to go further, it was as if his very being called to him to explore and claim the power for himself, but his better sense and exhaustion took hold. Turning, Knox left the hallway and joined Mic in the outer room.

"Tell me everything," Knox said, eyeing his metallic companion with a fair bit of suspicion.

"Perhaps you should rest first, then I can regale you and your group with the tale. This Labyrinth is much like a dungeon, so you will need a group with you if you expect to make progress within it," Mic said, but Knox shook his head.

"No, tell me now and I will pass it on," Knox said. "I've got to rest, but I won't be able to if I don't know."

Mic went on to tell Knox all he knew about the Labyrinth, which ended up being much less than he would have thought. The basic idea was the Labyrinth would have rooms filled with resources to be won by defeating the mobs inside. You would go through several rooms, each one progressively a bit more difficult until you reach a Guardian of the Labyrinth. Once you defeated a Guardian, you were given a part of an emblem that could be combined to release a massive amount of power.

Mic was lax on the details, like how many Guardians there were, but he assured Knox that the process of defeating the Labyrinth, or 'taming' it as he said, would take time and resources. The Guardians wouldn't reappear, but the monsters that served them would. And now that the door was open, if the monsters within weren't taken care of daily, they'd emerge from the Labyrinth and would become a threat. He guessed that they had a few days before the buildup became too much, but Knox was only going to give it a day.

He planned on returning tomorrow around the same time, after he'd slept and gotten his party ready. Bidding Mic farewell, Knox left to rest.

He'd only been asleep for what felt like minutes when whatever he was dreaming pulled him from his slumber. Aetex stood over his bed, looking down at him.

Aetex, the B Ranker he'd met while helping some captives of the pirates, had stuck around and been a huge help since their meeting, though he'd been all but absent in the last month and a half.

His features were mostly human, save for the pointy ears that closely resembled an elf and the gem set into his forehead. The gem seemed to shine with a sapphire light as he stood over Knox, his hands held outward as if casting some spell or enchantment. The man's skin was a grey that wasn't common in this area or any that Knox had encountered. Overall, he looked rather odd when compared with anyone else, but Knox wouldn't be the one to tell him such news.

What was more, the aura around Aetex had all but disappeared, whether this was because he'd been accepted into the system or he'd masked himself better than before, Knox wasn't sure. Either way, Knox had the unrelenting feeling that this man, Aetex, was stronger than he had been before.

"Can I help you?" Knox asked, rubbing the sleep from his eyes.

"You've damaged yourself," Aetex said, shaking his head. "Lay still and allow me to finish repairing what I can. The gifts Mah'kus bestowed upon me are vast yet limiting."

Before Knox could protest and so much as speak again, Aetex's hands erupted in blue light and a soothing presence washed over him. It was unlike anything he'd felt before, a mix between a cold bath and at the same time the warmest most comforting bath he'd ever taken. Both feelings worked at him in a perplexing show of opposites.

Knox could do nothing, but lay back and enjoy the feeling, though his suspicion couldn't help but rage at the thought that Aetex could be doing something harmful to him. He barely knew the man, part of his head told him, while another more comforting part remembered the pastry that had given him so much peace. The message that from the realms of dreams from this Mah'kus character that one was being sent to help him.

In the end, he relented and said nothing, allowing Aetex to do his strange magics. By the time he finished his quiet mumblings and the glow from his hands ended, Aetex fell to his knees.

"I've repaired the damage," he said, coughing into his arm. "You must be careful pushing your internal essence around like that, it isn't meant to be done like that anymore. You rubbed against powerful safeguards and did much damage to your pathways."

"Thank you?" Knox spoke the words as a question, still unsure of the help he'd been given.

One thing was for sure though, he felt great. No longer did he need to sleep or rest, his body vibrated with power as it did before he started the mess with the Labyrinth door. With this new rejuvenation, he felt ready to challenge the depths of the Labyrinth, but first he needed to check on Aetex and ask him a few questions.

Moving over, he helped the massively muscled man up from his knee. He stood taller than Knox by a solid head height, but he slouched in a way that spoke of exhaustion.

"You feeling alright?" Knox asked, letting the large man sit on his bed, as Knox sat beside him.

"Thank you, young one," Aetex said and suddenly Knox wanted to ask him how old he was to be calling him young one. He didn't look so old to Knox. But he held back the question in place of another.

"Who is this Mah'kus and why has he sent you?" Knox asked, being as straightforward as he could with the question.

Aetex looked at him, his orange eyes burning with an intensity that always made Knox feel a bit uncomfortable. He seemed to consider things for a long time, at least several seconds, before he finally spoke.

"He is my benefactor and a being of endless power," Aetex said, meeting Knox's stare with as much intensity as ever. "I was sent here to ensure that you be allowed a fair chance to succeed in your destiny. It is a task that normally he takes for himself, but he speaks as if one like him prevents him in this case. I know not all the doings of the gods, but I will be here to aid you should it become necessary, as it was today."

Knox tried to digest the information and found he had a hard time knowing what to say next. Aetex spoke of gods and endless power, did he mean Titans? The idea of gods wasn't well agreed upon, most just attributing the idea of gods to the Titans. Hell, even the Titans had been the thing of lore and make-believe before Knox himself became one such being.

"Is he as powerful as a Titan, like a fully developed one, not what I am, Titan Born?" Knox asked, his voice softening.

"He is the creator of Titans, him and his kind," Aetex said, smiling gently down at Knox, his own voice lowering to a softer pitch as he spoke. "You must have endless questions but know that you are on the right path. I can't be here to help with every possible outcome, but I am doing my part to thin the herd and discourage the pirate lord, the one who calls himself Dread."

"The pirates won't be a true threat as long as they can't get abilities," Knox said, but seeing a look flash over Aetex's face, his heart sunk. "They've figured it out?"

"They have, by a stroke of luck no doubt, but they've begun to display system abilities. Some are so interesting that it tempts me to partake in this Gowlen System," Aetex said, chuckling.

"You mean you aren't a part of the system? How is that possible?" Knox asked, his voice growing excited at the prospect of learning about new and interesting magics.

"I've been protected from the sight of the Titans, with that came the ability to resist the outside influences. Leaving me with access to my own familiar system, plus a few modifications done by my master," Aetex said, standing as he did so. "I must be off; my aid is needed elsewhere."

"Before you go," Knox said, standing beside his odd friend who towered over him. "Tell me why you want to help me, I don't understand."

"I've no need of a great calling to be helpful to one with a heart such as yours," Aetex said, putting a friendly hand on Knox's shoulder. "You remind me of a pupil of mine. He went by the strange name, Nick, and he had a noble heart, just as you do.

Hold to those convictions and be true to the man you are, you will succeed, even if sometimes it feels as if you've no chance to do so. Trust in yourself and the friends you've surrounded yourself with."

"Thank you," Knox said, the large man's words soothing him enough that he might take a small nap after all.

He sat back on his bed, ready to catch just a minute or two of sleep, and before he knew it, he was dreaming.

Figures of metal and power moved in the darkness, searching for something. He reached out with his mind and another feeling touched him, a powerful unyielding force. It shone with such brightness that the very void between worlds melted away. Then came the voice.

"You ate of the fruit of my brother. Know now the blessings of his kin."

Suddenly, Knox sat bolt right up on his bed, breathing hard. On his lap was a simple clear gem. What it did or if it had to do with the voice he'd heard, he knew not. Picking it up, he felt, well, he felt nothing. Deciding it must be worth something, he pocketed it and made his way out of his room. He was ready to challenge the Labyrinth, but he needed his team to do so.

He found Murdoch, Beth, Frederick, Terrim, and Dernal all sitting around a fire and trading tales of the adventures they'd had so far. Knox almost didn't want to interrupt them, but they quieted as he approached.

"The Labyrinth is open; are you guys ready to challenge what lies within?" Knox asked, he got a round of head nods and a few 'hell yeahs' from Murdoch and Terrim, but Frederick said nothing at first.

He met Knox's eyes and spoke. "I think I'm going to need to

pass. I'm making a lot of progress in the greenhouses and I'm not ready to use the spirits I'm communicating with for battle. And without them, my power is pretty limited."

"I understand," Knox said, though he wasn't sure that he did. But he knew better than to force someone down a path they didn't want to walk.

That left Murdoch as a melee fighter with crowd control abilities. Terrim as their main tank, he'd taken points down the branch of Guardian and became a powerful frontliner. Beth filled the role of backline ranger, she'd gone down the Beastmaster branch, taming a powerful grey wolf she'd named 'dog'. Finally, that left Knox to do the mid, frontline to backline hybrid role and Dernal to take the spot of healer.

They lacked a powerful practitioner that focused only on magic, but Knox had enough power there that he should be able to fill that role. The biggest hole they had in their party was a rogue type to check for traps and secret rooms. Beth had limited ability to set and discover traps, but it wasn't where her build shined, so they'd have to be extra careful.

As if reading his mind, Dernal spoke up with an unusual request.

"We need to find a fifteen-foot pole or branch, perhaps a couple of them," Dernal said, surprising Knox.

"What for?" Knox asked.

"Traps," Dernal said, cracking his neck to the side.

"Traps?" Terrim asked, but Knox thought he understood suddenly.

"I think he means for us to tap the area in front of us to trigger traps at a distance. Clever idea," Knox admitted.

So, they went out as a group outside the walls and gathered as many long branches as they could, cutting and shaping them to be most useful. In the end, they had five such poles, Knox planned on taking point and using them, but such preparations were important, and Knox was glad Dernal had thought about it.

With preparations made, they headed down to the Labyrinth,

ready to take on any challenge. It filled Knox with the same excitement as he'd felt when first running a dungeon. With sure steps, Knox took the first step into the Labyrinth, his party by his side.

CHAPTER 11
GUARDIAN OF LIGHT

THE HALLWAY LEADING to the first room was just big enough to allow them all to walk shoulder by shoulder. But Dernal took point, poking the ground and the walls with a long stick as they walked. No traps were found, and they reached the end of the hallway in safety.

It opened up into a rather large room without the neatly bricked face of the hallway. In the center of the room were three golems made of bronze-colored metal. Before Knox could ask them what they were doing inside the Labyrinth, they attacked.

They were unarmed, but one of them summoned fire while the other two ran for their group, fists raised. Terrim took his place in front of the party, shield raised and ready to intercept the incoming golems.

Knox erected a Prism Ward to catch the fireball, but the melee golems got there first, and with a casual punch, shattered the barrier. Runes all around them seemed to glow as they did, and something occurred to Knox. They had some sort of magic resistance.

Metal met metal in a resounding clash as Terrim's axe cleaved through one of the golems, bringing it crashing down. Protected against magic as they might be, they seemed to be weak enough to be affected by physical attacks.

The fireball hit Knox's team, momentarily enveloping them in searing pain. However, the fire burned out quickly, leaving the party enraged and ready to smash in golem heads.

The battle was short and sweet, ending with Beth putting several arrows into the magic-slinging golem and Knox's own axe taking down the second physical golem.

Murdoch just looked perplexed, walking up to the fallen golems then around the room, and said, "That's it?"

"I suppose so," Knox said, going over to the walls and pointing out odd places for Beth to check for any hidden doors.

"It's ore," Beth said, after only a few moments of looking at the walls. "This entire room is stuffed with it, iron ore by the looks of it."

"You sure?" Knox asked, running his hand over the veins of metal, it looked like ordinary rock to him but who was he to doubt her.

"I'm sure," Beth said, then looking over it again she nodded.

"So, we should get some people in here to mine," Knox said. "The golems were weak enough that most parties would be able to take them out, if they stick to this first room, I bet it'll be fine."

"Let's press forward first and get a team later," Dernal said, his voice a low grumble.

"I agree with short stack," Murdoch said, smiling down at Dernal.

Dernal for his part ignored him, but Knox knew better than to antagonize the healer, that was a quick way to find yourself in pain and stay that way.

Smiling at Murdoch and shaking his head, Knox led them toward the next hallway, leading them out of the room. With long pole in hand, Dernal began the work of hitting random spots with it. While doing this something extraordinary happened, fire spit out from nowhere burning the tip of his stick.

"Found a trap," Dernal declared, hitting the spot again and triggering another fireball.

It was on the ground, about halfway through the tunnel and to the very left, right where Murdoch would have stepped if they hadn't had any sticks to check for traps.

The rest of the way was clear, and they made sure to avoid the fireball spot. Reaching the end of the hallway the room led into a slightly larger room with twice as many golems waiting for them within. Spreading out, with Terrim in the front, they got themselves ready for combat.

Knox cast Mystic Armor on himself, then Mystic Veil on his allies. Next, he readied Lustrous Chains to cast on the group of six golems.

Chains of light wrapped around all six golems at once and the battle was on. Murdoch rushed forward, seeing an opportunity, and pierced one of the golems right through its visor, killing it. Terrim used an ability to close the gap, rushing forward with inhuman speed and crashing into the lot of them.

Beth moved to flank them and get a clear shot, so Knox took that opportunity to lash out with his Luminous Surge, since it would heal any friendlies in his path and harm his enemies. Light lanced out from his open palm and washed over the golems, knocking them all to the ground.

Wasting no time, Knox rushed forward and slammed down his foot, casting Radiant Ground. The floor pulsed with light and ripples of it spread out from where his foot fell. It was too much for the weakened golems and before they had a chance to do so much as swing a fist at the team, they fell silent.

"This Labyrinth is turning out to be a disappointment," Terrim said, raising his eyebrows at Knox.

"I was just thinking the same," Knox said. "Perhaps it gets harder the deeper we go? Maybe we are just stronger than what it was designed for."

"Hhrmm," Dernal said, gesturing with his chin at the golems.

Two of them were getting up, Knox noted that they had a silvery look to them, not the same bronze as the others.

"Guess they aren't finished just yet," Knox said, slamming his axe down on one of their heads, then repeating the gesture twice more before it fell still.

Terrim did a similar action to the other and the battle truly ended a few seconds later.

This room held more ore, a few veins that Beth couldn't recognize that Knox hoped would be worth checking out. No trap doors or secret areas though, which Knox found disappointing.

Moving as a group, they ventured deeper into the Labyrinth. So far, it had been nothing but disappointing and that continued to be the case as they defeated four more rooms worth of weak golems. Sure a few put up a fight, the gold ones were the hardest, but even they barely registered a threat to Knox's group.

Two days later and they still had done nothing more than clear out room after room of golems. If nothing else, they were a good steady source of essence. They even realized later that they could harvest Monster Cores from them, as odd as it seemed to do with a mechanical creature. Nevertheless, they'd faced nothing but the same, with a few color differences the deeper they got.

Mining the first dozen rooms was in full swing, and production of needed equipment was yielding a bounty of cool new items. Knox wished he had a chance to sit down and toy with some, but he didn't, his entire day being spent clearing out the Labyrinth and searching for the first Guardian.

It was nighttime and they'd called it quits, heading back for some well-needed drinks over the fire and a decent meal, when Beth discovered a secret door set into the stone. She'd barely been looking, but the more she'd practiced the better she was getting at locating secret caches. Mostly, they found reagents but this time it was a hallway.

"Should we check it out?" Knox asked. The party was exhausted and ready to retire, but this was an opportunity Knox didn't want to pass up if he could help it.

"Hhrmm," Dernal said, shrugging.

"I'm tired," Murdoch complained.

"Let's do it," Terrim said, cracking his neck to the side and yawning at the same time.

That left Beth to break the tie. All eyes were on her, and she had a critical look on her face, eyebrows raised and finger tapping on her chin.

"Can't hurt to take a look for a minute or two," Beth finally said, shooting a smile in Knox's direction.

She'd been warming up to him in the last few weeks, but Knox was careful to keep things professional between them as he didn't want to assume that she wanted to start things up again.

In fact, Knox had been taking Terrim's advice and talking to a girl named Sarah, with striking blue eyes and light auburn hair. She was one of the few that hadn't lost any family to the black sickness or the attacks that ensued. Her mother and father were tailors, working with the crews making armor and general goods. She had a sister, named Angie, but she was quiet and kept mostly to herself. Angie was two years younger than Sarah with dark hair and keen eyes.

Sarah had chosen Rogue as her Path, leaning into the Trickster branch and had been a huge boon to her party during hunts. Angie on the other hand had surprised her family by going the Elementalist Path, focusing her talent points down the Geomancer Path, or at least Sarah said as much.

Her parents had both taken the Scholar Path, they were well known bookworms and Knox was sure they wanted to pick a Path that wouldn't be huge on combat, but research instead. Many of the older folks made such choices, but little did they know at the time that each Path had its combat capabilities. So, despite picking a more learning-based Path, they were still endowed with power to defend themselves and as such, were encouraged to be a part of a party and go on hunts.

As a group, the two hundred or so individuals Knox cared for were leveling pretty well, the very landscape of the monsters around Luminar changing as they also grew stronger. It had the annoying effect of making hunts always seem a bit more dangerous than maybe they could be, but Knox never felt that fear being so much higher than the rest. He'd finally hit level 31, putting him firmly in the C Ranked equivalents and as strong as ever.

-Personal Status-
  -Name: Knox-
  -Level: 31 (C Rank, Tier 1)-
  -Essence To Next Level: 6,723/21,000-
  -Health: Great Tier 9-
  -Mana: Great Tier 9-
  -Stamina: Great Tier 9-
  -Mind: 123-
  -Body: 123-
  -Spirit: 123-

With how his attributes worked, operating at peak as long as he was within a certain level, his Health, Mana, and Stamina operated now the same as Dernal, perhaps even better since his would be the same as a Level 40 person normally. Dernal was still only level 38, the amount of essence required really jumping in the 30s. But he was close to hitting level 39, which put him only a few levels away from moving into the B Ranks, a feat he never thought he would achieve in his lifetime.

The system was special like that, but it also represented a fear that was growing in Knox's gut. The pirates had figured out how to use the system and would be growing stronger as well. If he couldn't find these Guardian's and retrieve this emblem of power, what hope would they have when the pirates came for them in force?

His mind turned back to his task at hand as they made it through the hallway leading to a new room, different from any they'd seen so far. The stones of the hallway lined the room beyond in alternating colors that had a dizzying effect on the party. Sitting in the center was a metallic man of blue, for a moment Knox could have sworn it was one of the Titan's from his dreams.

But no, it shared a similar design to the golems they'd been facing down below, save for the eyes. Instead of a familiar visor there were six smaller glowing eyes of white light. The metallic man held a blade in his lap, one hand on the hilt and the other hand resting on the blade. He spoke, his voice a rumbling low thing, and Knox felt the hairs on his arm go up.

As it spoke, runes of white, similar to what Knox could create, flashed over every square inch of its body. "You face the Guardian of Light. Make yourself ready and prove your worth, Titan Born."

Terrim stepped forward, shield ready, but suddenly the Guardian looked at him and raised his left hand in a stopping gesture.

"This challenge is for the Titan Born alone. You may watch, but if you interfere with the fight, know that ancient wards will ensure you never enter these sacred halls again. You've been warned," the Guardian of Light said, moving his gaze to Knox and tilting his head ever so slightly.

So, it is to be a one-on-one bout? No problem, Knox thought, doing as Terrim did so often, cracking his neck to the side and rolling his shoulders to loosen himself up. He'd been holding back most of the time, too afraid that his attacks might damage his own friends, or his strikes might be too powerful. It would be nice to cut loose and see what he could really do with his newfound power.

He re-cast Mystic Armor on himself, it shimmered into existence around him, providing him with armor nearly a match for what he used beneath it. Next, he swung his axe a few times while mentally going over his abilities. He had Void Grasp, Lustrous Chains, and Reality Ripple to tie up his enemies. Arcane Pulse and Luminous Surge to really punch opponents in the face with as much raw power as he could channel into the spells. Then he had moves like Ethereal Step, Solar Wings, Aetherial Step, and Radiant Rush all to help with his mobility.

But he wouldn't even need his entire kit, he knew that without a doubt. His sense, his most powerful weapon and defense, lay out around him like the finest webs of a spider's silk. Even the smallest twitch of his enemy would register in his thoughts, and he'd be moving before he even had a chance to digest the information, so powerful was the trait he'd picked up.

"I'm ready," Knox declared, and the Guardian nodded, beginning to stand. Knox let him, wanting it to be fair.

The moment the Guardian made it to his feet, Knox felt him begin to weave a spell together that was so familiar that Knox found himself mimicking the casting before he even realized it.

Two powerful Luminous Surges went off and exploded the air outward between the pair. The force was enough that it took Knox off his feet, but he rolled back into a standing position, taking a moment to check on his friends. His eyes registered they were fine, all of them backed up as far as possible against the wall, each with looks of apprehension to various degrees.

Knox's sense screamed and he twirled out of the way, only to activate Ethereal Step to avoid an incoming slash. The Guardian moved with a terrible speed, a trail of light that Knox recognized following him. The Guardian had just used Aetherial Step, a charge spell that left a trail of radiant light boosting his speed and slowing enemies.

Keeping clear of the trail, Knox activated his own Aetherial

Step, giving him the boost he needed to smash into the Guardian with all his strength in a mighty axe swing. The power of Illuminated Strikes and Searing Strikes activated, and his axe head became a blur of radiant energy.

The light infused attack smashed into the Guardian with a sickening crunch and sent a reverberating backlash up Knox's arm. It was strong enough that he dropped the axe and screamed in pain, but despite the pain and his screams, he was ready for what came next. Using his bracer, he caught the sword strike, it shattered a part of his Mystic Armor, but the blow barely dug into his physical armor.

Putting his hand on the Guardian's chest, he activated Arcane Pulse. The power was much more effective against the Light-based Guardian, throwing him back and off his feet. Knox took a deep breath, reached down, and retrieved his axe. The rooms light seemed to dim slightly as the Guardian struggled to stand, but Knox let him find his feet.

"You are powerful," Knox said, trying to buy some time as he worked out what to do next. He was a match for his opponent in so many ways, he wasn't at all weak like the smaller minions had been.

"As are you," the Guardian of Light said. Then, standing, his eyes flickered as he raised his hands and began to inscribe light into the air in front of him. "Feel the raw power of the Light and be cleansed!"

Knox had only the time to erect his Prism Ward before a wave of radiant energy smashed into him. His ward shattered but not before it sent a large amount of the attack into a heal. It was good too, because the raw power threw him off his feet and inflicted some serious damage before it dissipated. His opponent didn't wait for him to stand this time, rushing forward and swinging down with his sword.

If not for his sense, he would have died in that moment. Instead, he rolled out of the way, and struck out at his opponent's feet, dropping him to the ground beside him. Next, he rolled atop the Guardian, struck his sword from his hand and cast Void Grasp, tendrils of nothingness grabbed ahold of him and drained him of his powers. All the while, Knox slammed his axe into the Guardian's face, doing significant damage.

Just when Knox thought he had it, the Guardian sprouted wings of light and flew to the center of the room, light beaming off him in every direction. Then he slammed his foot down on the ground and the biggest Radiant Ground spell Knox had ever seen appeared. The damage was slight, but annoying. It made it hard to concentrate and focus on his sense, so he didn't dodge the punch that came a second later.

Back and forth they battled, punch traded for axe strike that rattled Knox's bones. It wasn't until Knox activated his newest ability, Chronicle Resonance, that he began to really get the upper hand. It did much of what he'd been using his sense for, predicting your opponent's next move, but combined with his sense it made him a god of war.

Before the Guardian even moved to strike, Knox was there countering it. Back and forth, Knox locked him out for the duration of his spell. It faded just as his axe went down on the edge of the Guardian's neck, severing head from body.

"Finally," Knox said, panting for breath, his muscles all strained to the max, and his Stamina at its end.

"You've won, claim your prize," the Guardian's head said, then it flickered and went out.

CHAPTER 12
FRAGMENTS

A CHEST APPEARED DIRECTLY in the center of the room and a pulse of energy shot through the Labyrinth, yellow with streaks of gold. It didn't hurt, instead, Knox felt himself uplifted and infused by the energy. What was more, he also got an influx of ten thousand essence, a staggering amount that took him that much closer to the next level.

"You did it!" Beth cried, running up to Knox and pulling him into a hug.

She held him there for several long moments before releasing him, blushing and taking a step back. Knox just smiled, happy that the coldness between them had begun to thaw.

"Thank you," Knox said, then turning to Terrim, he wrapped him into an awkward man hug, each of them using just one arm.

"Thought that guy had you for a minute," Terrim said, adjusting his helmet to better see Knox.

"He was surprisingly strong," Knox said. "Let's check out the chest and get out of here for the night."

It was late, Knox was tired, and so was his group. They wouldn't be doing anyone any good by lingering in the Labyrinth after slaying the Guardian.

Knox walked over to the chest and pulled the lid open. Inside of it sat a single item, a cracked piece of metal with golden coloring. It was hard to make out any details as it was clearly a single piece of something that had been cracked. But despite all that, he could feel power thrumming off of it and quickly took it from the chest.

"Let me see that," Dernal said, reaching for the fragment.

Knox handed it over, eager to hear what the seasoned Adventurer thought of it. Dernal held it in his hands, rotated it, and even squinted at it before handing it back.

"Well?" Knox asked, when Dernal didn't immediately give his opinion.

"Whatever it is, it gives off an aura similar to what I'd imagine an A Ranker would, though it's hard to say as I've never seen such an aura. Keep it close," Dernal warned.

This caught Murdoch's attention and he reached for it without asking. Knox moved it out of sight, pocketing it and gave Murdoch a wide smile.

"I think I'll hold on to it," Knox said, realizing what it must be after hearing Dernal's opinion. "I'm pretty sure it's just one piece of many that I need to collect."

Knox checked his quest and sure enough, it had a single piece of the emblem ticked off. It was reassuring and at the same time intimidating, to feel so much power from just a piece of it.

"Tell me again, where did your sister go?" Knox asked, confused by the rush of words that Sarah had thrown at him upon his return.

"She'd been talking about seeing some girl and she got it in her head that it was the cause of the black sickness, so she went to hunt it with her group. But her group came back without her.

Please Knox, please do something!" Sarah barely got the words out through her sobbing.

Angie had gone missing, and Knox was going to have to go after her. First things first, he needed to find her party and find out what happened. He found them, two girls barely considered adults, a rotund man with a shield, Frank if Knox was remembering right, and an elderly man who probably shouldn't be out hunting in his aged condition.

"You," Knox said, pointing at the rotund man. "Frank, right?" Frank nodded that his name was indeed that. "Good. Tell me what happened and why you left a party member behind."

Frank sputtered a few times and looked to the older man.

"Allow me to enlighten you," the elderly man said. "My name is Henry Hillcrest and I'm the de facto leader of this group."

"Henry," Knox said, warning clear in his voice. "Someone's life is on the line. I need answers and I need them quickly."

Henry seemed surprised that someone would speak to him in such a fashion and Knox could see a flicker of defiance cross his face, but it faded with a sigh.

"As you say," Henry said, clearing his throat. "Little Angie told us there was a monster that we could handle and set us on a merry little journey deep into the woods. However, she started seeing something that only she could see and talking about a little girl singing nursery rhymes. We told her it was time to return but she refused. You know how it gets that deep into the forest and at night the monsters are that much more fierce."

"So, you left her?" Knox asked, dumbfounded by the actions of this party.

"Hardly meant to," Henry said, shaking his head. "She started to attack us, saying she could see darkness in us and speaking like a madman. We had to leave eventually. Her magic is strong, and I can't heal through the damage she can output. So yes, we left her and reported in immediately."

"You," Knox said, pointing at the oldest and fittest looking of the two girls. "What Path do you walk?"

"Ranger," she said, her eyes averting from Knox's. "My name is Alice. I'm so sorry we left Angie."

"You remember the way back Alice?" Knox asked.

"I think so," Alice said, her voice coming slow and confused.

"Come with me, we are going to get her back," Knox said, cutting his eyes at Henry as they left.

"Good luck," Henry called out after them and Knox almost went back to yell at the old man but restrained himself.

Sarah came along and the three of them ventured out into the dark woods surrounding Luminar. It wasn't wise to go out at night, but Knox was so much more powerful than the monsters around the complex that he hardly gave it a second thought.

As they jogged, following Alice as she retraced their steps, Knox thought about the dark-haired little girl that had been appearing, mostly to him, but also to those about to be infected by the sickness, and he wondered if he ought to have brought Dernal as well. He knew he could burn away the blackness if he got to the infected soon enough or if they happened to be resistant, but his healing was mediocre at best.

"What level are you both?" Knox asked. He was pretty sure he knew Sarah's, but he didn't want to single out Alice.

"I'm level 18," Alice said, she held a torch and led the way through the brush.

Sarah gave Knox a look and said in an amused tone, "I'm level 21, you forgot I told you I leveled up yesterday?"

It was good that she could bring herself to smile, Knox thought, because there was a good chance her sister was in trouble and in pain, or soon would be if he had to purge darkness from her.

Sarah's smile faded nearly as fast as it appeared, as if the same thing occurred to her. When she spoke again, it was without any mirth. "You think she'll be okay?"

"We have to find her first, but if we can get to her in time, I'll not let the darkness take her," Knox said, doing his best to sound confident.

From there, they traveled in silence. Several Nolic's, wolves, and other monsters approached but never attacked. Knox was doing his best to allow his aura to surge around him, making all but the strongest monsters stay away. It was a useful technique, but it also made them very visible to anything stronger that might be looking for prey.

It took nearly an hour before Alice stopped and looked over to Knox. "This is the place we left her, I'm pretty sure at least."

Knox reached out and took the torch from her while surging his sense out as far as it would go. At first, he felt nothing, but he found a bag that Angie used to carry things not far off and gave it to Sarah. It had blood on it, and it was not a small amount. The ground around it was soaked as well and suddenly Knox felt foolish for not bringing Dernal.

Then, suddenly his sense touched against something, but it was gone a moment later. "This way," Knox called out as he sprinted in that direction, easily outpacing and leaving the two behind in the dark.

Knox reached the little girl seconds later. She held her farmer's sickle on Angie's throat, her head tilted to one side as if confused by Knox's presence. A dark energy pulsed around Angie and Knox knew something bad was about to happen.

Sarah and Alice arrived a moment later. Sarah screamed, then so did Alice, but Knox stayed calm, his power growing on his fingertips as he prepared to cast Luminous Surge.

"Let her go," Knox said, power thrumming inside of him.

The girl straightened her head and smiled, then her arm jerked. But Knox sense felt it coming before she did it and he let loose his attack.

The dark little girl flickered suddenly, disappearing before the attack arrived. However, the attack kept coming and hit Angie with its full force of healing. The various cuts on her began to close and she screamed in agony as whatever darkness had invaded her began to be purged out.

"Watch out!" Sarah screamed and Knox let his focus waver for a moment, ending the spell.

A sharp pain rippled up his spine as the dark-haired girl appeared, humming playfully along with the tune of Victory. Then as she wretched her sickle out of Knox's back, she began to sing it.

Victory, Victory, to the deep ones went the victory. Gone for now, we come again, victory, victory.

Knox nearly blacked out as the blade cut right through his armor and seemed to burn with an intensity that he'd never felt before. Before he could think of what to do next, he found himself slamming his leg down and causing a Radiant Ground to appear.

The girl shrieked and flickered away once more.

The burning stopped and was replaced by intense but manageable pain. Breathing ragged and blood pouring down his back, Knox turned to the three girls.

Angie was laying on the ground, passed out but breathing. Sarah was kneeling over her, crying. Alice looked scared out of her mind, her skin had gone several shades paler, but she said nothing. Then, right as Knox was about to look away from her, a single bloody tear fell down her left cheek.

Summoning forth the power to cast Luminous Surge, Knox let the spell loose on Alice just as she fell to her knees, the dark-haired child standing behind her with a wicked smile on her face.

Then, as if this were all some casual interaction, she waved goodbye and Knox felt her dark presence finally leave for good, or so he hoped.

Alice was coughing blood now, so Knox hit her with another Luminous Surge, then pulled her onto the Radiant Ground, that would heal her a little bit as well. But it wasn't enough to turn back whatever the evil little girl had done. Alice blinked and sputtered out, "I'm sorry." Before going still, her eyes looking out with the blankness that comes with death.

Knox didn't even know her last name, he realized, and for some reason that hurt even more. He lifted her off the ground, his sense confirming that life had left her body. Then he felt something stirring inside of her, a darkness, and he set her down. Tears streaming down his face he cast Luminous Surge on her several more times until all fragments of darkness had left her.

Why hadn't he found Dernal? He knew part of this life meant death, but avoidable death was something else entirely.

"Damnit! Damn, damn, damn!" Knox cursed as he reached down and picked her back up. She felt heavier than she ought to have on the walk back. Sarah carried Angie, she was a slight woman and easily handled. They walked in silence saying nothing, only sharing looks as they walked.

By the time they got back, a crowd had gathered outside the gate, including Dernal.

"Are they injured?" Henry asked, looking sorrowfully at Alice and Angie.

"Dernal, please heal Angie," Knox said, walking straight through the crowd and toward the area they'd been putting the dead to rest. He had one more thing he could do for the girl before the day was done, he could put her to rest.

He spoke with Murdoch to see if she had any family, but she'd lost all her family to the blackness, so it was just Knox, Sarah, Angie when she woke up, and the rest of his party there to put her to rest.

"I'm sorry I couldn't have been better, faster, smarter," Knox said, sparing a glance at Dernal and wishing he'd brought the healer with him. Hell, any healer might have been sufficient.

Dernal helped Knox shovel dirt over the grave and stayed after everyone else had left, leaving the two of them staring at a mound of dirt.

"Her injuries were severe," Dernal said, putting a hand on Knox's shoulder. "I doubt even I could have healed them in time."

"You don't know that," Knox snapped, but immediately looked to his friend with apologetic eyes. There was just so much emotion going through Knox right now that he couldn't stand it.

His spells had healed her a little bit, but it hadn't been enough. If he'd somehow had the power of the Labyrinth already, perhaps he'd have been powerful enough to save her.

"I'm so sorry Alice," Knox whispered the words, his mood darkening with every passing second.

The sun came up and suddenly an alarm was sounded. Three bells—they were under attack. Knox smiled, he wouldn't lose anyone today and those pirates better be ready to meet death. For he was death incarnate as far as they were concerned.

"To death," Knox whispered the words as he stood and retrieved his axe from the ground beside him.

CHAPTER 13
CHANGE

The battle was swift and not at all the massive attack Knox had feared would be coming. Instead, it was two dozen pirates again, more souls to feed the golem war machine of creation. Knox smiled as he heard the reports, all pirates accounted for this time and no casualties. He'd done it, slaying nearly half himself.

But despite the carnage he was able to rough, it didn't make him feel any better. There was a sinking feeling in the pit of his stomach that he couldn't banish, so instead he focused on keeping himself busy.

It was during one of his rare moments of solitude that he finally looked at the Journal of Ramses, opening it to see if any new entries had revealed themselves.

Journal Entry #6 – 0001-10 Titan Risen Standard Time

All the knowledge I've gained comes to naught when forced against the network of pathways within me. These Titans, for all their strength and guile, failed to understand proper pathways for teleportation.

However, I did learn a spell that allows for teleportation of a kind when in water or through areas of water, but I've yet to master it. I've come face to face with a being calling itself 'Titan Gowlen', he aids in my learning, but I fear its malfunctioning as it speaks of magic in terms that not even I can understand, which hampers my attempts to learn even the most basic of these new abilities.

I'm going back in to learn and will refuse to leave until I've mastered even this most basic of teleportation spells. From there, I should be able to work out more advanced methods and apply what I've learned to getting a portal connected to other places.

In fact, I am convinced that the circular device behind the throne is or once was a device used for basic travel and portals. But without knowing how it worked, it will take me several more decades to work it all out myself. But I am determined.

Knox turned the page but found it empty. Whatever power that kept the journal from revealing its secrets was still working strong. But he did learn something new, whoever this Titan of Water truly was, he was experimenting with the powers of teleportation. What if he worked out more advanced methods of teleportation using his Ethereal Step ability?

It was worth noting that he didn't have the academic background that Ramses had, but surely it couldn't be so hard. He pulled out his notebook and began to take notes about what he knew of the spell, and what he'd learned. There was much more to activating the spell than just thought, the projecting of Titan Gowlen had drilled the lessons into him for weeks on end to learn the spell.

After outlining in as much detail as he could the methods of the spell, Knox tried to imagine other ways it could operate. However, without any frame of reference it was a pretty difficult, maybe impossible, task. So, after a few pages of ideas and notes, he decided to seek out more information in the complex archives.

There hadn't been anything specific on teleportation, but he remembered a mention of something to do with portals. Mic found him as he was walking toward the archives and stopped him.

"Can I be of assistance?" he asked; he had two maintenance golems flanking him on either side.

"Just looking for information on portals," Knox said, not even looking up from his notes as he pondered the problems.

"The main gateway is offline; would you like me to assign maintenance golems to fix it?" Mic asked, this had the effect of shaking Knox from his focused attention.

"Come again?" Knox asked.

"The main gateway, the portal that connects you with other nations and Titan Complex's, it is offline," Mic said as if it were just some miniscule thing to mention that they had portals that could possibly connect them to others.

"Why am I just hearing about this now?" Knox asked, annoyance overriding any sense of frustration Mic was bringing on.

"We've many tasks that remain undone and with our current status as self-reliant, I felt that it could wait. But if it is a priority, I can assign someone to work on it," Mic said.

Knox pinched at the bridge of his nose. "Please fix it—where is it anyways?" Knox asked.

"The circle construct behind the command chair, it is the main gateway, but there are several smaller ones that will be easy enough to bring online that help navigate from one part of the complex to another. However, the current output needs to be increased if we make such changes. The Titan Engine can only do so much while also spreading at maximum distance."

Knox sighed. "Why do I get the feeling that the spread is something I can control as well, and you haven't told me?" Knox asked, closing his notebook and giving the golem his full attention.

"One would assume that you wanted to have the maximum range of influence, so I didn't mention it. I can make adjustments if you feel the power could be used better elsewhere?" Mic asked, his gaze downcast for a moment before meeting Knox's eyes.

"Prioritize keeping us within the field but everything else

doesn't matter for now," Knox said. "Can we pull the field back or just prevent it from going wider?"

"The field cannot be pulled back, but its rate of expansion can be slowed. I will see to it immediately," Mic said, turning and leaving with his two maintenance golems.

Knox stood there for several long seconds as he considered what he'd just learned. He was more than a little eager to experiment with portals and understand a new concept of magic, but there was likely to be danger in making such considerations. Doors worked both ways, for instance, and if any force powerful enough to have portals decided they wanted the complex for themselves, Knox would be powerless to do anything about it.

He decided that he would have it repaired up to a certain point, but not activated until he could learn more about how they worked. To that end, he went to the archives and began to search out anything and everything on these 'Gateways'. What he found was more helpful than he'd thought possible.

"I'm leaving for a few weeks," Dernal said, shocking Knox out of his study.

"What for?" Knox asked.

"John and Leo were going to try to make it through the pass as soon as the snow thinned, they'll have a surprise waiting for them if I don't go meet them," Dernal said.

"Has it been that long already?" Knox asked. The winter had been cold, but no snowfall made it to the Shadowfall Swamp. Hell, they hadn't even been getting much rain. Another issue for another time, but Mic had mentioned that the water collection tanks were getting low from their constant use. Knox would have to talk to Murdoch about rationing the water until they got more rainfall.

"With any luck, they'll have made it through, and I can bring them here," Dernal said, his face emotionless.

"What of the monsters of the Shadowfall Swamp?" Knox asked, but he guessed at his answer before he gave it.

"With the culling of the C Ranked you've been doing, it's left only a few powerful B Ranked Monsters. I'm confident that we can avoid them," Dernal said.

"Did you want to bring anyone with you?" Knox asked, a part of him thinking that perhaps he could go on the little adventure with him to gather up more of his friends.

"I don't think that wise," Dernal said, his voice a low rumble. "It would be best if I traveled alone. It'll be faster and safer if I'm not having to protect anyone else."

Message received, Knox thought, nodding his head along with his friend's words.

Dernal left the next day, taking supplies with him and saying goodbye to very few. It left a hole in Knox's group that he needed to fill: a healer.

"Tell me again why you think you'd be a good fit?" Knox asked; he hadn't even started the process of looking at healers yet, but Henry had flagged him down, somehow knowing Dernal would be gone for an extended period of time.

"You need a decent healer and I'm available," Henry said, his voice had a quality to it that annoyed Knox, but he had to admit what he'd heard about his healing abilities were promising.

"I'm going to be honest," Knox said, pinching at the bridge of his nose. "I'm not a big fan of yours after the incident with Angie and Alice."

A fire seemed to light itself behind Henry's eyes and when he next spoke, it showed. "I did what was best for the entire party.

That poor girl's blood isn't on my hands." Then, as if something occurred to him he added, "And neither is it on yours. Forgive yourself and let me help you."

"No," Knox said flatly.

The fire continued to burn in the elderly man's eyes. "Name another healer with my level and skill?" Henry asked, then looking around the room as if he were going to find them there, he said, "I'll wait." He folded his arms and gave Knox a stare that could only be described as a 'stern grandfather look'.

Knox wanted to pinch his entire face off in frustration but held back from pinching the bridge of his nose any harder. "Look, I need a healer that I can trust, and I don't trust you," Knox said, done sparing the man's feelings.

"I get that," Henry said, clearing his throat. "But you also need a healer that can perform at your level or close to it. With Dernal gone you want the best and that's me. Trust? Give me a chance to earn it."

Knox groaned. He had a point and it frustrated him to no end. "We are due to hit the Labyrinth in an hour. If you fall behind, you are done. If you can't keep up with the damage, you're done. You make any questionable choices that I don't like, you're done," Knox said. He knew he was being a tad bit too stern, but the wounds of Alice were still too fresh for him to act any other way.

"I'll be ready," Henry said, turning and leaving the room before Knox had a chance to change his mind.

Knox left shortly after to gather some supplies. The air was cold and the ground wet from a recent rain. They'd been challenging the new section of the Labyrinth for a while now and Knox had a feeling that they were getting close. Several teams were now focusing on clearing the Tier 1—as Knox called it—mobs from the Labyrinth while his party focused on dealing with the mechanical spiders that were the mobs of the second Tier of the Labyrinth.

The very first room held a staircase now that led to the start of the second Tier, which was helpful, but also a bit weird since a similar staircase led to the exact spot in the Guardian's chambers where the empty chest still sat. The Guardian didn't respawn like the humanoid golems, but still, Knox kept the area off limits just to be safe.

Having gathered his supplies, he met with his party at the entrance of the Labyrinth. Henry wasn't there yet, so he decided to break the news to them.

"Dernal is gone for a bit," Knox said, most of the group nodded, having known as much already, but Murdoch looked surprised.

"Where'd that little devil get off to?" he asked, his head tilted to one side in confusion. "This isn't because I asked him for help, is it? I swear that man avoids anything resembling work like the black sickness."

This was news to Knox, so he fixed his attention on Murdoch and asked, "What did you ask him to do?"

"Nothing really," Murdoch said, his hand going behind his head to rub his neck. "I just suggested that because of his many wise years and being one of the more powerful members of the community, that perhaps he'd want to get to know a few more prominent members of Luminar. Nothing crazy, I just suggested a few lunches or dinners. You should have seen the color he went at the suggestion."

"Dernal doesn't have a wide social group," Knox said, chuckling. "He left to go get some friends of his, they will be a boon to Luminar, so I supported him going. But I have to wonder if you scared him off sooner than he was planning on going?"

Murdoch pursed his lips and looked anywhere but at Knox. "Doubtful," he said, then seeing someone coming down the hallway he added. "Who invited Henry?"

"I did," Knox said. "I was trying to tell you all that he is going to be Dernal's replacement until he returns. But be careful, he doesn't have the same level of healing, so I will be focusing on topping everyone off with my offensive spells as much as possible.

But if we work carefully and wisely, we ought to keep the same pace we've held in the past."

"You will find my heals to be quite enough," Henry said, stopping just shy of the group. He nodded his head to all the party members. Frederick had finally joined the team again, meaning they had a party of six members now: Beth, Murdoch, Terrim, Frederick, Knox, and now Henry.

They'd kept most parties around five to seven people, but six was enough for what they needed to do. The spiders thus far hadn't proven to be much of an issue, instead they were more annoying than anything else, quick, and hard to hit.

"Move out," Knox said, and they entered the Labyrinth once more to try and find more Guardians.

CHAPTER 14
GUARDIAN OF WATER

THE AIR inside the Labyrinth had an earthy quality to it. Knox took a deep breath of it regardless, because the rich essence that covered almost every square inch made it as sweet a thing as he'd ever tasted. It was like someone distilled pure life mixed with all manner of nature and served it up to every sense, including his special sense.

Knox was hyper aware of the halls they walked, remembering, and pointing out where Henry should avoid traps and such. Henry for his part moved with a lithe grace not befitting his age.

Henry was perhaps eighty or more years old, a ripe age for someone in their village, and he'd lived there his entire life from what Knox had heard about him.

His skin wasn't as wrinkled as it appeared to be when Knox first remembered meeting him, whether that was due to the effects of the system or something else, he wasn't sure. The truth was, Henry, with his white hair and keen blue eyes, was the most talented healer they could have hoped for. He'd been a healer his entire life, never truly the main physician in their small town, but one that you could go to for smaller issues.

This expertise or desire to be a healer translated well to the system where he was given a Path to pick, and he chose wisely. His

Path was that of the Mystic with a focus on the Celestial Adept Path, allowing him to summon little Celestials to aid him in his healing. It was a Path Knox could walk himself if he was interested, but he wasn't, at least not yet.

Celestials, as far as Knox had seen, were balls of golden light and more ethereal than physical. Knox looked forward to seeing what other types of Celestials there were and more importantly, he was interested in trying to communicate with them to learn where, why, and how they came to be.

All the studying he'd done recently had reignited his desire to learn about all types of magic and why they worked the way they did. With each step down deeper into the Labyrinth, Knox's mind wandered. It rested on his mother's journals and how important they were to him. He'd brought his own notes on the subjects he'd found within them, but not the actual journals.

He'd discovered that she'd been wrong in some of her assumptions when studying the records of the Titan Complex, the archives. But he didn't hold such errors against her; in fact, it made him yearn for a conversation with her more than anything. Perhaps he could ask Frederick if he... but no, that wouldn't be right.

"You look like your mother, you know. More so than that father of yours," Henry said, totally shattering Knox's train of thought and even his physical focus. Knox tripped on a misshapen stone and fell flat on his face.

Getting up and brushing himself off, he moved to stand right in front of Henry. "You knew my mother?" Knox asked, his voice filled with more emotion than he intended.

"What?" Henry said, obviously flustered by having Knox in his face, breathing hard as he was. "Why yes, I've a memory like a steel trap. I was one of the few that got a look at her before she passed."

"How, and why have you never told me this before?" Knox asked, his eyes welling up on their own with excessive fluids. He blinked the tears away and stared hard at the man.

"Your father made it clear that we shouldn't speak of her and believe it or not, your father was a man we all respected," Henry said. "He grew up in our village before leaving to adventure. We welcomed him back when he returned from that life of nonsense to a life of hard work. A shame about his injury."

"Tell me about my mother," Knox demanded. "What was she like? What did she look like? Why did you meet her? Who else knew her?" Question after question poured from Knox's lips but Henry held up a hand to quiet Knox.

"No one knew much about her. They arrived in secret, buying up that house with gold and for several months stayed in seclusion. It wasn't until she was giving birth to you that I got to see her. You see, I was on hand to help with the birth, should any additional expertise be needed. Terrible shame that she caught a fever afterward. Poor Askar was never the same after she died, leaving you in his care at such a young age. If not for the wet nurses, we'd have likely lost you as well. But you fought hard to stay alive, the tiny thing you were."

Knox was overwhelmed by the information he was getting. As far as he'd been told, his mother had died during childbirth, not after because of a fever.

"You say my mother survived childbirth?" Knox asked, his voice barely above a whisper.

Henry seemed to sense something was off and looked perturbed. "Did your father not tell you anything about the matter? I don't want to put myself between you both. But I won't lie either. She was strong and healthy when she gave birth to you, it wasn't until a week or two later that Askar informed us she'd died in the night due to a fever. It happens sometimes, sickness lying in wait days or even weeks to strike when the patient is at their weakest."

"You saw the body?" Knox asked, a sinister thought filling his head.

"Well, no, but I believe the head physician at the time did, but

I wasn't called in personally," Henry said, his words almost a sputter as he spoke.

"And he is dead now," Knox said, knowing he'd died many years ago due to old age, leaving Henry as the main physician.

"Are you alright?" Beth asked after several long seconds in silence.

"My father never speaks of her," Knox said, shaking his head. "I don't know what to think, what to feel. I just don't... let's go find something to kill. I need to blow off some steam."

They found a room filled with spiders and Knox held up a hand, indicating he'd be taking them on himself. This wasn't so uncommon, and so his teammates all took positions around the room, ready to help if needed.

The clickity-clack of the mechanical spider legs were music to Knox's ears as he readied his axe to strike. There were six of them and they spread out circling Knox and ignoring his party. Henry had the most perplexed look on his face, but the rest of the party understood.

The first two lunged forward, striking with their legs sharp enough to score hits between his armor and draw blood. But Knox side-stepped them with the grace of a lifelong dancer. Striking out with his axe, using no magic or excessive force, he took a leg off one of the spiders. It was almost too easy, and he loved it. His sense was a finely tuned weapon that gave him more control in a fight than any other spell or ability in his arsenal.

Three attacked this time, with two more shooting out some type of water attack. It left only the tiniest path of escape, but Knox saw it as clear as day, weaving in and out, striking legs from unsuspecting spiders. The water they used was hot to the point where it would boil the skin if it made contact, so Knox was extra careful not to let any of those attacks land.

He did let several of the sharp-legged attacks through, but his armor, both mystical and physical, blocked any damage from occurring. At no point during the fight did he feel afraid for his life, it was enough that he almost stopped listening to his sense to even the battlefield, but it wasn't to be. Instead, he tore them apart, one leg at a time, until there was nothing but spider bodies wiggling on the ground, shooting out streams of water here and there.

Stepping up to one such spider, Knox crushed it under his foot and yelled in fury as he considered all that he had survived and still had yet to endure. His life was everything he ever wanted and at the same time not. The pain that came with the loss of friends and those under his care was enough for him to wish for a simple life, but the thrill of discovery and magic called at him with equal pull. He lived for adventure, discovery, and power.

It was the power he was putting on display right now as he finished off the final spider. The entire thing had taken minutes, much longer than if they'd all been involved, but his party knew that he had to blow off steam occasionally. He was the most powerful person on the team, hell, probably in the entire complex. Even Dernal couldn't match his speed, strength, and agility anymore.

Only Aetex stood above Knox as far as he could tell, but soon he'd surpass even the mysterious Ki'darthian.

Ki'darthian, such a strange word and not a race he'd ever heard of before. Knox didn't know all of the races of his world, but he thought he had a good accounting of many of them. Certainly, he knew more than most of the people he'd gathered to live here, that much he was certain. Perhaps Leo would know more about the so-called Ki'darthian and where their people came from. Aetex mentioned that he'd become a hybrid as well, whatever that meant. In the context he'd said it in, it sounded as if he'd been changed by the mysterious Mah'kus, but these were heavy matters that Knox didn't have the time to ponder at that moment.

"Found a secret door!" Beth declared; she was finishing her second look over the walls.

"That display of p-power," Henry said, his voice stuttering as he stepped forward with eyes wide. "You truly are one of the

Titans of legend." With that, he bowed his head and Knox began to feel very uncomfortable.

"Easy there, Henry," Murdoch said, slapping the old man on the back lightly. "You'll give our boy Knox a complex if you start bowing to him. Bad enough he likes to show off so much."

"I wasn't showing off," Knox said quickly, and all his party laughed in one way or another, some snorting and some hiding smiles behind raised hands.

The secret door led to a treasure room, a chest inside filled with odd gold coins that they split. They had the face of Gowlen on one side and an odd gear on the other side. They'd encountered the coins before but there wasn't enough in circulation yet for them to be more than curiosities.

The air was the key to finding the Guardian in the end. There was a heaviness to it that if followed, eventually led them to a room filled with steam and water.

They found the room where the Guardian lay in wait two hours later. It was a massive affair with a giant pool of water taking up most of the room and serpents formed completely out of water resting just above the surface.

"As before, it shall be again," the Guardian hissed the words, and its meaning was clear.

"Get back everyone, no one interfere with this fight," Knox said, his gaze lingering on Henry.

The elderly man, to his credit, gave Knox a confident nod and lowered his hands. He'd been ready to buff Knox or summon one of his Celestials, but this was a task that Knox had to do himself, per the rules of the Guardians.

Stepping forward, Knox faced off against the watery serpent and awaited its first attack. His armor shone with the light of his power as he cast Mystic Armor over himself. His power sat just out of reach, ready to be called down at a second's notice.

He was strong, he was powerful, he was not going to falter.

Even so, he didn't sense the first attack as it slammed into him from behind, hot water scorching his flesh and causing him to scream. Focusing on spreading his sense out, he caught the barest signs of movement and paid attention to it this time. A dozen little spiders made of water crawled all around him, attacks ready.

With a sudden buildup of power, he unleashed a powerful Arcane Pulse. It decimated the smaller spiders but, in that moment, the larger serpent chose to attack as well.

Knox rolled to the side, but even so, it was only barely fast enough to miss a giant spike of ice shattering beside him. It had the effect of blowing him off course and sending him stumbling and slipping to try and regain his feet. Another ice attack came and although he could sense it coming, the slick floor made it nearly impossible to do much more than try to attack back.

Raising his hands, Knox sent out a Luminous Surge. Power surged at his command and shattered the dangerous ice spike midair. A thousand little shards smashed against his armor, falling harmlessly onto the ground. It just added to the debris that would make maneuvering harder, but there was no helping it.

With such a debris-filled battlefield, Knox did his best to keep his footing, slashing out with his axe at the next ice bolt that came his way, shattering it. Something needed to change and quick, he'd been on the defensive this entire time. It was time to show this Guardian the power of the Light.

Using Ethereal Step, Knox instantly teleported a short distance, putting himself right in front of the monstrous water serpent. His axe came down and slashed harmlessly through it. He didn't realize his mistake until it was too late; whatever this serpent guardian was, solid it was not. Water slammed in all around and Knox felt himself being pulled into the small body of water.

The rush of the water blurred his senses and made it impossible for him to right himself. Meanwhile, something struck his armor over and over again, forcing the air out of his lungs and leaving him gasping. Thinking as best he could under the circumstances, Knox activated Solar Wings, hoping it would allow him to break free of the water.

He beat his wings of light with all the power he possessed. Inch by inch he made progress, but he wasn't sure it would be fast enough. Just as the corner of his vision began to flicker with blackness from lack of breath, his head broke free and he gasped in the sweet, blessed air.

The next moment, water covered him again and his Solar Wings failed. Thinking fast as he sank back into the depths of the water, Knox triggered Aetherial Step, allowing him to dash through the water and break the surface once more. The edge of the surface was only steps away, so he teleported the short distance, his axe lost in the rush to break the surface.

Standing before this new Guardian, unarmed and fed-up, Knox began to weave the magic of the Titans around him. He was Titan Born, damnit, and he wouldn't allow some simple Guardian to defeat him, not now!

Triggering Chronicle Resonance and Aeon Gaze simultaneously, Knox saw what he needed to do. The barest glint of metal could be seen inside the serpent, his gut told him it was this Monster's Core and the only way he was going to survive the next few minutes.

Checking behind his shoulder he saw his team, each of them with weapons ready and apprehensive looks on their faces. Knox smiled at them before turning back to his task at hand.

The serpent Guardian raised its head, ready to strike him down with ice and hot water, but Knox was ready. Using his sense, he located his axe, it was in the water but not so deep that he couldn't get to it if he had a second or two. Problem was, he didn't have any time. So instead, he improvised. Using Radiant Glyph, he added some temporary runes to his right gauntlet, turning it into a more effective weapon for crushing Cores.

Then just as an ice bolt came his way, followed by a dozen new water spiders, Knox jumped into the water. Swimming wasn't really an option with his heavy armor on, so he activated Solar Wings again, moving as fast as he could toward the Core and his victory.

But just as before, the serpent wasn't going to sit still and be defeated so easily. It came at him, swirling and whirling the water to make it hard for him to focus. Instead of relying on his eyes, he closed them and let his sense take over. There was a moment of panic that he squashed before he could truly see once more.

Like a thousand strands of silk connecting every possible movement and power, his sense reached out and reported back to him at the speed of thought. A lance of ice was coming for him, he pushed off it as it approached and leveraged himself closer to the core.

After several moments of tense movement and a few more ice bolts later, the Core came within view. He smashed out with his empowered gauntlet and struck something solid for the first time during the fight. The waters spun and rushed around him suddenly, before going still.

He'd done it, his eyes opened to see darkness all around him as he sunk to the bottom of the pit of water. Feeling toward the bottom, he found his axe and made slow progress toward the edge, slipping and falling in the muck at the bottom of the water. Hands reached out and helped pull him free just as he was about to lose consciousness, so terrible was the lack of air.

"You alright?" Terrim asked, his voice worried. Despite the tone of his voice, he wore a smile on his face and looked to be on the verge of laughing.

"I'm a bit wet," Knox said, chuckling back at his friend's ridiculous-looking, smirking face.

"We can see that," Beth said, she kneeled at the edge of the water with her bow out. "Did you get it or are we breaking the rules and killing it together now?"

"I think I got it," Knox said, spitting out a bit of water that had made its way into his mouth.

"Allow me to ease your pain," Henry said, muttering an incantation and a small orb of light appearing. It shimmered and pulsed, warm healing covering Knox's body and drying him out.

"That's a neat trick," Knox said, feeling his clothes go from freezing cold and wet to warm and dry.

"Celestials have all sorts of perks, I can't wait to meet my Champion, I'm sure his power will rival even your powerful strikes," Henry said, his old man voice surprisingly clear in that moment.

A chest appeared at the edge of the water and Knox retrieved the next emblem shard. By the size of each shard—both being equal—Knox could make a guess at how many more Guardians he had to face.

"I think there are six emblem shards total," Knox said. "That is assuming they are all the same size, and it ends up being a mostly circular emblem, as I'm guessing it is."

"So, you've only got to do this song and dance four more times," Murdoch said, his tone sarcastic. "Good luck."

"You've defeated two pretty easily, the next four won't be an issue," Terrim said, his reassuring words doing nothing to squash the growing feeling of apprehension that Knox was feeling.

"Pretty easily?" Knox repeated, shaking his head. "This one was harder than the last, but for a very different reason. Overall, if I knew how to deal with them, both Guardian's represented a mild threat compared to some of the things we've faced before."

"Then continue to be an insightful young lad and you'll be fine," Henry said. "I'm terribly sorry that I never told you about your mother, I always assumed your father told you about her."

"Not now," Knox said, holding up a hand. He didn't need to rehash those raw feelings just yet; he was too tired and too on edge still.

Having defeated a new Guardian, a stairwell leading downward appeared in the Guardian's room and in the starting room.

They now had access to more ore than they knew what to do with and Mic had decided, with some prompting from Murdoch, to use the extra metals to mint several coins to use as currency.

There were four kinds of coins, a copper coin that represented a hundredth of an average-sized Monster Core. An iron coin that was meant to be one tenth of the value of a Monster Core and the most common coin. Then there was the steel coin roughly twice the size of the iron coin and worth roughly one Monster Core. Lastly, despite the higher value attributed to it being three average Monster Cores, was the golden coin that they'd been getting out of the Labyrinth. Of course, the values would fluctuate as more cores entered the market and became more or less scarce.

Knox wondered if the coins he got from the dungeon, the Runemarks, would hold up as a currency within this new minting process Mic had created. Studying the two coins, he noted they were very similar, except for the gear on one side and the general appearance. One was very much gold and had no magical runes on it, whereas Runemarks clearly held some magic in them. Even with his new knowledge of runes and the archives, he hadn't come across what the specific collection of runes meant yet.

He had an idea that it was some type of preservation rune set, but it went deeper than that and he didn't know how.

Moving to the vaults, where the Monster Cores were being kept as a sort of bank, Knox felt the pull of all that unused essence. The idea of keeping so many Cores unused for the Titan Engine or for himself nearly made Knox sick, but Murdoch stressed the importance of having a stockpile until the currency really took. Eventually these would all be put into the engine, feeding the growth of the system, but for now, they acted as a backing for the currency.

A few older folks, Henry included, argued that creating their own currency was a bit over the top, but they had so little of the king's currency out here in the wilds that it only made sense. Trade and barter could only go so far when you wanted people to get paid and have incentives to keep working. Most of the people took it in stride, happy to exchange their daily or weekly supply of Cores for a hard metal currency.

It was during this daily in and out of running through the Labyrinth and helping the occasional hunting party, that a discovery was made. Deep within a cave on the coastline—where some of the stronger hunting parties had started venturing and even some fishing had begun—a stone pillar was discovered. Upon touching it, one party member reported that they experienced a surge of heat filling them and being transported someplace else with doors that they dared not enter.

A new dungeon had been discovered.

CHAPTER 15
WARNING

AETEX CAME BACK into town right as another attack by the pirates appeared. He single-handedly took care of them as Knox rushed to get together a defense. These pirates were different though, each of them was able to avoid the detection of the command chair and Knox's sense. If not for Aetex appearing when he did, they might have been caught off guard and lost several lives to the pirates before they could react.

It was a cold day, perhaps two hours into the early morning when Aetex greeted Knox at the top of the eastern defensive towers.

"They just don't learn," Aetex said, wiping a bead of sweat off his forehead. It made the gem on his forehead seem to glimmer as the sun hit the wet gem and, not for the first time, Knox wondered at its purpose.

"Do all Ki'darthians have a gem set into their forehead?" Knox asked, deciding that if he didn't ask now, he never would.

Aetex smiled down at him and let out a long-suffering sigh. "Not at all. Just the Erusha, the chosen of the gods, the champions of my people."

"Hmm, well, thank you for the assist," Knox said, gesturing to the bodies being picked up off the battlefield.

"I come with a warning," Aetex said, then he suddenly grimaced and held his ribs. "Sorry, been fighting off an infection for several weeks and it's digging deeper."

"Are you alright?" Knox asked, letting his sense fall over Aetex and gasping as he did. "You've got the darkness in you. Let me purge it from you and we can get you healed before it does any more damage!"

"Not necessary," Aetex said, giving Knox a weak smile. "I'm fine." The words barely got out of his mouth when his eyes rolled into the back of his head, and he collapsed.

Knox lifted the large man—he was notably heavier than Knox expected—as best he could and began to drag him to the healer's hut. He met Terrim along the way and the two of them lifted Aetex much easier.

"What happened to him?" Terrim asked as they entered the hut and set him on one of the many empty beds.

"The darkness has taken root, get Henry here now, I'm not waiting to purge the filth from him," Knox said, already light beginning to glow around his hands as he began the workings of Luminous Surge.

A hand shot up and Aetex's eyes opened, cutting off the spell.

"I can manage it, save your strength for what is coming. The Dread Pirate and his horde of undead pirates. They amass their strength for a final attack," Aetex said, but Knox just moved his hand away and began the casting once more.

To hell with his pride, Knox thought, he needed help, and he was getting it.

Luminous Surge went off and Aetex sat up, screaming in pain, Knox pressed into the spell even harder. It took an entire minute of casting on and off until any trace of the darkness was gone and Aetex had lost consciousness halfway into it. B Ranked or not, pain was pain and everyone had a limit.

Henry appeared in the doorway just as sapphire blood began to fall from Aetex's nose and eyes.

"Heal him!" Knox shouted, seeing Henry freeze up at the sight.

"Oh yes, of course," Henry said, and he began to chant words of healing.

Unlike the healing that Dernal used to do that returned the blood to the body and strengthened it, Henry's worked by showering the target with a deep golden-white light. He even summoned forth his little ball of light, the Celestial. It popped into existence and even Knox felt the healing effects its presence had.

Still, Aetex remained unmoving, and Knox wondered if he'd made a mistake.

"He's as healed as I can make him," Henry announced. "I'd wager he needs rest, give him time."

"He came with a warning," Knox said, shaking his head and wishing that Aetex was conscious to tell him more. "The Dread Pirate Captain is on his way and apparently, he's got an army of undead."

Aetex remained unconscious, but Henry assured Knox that he had been healed and his body just needed time. However, Knox couldn't help but feel guilty about his part in the matter. Had Aetex known something like this would happen if he was cleansed and that was why he'd been so adamant about enduring it? He didn't know and all he could do was hope that Aetex pulled through.

Murdoch appeared beside Knox in the community area they'd been using for large meals. "People are asking about the dungeon," Murdoch said, putting his food down beside Knox's untouched stew.

"What about it?" Knox asked, this was the first he was hearing about it.

Murdoch took the time to enjoy a warm spoon full of his stew before continuing. "Now that we are all basically Adventurers, people want a shot at the dungeon. They've heard the stories about what you can find within them. I'm a bit excited about it myself if I'm being honest."

"Too dangerous, this is an uncharted dungeon and there is no telling how powerful even the weakest of the paths inside the dungeon could be," Knox said, he was not going to send off a group into a possible death trap just for the chance at some loot.

"Not for us," Murdoch said, elbowing Knox. "Think about it. You are as strong as any Adventurer I've come across and with Henry's heals and our strength, what are the chances we can't at least clear out a small bit of the dungeon?"

Knox considered his words, but shook his head, no. "We have pirates at our doorstep and a Labyrinth to clear out. There just isn't time to do a dungeon run."

"But think of the loot," Murdoch said. "We might find a pivotal piece of armor and arms that will allow us to defeat the pirates or more Guardians. It is important that we try."

Knox had to admit that Murdoch had a decent point. Dungeon loot was powerful and better than anything they'd been able to make yet. Mostly due to the special effects certain items could have when coming from the dungeon. Those types of runic formations were beyond even him and he was the best at the runic system they had right now. Sure, they had Necromancers empowering items, but much of the actual rune crafting had to be done by Knox, taking away precious time he could be doing other things.

"Three days," Knox said, taking a spoon full of his lukewarm broth, he'd let it sit too long. "That is all I will give us. Whatever we can clear out in that time, it will have to be enough."

"Nice!" Murdoch said, followed quickly by, "Ow, that stew is hot." His own stew being fresh from the pot still held a wonderful heat to it.

Knox collected all the information he could about the dungeon from the person who'd found it. It was surprisingly little; he had entered the dungeon the normal way but hadn't gone into any of the paths open to him. He did say that the cave was a bit hard to see, them having only found it when one of their party members fell down a cliff and injured themselves.

Knox was pretty sure he'd be able to find it based off the directions he'd received, but he decided to take the party with him just to be sure. They wouldn't be going into the dungeon, only his party would, but he didn't want to waste any time going about it.

Aetex continued to sleep, nothing any of the healers did was able to rouse him, but his color had returned, and his breathing normalized. Whatever was keeping him under couldn't last forever and Knox fully expected him to be awake by the time they returned.

He also saw to it that the Labyrinth was continually explored, even the newest third Tier. In that Tier, Knox and his party had come across mechanical wolves that weren't much of a challenge, but showed much more intelligence than previous mobs, flanking and sacrificing themselves to get a shot in here and there. But Knox wasn't worried about it as they'd set a clear level window for those wanting to challenge it.

With everything taken care of, they set out early in the morning after Knox did a quick check on the pirates' locations, as far as the system was concerned, they remained clustered several dozen miles down the coast from where the dungeon was and even further from Luminar. The area of effect from the system had grown much, so much so that it encompassed the Mire Gloom Dungeon and the Guild Charterhouse.

They were both clearly marked on the map with odd runic symbols that Knox had looked up but found their meaning unclear. He could only imagine the turmoil the system would be causing to those Adventurers in the dungeon town or at the Guild Charterhouse. It was enough that Knox had been speaking with Murdoch about sending out an emissary of types to help them understand the system and the Paths, but so far, they hadn't been able to agree on who to send.

"Can I talk to you alone?" Murdoch asked, to which Knox nodded and let the rest of his party follow closely behind the party leading them. After they were a good distance back, Knox turned to Murdoch with a curious eye.

"What's up?" Knox asked, when Murdoch didn't immediately tell him what was happening with him.

Murdoch seemed off, nervous in a way Knox rarely saw him.

"I've been talking with a few of the elders, and they want to do an official election," Murdoch said, his voice even and not filled with the zest it normally has.

"So?" Knox asked, shaking his head. "You're the best man for the job and you enjoy doing it, you've got my support."

"It isn't that simple," Murdoch said, a touch of heat reaching his voice. "I'm not sure I want the job anymore."

Knox stopped and looked at his friend. This went contrary to everything he knew about Murdoch, so why was he saying it? Murdoch had always loved politics and working with people in general. Hell, he even chose his Path based off that love of messing with people. Sure, it wasn't all he was about, he still loved adventure, women, fooling around with friends, *women*, and life in general, but it was a core part of what made Murdoch, well, Murdoch.

"Is the responsibility too much?" Knox asked, he'd had similar feelings that he hadn't really had a chance to express to anyone else, so he brightened at perhaps having someone to share that particular burden with.

"That is part of it," he said. "But there is more to it."

"I can understand the responsibility part," Knox said. "I'm not exactly the leadership type myself but I've been thrust into a role as a Titan Born that I can't ignore. I supported you as a step-in mayor the same as everyone else when the time came. You are right for this job; you just have to trust that we will support you in it."

"We've lost nearly half our numbers either by death or leaving from the original group that survived the black sickness. I can't help but think that part of that responsibility lies on my head and it's much more real a feeling than I'm used to. I mean, when I was younger, hell even before you left, things were fun, exciting, and the weight of it all didn't ever occur to me," Murdoch paused his speaking to wipe away tears that began to form. "I don't know if I'm good enough, I'm not my father."

Knox didn't know what to say at first, but he trusted his gut and went with what first came to his mind. "You aren't your father and that's good. You are Murdoch, a man of respect and authority that doesn't shy away from a heavy load. Your father did the best he could with his situation, but this entire thing," Knox said, waving his hands around to indicate the system, "is more than I think he could have handled. But you. You, Murdoch, can handle this. Together, with the help of our friends, we can bear the weight."

"To death?" Murdoch said, a coy smile on his face.

"To death," Knox said, the saying feeling a bit morose given the circumstance, but Knox didn't want to dissuade his friend when he looked like he was coming off it.

"You know, with you as the Titan Born and head of Luminar, just by the fact that you are basically a Titan of Legend now, do we even need a mayor?" Murdoch asked, mirth still in his voice.

"We do," Knox assured him. There was so much to organize and work out with people in general, that not even Mic could handle it all. There had to be administrative help and Murdoch was the one to do that. "So, you'll put your name in the hat?"

"Only if you do," Murdoch said, his sarcastic tone making it clear he wasn't serious.

"As if," Knox said, increasing his pace. Murdoch did the same and soon they were right there with the two parties as they navigated toward the newly discovered dungeon.

The ground was still soft from a recent rain and the tracks from the group's first trip out there stuck out enough that Knox wondered if he ought to try and disguise them, but the mud turned to stone a few miles further out, so he guessed they'd be safe after all. The last thing he wanted was to give the pirates access to a dungeon to collect powerful gear and Runemarks. He cared less about the Runemarks, but if they got powerful gear, they'd be that much harder to deal with.

"Brandon," Knox called out to the head of the party that found the dungeon on the coast and entered it, alone.

"Hmm?" Brandon asked, as he slowed his pace to allow Knox to catch up with having to jog.

"Describe to me the runes you saw above the door again," Knox said.

Brandon did as much, and Knox was certain he had an idea of what the first path held within it.

"If I'm understanding it right, then we can expect an aquatic theme for the dungeon. Part of what he described had to do with water," Knox said to the group at large.

"Too bad we can't breathe under water," Terrim said, laughing.

But Knox didn't laugh. He'd been working on a runic cluster that might give them that very ability, but he'd kept it close to his chest, not knowing if it would work like he'd hoped. Basically, he took steel coins, the circles before they were minted and added row after row of runic formations. If the bundle of coins he had worked properly, they should produce air for a limited amount of time.

They could be recharged easily, in fact an entire side of the coin was done in a way to accept mana to recharge it, a simple task that Knox was sure he could teach the others. Figuring that a dungeon close to the ocean would require some swimming, he'd taken the idea he'd been working on ever since he had the trouble with the water Guardian, taking the five prototypes with him.

He'd begun work on a sixth, to work well with their group, but Frederick had once more decided to stay back and work with crops, so five would do fine for this adventure.

Frederick had separated himself more and more as a member of the party, much to the point where Knox was considering letting him just start or be a part of another group. It wasn't anything personal, but their schedules weren't really working. Frederick wanted to spend lots of time farming and researching his Necromancer magic with the other Necromancers, leaving him missing more than half of the Labyrinth clearing and hunting the party did.

He couldn't blame him, but it did rub Knox the wrong way if he thought about it too much. He was so committed, along with the rest of the party, to the goals and quests he had, that he couldn't imagine what Frederick's issue about it could be.

"You talk to Frederick much?" Knox asked Terrim, careful to keep his voice low enough that the entire party wouldn't overhear.

"You mad he didn't come?" Terrim asked, looking at Knox with a flat expression.

"A little," Knox said, shaking his head. "It might be time for him to have his own group, one with far less time commitments."

"I think you might be right," Terrim said, nodding. "He wants to be there for you, but the man has a lot on his plate. We all do, really. But we understand getting stronger is more than important, it's necessary if we want to survive. Just be glad he isn't listening to your father."

"Great," Knox said, stopping to look at Terrim. "What is he doing now and why am I always the last one to know?"

"He's been heard saying, after a few drinks, that we ought to abandon Luminar and let the pirates take it. Says with this system the world is changing and that you aren't up for keeping everyone safe," Terrim said, wincing as he spoke.

"He might be right," Knox said, lowering his voice even more, so much so that Terrim must not have heard.

"What'd you say?" Terrim said, leaning down as if his incredible height was the reason he didn't hear.

"Nothing," Knox said, smiling up at his friend. "The time may come that we need to flee and get more support, perhaps even from the Guild or the King, but now isn't that time."

CHAPTER 16
NAMELESS DUNGEON

"WHAT DO you mean it's right there? That's nothing but water," Knox said, looking over the cliff and into the great waters beyond, the Endless Sea.

"I'm positive it was right here, maybe the water moved," Brandon said, looking as perplexed as Knox felt.

Seeing as none of them knew anything about the sea and if it rose or fell with time, Knox decided it would be best just to camp out and wait to see. He didn't like the idea of starting the dungeon using his experimental coins. It had been meant to be more of a last resort, not something that got continual use.

"We'll wait it out and see," Knox announced, and they began the process of setting up a camp at the edge of the cliff where the great waters met land.

With camp set up, everyone went about their duties, some gathering firewood, others just relaxing, while Knox studied one of the coins he'd created, putting it in his mouth and testing it out.

It was an odd sensation, and he didn't quite like it, but it was working. He placed the coin back in his mouth and shut his jaws. A steady trickle of air filled his mouth, and he focused on exhaling out with his nose, it wouldn't do to get water in your mouth after all.

"Whatcha working on?" Beth asked, coming to sit beside Knox on a log they'd pushed over around a small fire, pushing the cold of the winter away as best it could.

Knox looked up from his work, spitting the coin out into his palm and showing it to her.

"That's gross," Beth said, not missing a beat. "Why are you putting coins in your mouth?"

"I've inscribed them with runes, and if it works, it'll give us a way to breathe underwater for a time," Knox explained. Pulling a fresh one out, he offered it to her. "I need test subjects, care to try it out? Breathe through your mouth and exhale out your nose. Oh, and don't swallow the coin, no idea what that would do but I doubt it'd be good."

"Okay," Beth said, drawing out the word.

She took the coin and examined it, then unceremoniously popped it into her mouth. After several seconds her eyes went wide, and she gave Knox a thumbs up. After a solid minute she opened her mouth and spit the coin out.

"It's weird and makes me slightly nauseated, but it works!" Beth said, handing back the wet coin.

Knox held his hands up. "You keep it, but don't lose it, alright?"

"Deal," Beth said, then an awkward silence began to grow between them.

"You doing okay?" Knox finally asked and Beth shot him a look that spoke volumes.

"Not really," Beth said. "I've dealt with loss before, it isn't anything new to me, but I'm feeling, I don't know, unwanted? I know I have the group and you guys won't leave me, but I've never dealt with feeling unwanted before. Why would Richard leave me? Was it something about me that he didn't like, is there something wrong with me?"

Knox had never heard Beth be so vulnerable before and it

shocked him into silence. Sure, he'd been around when she was hurting or mad, but this was different.

"It isn't you, you're perfect," Knox said, averting his eyes as heat rose up to his face.

"Yeah, sure," Beth said sarcastically. "You are basically a literal Titan now, how is that fair?"

"What do you mean?" Knox asked, confused by the sudden turn in the conversation.

"Nothing," Beth said, shaking her head and going to stand.

Knox put a hand on her arm, and she stopped to look at him.

"I know it's been rough but know that I still care for you and whether or not you feel the same level of intensity of caring that I do, I'll always be here to be your friend," Knox said, doing his best to express his feelings on the matter. He cared deeply about Beth, as a friend.

"What about Sarah?" Beth said, a flash of jealousy crossing her face.

"Well, I'm not a Kor Monk or anything," Knox said, laughing. Kor monks were famous for their celibacy, but based on Beth's reaction, she had never heard of them. "I just mean to say, I have needs—wait that didn't come out how I meant."

Beth raised an eyebrow. "As I told you before you left, I'll always be there to help alleviate any 'needs' you might have," Beth said, a sly smile on her lips as she leaned forward.

Knox raised his own eyebrows and couldn't help but lean in toward her as well. They shared a light kiss, nothing compared to the passionate times they'd spent together before he left to be an Adventurer, but it was nice.

"I'm open to exploring things," Beth said, her voice a breathy whisper. Then looking around to see that no one else was watching, she reached around and pinched Knox's backside. "But I'm not a side lady." She stood then and spoke a bit louder. "Let me know how things with Sarah go or if they end."

Knox watched her go, feeling like he wasn't a hundred percent sure what had just happened. He'd been trying to make her feel better and now she'd propositioned him? At least he thought that was what had happened, honestly the kiss had him a little dizzy of thought, so he just smiled and enjoyed the feeling.

Beth still cared for him, perhaps even more than a friend. But where did that leave Knox and Sarah? He'd just started things with her, she'd been super understanding about his time constraints and despite going somewhat steady for a month, they'd progressed very little relationship wise, only becoming intimate a week or two ago. She was beautiful and she obviously cared for Knox, he wasn't sure what he'd do about it, but he did know it could wait for another day.

"I saw that," Terrim said, throwing down some firewood and giving Knox a huge shit-eater grin. "Playing the field with multiple ladies, eh? You'll give Murdoch a run for his money."

"Two ladies at a time is never a good idea," Murdoch said, appearing from behind and startling Knox, who was completely distracted at that moment.

"I don't know what's happening if I'm being completely honest," Knox said, grinning. "I'm not sure what to do. I was just getting comfortable with the idea of Sarah. Sure, we aren't super serious yet, but still."

"Inter group relations might make drama during combat," Terrim said, keeping his booming voice low.

"Forget that, life is drama, live it up and see if you can balance both of them at the same time," Murdoch said, then seeming to hear his own words he raised a finger and said, "*Or... at the same time!*"

"No, Murdoch, just no," Knox said, rolling his eyes at his overactive friend.

Murdoch was just nodding along as if he hadn't heard Knox, likely imagining what it would be like to have a 'same time' kind of situation of his own.

"Who are you seeing now?" Terrim asked Murdoch, a little grin on his face.

"Oh, me? Well, that isn't important right now," Murdoch said, looking suddenly shy and nervous at the same time.

"Who is it?" Knox asked, trying to guess at who would cause Murdoch to become embarrassed like this.

"It's someone you know pretty well," Terrim said, on the verge of laughing out loud.

"Now isn't the time," Murdoch said, standing and looking around for something to do. "Perhaps we need more wood? I'll get more wood."

Knox stood and grabbed his friend's arm, not hard, but in a way that made him stop and look him in the eyes. "Just tell me," Knox said. "Who could it be to make you so jittery?"

"He's been seeing Angie," Terrim said, unable to hold his laughter back he bellowed out several loud laughs.

Knox wasn't laughing. "Really? After everything she's been through, she doesn't need emotional pain that comes with dating you Murdoch," Knox said, he didn't understand why he was getting so heated about it, but after saving Angie he'd felt protective over her, and Murdoch had a reputation.

"Hey now," Murdoch said, looking truly offended. "I'm not that bad."

Terrim and Knox both shared a look and then gave Murdoch a leveled stare.

"Okay I can be... insensitive at times, but I truly like Angie. She's a sweet girl who listens to my prattling without making me feel less for it. It isn't like I'm just using her for sex," Murdoch said just as Beth happened to walk close to the fire again.

"Whose Murdoch using for sex now?" she asked, and Murdoch's face went red, whether from annoyance or embarrassment Knox couldn't tell.

Murdoch took several deep breaths, then turned to leave, Knox let him go.

"We will talk about this later," Knox called after him.

"What'd I say?" Beth said, looking from Terrim to Knox.

They both shrugged, Terrim laughed, and Knox left.

Several hours of waiting was getting to Knox, so he decided he was going to take a swim. The air was cold, but the water was colder. Stripping out of his heavy armor, he wanted to be able to swim around easier, so he cast Mystic Armor on himself for a measure of protection and tied himself off with a thick rope.

"I'll go take a look to verify it's a dungeon or that we are even in the right place, but keep hold of the rope and be ready to pull me out in say, ten minutes?" Knox said the last bit as a question and got head nods from his party. "Good, let's do this."

Taking several deep breaths, Knox got himself a running start to jump into the water. He knew how to swim, but he hadn't been the most powerful swimmer before becoming a Titan Born. Now though, he had strength to rival the strongest on the planet and swimming had become much easier. The coin was cold on his tongue, he pressed it to the roof of his mouth, hoping it wouldn't slip down his throat when he exerted himself.

The water hit him like a burst of painful needles all across his body. He nearly swallowed the coin the moment the pain lanced up his body, but he managed to get it back into place. Squinting his eyes, he tried his best to see, but the waters rushed all around him and made it difficult.

Making it to the surface, he looked around and saw he was already being swept out into the great waters as the water came and went against the edge of the cliff. Activating Solar Wings, he plunged back into the water and toward the cliffside. His eyes burned from the salt in the water, but he could see, if only barely.

There was indeed a cave down here under the water, so Knox swam for it, thinking as he struggled to swim downward that perhaps keeping his armor on might have been a wiser choice. He could use the help to stay toward the bottom of the water, but there was no helping it now. Instead, he focused on the cave and made his way inside.

Turned out the water filled the entrance and a space a hundred or so paces inward, but then opened up to breathable air. Knox slipped the coin from his mouth and put it away in a pouch at his side. Pulling himself up and onto dry land, he saw the dungeon entrance.

Unlike the Dire Gloom Dungeon, there was no building around the dungeon entrance or a guard looking to see your papers. Instead, it just stood there, a monolith of stone with glowing runes down the center of each side. The glow was bright enough to illuminate the dark cave with enough light to see by, but not much more.

The rope prevented him from moving much closer, it must have gotten stuck on the entrance of the cave, so Knox just looked at it and admired the beautiful sight. The runes were many he knew now, each one being a cluster of smaller more complicated runes. These particular ones had to do with preservation and transportation. The dungeon itself was somewhere deep underground, or at least that is what Knox theorized.

Knox was about to start on his way back when a shadow from the far side of the opening moved. Going to his side, he pulled free his axe, unbuckling it from his leg where it had been safely strapped down.

"Who's there?" Knox called and several more of the shadows moved, followed by a hissing sound.

Two beings slunk into the dim light of the dungeon and Knox gasped. He'd never seen anything like them before, they were naked for one, or mostly so. Each one had odd translucent skin that made it possible to see muscles just below their skin. Their eyes were black orbs twice the size of any race Knox had seen before. They held spears with what looked like shells sharpened and attached to the ends. They had webbed hands and feet, their skin looking more like scales than flesh.

The one that wore some clothing, had what looked like fish

scales covering his nether region. The other, a female by her anatomy, wore nothing at all, but her body was covered in red, blue, and green painted stripes. They were patterned in a way that almost resembled runes, but just different enough not to be anything that made any sense.

Then they spoke and Knox was even more startled, as they spoke common.

"You trespass on our waters," the larger of the two said, the one with nether coverings. "Leave or face the might of the Ahtora." With that, he clanked his spear down and puffed out his chest. There was a shell around his neck and as he spoke it glowed with obvious runes. Perhaps it was translating his words or doing some other useful magic? Knox wasn't sure, but he wasn't about to give up a chance to run a dungeon after all the time he'd sunk into it.

Moving slowly so as not to startle them, Knox returned his axe to its holster and held his hands out in front of him. "I'm not an enemy. I am Knox, Titan Born of Light." Knox wondered suddenly if his system area of effect had pierced the water yet or not—he'd have to check when he returned.

"Titan? You make tall claims for a human," the shell wearing Ahtora said. "You may call me Atar, I will face you in combat. Prove to me you are Titan, show your vast powers or be proven a liar."

With that, Atar stepped forward and twirled his spear, it whistled in the air and Knox could feel the power thrumming off him. Using his sense, he took a look and was surprised to find he had the aura of a C Ranker, and it was bright enough to suggest he was close to B Rank. That was fine with Knox, as he had the attributes of a peak C Ranker, plus access to two Paths.

Knox sighed and pulled free his axe again, shifting his grip on the handle, he stared hard at his opponent.

"We don't need to fight, but I will if you wish to see my power. Ready?" Knox asked, tilting his head ever so slightly and cutting loose the rope around his waist.

Atar tilted his head as well and the battle was on.

Knox struck first, feigning an axe throw only to use his spare hand to cast Lustrous Chains. Strand by strand, the chains shot up, entangling Atar. The man cried out in surprise, flinging his spear with frightening speed. If not for his sense, Knox wouldn't have known what to do or be able to react in time, but he had it and his teleportation step spell went off, dodging the attack.

Knox closed the distance, axe in hand, and rose it to strike down a killing blow. But Atar wasn't finished, his body began to glow, and the chains shattered. His spear appeared out of nowhere in his hands once more, smacking Knox's axe blow to the side, following up with the blunt end into Knox's stomach.

Groaning, but focusing on his sense, Knox dodged two more attacks and raised his hands activating Luminous Surge. He blew the fish man right off his feet, slamming him against the dungeon pillar. Atar grunted in pain but managed to make it back to his feet within moments. Knox leaned into his sense and, ready for any attack that might come, activated Solar Wings.

If he wanted to see the power of a Titan, then Knox might as well look the part. Lifting himself a few feet from the ground, he hovered over his opponent. Instead of being awed by his performance, Atar moved his hands and chanted something. Water came streaming out of his palms, slamming into Knox and throwing him back.

Unarmored in anything but his Mystic Armor, Knox felt the crushing blow in its full glory and smiled. It had hurt for sure, but this being lacked the raw power to finish him off with techniques. His wings still active, Knox landed lightly on the wet stone. Then using Astral Projection, his newest Mystic ability, he projected a copy of himself and closed in on the fighter.

It worked to draw his first attack, giving Knox the time to cast Void Grasp, followed by Reality Ripple, ensnaring and slowing his opponent. Knox rushed forward, his sense guiding him, and swung his axe, it shone with powerful light. Suddenly, he heard chanting behind Atar and a wall of ice appeared in front of him.

It shattered under his blow, but still it stopped him from dealing the blow that would have ended the fight.

"Enough," Atar said, his body glowing again, and Knox's spells dissipated.

Another voice spoke in a language Knox had never heard of, fast and almost musical. Atar looked at the painted lady who'd obviously been the one to cast the spell and replied in the same language. Then looking back at Knox he said, "You are one of power, though I do not recognize you as a Titan. Do you wish to challenge this place?"

"I do," Knox said, careful to keep his weapon ready if any hostile moves were to happen.

"I will permit it. Wait until the water recedes and you may proceed," Atar said, then just like that he turned and disappeared into the back of the cave.

"What about my people, I wish to have several teams do the dungeon in the future," Knox called out into the darkness, but got no response. This was a problem, but one that he'd deal with on another day. Surely these people, the Ahtora, wouldn't be a problem later.

Knox hoped that he hadn't just made a new enemy, but there was no dealing with it right now, short of walking into the darkness to get another audience with them. So instead, he tied the rope back around his waist and jumped back into the freezing water.

They had a dungeon to do, and Knox found himself getting excited about it now. If someone like Atar could run the dungeon, then his team might have a chance to clear at least a few floors before it became too dangerous.

CHAPTER 17
DUNGEON RUN

KNOX USED Ethereal Step to get out of the water, unfortunately though, the spell didn't have the ability to remove the water covering him and he shivered in the cold afternoon air. Moving over to the fire he sat down and began to strip. He needed to get out of the wet clothes and into something dry fast.

He was hyper aware of the audience around him, but his chattering teeth prevented him from saying much more than the fact that he needed his 'dry' clothes. Terrim got them for him and stood guard while Knox changed, blocking most of him from view. When he was in dry clothes and sitting in front of the fire, he finally spoke. He told them all about the fish people he encountered and the battle that followed.

"And then he said that we could use the dungeon, but only after the water recedes, which means the water must go down eventually," Knox said, using an extra shirt to dry his hair off some more.

"You sure you didn't hit your head down there?" Murdoch asked, smiling. "You weren't down there for very long."

"Just get ready to run the dungeon, I don't know how much time we have, but I did notice the water has gone down since I took a dip. Shouldn't be long now," Knox said.

Because they had time to waste, they ended up playing some dice games after everyone had gotten dressed in their armored best. Brandon and his group armored up as well, Knox told them to keep guard up here in case someone was to come along. They had instructions to flee if any pirates came by, but otherwise hold the ground as best they could.

The water receded enough after an hour or maybe two, time passed so quickly while playing dice. The group walked down the side of the cliff, there was a path that allowed for decent access as long as you were careful, which they all were—except for Terrim. He fell, nearly taking poor Henry with him. But as much of a sturdy brute Terrim is, he was fine and just got to the bottom a bit faster than the rest of the party.

"I'm worried about the potential need to swim," Henry said when they reached the bottom.

He'd been given a coin to breathe the same as everyone else, but Knox hadn't considered his age and how well he could or couldn't swim.

"You can't swim?" Knox asked.

"I never learned," Henry said.

"Me neither," Terrim said, shrugging. "The coins will keep us breathing, so as long as the water isn't too deep, we'll be fine."

"I hope so," Henry said, looking around nervously.

Their bodies were enhanced under the system and the levels that had been gained, so Knox wasn't terribly worried about Henry not making it through the dungeon. He was likely as sturdy as, or more so, than Knox was before he became a Titan.

Knox regarded his group as they made their way to the dungeon pillar. "Just put your hand on it and wait," he instructed, seeing their confused looks.

They did so and a few moments later they were inside the dungeon, a barren cave with another obelisk that could be used to return behind them.

"We set up a camp here and we try at different parts of the dungeon," Knox said by way of informing them.

They all nodded, each of them in various stages of awe as they looked around the barren dungeon room. It wasn't such a shock to Knox, seeing as it looked the same as any other dungeon he'd been in, but something was new.

The words above each of the dungeon doors made sense to him now, being the Runic Language he was learning from the Titans!

Well, perhaps making sense was a strong turn of phrase. It was something he could understand, somewhat. For instance, he knew it spoke of danger, water men, and a reward for defeating a champion. His grasp on the language of the Titans was still tenuous at best, and without reference he was hard-pressed to just know exactly what it was trying to say.

For example, there was some kind of modifier that was attached to the 'water men' that meant something, but what that was Knox didn't know. Maybe it meant dangerous, but it could just as easily mean friendly. There was a small notation on the bottom that raised his spirits, it seemed to be a system message denoting the strength or level range of the path forward, this much Knox could make out.

It was saying, roughly, that those that they will face are at the fifteenth level of advancement. Now, whether that means all of them or just the champion, or perhaps that those challenging should be that level, again, Knox wasn't so sure.

"You can read that?" Henry asked, sauntering over to stand beside Knox.

"More or less," Knox said, sharing with Henry what he thought it said, Henry just nodded along.

"So, we are well-suited for this path, being all of us over level 20?" Henry asked and it was Knox's turn to nod along.

"You hit level 20?" Knox asked, surprised by the speeding growth of Henry and really all those under his care. Daily monster slaying and collecting of Monster Cores really went a long way in power leveling a group of people.

"I did," Henry said, smiling. "And in doing so, I gained talent access to my Celestial Champion. I'm eager to meet the fellow and see what he can do."

"Can I ask you a question?" Knox asked, something occurring to him that ought to have been more in the forefront of his mind than it was.

"Anything, lad," Henry said, reaching out and touching the runes above the doorway. Nothing happened, so Knox held back from telling him to stop.

"Everyone, well most everyone, seems to be okay just changing their lives and becoming Adventurers. It should have occurred to me sooner, but most of you, well sort of all of you, always scoffed at the idea of adventures, so what changed?" Knox asked.

Henry didn't answer at first, considering the question with the sage wiseness of someone who'd lived a long while.

"In a way, we had little choice but to accept it," Henry said, but held up a hand to stop Knox from responding. "But it was more than that. We've all spoken behind your back, marveling at the power you've displayed in our defense. The idea that maybe we could wield such power as well, despite our age or inabilities, went a long way to convince most people."

"But at the end of the day, it felt right to us. We've always lived the harder side of life, so far out from anything resembling civilization. We followed you for the sake of safety, never expecting we'd eventually get access to the very power that could do such marvelous things, but here we are. I guess what I'm trying to say, lad, is we all have a part of us that wants power and the ability to effect change. You've given that to us. Hell, we don't even think of ourselves as Adventurers, just normal folk who have the power to make change."

Knox nodded along as Henry spoke, wondering if he had his hand on the root of the matter or if everyone just had their own reasons. He decided it must be somewhere between the two, as nothing was ever so cut and dry. He was grateful, regardless of the reasons, that so many decided to stay and follow him. Taking up power and fighting for the betterment of everyone's lives, it was all part of a glorious vision that Knox was beginning to imagine for Luminar.

The only issue being a horde of pirates that outnumbered them and somehow had gained access to the system through voice commands. That was another matter that needed more consideration, how had they stumbled upon the keywords needed to access the system? Was it by chance or perhaps one of his three more lively golems weren't as under his control as he thought? No, it wasn't worth worrying about right now, if they were meaning to betray him and they had the means to do it, they could do far worse.

Plus, Mic had assured them that such actions would be impossible due to the constructions of the golems themselves. But of course, he had only Mic's word on that, as the golems were fairly advanced runecraft and Knox was only beginning to crack that nut of knowledge. So much to do and so little time to do it, yet he found himself off on a dungeon adventure. Swallowing hard, Knox walked back to the small camp to inform the team it was time to set out.

"As far as I can tell, we will face some sort of water men inside," Knox said, pointing at the runes as he spoke. "Whether that means it'll be like the tribe I encountered above, the Ahtora, or something else entirely, I do not know."

Knox took stock of his team before they went any further. Terrim was outfitted in heavy armor, a shield, and a new axe that was a step away from the traditional woodcutter's axe. It had two bladed sides, both around the same size as his normal axe—which is to say, twice as big as Knox's normal-sized axe. Under Knox's sense, it blazed with runes that would assist in cutting, piercing, and slashing away at victims.

Beth wore mostly leather armor, some plates added here and there in an overlapping manner that one of the maintenance drones had suggested, calling it the style laminar armor. Each of those little overlapping scales had individual enchantments to keeping them strong and protective. Her bow was new as well, but it looked like nothing fancy, until you looked with a magical sense, then it shone like the noonday sun, each and every space taken up by reinforcement and damage dealing runes.

Meanwhile, Murdoch wore a simple steel breastplate, and leather under armor. It was a soft and supple leather that allowed full range of motion and wouldn't do well for stopping any attacks, or at least it appeared that way. With the softness of the leather, Knox had been able to put many runes into it, turning it as hard as iron, but not quite up to the strength of his steel breast-plate. His blade was the same old one he'd always used, but reforged with runes, almost all focused on speed enhancement, per Murdoch's own request.

That left old Henry, wearing a simple outfit with some hard-ened leather covering his chest and vital organs, including his head. They'd all been enchanted as well, but Henry had to be careful that the armor didn't reduce his range of motion, since much of his spell casting required grand flourishes of his arms. Or at least they did when Henry did them, Knox knew for certain that curt small gestures worked well enough as well, but to each their own.

Knox's own style of casting was doing the bare minimum to get the spell to work, then load it with as much mana as possible. That resulted in a more bang for your buck kind of casting, but that wasn't to say there wasn't a place for the way Henry was doing it. He could get more subtle increases in how the spells worked, healing more delicately and effectively. Or sending out bursts of power and hitting only that small area you wished to hit, instead of how Knox did it, smashing everything out of his way.

That led Knox to his own armor choices. He'd fashioned his armor after his original suit and some that he'd found in the armory. It had much by the way of decorated leather and cloth, all filled to the brim with runic formations. And of course, he had a breastplate made of the finest steel, the inside inscribed with enough power to make it as hard as anything he'd worn before. He also cast Mystic Armor over it all, the translucent blue armor overlapping perfectly with his current armor.

Mic had given them all a quest to explore the dungeon, and Knox assumed it would update as he'd seen them do before as they made progress within it. But for now, it promised a reward of 5,000 essence to defeat the first path of the dungeon. So many quests were coming and going that Knox barely had time to really focus on them. Instead, he just accepted that they were a method of driving civilization forward as a whole, at least in Luminar.

"Follow me through, Terrim here in front, and be ready for anything," Knox said, stepping over the threshold and into the long hallway that would lead them to the first room of the dungeon.

Each of them took places two by two, with Henry taking a lone spot at the end, ready to heal any that were injured. During idle chit-chat, Knox had told them all about his own dungeon experience, hoping that it would help them relax, but he could see now it hadn't worked. Each and every one of them were stiff and anxious, the mystery of what lay ahead being too much for them.

Knox decided to focus on himself, sweeping out his sense down the corridor. According to what he'd learned, they wouldn't have to worry about traps in the first corridor, but they'd brought several folding metal rods to check for traps later in the dungeon. It had been Knox's idea, as carrying around ten-to-twenty-foot wooden sticks wasn't practical; however, Mic knew plenty of ways to work with steel and they'd come up with a metal rod that would work in place of the sticks, likely lasting much longer as well. This was their first use of them though, so who knew if they'd be effective or not.

They reached a massive room, half filled with water that snaked throughout it. A cavernous ceiling was covered in glowing moss that sent long shadows throughout the area and the air itself was rich with essence. Back in his days before the system, Knox would have loved sucking up all the stray essence, but now he had to wait for his body to naturally suck it in when defeating monsters, or in this case, Ahtora.

At least a dozen Ahtora were visible here and there in the massive chamber. They were separated into groups of two all the way up to a single group of five toward the back of the room. Knox knew by experience that they'd likely be able to pull small groups and slowly clear the dungeon room. Why the dungeon had chosen the water folk to be its monsters was anyone's guess, but it made him wonder if the Ahtora above were okay with their likeness being used or having to kill their own for essence.

Pointing at a group of two about thirty paces away, Knox said, "Let's start by taking them out and we will move our way through the room, one group at a time."

Terrim nodded and stepped forward, shield leading.

The pair of Ahtora saw only when he was about ten paces from their face, clearly a dungeon specific eyesight issue they must have, but Knox wasn't complaining. It would allow them to clear this room without being overwhelmed.

Of the two translucent-skinned figures, one had armor on—it was made of shells overlapping and he had a sort of rigid sword that could have been part of a fish at some point—while the other one was naked, save for some seaweed dangling around its midsection. A bolt of ice smashed into Terrim's shield before he could close the gap on the pair, it had come from the less dressed of the two. The armored one stepped forward and swung with his sword and the fight was on.

Knox acted first, using his curt hand movements, and uttering the runic words to his most used spell, Luminous Surge. It blasted the weaker caster on its ass, just as Terrim threw back the armored fish man and struck him with his axe. An arrow appeared in the Ahtora's unarmored neck, followed closely by a slash down its face by a flanking Murdoch.

The fight was over before it had a chance to start, Knox's axe ending the caster before they could make it to their feet. It was clear this floor was going to be a pretty easy clear, but as with the dungeons he'd faced before, he knew it would get harder.

"It amazes me the strength we have now," Henry said, rolling his neck in a way Terrim did, the cracks Knox heard making him a little concerned, but the old man seemed alright.

Knox thought back to his first dungeon run and the strength of the giant rats, his body just in the early ranks he'd been had all but changed, giving him superior strength over a normal person. Now he had an entire village of people stronger than most, his village alone would be enough to fill up half or more of the dungeon town around the Mire's Gloom Dungeon.

Knox wondered suddenly, and wished he'd asked Dernal about it, but how common exactly were Adventurers outside of the edge of civilization? Was it so great a number that the change to the Titan System would unhinge the world or was it only out here in the edge of the kingdom that such a disparity was shown? *Surely it wasn't so common,* thought Knox. His spread of the System was sure to turn heads.

Moving as carefully as they could, they took care of each group in turn, the casters being the worst of the bunch, but as long as Knox hit them fast, they had little chance to do much more than dent Terrim's shield. On one occasion, an ice bolt had gotten past him and hit poor old Henry right in the chest, but it hadn't done more than taken the wind out of him. It was good to see he was sturdier than he appeared, because he didn't appear to be sturdy at all. Even his skin looked like it might crack open at a moment's notice. Yet, with all that being said, he remained strong and in a single piece.

They reached the final pull, a group of five Ahtora, one of which wore a headdress of shells and had a spear with a sharp stone affixed to it. They hadn't faced this variety yet, but Knox wasn't worried.

"I'll hit them with my chains first then focus on getting the casters down next," Knox said, nods from each of the teammates told him that they were ready, and the attack began.

Throwing out his Lustrous Chains spell, Knox positioned himself to Terrim's right and used Arcane Pulse. It had more of a wide range and chance to disrupt enemy abilities mid-cast. As it happened, Knox was too slow this time and three lances of ice came shooting for the group a moment before his cast slammed into them, throwing one of them to the ground, but only taking the other two back a step.

Working fast, using quick and curt hand movements loaded with power, Knox got a Prism Ward cast off just as the attacks landed, blunting their blow on Terrim. His shield was really taking a beating and Knox might have to take a look at it after this pull. Each dent it sustained meant a chance at disrupting the runes inscribed on the back.

An arrow caught the fallen caster, ending it while a swift cut from a flanking Murdoch opened the throat of another. Terrim struggled to hold off the spear-wielding man and the club-holding warrior, but Knox knew he needed to take care of the caster first. Just as he squared up against it, the caster finished a spell that covered the spear-wielder in an armor of ice, making him look much more intimidating.

Using Ethereal Step, Knox stepped through the void and appeared beside the caster, axe raised. He felt another spell charging up in the caster, but his blow fell first, and the backlash of the spell sent him whirling backward and into the water. Using his sense, he confirmed he was dead, before turning back on the two warriors. They were a match for Terrim, beating him back step by step as he tried to get a swing of his own in here and there.

An arrow smashed against the ice armored one, but it glanced off harmlessly. Just when Knox was about to yell for Beth to focus on the other one, Murdoch took him across the face, forcing him back a step. When he stepped, a flash of light and a moment later, he was covered in vines, wrapping him up thoroughly. Before Knox could work out what spell or ability had done that, Knox watched as Beth let loose arrow after arrow in a display of speed that could be nothing other than her Rapid Fire ability.

The warrior succumbed to his injuries, leaving only a lone fighter covered in ice armor that moved like leather over him instead of the rigid frost that it was.

"Time to end this," Knox said, beginning a cast of Luminous Surge that would encompass everyone and attack his opponent.

"To death!" Terrim cried, throwing his shield down and taking his axe in two hands. The giant of a man loomed over the spear-wielding warrior and swung with all his might. The spear took him under the arm, but it wasn't enough to stop the ice crushing blow.

The fighter fell just as Knox's spell washed over the group, the final hit being enough to end as he fell to the ground. They'd done it! They'd cleared the first room.

"Good job," Knox said, panting from the exertion of the fight.

"Let me pass," Henry said, pushing Knox aside to get to Terrim.

"I'm fine," Terrim complained, but Henry fussed over him anyway. "It barely got me."

"You are bleeding pretty bad, let me heal you," Henry said, his words turned soft, and his hands did grand gestures that Knox recognized as being way over the top, but they worked, closing the wound and healing Terrim.

"Let's check for Monster Cores, these were much stronger than the rats I faced in the Mire's Gloom Dungeon," Knox said.

Sure enough, they found a few intact Cores on the stronger of the Ahtora, but most were empty.

One room down, a few more to go.

CHAPTER 18
AHTORA KING

THE NEXT ROOM was just what Knox expected, a more advanced version of the one they'd just faced. Groups of three to six, each one with a spear-wielding Ahtora and anywhere from two casters to a group with all warriors. It was much as the Dire Gloom Dungeon had been, where the room was a village of sorts, but it wouldn't be so easy, as the ratkin had been.

"See the watch towers over the water," Knox said, pointing at the three distinct towers breaking the surface. "See how each of them go right down into the water. I can sense another watch and several more Ahtora down below. Let me think about the best way to deal with this."

If Knox's hunch was right, they'd need to take out both the underwater lookouts and the above the surface one at the same time, or risk tipping off one or the other. So, who would be best suited to one-on-one a warrior under the water? Knox knew that he would have to be the one to do it, perhaps Beth could take care of the one standing out in the open with a well-placed arrow, but Murdoch should be close to end him just in case the arrow failed.

With a plan ready, Knox shared it with his teammates, and they nodded in turn.

"Wait for a twenty count once I go below the water, then act. We will start with the easternmost one, then make our way west. Do not attack a new tower until you see my head break the surface and give you a sign," Knox said.

"What kind of sign?" Beth asked.

"I'll just wave," Knox said, shrugging. "Let's do this!"

Knox moved as silently as he could toward the water's edge, it snaked through the room just as it had the previous one, except that this room had patrols within the water whilst the last one hadn't.

Reaching the edge, Knox slipped in, looking around as he did for any reaction from the surrounding patrols. No one noticed him and his sense confirmed it. If he approached from the side, the watcher below the water seemed to have his attention fixed to the south, then Knox should be able to catch him off guard.

Turning to his team he judged the distance good enough and waved before sinking below the surface. All he had to do was stop trying to swim and his heavy armor took him down swiftly. He was strong enough to swim with it on, stiff as it was under the cold water. Knox was glad for one thing, the water wasn't salty, so his eyes didn't have the same burning sensation that they'd had when diving into the cave.

Knox made it, counting all the while in his head, to the edge of the underwater tower. His axe was ready and as of yet, the guard hadn't noticed him. Just as the count ended, Knox lurched forward but the Guard moved faster than Knox thought possible underwater, spearing out and striking him on the cheek, drawing blood.

Surprised, but confident that he was the stronger of the two, Knox pushed the coin around in his mouth, before striking out with his axe. The blow took the surprised warrior in the neck, ending him. His neck wound let out an immense amount of blood and suddenly Knox saw a flaw to his plan, this blood would be noticed.

Sure enough, a close patrol narrowed in on him halfway back to the surface and were swimming with insane speed, targeting Knox. Raising his hands Knox tried to cast, but without the verbal component he couldn't quite get the spell to go off. Instead, he focused on one that didn't require a verbal component, Ethereal Step, his body appeared on the surface, red blood all around him from the fallen fish man.

Knox didn't wave, instead going right back into the water to face his attackers but kept his head just above the water to cast his spells. A flash of light struck the incoming warriors with enough force to splash water noisily. Luckily, Beth and Murdoch had taken care of the other tower guard, meaning no more came to join the fight.

Focusing on the closest of the fighters, Knox cast Arcane Pulse, followed by a slash across the other's chest. Within seconds the two had fallen, leaving him surrounded by more red blood but alive. He was just far stronger than them, to the point that for even two of them, in their own element, stood little chance against him.

Knox swam closer to the next tower and signaled the group with a wave. Beth waved back and Knox submerged. It was all the same this time, the guard being less surprised than Knox cared for, but in the end, he died, and his blood didn't attract a patrol this time. However, on the final one, Knox attracted a group of five and he decided to Ethereal Step to the surface to get aid from his party during the fight. No one, no matter how strong, was invincible, and five to one in the water wasn't odds Knox liked.

However, it appeared his team was already mid fight. A group of three slammed their ice and weapons against Terrim, as Murdoch tried to weave his way to the front, his blade flashing. Beth was kneeling over Henry, who'd fallen on his ass, bleeding from his neck.

Knox grimaced and ran for Henry, the spell already on his lips as he reached him. Stuffing it full of power, he cast Luminous

Surge and Henry's neck stopped bleeding, but a raw, red line where he'd been stuck was left afterward. But it was enough to bring him back to consciousness.

"Oh my, that hurt," Henry said, then seeing the group coming behind Knox and the three they were already fighting, a steel settled over him. "I've got this." He stood and began to chant loudly, waving his arms about.

Knox couldn't spare him anymore attention; turning, he cast Void Grasp on the location just in front of the five coming for them. Shadowy tendrils reached out of the ground and began to entangle them. Because Knox needed the time, he also cast Lustrous Chains, the two spells working together to all but stop their forward momentum for a moment.

However, the casters, all three of them, could still cast their spells. Bolts of ice came hurdling for the group and more importantly, right for Terrim's unguarded flank. Putting himself between the attacks, Knox closed his eyes and leaned heavily on his sense. One at a time, he swung his axe, knocking each ice lance from the sky in a shatter of ice and cold.

Opening his eyes, he jumped into the battle between the two fighters and the one caster. His axe took the caster's arm off with one mighty blow, then a swift kick to his chest brought him to the ground to bleed out while he dealt with the closest warrior.

A spear of ice came for Knox's face, but he easily dodged it, letting it strike the warrior on the other side. It cried out and Knox just smiled, slamming his axe down with the power of a Titan, shattering shell armor and drawing blood. The warrior crumbled under the attack at the same moment that Terrim finally got a decent hit in, taking the last of the three down.

Turning to face the final threat just as Void Grasp and Lustrous Chains dissipated, the group formed up behind Terrim. Knox was in no mood to wait out the enemy's charge, so he cast Ethereal Step, dashing forward and leaving a trail of light that boosted the speed of all allies that followed it. And follow it they did, all but Beth and Henry, who preferred to fight from a distance.

Terrim, seeing Knox rush forward, used an ability of his own to Charge forward as well, bowling over the lead spear-wielding fish man. Then, with his axe glowing with power, he struck downward, getting the first kill of the new group. Then just as another warrior faced him, he slammed his shield forward, bashing it in the face. Just as Knox was finally finishing his first Arcane Pulse to interrupt the casters, Terrim leapt into the air and slammed right in the center of the casters, throwing them all backward and interrupting their spells.

Knox let his jaw hang open just a bit as arrows and thin blades finished off the stunned figures. It was during the final moments of the fight that Knox noticed a golden-armored figure appearing with a massive sword and had pale, almost snow white, skin. It glanced over to Knox and nodded its head before disappearing in a flutter of golden light as the final fighter was taken down.

"Who the hell was that?" Knox asked, the figure had been nearly as tall as Terrim and much more muscled, wearing fantastic armor that glowed with thousands of tiny runes.

Henry limped up to the front of the group and smiled wide. "That was my Celestial Champion," Henry said, then frowning added, "But I can only summon him once a day, perhaps I should have saved it for later."

"Yeah, I had it without its help," Terrim said, a smile of his own forming on his lips. "You see that Knox?"

"I did," Knox said, returning the friendly smile. "You really showed off what the Warrior Path can do. Why don't you do that more often?"

Terrim shrugged, "So far, you've all had it fine, no need for me to do much other than pull their attention. But I wanted to cut loose a bit."

"Fair enough, it helped, good job," Knox said, reassuring his friend. He was sure his friend had even more up his sleeve and this dungeon was the perfect place to get a feel for it and the extent of his party's abilities. Although, if Knox was being honest with himself, the Celestial Guardian was a bit too much for what they faced. Henry ought to have saved it for the boss, which might be the next room, though he was unsure since all dungeons and dungeon paths differ to a certain extent.

The rest of the room was easy in comparison, they took their time and killed every single Ahtora they could find, a healer-type mob being the only big surprise they came across.

"There is a good chance that this next room will be the boss room for the first path. Be ready for anything, but if the theme continues, it'll be an Ahtora of some kind. Perhaps a champion of theirs with all the abilities they've shown so far. Since we don't know what we are getting ourselves into, I'm going to split the party just in case it's needed," Knox said, thinking back to how the dungeon boss fights had gone before, he was sure it would be necessary.

"Terrim, Henry, and I will take on the boss, while Beth and Murdoch focus on any additional Ahtora that show up during the fight. If it appears none are coming, then we can adjust and focus up on the boss. Remember, the boss will have deadly moves and abilities, we have to be careful to avoid them and recognize when we can block attacks and when they need to be dodged. I wish I could say this will be easy since we are so much stronger than them, but boss fights aren't ever easy, so be careful."

They were cautious in using their long metal poles on the ground but the passageway from the second room to the third remained as the others had: trapless. Knox was starting to think that perhaps the first path of the dungeon wasn't ever going to have traps, which made sense that it was that way. More of an introduction to the rest of the dungeons than anything else.

They reached the end of the corridor and a runed door opened to a massive pool of water with only a foot or two ridge around the edge. It was clear this fight would be water bound and Knox looked over his shoulder to his party. They seemed to understand as well, pulling out their coins.

"Arrows won't be very effective underwater," Beth said, shaking her head.

"Spells can't be cast if words can't be spoken," Henry added.

"That is why I'm going in alone," Knox said, cracking his neck to the side. "I'll draw it to the surface, whatever it is, and we will fight it from the edge. Have the coins ready just in case you fall, but we won't be accepting such an overwhelming disadvantage."

As if the dungeon was responding to Knox's words, it rumbled and several platforms appeared in the water, each one big enough to fit five people and close enough that you could jump from one to another with system enhanced legs.

"That's mildly better," Knox said, considering the new terrain. "The plan remains, find a platform, be ready to change and move as needed, but I'll go get the boss and bring it to the surface."

The water's edge began to tremble and suddenly tentacles began to rise from beneath the surface. A massive creature of the depths appeared and atop it rode an Ahtora with a crown of shells and gold.

"You have trespassed the domain of the Sea King," he said, his voice booming with magical enhancements. "Face me and die."

"To death?" Knox said, looking around at the faces of his teammates. Terrim took up the call, but the rest looked wary of what awaited them.

"To death," Terrim called, hopping to one of the platforms, shield raised and ready for combat. Knox followed him, moving closer to the massive sea creature that awaited them.

Beth stayed on the edge and shot off an experimental shot, stabbing a tentacle that began reaching toward Terrim. The creature screeched and blackness covered the water all around it.

Whatever it was doing, the water was no longer crystal clear, and Knox didn't know what else would await them in those murky depths.

"New plan," Knox said, shouting loud enough to be heard by all his teammates. "I'm going for the King; you guys deal with the tentacles. Beth, try and keep me in a single piece if you can."

She had the best reach with her bow and sense or no sense, there were a lot of tentacles sloshing about in the water. Knox would do well to keep clear of them and face the King in single combat. Strong as he might be, Knox was sure that the beast below him was the main challenge.

Running forward, Knox cut at a tentacle, dodged another, and slipped below a final one before reaching the massive body. Its skin was lumpy and rough, but he had to do what he had to do. Grabbing hold of some flesh he reached up and began to climb. It was easier than he'd imagined, but he was hard-pressed to fight back the tentacles as he climbed. Luckily, Beth had his back. Just as one came dangerously close to striking him free, she caught it with an arrow that seemed to burst into flames as it made contact.

Good save, Knox thought, as he made it to the head of the beast and faced off against the so-called King of the Ahtora.

"Ready to die?" Knox shouted, getting the fish man's attention. He wore armor as translucent as his own skin, but it was full plate and covered even his head. He wielded a massive lance made of the same material and atop his armored head was a crown of shells. Despite all that, it was his height that caught Knox most off guard, he was easily two or three feet taller than Terrim, and Terrim was at least that much taller than Knox.

Knox almost wanted to call Terrim up here just to give him a chance to feel what it was like being him, but there was no time for that silliness. Laughing in glee and with a large dose of apprehension-filled excitement, Knox slashed at a tentacle that tried to slap him free. Blood sprayed all around them as the tentacle left, and the king advanced.

Raising his hands, Knox let off a solid Luminous Surge

right into the king's chest. Though the attack clearly hit, the king kept his footing and his armor shimmered as if nothing much had happened. Thinking fast, Knox threw out a Lustrous Chain attack to bind him down, but once more, his armor shimmered and the chains never took full hold, breaking to dust instead.

"You're immune to magic or highly resistant to it," Knox said, realizing that the king's armor must be the culprit. He had his axe though, and his magic still worked, just not his offensive spells.

"Doesn't matter, you're still dead," Knox said, just as the king closed the distance, spearing out with his massive lance.

Focusing on his sense, Knox dodged but the speed of the attack changed mid lance, and something hit his arm—only a glancing blow, but the Mystic Armor around him flickered and faded to nothing.

"Oh," Knox said, slashing out with his axe and hitting the weapon full on, "you can negate my defensive magic as well, eh?"

"You are no match for the King of the Ahtora," the king said, his eyes locking with Knox's.

"You underestimate me," Knox replied, though he knew talking was pointless. However, it did buy him precious moments to think. "I will crush you beneath my boot."

The king laughed and was about to respond when Knox used Ethereal Step to appear to his side and bring the axe down on his neck. The blow hit armor, but the king grunted and went down from the force of it. Knox didn't let up, kicking hard, and slamming his foot down on the king's arm. His weapon fell free and a pulse of power that Knox recognized shot out in all direction, pushing him back.

"You just blasted me with my own power?" Knox said, surprise evident on his face. "No more free power for you."

Knox rushed forward, wishing he had a shield as the lance came for his head. His sense told him where to go to avoid it, but once more the attack surged mid strike and nearly hit him anyway. Rolling harder to the side than he meant to, he lost his footing and cursed. Then, casting Solar Wings, he caught himself mid fall and landed back on his feet.

Before the king could figure out a way to suck in that magic as well, Knox canceled the effect and activated Aeon Gaze. He saw it then, the great weakness of the armor as if someone planted the seed of an idea in his mind. Yes, it could suck in magic, but it had a limit, which is why it was able to expel that power. But if it got too much too fast, then bye-bye armor.

Trusting that his ability wouldn't lead him astray, Knox adjusted his plans. The first Arcane Pulse hit the king with little effect, but Knox continued the onslaught, much to the king's enjoyment, laughing the entire time, letting the attacks come.

Just as the armor reached capacity, Knox's sense could feel it now that he'd been made aware of it. The King pointed his lance and power, raw and intense, shot out at Knox. Barely dodging it with Ethereal Step, Knox teleported out of the path of the massive attack.

"Damn," Knox cursed, seeing that over half the armor's stored energy had been shot off. He needed to move faster, and with more power.

He resisted the urge to take off a suppression band, as the side effects were just too much for a fight that wasn't of deadly importance. Knox knew he could beat this foe without the help of his untapped potential power, he just needed to focus and do it.

Luminous Surge followed by a powerful fireball from Radiant Glyph, and the armor was filling once more.

"Keep feeding my armor," shouted the King as he leveled his lance for another attack.

Knox shook his head and stepped close enough to smash his axe head into the lance, causing its beam of power to smash into the creature below, dealing a bloody gash across its head.

It began to writhe and shake, both the King and Knox losing their footing atop it. Knox wasn't done yet, casting spell after spell, loading it with as much power as he could, but he needed more, just a little more. From down below came a pulse of arcane energy striking the King with a powerful, yet measured attack.

Knox turned in time to see Henry standing with his arms flailing and another Arcane Pulse being unleashed by him. Somehow, he knew that Knox needed help and he was forgoing his healing focus to use some of his core Arcane abilities.

Knox turned to see the King preparing another attack just as he unleashed his own Arcane Pulse. It released, an entirely different animal than the precise and powerful attack that Henry released. Instead, it pulsed with overwhelming raw power that was Knox's trademark type of magic.

His attack hit the weapon just as it filled with magical energy and suddenly the king's weapon had too much magic. It began to crack, and a hideous screech filled the air as it exploded. Knox was thrown from atop the sea beast, shards of the weapon piercing him in several places. Pain became his reality as he fell, and he knew that he'd made some kind of mistake. He wasn't meant to be falling, no, he was meant to be defeating something.

Water, cold and harsh, consumed him and he was in a pool of blackness, sinking ever deeper. His mind struggled to latch onto any thoughts, but suddenly another sense, one not bothered by something like a blow to the head, washed around him and he knew where he was—sinking below the surface and soon to be dead if he didn't do something.

With a sudden burst of light, not his own, he felt his thoughts begin to clear. His sense told him that one of Henry's Celestial balls of light had healed him, so he did the next thing that was required of him. Focus. He placed a coin in his mouth and spit out any water. Suddenly the pain in his chest subsided and he was able to breathe once more.

He had to swim, ignore the pain, *swim*. But which way was up? He felt out with his sense and caught hold of a familiar bunch of people and decided they must be up. So, turning himself around he swam, pain and blood all around, he swam with all he had.

His head broke the surface just as his strength began to wane. Strong hands pulled him ashore and friendly voices spoke all around him. Sensing that he was safe, Knox let himself rest, spitting the coin out and taking a breath of refreshing essence-filled air.

CHAPTER 19
LOOT

Knox kept himself from passing out or letting himself drift off to sleep, and he overheard Henry as he lay there with his eyes closed.

"That boy takes too many risks! What if we weren't able to get him out in time? Foolish!" Henry said, and no one else said anything at first, until finally Terrim spoke up.

"That *fool* just kicked the boss's ass and saved our bacon. I'd suggest you not talk about him like he's some irrational child."

"Yeah," Knox said, groaning as he sat up. "What he said."

Opening his eyes Knox saw Henry go red and he just smiled, nodding his head.

"I didn't mean to suggest," Henry started to say but Knox held up a hand to forestall him.

"You meant what you said and that's fine. We are all able to have our own opinions here, we are a group not a solo party. And to speak to what you said, you are probably right. I was reckless and stupid, but I didn't see any other way. If you do, give me options and I'll gladly take them," Knox said.

"I understand," Henry said, his eyes downcast.

"Now I've got an important question," Knox said, standing

and rubbing his hands together as his eyes panned across the room.

"What's that?" Murdoch asked, following Knox's gaze, and then sighing. "Ah, that."

"Who's ready for Loot?" Knox declared happily.

A single chest had appeared in the middle of the room, the giant monster and the King's corpse all gone, which was a shame as they hadn't collected any Cores from them. It shone from the light that filled the ceiling, even giving off some of its own light. The chest was gold and Knox was ecstatic to find what was inside.

Knox hoped that it was not something so simple as a warming rock, though the runic formations from that rock had been useful. Knox had added temperature auto adjustments to most armor's he helped craft, adding a level of comfort that you wouldn't normally have in such hot and bulky armor.

But no, a gold chest would have something fabulous, Knox was sure. It was just a matter of getting over there and finding out. Leaping from one platform to the next, each member of the group slowly made their way over. Henry was spry for an old guy and wasn't even the last one to arrive.

"After you," Beth said, gesturing to the chest.

"So, whatever this item is, it should go to the person who most needs it," Knox said, getting ready to explain dungeon points and how Dernal had done it, but Murdoch interrupted him.

"Of course! Now pop that chest and let me see what item I am getting!" Murdoch said, his hands rubbing together in antici-pation of whatever they'd find inside.

"Har har," Knox said, reaching down and pulling the lid open on the dungeon chest.

Reaching in, Knox grabbed hold of something and pulled it out. As it was with chests, the item was big enough that it ought not to have fit inside, but it worked regardless. Smiling at the translucent item, Knox handed it over to Terrim to inspect.

"How does your new shield feel?" Knox asked after giving

Terrim a moment to heft it and do a few practice bashes into nonexistent enemy faces.

"It's oddly, *light*. You think it is going to be sturdy enough?" Terrim said, his shield so translucent that he could look straight through it if he wanted.

There was all the chance in the world that this shield had special magical absorbing properties just like the King's armor and lance had. Knox studied the item with his sense and decided that the runes were ingenious and warranted further study. They were all placed around the edges, visible only by his sense and so tiny that he really had to focus on the formations to work out what they said.

It was a bunch of runes meant to make sturdy and reinforce the item. Only a string or two had anything to do with gathering power and releasing it, which meant the process of capturing magic wasn't as complex as Knox first anticipated. He might be able to craft armor that did the same if given enough time. However, several of the runes seemed designed to flush power into the metal itself. Though, it didn't call it metal but referred to it as a type of glass.

Material types were important to declare when setting up runic formations, as each had different tolerances that had to be respected. For example, making steel too much harder could make it brittle, but making cloth harder on impact or soft leather, was an easier process.

"I think that shield is made of glass," Knox said, reaching out and taking it from Terrim, who happily offered it up for inspection.

Feeling the outer edge, Knox grimaced as he cut his finger on a sharp edge. It was definitely glass, but glass as hard as steel, if not a bit stronger based on the runic formations ingeniously added to it. If he was understanding it correctly, damage beyond the strength of the material would cause the very edges to chip off, instead of outright cracking. While a genius idea, it also meant that eventually the runes would fail as they were located about an inch or two off the edge of the shield.

"This shield is meant to absorb magical energy and release it on thought from its bearer," Knox said. "It is as hard, if not a bit harder, than the strongest steel we have access to, but it isn't invincible. We will have to watch the edge and make sure the runes don't get disrupted."

Terrim took the shield back and shrugged. "Glass or not, if it can take a hit, I'm happy to have it."

"He has a shield already, maybe *I* need a shield?" Murdoch spoke the words as a question and Knox shot him down with a single look.

"It goes to who needs it most and you know damn well you can't properly use a shield," Knox said, then reaching down and picking up Terrim's old shield he hefted it to test the weight. "However, I might be able to use this to help off tank."

The shield weighed practically nothing with his maxed C Ranker attributes. He could imagine several instances where a shield would be handy, he'd had one for some time when first running dungeons and knew how to use one with his axe. This particular shield was covered in dents and one corner had even been bent down ever so slightly. It wouldn't last much longer after the dungeon, but perhaps he could put it to good use until then.

"Here's the plan," Knox said, throwing the shield over his shoulder and securing his axe in place. "We rest for the night and take on the second path tomorrow, however, I think after the second path we will call it. Based off the first boss we won't stand up against a full clear, but who knows what awaits us."

"As you command," Murdoch said, saluting Knox.

Knox laughed and did a feint punch for Murdoch's head, but the quick little shit, dodged and came back with his own feint. Knox flinched, despite knowing he could have dodged such a strike, Murdoch's speed notwithstanding. Knox's own speed and sense made him a terrible sparring partner.

"Hit me with a spell," Terrim said as they walked back toward camp.

Knox smiled and decided that perhaps it ought to be fun to test out his shield. After several attempts to make Terrim appear as his enemy in his mind, he finally got his attacks to treat him as such.

Casting Luminous Surge right at Terrim and picturing him as the King of the Ahtora, an enemy wanting to harm his friends, the spell smashed into him. It began to glow a gentle white light as it absorbed the magic and before Knox could say anything, the magic released back toward him. If not for a quick teleporting step to the side, it would have hit him too, the speed of the attack just as fast going out as it was going in.

The rest of the night was spent joking over the fire and listening to stories Knox told about his other dungeon adventures. How he'd had to deal with a grumpy Caleb, learned several cool techniques, and how Dernal had helped him through it all. For the hundredth time, Knox tried to pull in the essence around him, but found that his body couldn't or wouldn't do it as it used to.

However, as he focused on the essence around the dungeon, especially thinking back to the rooms in the path they'd taken that day, he noticed the essence had dropped dramatically after each fight. Whether an indication that the system operated similarly to how he'd been taught to draw in essence or perhaps the dungeon recycling it, he didn't know. But he'd gained a fair bit of essence from the run, and more importantly, so had his team.

Life was wonderful when looked at from the point of view of a day-to-day basis. Knox was an Adventurer, and not only that, but he was also adventuring with his own friends. What more could he ask for? Several darker thoughts came unbidden, but he pushed them down. Sure, there were responsibilities and worries to be had, but this night, he was happy.

The next morning, or at least what they guessed was morning time after everyone had sufficient sleep, came quickly. They brought the fire back to life and cooked some sausage made of monster meat that one of the villagers had been making mass quantities of, then cracked several eggs collected from the few chickens that had survived the trip thanks to Mr. Tome.

There was so much needed to keep a population fed and happy, food variety being one of them. But those were worries for those left in charge after Murdoch and Knox left. That of course being the council of elders, one of which was with them now, Henry. But the others, all four of them, were well-equipped to keep the place running in their absences.

Knox knew for a fact Murdoch was enjoying the time off, though he was doing better now, he'd struggled with the responsibility that came with the office of mayor. It didn't help that he doubted himself now that open elections were about to happen. But Knox knew of no one else better suited for the job. Murdoch had a big heart and cared for the people of Luminar.

Thinking about those that chose to come to Luminar made Knox suddenly consider those that did not and wonder if they had made it safely someplace. Perhaps they could send out some scouts to inquire after them, with the power of the system behind them it isn't like there are many that would be a threat to a small team of scouts. Knox decided that he would do that as soon as he got back. But who to send? Beth's name came to mind as someone who could lead the group, but it would be important to have a healer and perhaps a diplomat with them as well.

Then of course Knox would have to make sure they got out of Shadowfall Swamp safely himself, then he'd need to figure out a way to know when they needed escorting back in. Then it hit him, and he almost smacked himself in the head for being so dense. Dernal had taken a stone with him, one of the shadow stones that kept monsters away, but they still had half a dozen more from looting pirates. Satisfied he'd worked out the details for now, Knox focused back on the task that lay ahead of them.

"There is no telling what awaits us on this second path but know that it will be more difficult than the first," Knox said, then examining the runic language above the door he sighed.

"Actually, it looks like this area is a puzzle corridor where we will face traps as well. It is marked for level seventeen, so it should be within our capabilities. Let me take a look at the others real quick," Knox said, moving to the next.

In total there were six doors in this particular dungeon, and he looked at each runic script at the top and realized there was a pattern. Level 15, 17, 19, 21, 23, 25. Each one was two levels more difficult than the last, which meant that he was out leveled for this dungeon entirely. Regardless of what the runic language said, that level 15 boss had been a challenge for him, despite being twice its level.

Of course, he'd faced it alone instead of five on one, so that obviously would change the dynamics of the fight. Every other path was a trap and puzzle room, with the final one saying something about being a 'world challenge'. That might mean it was a themed adventure similar to the ones Knox had dealt with in the Mire's Gloom Dungeon.

Should we skip the trap and puzzle paths and try for the direct challenges instead, Knox wondered. He asked the party the very same thing and it was Henry that spoke up first.

"I'm a bit of a puzzle whiz myself, I'd love to give it a go."

"Very well, it could be our last path we try, but if you think you're up to it then I support you," Knox said, stepping into the first hallway and removing the long metal rod to check for traps.

It was a good thing too, because only ten paces ahead they set off a pit trap, then a fire trap just to the left of it. Luckily for the party, they were all one and done traps. Knox took Beth aside and pointed at a location of a trap that he could see thanks to his sense.

"Can you sense that trap?" Knox asked.

Beth squinted her eyes and held her hand out in front of her. "Barely, if you hadn't said anything I don't think I would have known it for what it was. But if that is what those traps feel like, then I can sense another just five feet ahead."

Knox stretched out his sense some more and sure enough, another fireball trap was set into the ceiling. Just below it was an empty space covered by a thin sheet of stone. With Knox focusing he saw that most of the traps were easy enough to discover. Focusing on the pitfall trap, he asked Beth to see what she could feel. Again, she said that she hadn't realized what it was, but had an idea now.

Next, Knox took her up to a fire trap to show her how to disarm it, assuming he could replicate the one or two times he'd done so with John's help. He triggered the first one within minutes of trying to disarm it, but the second one they successfully disarmed, mostly due to Beth taking over. She had nimble fingers and a light touch, both necessary when dealing with traps.

From there on, they continued to trigger the traps, figuring there would be more practice down the line. Making it to the first room, a square room with a pedestal in the middle, everyone found a place on the wall to relax while Knox and Henry looked over the puzzle.

It was a simple tile puzzle, there was a single space missing, and you had to move them around to complete a runic formation. Luckily for them, it wouldn't be guesswork like it had been with Leo, because Knox knew what rune it was trying to say, a simple 'Open' rune.

"It should look like this," Knox said, tracing out the rune in the air with his Radiant Glyph ability.

To Knox's surprise, the room seemed to shiver under the weight of his rune, almost as if he was straining to obey. However the door to the next room remained shut, but he wondered if he could force the matter if the puzzle failed.

Interesting, Knox thought, *very interesting.*

With his help, Henry worked out the puzzle within minutes and they were on to the next challenge. Traps, puzzles, all fell before them much faster than Knox would have guessed until they reached the final room. Henry worked out the puzzle in the last room as the room was filling with water rather quickly. If not for Henry and his affinity for puzzles, they'd likely have not made it through the rooms.

The chest, loot for a path complete, sat before them. It was a silver chest and Knox reached into it, pulling free a smallish item. Holding it in his hand it took him several moments of looking over the runic formations to work out what it was meant to be. When he did, he handed it over to Henry and explained what he thought it was.

The item itself was no more than a bobble on a thin chain, made of a blue metal that Knox could have sworn he'd encountered before, but he couldn't quite remember where, perhaps the armory. The blue iron bars! They hadn't had much luck using the blue iron in armor, but it had made some pretty fantastic weapons.

"This is a blue iron bobble," Knox said, placing the item in Henry's outstretched hand. "As best as I can tell, it is a focus of sorts. It'll allow you to cast your spells through it, magnifying their effectiveness and raw power."

"You should keep this," Henry said, shaking his head.

Knox shook his head. "It goes to who needs it the most. Besides, I've no problem unleashing powerful, raw spells. If instead it concentrated my spells and gave them better aim or finesse, then maybe I'd take it."

Henry relented, taking the blue iron bobble and holding it in his hand he began to cast a spell. The bobble, the chain wrapped around his hand, began to glow ever so slightly. The spell went off and Knox felt a warm wash of power go over him, as if he was being healed despite not needing any healing.

"It feels... easier," Henry said, struggling to put words to the experience.

"I don't know all of what those runes mean, but it should enable you to cast more, cast faster, and cast harder," Knox said, explaining a bit more of what it might be able to do.

"Fantastic, with this in hand perhaps we are ready to take on the third path before calling it a day?" Henry asked, Beth and Murdoch both nodded, having been bored most of the day up to this point.

"We could use a bit of exercise after all that," Terrim said, and Knox crumbled under the combined gazes of his friends.

"Fine," Knox said, turning to make their way back toward the entrance. "But after this, we leave. I planned travel time into our little expedition, and I don't want to leave Luminar unguarded for too long."

CHAPTER 20
NAGA COMMANDER

THE PATHWAY OPENED up to the first room and Knox had to scratch his head. This room was hot and not only that seemed to be made of bubble rooms and corridors, each one filled with serpentine humanoid figures. They had tails of a snake and fins around their heads, but then they had hands and faces like a humanoid. Knox knew nothing about what kind of monster they could be, a part of him wishing Dernal was here to tell him if they'd be a threat or not.

Like the fish people these had two noticeable varieties, a bulky more muscled snake like creature and a lean shorter kind. If his sense was any indication, the shorter thinner snake-like figures had magic and powerful magic at that. Whereas the brute-looking ones showed almost no signs of magic on them.

That is to say, except for their weapons. They held anything from maces to axes to spears, each one glowing with deadly potential. Then there were the cracks in the ground letting out wave after wave of hot air.

"Underwater, but not," Beth said, reaching out and touching the water tunnel, her hand went right through.

"I suppose we could take a short cut through if you guys don't mind getting wet," Knox suggested.

"Or we could follow the path and stay warm and dry," Beth suggested back, winking at Knox.

"I vote dry and warm," Terrim said, nodding ferociously.

"I second that option," Murdoch said, then turning to Henry, who nodded, he added, "It has been decided. We will stay dry."

Knox wanted to remind them that when it came to dungeon directions and calling the shots, it wasn't a voting system, but they had a good point, he didn't want to be wet either. So, nodding along with them, he set out, shield ready alongside Terrim and his magic capturing shield.

The first group they approached had two brutes and one mystic—what Knox was calling them in his head.

"Focus on the smaller one first, magic shield or not I think it's likely the biggest threat," Knox said, they were hid behind a rather large boulder, close enough that if they left cover it would start the encounter.

"Got it," Terrim said, cracking his neck to the side.

Terrim went out first, catching all three of the serpentine hominoids' eyes at once.

"You trespass on the lands of the Naga, flee now or die," the smaller Naga said, her voice—it sounded more feminine than not —had a hissing quality to it.

"Eat shit," Terrim said, kicking a rock at his feet right into one of the brutes.

Knox couldn't suppress a laugh and joined his friend's side with his shield raised.

The smaller Naga hissed and began to chant, her arm swirling the water above her as she did so. The brutes came then, each twice the size of the smaller Naga and with muscles that rivaled even Aetex.

Knox held out his hand and cast Lustrous Chains on them, just as an arrow shot out catching one in the eye and dropping it instantly.

"Good shot!" Knox yelled, as he braced himself to catch the second brute.

The blow hit from the large Naga's mace rattled Knox's shield but didn't move him an inch. He was still close to twice this beast's level, and it showed in that instant.

Terrim was open to catch the strands of water that lashed out like snakes from above. Each one he caught caused the magic inside the water to be undone and drench him with ice cold water. The heat from the vents in the ground were so intense that within seconds he was a steaming mass of red irritated flesh.

A wash of golden light fell on him, and Knox noticed he unclenched his teeth, just in time for another water snake to come undone. Counter attacking the brute before him, Knox took the snakes weapon arm off at the elbow, red blood spraying out and covering his shield. Another arrow took him in the chest, followed by half a dozen more a moment later. Rapid firing was enough to end him. Knox heard Beth call out as a snake made of water slapped into him.

It didn't do much, Knox catching it on his shield. Then throwing the shield aside, he rushed forward with a focus on his sense. Bobbing and weaving through the water snakes, he approached the caster. Before he could reach it there was a cry of anger from behind him and he felt a power unleash from Terrim. Dodging to the left, the power slammed into the caster Naga, taking it off its tail and onto the ground. Wasting no time, Knox jumped atop it and hacked away its remaining life with his axe.

The first battle was the easiest of the opponents they faced in the first room, each one being more and more tricky to the point that Knox wasn't excited for the second room. He figured it would be a painful experience, despite their victory being a foregone conclusion due to their levels and experience, it wouldn't be an easy feat.

Sure enough, it was not at all an easy task getting through the second room. When Knox had codenamed the larger Naga 'brutes', he hadn't yet seen the four-legged fish monstrosities that awaited them in the second room. The only good thing being that they discovered that the collars they wore were to keep them from rampaging on their own kind, so by the end of the room run it was actually quite easy as Beth took out the magical collars with a nicely aimed shot.

It turned out that there was a third room before the boss fight, and it wasn't easy either. Still, the giant brutes, which were hard to bring down even for Knox, turned out to be their saving grace. There was a pen of them and doing her sneaky thing, Beth was able to set them free and they rampaged through the large third room, killing over half of the army that was present there and sending the rest into a panic. By the time they got some of them under control, Knox and his group had cut through the entire army. And it *was* an army, gathered together in ranks and geared out better than any of the other groups.

That brought them to the final room where the boss awaited them. The room ahead was simple, a sphere with a pyramid of sorts in the middle where water ran out from the top, spilling over the sides. Atop the pyramid stood a single figure, as tall as the giant brutes but with an aura that was a magical match for any of the mystic Nagas.

"You face General Naga-shee, leader of the Naga. Come forth and meet my troops in combat," the General said, his voice booming magically throughout the room.

A portion of the pyramid opened up and a group of five Naga came out, each one armored in unique sea-style gear, fish scales and shells.

"Looks like we fight these groups and then get a shot at the General after?" Knox spoke the words more as a question than anything else, but no one answered him. Instead Terrim stood, shield ready and the group stood behind him. It had been a long day, and it was about time it was over, if he had a way to tell time he was sure it would be well into the night by now.

So, the fight began with lances of water and ice from the two smaller Naga in the back and three of the smaller brutes led the way. One even had a shield, which was a first for them.

The shield one zipped forward ahead of the rest, slamming

into Terrim and sending him back a step. Knox used this moment of distraction and placement to slam his shield into the Naga's face, followed by a slash of his axe.

It cried out but showed remarkable resolve by keeping his shield raised and in place, protecting most of its vital organs despite the cut running down its arm.

The other two caught up and the fight was on. It lasted much longer than any of the previous engagements, arrows flying with deadly accuracy and bolts of ice doing the same. Henry really had his work cut out for him as the battle continued, Beth took a vicious blow to her shoulder and Murdoch an axe to his gut.

All in all, the fight was a lot more balanced than it should have been, a reminder to Knox that this dungeon wasn't pulling any punches. It was almost as if it knew they out leveled it a bit and it was going for the throat where it could, like targeting the weaker party members and draining their healer.

After the first fight, four more followed. Each one slightly harder than the last until the final one hit them, almost leaving Knox with no choice but to pull a suppression ring. However, it worked out and he kept his powers in check, relying heavily on his sense and dealing almost every killing blow on the last fight.

That just left the boss. He boomed out magically enhanced words, bidding them to meet him atop the pyramid and they obliged him. Moving up the water, Knox checked on Henry, he was lagging behind and clearly at the end of his ropes.

"We need to strike out as a team, everyone pull out all your punches and hit him hard and fast. That Guardian ready to be used?" Knox asked Henry, to which he got a reluctant nod.

"It's an exhausting spell to cast but I think I can manage it," Henry finally said, catching his breath.

"Good, make ready, and remember, no holding back. Let's give him all we have right at the start," Knox said, hoping to hell his strategy would pay off.

The Commander of the Naga wore magnificent armor, all iridescent and shell-like. He wielded a mighty spear with a shield and a massive helmet that almost gave him the look of a dragon. He stood some ten feet tall and slithered closer as they approached.

At first, Knox assumed perhaps he was meaning to attack before they made it to the top, but he stopped at the edge and spoke.

"You've my word as Commander of the Naga that I will fight fairly and honorably. Come forward and meet your doom."

"Not likely," Murdoch muttered, and the snake-like head snapped to him. Had he heard from so far away?

Murdoch didn't look directly at him, and Knox couldn't help but take a breath in apprehension.

This fight wouldn't be easy, but they were ready, and he knew it.

The five of them made it to the top of the platform, ready to fight the giant of a Naga. Terrim took the lead, shield ready with Knox on his flank ready to support him. Henry stayed in the back where he hoped it would be safest, Beth at his side with bow ready. Murdoch was on Terrim's other side, ready to strike forward and get a blow in whenever the chance opened up to him. Together they stood strong against their foe.

The Naga attacked first, his powerful lance coming down on Terrim with deadly speed. Knox saw it coming, but did nothing until the Naga was fully extended. When he could go no further, Knox shifted his weight from his back foot to the front, lunging forward, axe ready. His blow hit armor, but smashed with enough force that he knew that the Naga commander must have felt it.

Responding to the blow, the Naga shifted on its tail, his lance nearly bowling Knox over as he withdrew. But the others hadn't been idle either. Murdoch found an opening in the armor and a flash of red blood followed. Next came arrow after arrow, only one in three finding a mark between the armor, but Beth was using her Rapid Fire arrows and they came quick and deadly.

Back and forth they struck, each blow slowly bringing down the boss's health. It was during this exchange that something occurred to Knox. They really were overpowered for this area when they worked together. This fight might not be as dangerous as Knox had thought.

Of course, that was when the boss shot out a wave of ice that stuck all of them fast on the ground. The giant Naga came in swiftly, smashing into Terrim, the only one not affected by the magic and suddenly it was a one-on-one match.

Using his axe Knox began to chip away at the ice, seeing the others doing likewise. All but Henry, he just began to cast a spell, a long and complicated one that Knox was sure he remembered hearing before.

Meanwhile, Terrim screamed in pain as a blow got past his defenses and drew a line of blood on his face. Back and forth they fought as Knox and the others struggled to get free. But it wasn't meant to be, the ice was just too strong and too much. Knox cursed his freezing feet and began to cast a spell of his own, hoping Luminous Surge would do the trick.

It blew away a fair bit of the ice but didn't do the trick on the first go. Before he could get off another cast, he felt a spell finish and looked up to see a massive Celestial in golden armor appear on the battlefield.

"Do not fear, mortals," it said, the voice that of an actual angel, warming each of them to their core upon hearing it. The Celestial had a massive spear and he slammed it on the ground, shattering the ice off all their feet just as Terrim fell to the ground, too still for Knox's liking.

"Help him!" Knox screamed, already getting ready to cast his own spell on his friend.

With a look to Henry, who nodded, the Celestial acted. He had precious few seconds on the battlefield and Knox just hoped he'd be able to help Terrim in time. His own spell went off, but it didn't seem to do much to the still form of Terrim on the ground.

"Oh no," Knox said, rushing forward to try and put himself between the attacking Naga and his fallen friend, but the Celestial got there first.

With a magnificent show of power, the Celestial caught the spear of the Naga with a single hand, smashing its own spear into the chest of the attacker. The Naga cried out, but the Celestial wasn't finished. It released the spear and placed an open palm on the Naga's chest, a golden pulse of light later and the Naga went flying backward on its ass.

Then turning, the Celestial knelt over Terrim, heals streaming out of his outstretched hands. Looking up it spoke.

"I've done what I can, he yet lives but my time here has ended. Fight well, soldiers of purpose."

And with that, he faded from the battlefield like he was never there, leaving a deep stillness in his wake. Terrim stirred, groaning in pain but alive.

"You're done!" Knox yelled, pointing at the Naga with his axe and looking to see that the rest of his party was ready. An arrow slamming into the tail of the Naga signaled that Beth was ready and Murdoch stepping forward, sword ready, told Knox he wouldn't stand alone.

Shield at hand and axe ready to strike, Knox used Ethereal Step and cut a line across the Naga's face, moving all the while to catch the Naga's blow across his shield. Then, before the Naga could use its superior strength, he rolled back and Murdoch appeared to cover his exit. Several precise slashes and stabs later, the Naga screamed in pain. That stopped when an arrow went right into his mouth through the slits in the helmet.

A gurgling roar of pain followed as the Naga ripped free the arrow and seemed unable to speak. However, voice or no, it seemed still able to do magic. Lances of ice formed around it and struck out toward all targets, including a wobbly Terrim. Knox leaned into his sense and threw his shield, intercepting the ice lance meant for Terrim, but in doing so leaving himself open for attack.

The lance of ice hit him like a ton of bricks, knocking the air from his lungs and bringing blood into his mouth. Spitting the blood out and rolling to his feet, Knox eyed the battlefield.

It was close, with Terrim still disoriented they didn't have the defense they needed, but the Naga looked worst of them all, a gaping bloody wound in its chest.

"Give it all you've got!" Knox yelled, springing to his feet to do the same.

Aiming at the hole in its chest, Knox cast Arcane Pulse followed as fast as he could by a Luminous Surge that was packed to the brim with power. The first attack staggered the Naga back just as a rain of arrows appeared overhead, doing steady but insignificant damage. Next, Murdoch appeared, speaking over the din of battle and confusing the Naga who just looked at him as he carved flesh away one strike at a time.

Terrim made it to his feet, his eyes going wide as realization of the battle came upon him. He acted without thought to himself, taking up his shield and charging into the fray.

Knox cast chains all around the Naga, golden links holding the Naga in place as they hit it with their combined force of will and action. The Naga never stood a chance against their onslaught.

Between Murdoch's honeyed words, the chains that bound it, Terrim's powerful attacks, and the rain of arrows, it fell still after only half a minute.

"The battle is won!" Henry said, sounding both more exhausted than Knox had ever heard him and at the same time more excited than he'd previously shown.

"Loot better be worth it," Knox mumbled under his breath as a chest of Blue Iron appeared. He'd not encountered one such as this before, but it had a luster to it that made it feel even more special than the golden chests they'd gotten previously.

Reaching in, Knox grabbed hold of something stiff and pulled it free.

He looked to Beth and smiled.

It was a bow and a powerful one at that. Based off the runes it had the ability to conjure something, as well as infuse your arrows with a touch of extra force. Handing the elegant yet simple looking oak bow to Beth, he nodded at her to try it out.

"No, not with an arrow, try just pulling back the string," Knox said, prompting her into doing what he was sure the bow was meant to do.

She did as Knox bid her, pulling back the string and where an arrow would normally go sprung to life a sparking blue arrow that didn't so much as glow as it gave off a faint feeling of power. She let loose the arrow and it shot through the air much the same as her normal arrow would, but then she nocked a physical arrow and tried again. The arrow shot forth with such speed that it cracked the air and it seemed a measure of that power used to summon forth a magical arrow could still be felt on the physical one.

"This is so badass," Beth said, twirling the bow in her hands and handing over her other bow to Knox. Apparently, they thought that he should be the recipient of all spare weapons.

"It has a few other perks that I can't quite make out, but I think they have to do with increasing the output of abilities or something, I'll have to research it a bit more when I get back to town," Knox said, then turning he began to descend from the pyramid and back to their little camp area.

CHAPTER 21
BACK TO IT

THEY EXITED the Dungeon the way they'd come in, except when they emerged, they weren't alone as they had been when entering. Instead, several dozen Ahtora stood around, as if waiting for something. A great cheer went up among them as Knox blinked in confusion.

"You did well for your first time in, defeating both our King and our great enemy, the Naga General," Atar said, the necklace pulsing with power as he spoke, translating their words.

"You witnessed our victories?" Knox asked, confused.

"Yes, we activated the viewing stones," Atar said gesturing to the spire of stone as if it were a common thing to do such.

That's a trick I'll have to learn, Knox thought, walking up to the translucent-skinned Atar, he held out a hand.

Atar took it and they shook.

"I'm thankful you allowed us passage and we hope to return someday to let more of our kind challenge it. Would that be alright?" Knox asked, trying to keep himself from biting his lower lip.

"You have earned our respect, and as such, you may deal with our chief in this matter. Return in thirty cycles of the great light in the sky and you will be well met. Until then, avoid the shadows and walk in the light," Atar said, then bowing his head they began to leave, a few at a time.

Knox let them go, thinking on his words and what implications they might have to their current predicament, dealing with shadows and goo that threatened to overtake the mind and kill the host. Did they know of these things or perhaps it was just a saying among their kind. One thing was certain, he'd need to return here and try to make allies of these strong people.

If they had a dungeon and means for their entire people to train within it, then they'd be strong, stronger perhaps even than Knox.

"That was epic," Terrim said, slapping Knox hard in the back with a friendly blow. "We are definitely doing that again. I mean, it was like the Labyrinth, but we actually get to help with the boss fights, and we find epic loot inside!"

"Let's get home, but I agree. We will have to return," Knox said, then thinking about it and the winter coming to a close within the next month or two, he added, "We can also challenge the Mire's Gloom Dungeon, I bet we could get closer to a full clear at that one, but you'd all have to register with the Adventurer's Guild to get access."

"You think they'll be suspicious of so many new Adventurers?" Henry asked, then looking a bit abashed he added, "Or ones as old as me?"

"I think they'll be suspicious, but I think they are already suspicious of me, so what could it hurt to confuse them a bit more? Besides, when the system hits that area, they'll have a whole new sort of confusion and issues to deal with," Knox said, hardly able to imagine the confusion and chaos it might cause.

They met up with Brandon and his party and made their way back to the complex. It was an easy journey, only disrupted by the occasional monster attack—they were getting stronger that much was plain to see—and an unfortunate encounter with a Dire wolf that had been infected by the black goo.

The Elder's greeted them as they returned, Murdoch taking over that portion of the responsibility and hearing their reports while Knox left to go study up on the runes that were connected to the new weapons they'd gotten. But first, he confirmed that the new dungeon was in fact inside of the area effect of the system, meaning the Ahtora would have system paths if they wanted.

He made it as far as two stairwells down before three golems barred his path.

"We need to speak with you," Edgar said, his tone its usual reserved and level tone.

"Yeah, we's got a few things we need from you," Borris added, causing Edgar to shake his head.

All the while, Vlad stood in silence, his posture stiff as always. The three of them looked the most unique out of all his golems and it wasn't just the armor that did it. They'd taken to wearing different colored scarfs, likely in an attempt to look unique.

And beside that it looked like Vlad had done some work on his left arm, it appeared bulkier than it had before. That is when Knox noticed that each of them had specific changes. Edgar for one no longer had a visor for eyes, but two perfectly circular eyes. Whereas Borris had four arms! It was hard to notice at first because they moved in time with each other, each one only had three fingers, but it was clear they'd been experimenting with their form.

If they could do that much, what else had they changed about themselves?

"How did you accomplish these changes?" Knox asked, his hand slowly settling on his axe. If he didn't like their answers, he'd be forced to put them down. Perhaps they'd been the leak after all, and he was too blind to see it before.

"Us first," Borris said, uncaring of the tension that had suddenly grown between them. "You give any thought to giving us what we want?"

"What is it you want?" Knox asked, his grip tightening and the strap clicking out of place around his axe head.

"You know," Borris said, gesturing to his crotch area. "Those maintenance golems will do all sorts of changes for us, but they won't give us nothing in way of man parts!"

Knox couldn't help it; he snorted and relaxed his grip a bit. If it had been the golems guided by Mic that made the changes, then he was less worried they were changing their personal runic formations. Just to be sure, Knox focused on his sense and briefly looked over the many hundreds if not thousands of lines of runic formations, but it was no use. They were too vast to notice if anything had changed from just a quick glance.

Vlad shook his head and spoke, "It might seem silly to you, but we want some of the pleasures of life back. Mic has made it possible for us to eat, taste, and even feel more than before. But he says you will have to be the one that allows genitals."

Vlad was a serious fellow and he spoke in that same serious manner, which only made Knox snort the more. It was such a ridiculous ask that he couldn't even begin to consider it, but then he let himself be placed in their shoes and think as they might be.

They were likely missing their physical form and all that came with it. On top of all that, they were on a short leash of sorts, keeping their actions in check by runic formations that they couldn't disobey if their lives depended on it. He'd basically forced them into servitude in exchange for their lives and Knox suddenly didn't see the humor in their situation any longer, he felt sorrow.

"I'll talk to Mic about it," Knox said, and he meant it. As odd as it would be to have anatomically correct golems walking around, he had to consider their feelings. But first he had to know something.

"We are grateful," Edgar said, blinking at Knox—something he hadn't been able to do before.

"Can you lie to me?" Knox asked, then clarified. "Can you physically lie to me, does the runic formations allow it?"

"They do not," Edgar said, seeming saddened by the fact. "We might get away with half-truths, but an outright lie is prohibited, although silence is not."

With that, Edgar looked at Vlad, who just shrugged. Vlad had always been good at silence.

"Did you betray me to the pirates, is that how they know how to access the system?" Knox asked his burning question.

"Why would we want to help our enemies?" Edgar asked, though Knox noted that he didn't actually answer the question.

"Answer the question," Knox said, staring down the pirate golem.

"I did not reveal any secrets to the pirates and to my knowledge neither did my companions," Edgar said, each word said carefully and skillfully.

"And you two?" Knox asked, he wasn't going to let it rest until each of them had said as much.

"I'm no traitor, I like my life here, well most of it. I miss the warm touch of women and the like," Borris said, shaking his head. When Knox just stared him down, he finally said, "No, I didn't betray yous."

"I've not betrayed any secrets to our former kin, the pirates," Vlad said as Knox's eyes fell on him.

"Or anyone else?" Knox asked, looking to each of them.

"Or anyone else," they all said in unison.

Satisfied with their answers, Knox bid them farewell and found Mic attending the Titan Engine.

"These changes that the three pirate golems are getting, they don't affect their loyalty or runic pathways built out to keep them loyal?" Knox asked, lifting his hand in greeting.

"And hello to you too. I've kept this place together despite several critical issues that arose. Also, you'll be happy to hear your friend Aetex, the large muscled one, is back on his feet and left this very day out to fight 'evil and evil doers' as he put it," Mic said, the golem had undergone a few upgrades himself, looking far more human than he had before. He had two eyes, each one blinking to show his impatience, clothing, and a face with a mouth and movable muscles on it, or whatever passed as muscle for golems.

"I get it, you've been busy, sorry but I've got a lot on my plate as well. Can you please answer my question?" Knox asked.

Mic blinked, then grinned before answering. "All of these cosmetic upgrades do not affect the core runic programming each golem has within itself. We must serve you; we must be honest, we must not take any action that might result in harm to you or your people, along with a list as long as my memory that keeps us tied in knots if we were to try to betray you in any way. That includes the three 'pirate golems' as you call them."

"What do you think about their request for genitals?" Knox asked, he grimaced as he did, such an awkward conversation that he wished he didn't have to have. Who was going to want to sleep with metal men anyway, why did they care so much about this?

"I find the idea disgusting, but doable if you'd like them to have the *upgrade*," Mic spoke the last word as if it were dirty and hard to get out.

Knox thought about it for a long while before answering him, considering all the angles he could and in the end, he couldn't see why not. "I want new Runic formations added to each of them that will not permit them to use their new genitals without the consent of any receiving participant. I can't have them finding a way around it and forcing themselves on someone. If that were to happen, I'd not be able to live with myself."

"Sexual assault of any kind would be a severe violation to their current runic formations, but I can think of a few ways to tighten it up, adding extra layers atop what they currently have," Mic said, nodding his head and blinking several times as he considered ways to strengthen their restrictions.

"Fine," Knox said, hardly believing he was about to give the order. "Fit them with genitals but ensure they know they must be covered at all times. The last thing I want to see is that."

"Understood," Mic said, then before he could say more, Knox bid him farewell, and he escaped into the depths to get some reading and study done.

The rest of the week went off without much issue. Though they did have reports of the monsters growing stronger around the base and further out. This was to be expected as the general population grew in strength, so did the system as more Monster Cores were fed into the Titan Engine.

Knox met up with Aetex when he appeared inside Luminar one afternoon, giving Knox several B Ranked Monster Cores.

"Use these to grow in power, either yourself or those closest to you," Aetex said, handing them over.

A dozen B Ranked Cores were too powerful to pass up, but Knox had to wonder why Aetex didn't want them.

"Why not use them yourself?" Knox asked.

Aetex flexed his muscles and looked up into the sky. "My time here draws closer to an end. I've accomplished much getting you as far as you've gotten in a single piece. I fear that soon I shall be walking a new path, outside of this fair planet."

Knox frowned. "You're leaving soon?" He asked. "But why and where, surely Luminar can be your home as it is for so many others?" Food supplies were flourishing, and arms and armor supplies were at an all-time high.

"Mah'kus leads me to be where I am needed, be at peace, friend, for I shall not leave when you are still at need," Aetex said. "Do you wish to join me in the hunt? I've got my eye on one you'd call an A Ranked Monster, powerful and deadly, but injured by something even more powerful. I believe it is weak enough now to be slain."

Knox was level 33 now, but hardly a match for an A Ranked Monster and neither would Aetex be. However, while looking at the man, he noticed that his aura had shifted and changed into the impossible. The normally yellow aura had taken on an orange tint, meaning he'd broken into the A Ranks.

"Ah yes, I've grown stronger since you purged that evil from within me. A realization allowed me to break into the higher ranks, if only barely," Aetex said, smiling down at Knox. "Shall we go hunting?"

Dernal had still not returned, and Knox had many responsibilities to attend to, but missing a fight between two A Rankers was just too much to pass up on.

"I'll go, what kind of monster is it?" Knox asked, his curiosity growing.

"A wolf actually, I've been calling it Fenrir after an old legend I heard some time ago. A mighty beast worthy of the title," Aetex said.

"Fenrir," Knox repeated the name in a whisper as he followed Aetex out and into the wilds.

The very air around them seemed charged with power as they ventured to the edge of System controlled territory. They moved in silence and despite sensing several strong monsters, none of them turned out to be this mysterious Fenrir. It wasn't until they were only a few paces away that Knox sensed it.

Like a wave of sudden power emanating all around, he flinched back in surprise, but Aetex wasn't caught off guard. A massive nine-foot-tall wolf sprung from cover. It had somehow laid so still, it had avoided Knox's sense and appeared as a large boulder.

It growled and clashed with Aetex in a mighty show of power, pushing the powerful champion back. Knox didn't wait for an invitation, though he was just there to watch, he couldn't help but step in to do something.

He doubted his attacks would be much help, but perhaps he could tie up or slow the wolf. Casting Void Grasp first, he quickly moved to Lustrous Chains, each one shattering nearly the same moment they touched the powerful monster. But it was working to slow it, even if barely. Knox kept the casts up, even doing a Radiant Ground smash to add a touch of damage. But he needn't have worried, this wolf was not the mighty dragon they'd faced before. No, it was much weaker and Aetex had the fight well in hand.

He punched and kicked the wolf around the field of battle like it was a plaything, only stopping to summon up powerful swaths of light that cut through it with impressive force. Knox was in awe of the power being displayed here, power that he could obtain if he got the emblems inside the Labyrinth, or at least that is what he told himself.

The fight ended much faster than Knox would have guessed, with a beam of energy shooting right through the wolf's eye, killing it.

"Wasn't that a wonderful fight," Aetex said, putting his hands on his waist. "Waste not though, let's get to work bringing this corpse back to your people."

And they did, together they moved the body back where the hide and meat could be stripped from it and turned into useful materials and food for the masses. The entire experience felt like a dream and suddenly the idea of Aetex leaving filled him with not a little dread. But he knew that in the end it was only his power that he needed to grow if he was to stop the threats coming.

The battle with the Ahtora King rung through his mind and he doubted himself for a moment. How much easier it had been with his party at his side, perhaps sharing power was the way to greatness and not hording it? Knox remained unconvinced as he went back to his daily comings and goings.

CHAPTER 22
RESPONSIBILITIES

THE LABYRINTH REMAINED CLEARED out for the most part, parties filling it to clear out the monsters they knew they could defeat, but leaving the newest tier alone until Knox and his party could get a feel for it. That was what awaited Knox and his party as they gathered together, ready to challenge what new foes they'd find within.

"So, what do you think we'll find in the next tier of the Labyrinth?" Murdoch asked, polishing his blade as they walked.

"Hopefully no more spiders," Terrim said, shaking his head. "I do not care for those spiders."

This likely had to do with his repeated burnings he'd received at the hands of the water spiders, but Knox let them talk as he wondered about the same topic.

"As long as I can shoot them and Dog can eat them, I'll be happy," Beth said, looking down at her powerful alpha wolf she'd tamed, naming it Dog. Why she'd chosen to leave Dog behind when going to the dungeon, Knox hadn't asked, but it would be nice to have another melee fighter to help with damage dealing.

"Focus up," Knox said as they neared the stairwell down. "Whatever we are going to face, it'll likely be mechanical like the others and slightly harder to kill than the last tier. Everything else is just a distraction."

The group fell silent as they entered the next tier of the Labyrinth and saw their surroundings. It was vastly different than the first two they'd challenged. For instance, instead of rocky hallways and rooms, it was a wide-open area with trees and a sky. Well, not really a sky, Knox realized as his sense washed over it, more of an illusion of a darkened sky to mirror the actual sky.

Besides that, Knox felt several hard to focus on targets that immediately triggered a warning in his mind.

"Shields up," Knox called just as the first of the pack hunters jumped from their hiding place.

Wolves, shrouded in the darkness and seemingly wrapped in shadows themselves, rushed out to meet them. They were mechanical, as were all monsters they'd faced down here, but they had a magical aura of darkness shrouding them, so it was hard to really see their mechanics.

Knox caught one on his shield and the fight was off to a rocky start, as he tripped on a rock and nearly fell backward.

Terrim was luckier though and slammed his wolf back with an ear crunching clang and thwack. Dog appeared before Knox, grabbing the wolf there and ripping a mechanical chunk from it. A moment later, Knox found his footing and began to rain down hell on the other three wolves just appearing. Beam after beam of Luminous Surge hit them and the attacks hit with great effect, each one outright killing or pulling back the shroud of darkness on them.

He was in his prime against the element of Darkness, and this was one floor of the Labyrinth that he was sure they'd be able to speed run through. Gathering his power, he struck out again and again, his axe strikes infused with Light and his stomping foot bringing the pain of Light to each wolf.

The fight was over before a single true injury could be had and they continued to fight the wolves this way all the rest of the day and into the next day. Knox was getting a wonderful amount of essence and his group's level was averaging closer to twenty-five by the time the week ended.

They found the Guardian's room on the eighth day, Knox's light illuminating a hidden passage that led to a massive wolfman, shrouded in darkness and standing waiting to be challenged.

Instead of saying the usual line about only Knox challenging him, the wolfman seemed interested in watching Knox and saying nothing at first.

"Are you ready, Guardian?" Knox asked, his curiosity getting the better of him as he waited.

"Curious that you should take the mantle," a low voice responded; sounding almost as if it came from a great distance and spoken through the wolfman.

"Why is that?" Knox asked, thinking he knew what mantle the wolfman had to mean, becoming the Titan of Light.

"A weak human, of all the species to carry the weight, very rarely do humans last through the initiation process. Does that news darken your thoughts? As well it should, for you face a Guardian of the Dark and I will not hold back my power as my brethren do." The last bit of the sentence turned into a growl of words, as if the wolfman were taking over and the distant voice being pushed back.

Just like that, the wolfman lurched forward, its speed impressive but not a match for Knox's. Using his sense, he tried to guess where to move to avoid the strike, but a shocking realization hit him, and he had to roll away to avoid being hit. His sense hadn't been able to pick up on the wolfman's movements. Instead, where he ought to be, was a void or a darkness that he couldn't read.

"Hah, you will find many of your tricks will not work on me," the wolfman sneered the words, slashing with clawed hands for Knox's throat.

Knox was still faster and saw the attack coming. However, it felt weird after relying on his sense for so long. He almost took a wrong step, but he got his shield up in time to block a slashing blow. The wolfman had three-to-four-inch claws on each of its deadly fingers.

Back and forth they danced, Knox the faster one but the wolfman's movements were aggressive and gave no time for him to think of a plan of attack, much less time to cast a spell.

He needed distance to try and get a spell off, so he used Ethereal Step to teleport across the room and immediately began the workings of Lustrous Chains. The spell went off with the wolfman halfway across the room already. Chain after chain shot up to entangle him but Knox wasted no time in starting to cast Luminous Surge. He needed his powerful Light-based spells if he were going to have a chance here.

The spell went off, raw and packed with power, but the chains shattered against the wolfman, and he dove to the ground, running on all fours and dodging Knox's first strike. Frustrated and ready to even the playing field, Knox had just enough time to inscribe a short runic formation with Radiant Glyph.

The room erupted in brightness from the runic formation for Light, amplified by the properties of his talents. The wolfman suddenly appeared in Knox's sense once more. The attacker paused for only the briefest of moments before charging forward, claws out and ready to rend flesh.

With his sense working, for at least the half a minute or so he could keep the spell up, Knox easily dodged the attacks and countered with his own axe swings. Steel met flesh and blood poured out freely from half a dozen cuts on the wolfman. It had no armor, wearing nothing but its fur, and it was paying the price for it.

The Radiant Glyph flickered out and suddenly the darkness that followed was deeper and more troubling than what had been there before. Knox heard his teammates cry out something, but he couldn't hear. Instead, there was the sound of a little girl laughing, then pain in his neck and gut.

Then he felt the presence in his head, invading his very thoughts. He fought back as best as he could, his mind was his own sanctum, and he wouldn't let it fall! Clinging to that thought and the power of his mental fortitude, he pushed and pushed until he felt something give. All the while, his body began to pulse and burn from a dozen or more wounds.

Then just like that, the darkness receded enough that Knox could see, and what he saw gave him pause. Where the other Guardians had all been mechanical or magical in nature, this wolfman was very much flesh, blood, and magic. Something wasn't right here, and Knox needed to end this fight immediately.

Slashing out, his first strike came up short, glancing off a newly formed set of darkness imbued armor that the wolfman now wore. It clung around him like the carapace of a bug, leaving very little room for attacks to get through. Raising his right hand and letting his axe fall into a loop at his belt, he cast Luminous Surge, catching blows on his dented and mangled shield.

It was all too much for the poor shield and Knox felt when a section of the front armor buckled. It went flying to hit against the far wall and left his arm exposed, a fact that the wolfman took advantage of immediately. His slash nearly disrupted Knox's casting of the spell, but he held on and released a powerful blast of light.

The wolfman's armor was nothing against the light and within moments, Knox could hear flesh sizzling as the strike found its mark. Pulling free his axe, he swung and felt Light infuse each strike. The armor that the wolfman had summoned shied away from the light, so that each strike was nearly a mortal wound, cutting deep and deadly.

It was only a matter of a minute after Knox found his footing in the battle that he delivered a deadly blow to its neck, bleeding it dry.

The wolfman uttered his final words before dying and Knox shuddered to hear it.

"We are coming."

Examining the body afterward, Knox discovered the skeleton of the wolfman was very much a mechanical skeleton, but how had it grown flesh and been so highly infused with magic? Knox didn't dare to assume he understood the Labyrinth and the secrets that lay beneath, but he'd thought he was getting a handle on what to expect. Apparently, he was wrong.

Collecting the next emblem, he looked at his team, they'd gathered up to examine the wolfman as well.

"We only have three of these left to gather. Once I've done that, we will be ready to face anything that comes our way," Knox said, feeling less confident than he sounded after that last battle.

"You just stood there," Henry said, throwing another heal to address the many slashes that had made it through. "Why did you let him attack you without covering yourself?"

"It attacked my mind, somehow," Knox said, shaking his head. "I was lucky that I could even push it out, it nearly overwhelmed me."

"It nearly killed you while you stood there," Terrim added, looking at his friend with a very serious face. "Are you sure you are up for three more, especially if they are getting stronger? Who knows what you'll face after that wolfman."

Knox didn't answer at first, just looking at his team and wishing Dernal was back already. It wasn't that he wasn't getting used to using Henry, but he wanted to bounce theories and ideas off of Dernal. That, and there was a comfort that came with having his powerful friend around. He cared for Dernal and worried for his friend.

"Let's get out of here and find some rest. Also, tell the wood-cutters that we unlocked an endless source of wood down here, that might come in handy," Knox said.

They cleared a dead man's zone around the complex and used

the trees to add a sort of palisade around the already strong wall for extra defense, but with this much wood they'd be able to assist in building now as well.

Knox checked his status and saw he'd gotten a fair bit of essence from the last fight, but still not enough to level up anymore. He had so much on his plate between doing runic formations for materials, arms, and armor, and his own personal research. He'd even tried to look more into the personal journal of Ramses, but no new entries had made themselves present.

He needed power more than anything else, or many powerful people at his side. Once more he longed for Dernal and his return with John and Leo. Sure, they wouldn't be as invested in Luminar as he was, but he knew them well enough that he thought he understood what motivated them. They would help because they could tell Luminar and Knox needed it.

With so many signs of the Darkness coming and several new disappearances as of late—two hunting parties had been wiped out or lost to the Darkness—he needed all the help he could get. Then there were the pirates and the threat they posed. If he thought about it too much it was a bit overwhelming, so he focused on what he knew he could change and effect. He would grow stronger, claim the emblems, and fuse them back together. He would be a champion of his people and end the threats as they appeared, Darkness or pirates or even the Guild Charterhouse if they decided to come around.

That was something else he worried about, the Adventurer's Guild. He knew the system was only a hair's width away from encompassing it now and it might have already taken over the Mire's Gloom Dungeon. Eventually those powerful Adventurers would work out a source and come to Luminar, he just knew it.

"A lot on your mind?" Beth asked, taking Knox's hand in hers and squeezing it.

He didn't pull away but welcomed the warm touch of another person. It was a friendly gesture, though a part of Knox wanted it to be more.

"Yeah, I'm worried about so much at once I feel like I'm going to forget something important," Knox said, looking up as they made it to the staircase.

The room down below was wide open, but the staircases allowed for two people shoulder to shoulder to pass. It had the same ancient metal design the rest of the base had, with a bronzed look to it, but Knox knew it was sturdy enough by way of Mic.

He could smell Beth from this close, and the familiar touch of her skin sent tiny bits of lightning dancing up his arm. But as they walked, his mind wandered back to Sarah and the commitments he'd made to her. Knox took his hand back and gave her a friendly smile.

"Don't worry so much," Beth said, seemingly unaffected by the gesture. "Remember, you've got us to watch your back, so if the weight ever gets too great, just share it."

"Just share it," Knox said with a smile on his lips. She was right of course, he didn't have to bear this weight himself, he had people he could talk to, and unload some of his worries on, least of which was Beth herself.

"It helps to just talk about it," Beth assured Knox. "Trust me, I'd know."

Knox could tell she'd been feeling better, so perhaps she'd found someone new to confide with? That was good news and let a single worry of Knox's drain away. He'd been worried that she was going to turn cold and distant to people after so much that had happened to her, but that wasn't the case at all.

"You know what, Beth?" Knox said, his hand slipping around her waist and drawing her close into a side hug.

"What?" She asked, her tone sarcastic.

"You are just the best," Knox said, leaning over and kissing her on the forehead. It was a friendly gesture and not meant to be romantic, but when Beth looked back up, he could have sworn he saw something in her eyes.

Shaking his head and releasing her, a voice called out Knox's name. He looked up to see Sarah waving meekly at the pair of them as they exited to the surface.

"I better go see her, I've been so busy lately I've hardly given her any of my attention," Knox said, sighing.

"Take care," Beth said, but again he swore he heard a note of something else in her voice, was it longing or was he just imagining it?

"Knox!" Sarah exclaimed as he drew nearer. She pulled him into a warm hug and planted a passionate kiss on his lips. Knox returned the gesture and for several seconds they stayed locked in the throes of passion.

"Hello to you too," Knox said as she released him.

Her blue eyes washed over him, and he felt himself being pulled in by them. The touch of her body against his as she pulled him closer nearly took his breath away. She was on the Rogue Path and wore an outfit to match, skimpy black leather that covered less than Knox thought was optimal for combat. Though, right now he wasn't complaining.

"Did you give any thought to my idea?" Sarah asked and suddenly Knox had something else he had to worry about. He'd all but forgotten that she'd asked him to consider her for a place on his team, seeing as they didn't actually have any official trap finders. Knox had assured her that they got by fine without a Rogue, but she'd pushed the matter and Knox had all but forgotten.

"Well," Knox said, rubbing at the back of his neck with his arm as they made their way toward the dinner hall. "I told you before Sarah, we are all set on trap detection and our team is pretty solid. I can't go around messing with something that works well already."

"So, you won't even consider it," Sarah said, seeing through Knox's words and to the root of the problem. Then she surprised Knox by saying, "I bet if Beth was asking, you'd jump to give her a spot."

Knox's face reddened noticeably but he did his best to shake it off. "It isn't like that with us anymore. Please don't be jealous."

"Jealous!" Sarah practically yelled the words. "Oh no, I'm not jealous. My boyfriend spends all his time with an ex-lover who is touching him and flirting with him every chance she gets, but no, I'm not jealous."

Knox had a feeling that perhaps she was just a tiny bit jealous, but he was wise enough not to say those words. Instead, he put his foot in his mouth another way. "You aren't even strong enough to join our party anyway, it would throw off the entire balance of the team."

That hadn't been the right thing to say, Sarah went from looking pissed to looking hurt. "I'm not hungry anymore," she said just as they reached the open doors of the dinner hall.

Knox let her go, unsure why relationships had to be so complicated. Perhaps this was all for the best, without any relationships he'd have less to worry about, not that he remembered everything anyway.

Finding a seat beside Terrim, who was eating happily with Danielle, Knox ate his stew in silence. The warm broth unable to fill the void that was forming in the pit of his stomach.

CHAPTER 23
RETURN

Sᴀʀᴀʜ ᴡᴏᴜʟᴅɴ'ᴛ sᴘᴇᴀᴋ to him after that day and the following two weeks sped by as the team challenged the Labyrinth, growing closer and closer to finding another Guardian. It was at the end of two weeks of clearing out the Labyrinth that they found the next Guardian and Knox slew it with almost no issues. The mechanical creature was a being of ridiculous strength and firepower.

It threw balls of fire and punched through Knox's armor like it wasn't there, but it was slow and lumbering which made it an easy target to avoid and kill with some measure of haste. The Guardian spoke all the right words, none of that wolfman funny business, and Knox was one step closer to connecting the emblems back together and unlocking some untold power. Of course, two weeks of straight training and gathering of essence didn't go to waste, he reached level 34 and they celebrated with drinks.

Knox kept himself purposely distanced from Beth, despite the fact that he was pretty sure Sarah wasn't going to be taking him back, but Beth had no qualms about being her old self, flirting and hitting him with sexually suggestive remarks whenever he let his guard down. It was fine for now, and she seemed to respect his desire to be alone in principle if not in action.

At the end of the two weeks and a few nights after they defeated the fourth Guardian, Dernal appeared back in Luminar in the middle of the night. Knox went out to meet him as soon as he was told—he had given a standing order to be informed if Dernal returned by the golems that kept watch.

The golem that came to him told him that Dernal was in the dinner hall, so Knox went there first to check. The building was massive, made of the same metals that covered most of Luminar, but it had long windows up the high walls that let in sun during the day and moonlight in at night. Besides that, there were three massive fireplaces that provided ample light when you had them all lit.

Currently, only a single fireplace was lit, the centermost one, and it provided enough light to see by, but not much else. So, when Knox entered and saw that Dernal wasn't eating alone, he grew excited, however, the two people sitting beside him weren't exactly who he expected when he finally got close enough to see them.

"Good to see you Leo," Knox said, grasping the blue man's arm in greeting and sitting beside him.

On Dernal's other side sat a man that Knox hadn't ever wanted to see again, but here he was.

"Not good to see me, eh?" Caleb asked, then chuckling he slurped loudly at his soup.

"Where is John?" Knox asked, ignoring the one-armed man he knew as Caleb.

Dernal grunted, cleared his throat, and spoke. "Went to check out the markets at the dungeon, that, and hopefully to get us back in the rotation."

Knox nodded, ready to ask the question he wasn't sure he wanted to say out loud. His not so better sense won out and he gestured to Caleb.

"Why did you bring him here?" Knox asked.

The man was a horrible person, Knox couldn't understand what would motivate Dernal to bring someone like him here, someone who might betray all their secrets.

Caleb chuckled again and kept eating his stew. Knox really hoped it was hot enough to burn the inside of his mouth, but he held his tongue in saying as much.

"Found him wandering, figured Mic might be able to help with his missing arm. Can't afford the healing it would take to grow it back," Dernal said, as if he hadn't just invited an asshole into their midst.

"And you aren't worried about him siding with the pirates or giving away our location to the Adventurer's Guild?" Knox asked in a hushed whisper, but he was sure Caleb still heard him.

"Come now, Knox, he isn't that bad," Leo answered, and Knox gave him a flat look. They'd been with him longer than he had known him, so their judgement on the matter would be more sound, Knox knew.

"Adventurer's Guild already knows, and he wouldn't sign up with pirates," Dernal said, not taking his eyes off his stew as he ate.

Knox was ready to flip the table after hearing Dernal speak, but he held his cool. "What do you mean they already know? How could they?"

"I told them," Dernal said, finally looking up from his stew and hitting Knox with a level stare.

"Why would you do that?" Knox asked, suddenly very confused.

"It is proper protocol and they'd have found out eventually," Leo said, shrugging as if it weren't a huge betrayal.

"He's right," Caleb said, slurping loudly at his stew. "You're secret hiding hole belongs to the Adventurer's Guild now; they'll come and take it away from you in the name of fairness and all."

"They won't," Dernal said, elbowing Caleb. "They'll want to poke around, but the world is changing. They'll have something to say about it for sure."

Leo finished his stew and turned to Knox. "You have grown

considerably since I last saw you, you mask your aura well, but I can still see traces of red. Have you truly made it to the A Ranks and above?"

Knox shook his head before responding. "My aura is different as a Titan Born. What has Dernal told you so far?"

"Not much, but the basics I take it," Leo said, his eyes flicking over to Caleb. "He found us stuck in the snowy pass and we'd found Caleb some days before, so there hasn't been much by the way of private conversations."

"You can say whatever you want in front of me," Caleb said. "I'm basically useless without my arm, so who will I tell?"

"You aren't useless," Leo said, it had the tone as if it was something Leo had said many times before.

"Oh sure, I can hold a shield or a weapon, but not both," Caleb said, snorting into his stew.

What is the deal with people losing their arms and being assholes, Knox wondered as he thought about his father.

"Perhaps Mic can help with that," Dernal said, catching Knox's eye.

"What do you mean?" Knox asked, not following his train of thought.

"Perhaps an artificial arm could be attached?" Dernal asked and Knox considered it.

He thought about how the limbs worked currently and the advanced modifications that would have to be done for it to work for a humanoid body that wasn't completely mechanical. It might be easier than he thought, but it would be up to Mic if he thought it could be done.

"I can have Mic look into it," Knox said, wondering suddenly if his father would be interested in such a modification.

"Askar already asked Mic, he was told that he would look into it some months ago, perhaps he's made progress since then?" Dernal said, taking Knox by surprise.

"Let's go find out. Caleb, you can stay here and finish, Dernal and I will go," Knox said, putting a hand on Caleb to keep him sitting.

He struggled for a moment, but when he felt the power behind Knox's grip, he seemed to understand something and muttered under his breath. "Of course, you are."

They found Mic in the command room sitting on the control chair, tending to one thing or another. The room was large and cavernous, but it had been cleaned up plenty since he first discovered it with a dead titan atop the throne. So much had changed since then, but the room still left him with a foreboding sense of destiny.

"Is it possible to replace a missing limb on a human with one of the golem's limbs?" Knox asked, interrupting the golem in his duties.

"It is not only possible, but I've scheduled a time with Askar to be fitted with a new arm already. Two days from now," Mic said.

"And when were you going to tell me about it?" Knox asked, it wasn't that he was frustrated but something about this entire situation felt odd.

"Askar bid that I keep it a secret until we were sure it would work, I believe he wishes to surprise you," Mic said, his eyes blinked several times as he waited for Knox to respond, but Knox wasn't really in the mood to reply in a nice way.

"Can you do this procedure for another?" Dernal asked.

"With a little preparation, yes, I believe I can adapt the procedure to anyone," Mic said.

Knox cleared his throat. "Dernal, I'm not sure that's a good idea. Where has Caleb even been this entire time? How do we know he is on our side?"

"He is loyal to no one but himself, that is true," Dernal said. "But he feels helpless after losing his arm. Surely, you can understand that feeling having known your father. This is a solution until a real arm can be regrown through magical means, very expensive magical means."

"But I don't trust him," Knox said, feeling as if he were having to repeat himself.

"You don't have to," Dernal said, his voice steady despite Knox's own rising in anger. "Just help him."

"Fine," Knox said curtly. "But I don't want him here afterward. See that he is given supplies and directions out of the swamp. You can even guide him so that he doesn't take one of the black stones from us."

"Hhrm," Dernal said, then added. "Fine. I'll see to it."

The next few days were ones that went by swiftly, if with a bit of awkwardness. Mic did his procedure on Askar and then Caleb, giving them arms up to the shoulder that looked more like armor than anything else. He said that they'd have normal strength over time, but that it would take a few weeks to get to that point. It was all super advanced Runic formations that Knox didn't really have any desire to understand in that moment. He was far too upset at the events playing out in Luminar.

Of course, he knew that perhaps he shouldn't be, but he really didn't like Caleb and now his father going behind his back and Mic actually going along with it, it was more than he wanted to deal with right now. It wasn't like he couldn't feel happy for them, he was glad they were getting access to their entire bodies again, but it was just hard.

However, all of those feelings fell to the wayside when a golem came in a rush, informing him that they were under attack. A pirate army had arrived.

Knox ran from his bunk area and through the stone covered roads toward the command center. He had to see how many they were dealing with and rouse anyone that wasn't already up and ready to fight. It was midnight, perhaps later, but Knox hadn't been sleeping much, nor did he need to sleep every night. Instead, he spent his time studying one thing or another. With his notes discarded and his feet moving as fast as they'd carry him, he made it to the command chair.

"Move," Knox said, sliding into place where Mic had been moments before.

Each attack from the pirates so far had been something they could take care of, with each attack after the first getting a bit harder to manage, despite the growth of those inside Luminar. However, the force of red dots coming to the east gate was nothing short of a true army. His display told him that five hundred and fifteen combatants were on their way. They had at best, half those numbers, at worst even less.

"How many golems do we have that can do battle now?" Knox asked, he'd been told before, but the numbers changed daily.

"One hundred and eighty-three," Mic said. "If you add the maintenance golems throwing rocks from above, it would add another one hundred and four."

When did we become outnumbered by golems? Knox thought, as he calmed down ever so slightly. The odds weren't so bad in their favor after all, perhaps they might even make it out of this in a single piece. Yes, positive thinking is what he needed now.

"Get them to the walls and make them ready," Knox ordered. "We are going to war."

"At once," Mic said, pushing Knox aside to take the command chair and issue orders.

Knox wasted no time, rushing out the door and heading to the east gate where the battle would take place. He knew nothing of siege tactics, but he knew enough that they should let the walls protect them and rain hell down on them from above. Stopping off at his room, he grabbed the bow he'd taken from Beth and a quiver of arrows he'd gotten.

Shooting arrows at armored enhanced targets wasn't a sure way to get a kill, most had the speed to just avoid getting hit, but when fired by someone equally strong, the speed was vastly faster than what a normal archer could accomplish. The draw on this particular bow was so strong, in fact, that some level fifteens couldn't even draw it to its full length.

Feeling more prepared with a bow in hand, Knox made it to the eastern wall just as several small pockets of people began to gather, followed by rows and rows of golems, ready to give their all. He found Sarah in the mix and relayed to her a secret, but dangerous mission. She nodded that she understood and left to gather two more Rogues that would assist her in her mission. It was a simple plan and might not be necessary, but Knox wanted all his paths covered.

The golems weren't as strong, most of them, as he'd like but they each had special system abilities that gave them an edge and Knox would use all he could get at this point. Seeing the three unique looking golems, Vlad, Borris, and Edgar, at the head of a portion of the golems, he made his way over to them.

"Are they ready to fight?" he asked, looking over the gathered forces with small appreciation.

"Ready and willing, not that they have much of a choice in the matter," Edgar spoke for them, as he did most times. Borris looked like he was going to say something, but a glare from Vlad silenced him.

"You have a choice of sorts," Knox told him. "If you want to sit out this fight, I'll allow it."

The wheels seemed to be turning in Edgar's head as he considered Knox's words, but surprisingly he shook his head 'no'.

"There is essence to gather, and we can always be stronger, ain't that right boys?" Edgar said, elbowing them both. "Plus, we have a bit of goodwill toward you after a certain modification process. Just gotta find a willing participant and get her to sign off and all that."

Knox nearly facepalmed. They'd been given mechanical genitals of a type but had their base code modified to prevent any untoward behavior. It wasn't Knox's favorite topic of discussion, so he skipped over it and just nodded.

"Get your elemental golems atop the walls and be ready to call down whatever they can on the pirates' heads, arm your physical golems with bows, crossbows, anything really, give them rocks if you need to, just have them ready," Knox said, but his words weren't necessarily needed. Already, forces were beginning to file up the walls in rows of two. "Mic gave orders already?"

"Yeah," Edgar said. "But I like yours better."

"Thanks," Knox said, shaking his head and heading over to his party and the elders gathered around Murdoch.

They'd had the elections over the last week and Murdoch had won, like Knox figured he would, but he stressed the importance of keeping a council of the oldest and wisest together to help guide him, hence the elders remained at his side. Nodding his head to each of them, Knox came to stand beside Murdoch and listened as he gave orders of his own.

"Who is controlling those golems, make sure they leave room for our strongest ranged fights to attack. What? No don't push them just ask them to move aside," Murdoch said, relaying messages to runners who then dispatched his messages.

"Let's find a place on the wall, do you have a bow?" Knox asked Murdoch, who turned and showed that he did indeed have one.

Bows were more effective for combat over crossbows for the simple fact that the higher draw strength was beyond what Mr. Tome could create in crossbows. Even he'd stopped making them as he grew strong enough to draw a bow at double the strength of a crossbow. Sure, they'd made advancements in the rune scripting to strengthen the components of the crossbows, but it was a lot of work for very little payoff when you could just fire it from a bow.

"Follow me. Elders, I have to insist that you go to the command center and take a contingent of guards with you," Murdoch said, his words much more stern than Knox had heard from him in a long time.

They gave no protests, just nodding one by one and leaving. Two parties leaving with them, one of which was a rather strong party featuring Henry as their healer since Dernal had returned. Knox was about to protest having a group with such effective combat means being pulled away, but a voice cut through the stillness of the morning and a pit formed in the bottom of his stomach.

"I am Captain Dread of the Privateers of the Eastern Seas. We have come to speak with your leader, send him out to parlay or we will tear down your walls. Violence isn't necessary, but we have no qualms about showing our strength."

The voice was dark yet booming in its volume. It had a quality to it that made Knox want to both throw up and take a bath after hearing it. Without seeing the face, Knox was sure of one thing, something was wrong with this Captain Dread. His sense bombarded the location of the voice and had nothing in return but a void in the space where the captain ought to be.

"He's able to hide himself, I wonder how many more are hidden from us," Knox said, mostly to himself but Murdoch overheard him.

"You think it's even worse than what Mic said, how many more could he have?" Murdoch asked.

"Let's get to the wall and find out," Knox suggested, signaling for his party to follow.

Knox hung back to speak with Dernal and Leo as they walked.

"You've made enemies," Leo said, whether a question or a comment Knox couldn't tell as he spoke in such an even tone.

"But I've also made allies," Knox said, looking around. From the western gate he could feel Sarah and two other rogues sneaking out of the complex to try and get some much needed help.

His plan was simple, get reinforcements. But the execution and time required was the issue. Sure they had walls to protect them and buy them time, but not much was certain when you were dealing with literally hundreds of enhanced humanoids. Hell if one of them were strong enough, like this Captain Dread, he might be able to force himself into the complex without much effort.

But if Knox was right about the Ahtora and their strength, a flanking force would be enough to make these pirates think twice about attacking. Unfortunately they had no guarantee that they'd help or want to risk their lives in defense of Luminar. Knox had told Sarah to relay to them much about Luminar and how important it was if they wanted to walk the Paths offered to them. He even gave her permission to share the words that allowed them to train their abilities, if they hadn't yet worked it out themselves.

"I can't get a sense of this Captain's strength," Knox said, looking to Dernal one of the few he knew that had a keen magical sense. It wasn't uncommon of course, all beings that hit a certain threshold got the ability to sense magical energies, but it was hazy at best for most. Dernal had a clear view of most auras and as such Knox hoped he saw something he couldn't.

"Hhrm. I sense nothing," Dernal said after a moment of concentration. "In fact, I'm having trouble getting a read on any of them."

That was news to Knox as he could at least tell the general strength and power of the troops surrounding Captain Dread. It was faint but he'd put most of them at the level 15 to 25 range based off of auras, with a few exceptions that blazed like fires admit embers. Perhaps Knox's sense was even better than he gave it credit for, it never ceased to surprise him.

"I can sense them all pretty well. Overall, we are pretty balanced I'd say, but they have several higher leveled beings, probably twice as many as we have, so that'll be an issue. But none of that bothers me as much as that Captain Dread," Knox said, they'd finally reached the top and, in the distance, at the edge of the deadman's zone, was a mass of blacks and browns—the favored color of the pirates.

Knox was about to ask if anyone had any type of looking glass to help him see when Mr. Tome walked up to him, handing him such a device. He smiled friendly and headed down a few spots where he pulled free a massive boomstick with several barrels connected to each other and unfolded a tripod for it to stand on its own.

Looking over at the impressive looking weapon, Knox was about to ask how it worked, when he felt a surge of power. Putting the looking glass up to his eye he saw an aura of darkness covering the entire force and suddenly his sense cut off, unable to sense anything about that location.

However his eyes worked just fine and he found, standing a good foot taller than those around him, Captain Dread. He wore a hat that was all to common among the pirates they'd faced, likely meant to help against the rain they encountered out at sea. And around him was a black coat that seemed to seethe with black energy. His long coat snapped around him as if caught in gale winds, but the stillness of the night lay around Knox and his followers.

He was working some type of magic, gathering powerful darkness around himself. But what would he do with it once he was finished?

"It's just a veiling spell," Leo said, his eyes pinched in concentration.

"You are sure?" Knox asked, wondering how he could know that just by looking.

"I've experienced a great many spells," Leo said, "despite most of them not working now that I've chosen a path, I can still sense the workings well enough. He isn't part of a path either, or at least he is working magic that I'd find difficult given the changes made to my body."

Knox nodded. "Good," he said. "What do we do about his demand? Murdoch you feeling up to it?" Knox raised his voice to carry over to where Murdoch stood.

"Only if you and Dernal come with me," Murdoch said, rolling his shoulders and cracking his neck.

"You think it's safe?" Knox asked Dernal.

"Hhrm," Dernal said. "Seems that we have little choice. I've faith you can keep us alive if we need to escape. Besides, stories tell of a pirate code that they follow, part of that has to do with parlays and the like. Perhaps ask your metal friends?"

Knox agreed, moving over to find the trio of pirate golems and asking them their opinion on the parlay.

"He'll keep to it," Edgar assured him. "He's a powerful asshat that kills indiscriminately, but he's fair or at least he was when we were last employed by him. He looks right scary even from this distance though. We won't be going with ya, you understand right?"

"No one asked you to, just be ready to defend our walls should something happen," Knox said, feeling less than pacified by Edgar's words.

"Let's go talk to Captain Dread," Knox said, trying and failing to sound overly confident. He was worried about a multitude of things, but trusting a pirate's words were the worst of it at the moment.

"To death?" Murdoch asked and Knox snorted.

"I'd rather not die, but hell, why not," Knox said. "To death!" He called out the words loud and clear and the crowd answered it.

"To Death."

CHAPTER 24
PARLAY

KNOX WAS WORRIED that perhaps the Captain Dread fellow expected them to walk right into the ranks of his army to parlay, but after exiting the gate with Murdoch and Dernal, he saw the Captain, along with two others, moving out to meet them in the center of the deadman's zone. The air was oddly warm that night, the coolness having been sucked from the air by the workings of the magic.

Dead leaves crunched underfoot as they walked and Knox stayed silent, going over in his head what he might say or do to prevent the incoming battle. Perhaps there was nothing to be done and the path they were on was set, but he had to think that wasn't the case. This pirate had no way of knowing how many awaited him inside the walls, perhaps he was just probing for information and not a full takeover.

Whatever his intentions, the spell he'd worked over his people seethed and bubbled darkness in a way Knox had only ever felt when dealing with the black ooze. Had this pirate somehow figured out a way to harness the powers of darkness like Knox did with the powers of light? Surely not.

"You nervous?" Murdoch asked, his voice was sound and

confident now. "Don't be, just let me speak and work my magic. Give me five minutes and I'll have him eating out of our hands."

"Don't be so certain," Dernal said, his eyes narrowing at the incoming pirates. "I'd wager he can resist all types of magic. I can't sense him, but I can feel the weight of his power."

Knox knew what he meant, as they got closer there was a sort of pressure in the air that tightened around his senses. It wasn't the same as seeing an aura or measuring the magical output of something, but more of a side sense that you'd normally miss so focused on using your primary sense. As it was, Knox didn't like the feeling of pressure that this being exerted and he wondered if he would be a match for him, rings of suppression on his fingers or not.

His finger slowly traced the remaining rings he wore, he'd taken one off for each rank he'd passed, leaving him with six total, most of which were on his right hand. Even with the ability to make himself equal power to a B Ranker, Knox wasn't sure it would be enough against this Captain Dread. Was he truly an A ranked being or beyond that? Why had someone with so much power turned to a life of crime and piracy?

Because power corrupts, Knox thought, his own power tempted him in ways he dared not focus on for any length of time. His most private and darkest thoughts remained just thoughts, never given any focus or will.

But now wasn't the time to start doubting himself, now was the time to show this pirate that he was no push over either. Focusing on his power and the veil he tried to keep over it, though it wasn't really needed most times as the system did a fine job holding it back by default, he released it. Power bright and terrible flashed around him as if he'd let off a spell, but it was just his aura, burning around him like it would the tip of a match.

Murdoch and Dernal took steps away from him, so heavy was the pressure his aura gave off, but they continued to walk, not wanting to show too much alarm in front of the enemy.

"I'll remain silent and let my aura do the talking," Knox said to Murdoch. "Do your best to talk a way out of this."

"Right, just don't get too close, your aura feels like a weight on my chest that I can't push off," Murdoch complained.

"Hhrm," Dernal said, taking another half step away.

Another minute or two passed and they found themselves standing some twenty paces from the trio of pirates. Enough that they could talk normally and be heard, but not so close that anyone would have an advantage over each other. The two auras, one dark and sinister, the other bright and terrible, clashed against each other, neither fully able to push back the other.

"Well met," Murdoch said, breaking the silence. "I hope that we can settle this matter without blood."

Captain Dread smiled, but it was a wicked thing that had no place on his face and looked more threatening than it did friendly. His face was that of a nightmare, his eyes orbs of darkness without end, his flesh a pale color devoid of life. It was as if what stood before them was already dead, yet here he stood, shifting about as he prepared to speak.

"I'll take half," he said, his voice like darkness preconized.

"Half of what?" Murdoch asked, clearly confused.

"Your population, dead or alive, I don't care, but I will take half," he said.

"Uhm, well no," Murdoch said. "I would think that we could work out a better way than just giving you half our population to kill."

"Not to kill, dead or alive, they will serve my purpose," he said, his voice so devoid of emotion that Knox cringed slightly upon hearing it.

Then Knox looked at the two beside their captain and realized something. They were undead, or at least their flesh was literally melting off their faces and one had a glowing socket of darkness instead of an eye. And the way the two flanking him stood absolutely still was another clue, he must have taken the path of the necromancer or perhaps he was a powerful necromancer before the system exerted itself.

"Again, no, but perhaps we could offer you some supplies or compensation and send you on your way? I know you lot are said to enjoy gold, we have plenty we'd be willing to share," Murdoch said, then his bearing changed, and his voice grew thick like honey. "Take the deal and leave us be." His words were thick with power, but neither of the three flinched nor showed any reaction.

"Your magic is weak," the Dread Pirate said, shaking his head. "I see only one among you that is a threat to me, and my spies tell me we outnumber you severalfold, even with your toy men on the walls."

Knox had enough of this, and he stepped forward to speak, his aura shifting dangerously around him like a cloak of power. "You will not survive such a battle, I will see to that personally," Knox said, pushing power into his aura and willing it to smash against the powerful necromancer.

"But I will," the Dread Pirate said. "You see, this is just a test. I know that this 'system' that has infected my men and tries to exert itself on me, comes from your little town. You've killed my pirates, stolen my magical secrets to protect yourself, but you do not know the extent of my magic. I am able to draw in monsters as well as repel them. This parlay has ended, no accord could be met, I will enjoy the scent of death that follows."

And with that the Dread Pirate turned and began to walk away, his two bodyguards walking behind him, protecting his exposed back. Knox wanted nothing more than to rip off as many rings as he could handle and shove a Luminous Surge right up his backside. But he knew that he couldn't or shouldn't, since he'd leave himself vulnerable and unable to protect his people afterwards. Where was Aetex when he needed him.

The command chair hadn't shown him anywhere in the system-controlled lands and Knox had no way of summoning him. With Aetex at his side, he might be confident enough to take on this army, but as it was, things didn't look good.

And what was that bit about being able to call powerful monsters to his side? Surely, he didn't mean to say that his orbs had two effects after all? Knox hadn't learned much about how they'd worked, so cloaked in darkness as they were, and the runic formations were some of the most complex he'd seen.

"That didn't go well," Murdoch said, rubbing at the back of his neck. "All those talent points into diplomacy and it didn't even do a thing to that beast. I did, however, get a feel for his intent, an ability of mine."

"And what does he intend to do?" Knox asked.

"To kill us all," Murdoch said, shaking his head.

"Hhrm," Dernal said.

They walked back to the gate unmolested and rejoined their forces on the wall to wait for the inevitable battle that was to follow.

Knox was in no hurry to start the battle, so the next few hours of waiting were good really, if a bit nerve racking. Why weren't they attacking already, what was this Captain Dread fellow doing? With his eye glass he saw them hard at working cutting trees down and fashioning ladders, but did he really think it would be enough to get them over the walls?

Sure they were tall enough, but what would stop Knox's people from just smashing them with magic, arrows, and their own siege weapons. They had several large ballista maned by golems, ready to unleash hell at the first sign of conflict, but so far nothing was happening. The waiting was the worst part Knox was pretty sure.

The battle would be terrible and bloody, but mostly on the pirate's side and not Knox's as the walls offered them some protection, but the waiting for it all to come to pass was near maddening.

"Are you sure you don't want me to try and hit them from this distance?" Beth asked, she was as squirmy as Knox felt, eager to get the battle started so that adrenaline would take over.

"Let them attack first, once they start their march, then we will answer in kind, but not before," Knox said, holding to what he felt was fair.

Of course, nothing in war is truly fair and he had no idea if they were just stalling while rogues or spies of some kind made their way behind enemy lines. Perhaps they had sappers digging below the ground to mess with their walls? He'd learned as much in what little he'd read about sieges, which was really remarkably little.

Mic assured him that such tactics wouldn't be useful as the walls connected far down below and couldn't be destabilized by mere digging. He described Luminar as more of an egg, where the top had been popped off and sat at the surface.

The waiting continued well into the morning hours, but the dark mist that covered the pirates thickened in the light, seeming to resist it. Suddenly they found it hard to see much of anything of what they were doing, and Knox became alarmed. That was when the first roar filled the air, cutting the silence that had stretched for so many hours.

Knox reached out with his sense and caught ahold of a monster coming in fast, flying above the trees at a terrible speed. Whatever Captain Dread had done, he'd begun to call monsters to his side. However, the monster didn't come to his side, instead, the giant bat came straight for Knox.

"Arrows ready," Knox called, nocking his own arrow and sighting the bat as it dove. Clearly the bat was B Ranked by its aura, but Knox had no doubt that several hundred rune-reinforced arrows would be enough to dissuade it. "Release!"

As one, arrows poured out and struck the bat, shredding its wings and causing it to fall hard into the ground. Before it could get up, Knox used Ethereal step and slammed his axe down into its spine, ending its life. He had to make it quick, but he noted with surprise that it had already landed on its head, likely injuring it bad. But the illusion held of Knox being the superior foe, so when his cooldown ran up, he appeared back on the wall with his team.

"Don't want to get the Monster core?" Dernal asked, and Knox grinned.

"Had to make sure that pirate thinks I'm as strong as he is," Knox said. "Wouldn't do to waste time collecting the core."

"Send out a rogue to go collect it, that is valuable essence," Leo said, sharing a look with Dernal.

Knox did so and they were in and out before anything else attacked them. It wasn't until nightfall that more action occurred, and Knox's people were beginning to tire from all the standing around.

The veil that hung so tightly around the pirate army broke and suddenly they were on the march, a loose band of slow-moving targets.

"Begin bombardment," Knox said, and the first wave of arrows went to join their ranks.

CHAPTER 25
ATTACK ON LUMINAR

ARROWS SCREAMED through the air as they went to meet their targets. Knox imagined that the enemy would scream in defiance or at least bring up shields, but neither case was true as arrow after powerful arrow ripped into them, snuffing out the life of many. It was a scene like no other that he'd witnessed before, yet as insane as it seemed it was his reality now.

"Focus on the ones with the ladders," Knox yelled above the din of battle, his own arrows finding purchase among the hundreds of invaders.

This wouldn't be as bad as he'd thought if they just let themselves get hit so hard with their arrows. Not only arrows of course, as they drew nearer magic began to fall from the sky, giant rocks appearing out of nowhere to smash dozens of pirates, balls of fire splashing here or there, and ice rooting a few pirates at a time as it smashed down. Then came Edgar and Borris's spells, they were more advanced and had learned quite a bit more than their newer comrades.

Edgar weaved together fire and ice in an impressive display. A huge chunk of ice formed only to be blown apart above their heads by fire, spreading it out in a vast circle of death. Screams filled the air after that particular attack and Knox watched in awe as Borris, silly and slow as he seemed at times, wove together a powerful force of wind and ice. It streamed down into the forces arrayed against them and cut with reckless abandon.

Ladders were shattered, but there was always another one, or a dozen more pirates ready to step up. Captain Dread stayed far in the back, working a spell of darkness as his forces were being torn to bits. Knox's sense, as crippled as it was trying to sense Captain Dread, pulsed and wriggled now as Knox focused on the man. He was working something big and Knox needed to do his best to disrupt it.

Taking his bow, he aimed, then loosed an arrow that he hoped would find its target. It missed by ten or more paces, the bow at its very limit unable to go that far. Turning to Beth, Knox indicated his arrow and his target.

"Any chance you have an ability that would let you close that distance?" Knox asked.

Beth shook her head, but she seemed to be considering it anyways, looking here and there.

"I could Camouflage, an ability that I have, and try to flank him, putting myself within range to use my Aimed Shot ability. Or I could send Dog after him and hope he returns in one piece. He has an enrage now that might even the odds," Beth said, shrugging slightly as she saw Knox's expression.

"No, I can't risk anyone when we have the safety of the walls," Knox said, then considering going down himself he mentally went through the worst-case scenarios and decided that it wasn't worth his life either.

"Ladders are coming," someone called to Knox's left and sure enough, against all odds, a few ladders were being put into place. It was amazing what people could do even as death rained down all around them. A fierce darkness lingered around the attacking force as they moved, whatever it was, it hindered Knox's sense and gave power to the attacks in a way he'd never encountered. Pain must seem like a distant thing to them, as they began to climb the ladders, blood pouring for multiple wounds.

"Get the fighters in place, archers step back but keep the arrows flowing," Knox called, but as he did so he noticed their supply of arrows, so vast he'd thought before, were dwindling already. Just as he thought that a maintenance golem appeared to fill his own bucket with another three dozen arrows.

"Mic says arrows are being made as swiftly as possible, but the supply will run short within the hour," the golem said, before disappearing into the lines of golems and people.

They had several thousand arrows to start with, but having so many swift archers releasing arrow after arrow, the supply was running dry. Despite the fact that it seemed every pirate had at least an arrow or two in them, they still came on as if unaffected by such wounds.

Then the back line of pirates, these mostly unaffected by the arrows that were targeting the front line with the ladders and such, came into targeting range. There was a bit of a pep in their step that Knox found disconcerting and he found out why as the first one began to cast a fire spell.

Black fire swirled overhead and launched its way toward the wall. Several runes of the wall flared to life, ancient and powerful, stopping the magic attack before it could harm any of the defenders. Knox hadn't known there was any magical protection on the walls, but he'd have to give Mic a big kiss on his metallic cheeks for ensuring they still worked, if it was something he even had a hand in.

The first few pirates made it to the top of the wall and fighting broke out, hand to hand, weapon to weapon. It was during this brief period of time where fighting broke out on the wall that several things happened. First Knox realized why the mass of pirates that were bleeding and filled with arrows didn't stop or slow, or at least Frederick told him why a moment before he might have realized.

"Those are undead, they won't go down easy," Frederick said appearing at Knox's side, several ethereal white spirits garbed in battle armor and weapons floating above him. Knox saw them swoop in to save a weaker golem and take the head off one of the undead, killing it instantly. "Head removal or excessive damage to the brain is the best way to deal with them, aim for the head!" Frederick called out to the battle at large.

Knox took up the call as well and soon the undead pirates were being dropped and their corpses thrown over the side. The next thing to happen was a loud cracking noise as something in the wall gave way against a powerful spray of black fire from Captain Dread himself. Knox hadn't been told but he was sure that they'd just lost a measure of their magical protection.

Sure enough, black fire, black ice, and all manner of blackened elements came hurdling over the wall and in some cases hitting defenders. They lost the most men and women in those first few seconds, but the people of Luminar had been trained to use their powers and they did so with alarming effect.

Powerful wards and barriers began to be erected by the caster types and Knox added his own force to the wards, casting as wide a net of Mystic Veil as he could, followed closely by both Prism Ward and Radiant Glyph—he'd been studying up wards against magical and physical damage, so he did his best attempt to recreate what might have been on the wall.

It was enough that the next dozen or so attacks barely did anything by the time they made it through the wards and such, but still, they continued to come. Which meant Luminar's casters were now tied up in defense and more and more ladders were making it to the walls.

That is when a wave of golems appeared wielding daggers, maintenance golems Knox suspected, they turned the tide by nature of their fierce attacks. Stabbing for eyes and brain damage several were lost within moments, but they kept coming, bringing down ladders with them as they fell into the horde of undead.

All around Knox, battle raged on, archers used up the last of the arrows, while casters kept up as many wards as possible, casting them one after another to maintain the effects as powerfully as possible. It was a hellish nightmare in Knox's opinion, but there was a job to be done here.

Stopping his casting of wards and glyphs, Knox focused on all the forces right in front of him and let loose a powerful Luminous Surge. The undead screamed at the contact with the light and his own troops stood a little taller as they were healed from minor injuries. Next he slammed down his foot and cast Radiant Ground, spider web cracks spreading out from every direction to deal damage to foes and heal allies.

Getting to the front of the walls, where three ladders were resting against the wall, Knox cast Arcane Pulse, ripping them to pieces and sending several dozen undead flying into the casters of the army who were very much still alive. By a rough count it looked like Captain Dread had a force of a hundred or two living and the rest were undead minions. How he was able to maintain so many undead Knox didn't know, but it was a testament to his power.

The battle was turning to their favor and Knox felt that victory must be close at hand as the last of the ladders were turned away and the undead slain.

"We are basically out of arrows, but the last hundred were saved for those with the most skill, like me, and we took care of many of the undead from a distance," Beth said, her own supply of arrows still numbered in the dozens. Reaching down Knox took another dozen, grasping hold of his last arrows, and gave them to Beth.

"They aren't fleeing yet, so make them wish they could," Knox said, knowing that each arrow she fired would be a kill shot.

"Should have left a ladder or two up," Terrim said, sauntering over with his shield raised and ready to catch any projectiles.

"Doesn't look like it matters, look what is coming," Knox said, seeing a dozen undead carrying a massive tree with many thick branches being used as handholds. "I think they are going to try and slam down our gate, between the magic they have and the size of that tree, they might be able to do it."

"Good," Terrim said, a wicked grin on his face. "Let them come."

The ram reached the gate, Beth focusing on the ones carrying it, but they wore metal helmets that completely covered their heads, so none of the shots were lethal.

"I don't get it," Beth complained. "They won't be able to see a damn thing, but they are still making a beeline for the eastern gate. Unfair little asshats wearing those helmets."

"They are being guided by Captain Dread," Knox said, looking over the battlefield they'd managed to kill at least half of the forces against them, with their own side only taking marginal damage and deaths. "I should go challenge him now while his troops are distracted."

"That's madness," Leo said, appearing at Knox's side through the crowd of people all around. "We should maintain our wards, reinforce the gate, and keep weeding down the attackers. They'll retreat soon if they have any kind of sense."

Knox didn't know if his logic was sound or not, but he was itching for a fight and that Captain Dread was the one to give it to him.

"I'm sure I can make it to him without being detected, once he's dealt with the pirates will fragment and no longer be such an organized threat," Knox said, biting his lip as he prepared a mental route through the forces and to Captain Dread's side.

"I'll knock you senseless myself if you take that unneeded risk," came a voice Knox knew all too well—Dernal. "Let the fight play out, I've a feeling this was just a poke and prod at our defenses and not the real battle, otherwise why use such a poor fighting force as these weak undead?"

"Listen to your friend, he speaks sense," came a voice Knox didn't want to hear right now at all—Askar. "Being an Adventurer isn't about risking your life for no reason, have sense boy and follow the example of your elders."

Turning to Askar, Knox froze. The man looked good compared to the sunken eyes and gut he'd had before. Knox had spent enough time not paying attention to Askar that he hadn't noticed how tall he seemed when he stood up straight, or how powerful his muscles seemed now. And beyond that, Knox's sense, detected true power there. Not enough to match Knox's own, but Askar was a step and more above the rest here, minus perhaps Leo and Dernal, who burned like bonfires amidst candles.

Sure, Askar was close to their power, but on the cusp of C Ranked, to use the old measure of power. Leo had grown much stronger since being admitted into the system, somehow catching up to Dernal in almost no time. Dernal seemed the slowest to progress, though Knox knew he went out on hunts and regularly collected essence.

"Don't talk to me about what is right," Knox said, turning away from Askar. He had a new arm, it was a bronze color and looked like an armored gauntlet, but changed physically didn't mean he changed inside. "Able-bodied fighters are needed down behind the eastern gate; I suggest you go there."

Knox knew that his father wasn't moving, but he waited until finally his footsteps could be heard heading for the gate below, he even began to call out and gather a force with him. Why anyone chose to follow his words was beyond Knox, but soon the eastern gate would be well defended. Askar was a Ranger by Path, but he'd taken the branch of Warden, which enabled him to focus on close quarters fighting and natural magics.

The darkness was beginning to fade in favor of the coming sun, but Knox knew this battle wasn't over yet. He had to do something to stop Captain Dread, but everyone seemed dead set against him going out to fight in single combat.

"Fine," Knox said, a little more heat in his voice than he meant. "I can't go fight Captain Dread, but I don't think we should let our gate be damaged either. Let's open the doors and let the undead meet our own forces. We outnumber them now and with the help of our ranged attacks above, it'll be a swift massacre."

"Gates can be mended, it is better that we break them down as much as possible before they get through, it'll save lives that way," Leo said, and Knox knew he was right. Damn him, but Leo was wise beyond Knox's own years. Knox wanted nothing more than to hasten the end of this terrible battle.

That was when everything changed, at the edge of Knox's sight, he'd sensed the Captain Dread working on a spell, but as it unleashed Knox felt the full extent of its power and it was just that, raw power laced with intent and dark magics. It washed over the fallen undead and their wounds, including heads rolling back to bodies, began to knit together. Suddenly, Knox wasn't so eager to open the gate as several hundred fallen undead rose to their feet and screeched at them with a rage they hadn't had in their first life.

Running at the gate full speed, these undead began to climb the walls, finding footholds where there shouldn't be any. Over half fell, but more just kept coming. At the same time the banging of the eastern door began. Knox froze for a second, unsure of how to handle this change in the battle.

Snap out of it! He screamed internally.

"This isn't the end," Knox muttered the words, then closing his eyes he jumped into the fray, several dozens of undead made it to the top and fought with twice as much ferocity as before, but without weapons or care for their safety. No, they just swung out with boney claws and gnashing teeth.

Scarlet, Knox's axe, cut deep and deadly into the zombies, removing heads with each swing and slowly bringing the balance back to their side. But it was too much, the gate was beginning to give as spells were thrown into it as well, the wards set above the wall unable to protect the gate. All of it together was too much, they'd be overwhelmed if something didn't change soon.

"We should abandon the top of the wall, begin moving our forces to the stairs," Dernal said, putting a hand on Knox's shoulder and getting his attention.

He had been so busy fighting and slinging spells that he

hadn't noticed that several of his men and golems had fallen. They were being outnumbered, with a steady trickle of undead.

"Right," Knox said, cutting off the head of one that just made it to the wall. "Move out forces, go, go!"

The calls were made, and it would have been faster, but their side refused to leave dead bodies behind for the undead to claim, so they were forced to fight all the harder to claim their own dead. Who knew what Captain Dread, who so far had worked in the background to change the course of the battle, could do with their own dead if they were returned to his side.

As they retreated more and more undead took to the walls and eventually, they had a force of over a hundred rallied against them. Knox used his spells to great effect, using both Radiant Rush and Ethereal Step to make their escape all the easier, while pushing back the enemy with powerful casts of Arcane Pulse, Luminous Surge, and as they made the final decent off the top of the walls, Void Grasp and Lustrous Chains.

Terrim held the front line, pushing back half a dozen undead at a time alongside four other shield wielding paths, from Mystic Templars to Guardians to a powerful Death Knight Necromancer with swirling bones all around him.

Knox took a second to watch the Death Knight work, he was someone Knox knew little about besides his Path. His name was Hank, and he was a badass. At his side fought a fallen ally, raised to fight as his undead, stabbing and killing other undead with precision. Meanwhile he erected barriers of bone and flesh to defend himself, even going so far as to wrap his opponents with spectral chains that seemed to be made of spirits themselves.

Then between his strikes with his massive sword that he wielded with grace beyond his own size, he shot out Plague Bolts, each one taking chunks off the undead they hit. As his sword swung and struck, it too began to glow with a greenish/ghoulish light. The darkness surrounding his blade was almost the same as what Captain Dread seemed to be using, but this one had more of a green tint to it.

Go Hank, Knox thought as he bisected two undead at once, ending their ability to do much more than crawl forward. When they did crawl forward enough to be a threat, the shield barriers just slammed down boots on heads, ending their lives for good.

Despite all this, the battle was a losing one and Knox realized it just in time for the gate to collapse inward and another rush of undead to come storming in.

"I should have taken care of Captain Dread!" Knox yelled over the din of battle to those around him as he made his way to the ground, where Askar stood in front of a mass of undead, cutting his way through them like a scythe before the grain. All around him people fought and fell, but Askar was a sight to behold, dodging and twirling in a way he would never have believed possible.

"You might have to now," Leo admitted, as hundreds of renewed undead joined the fight. Their losses were still minimal but with such a force against them, it wouldn't stay that way for long.

That is when the horns were sounded in the distance, a melodic sound that filled Knox with a sudden hope. Had she done it? Had she gathered the Ahtora to help after all and so fast?

Suddenly, a large force of undead began to retreat and Knox flexed his sense to get a feel for what was happening, since he no longer held the top of the wall.

A force of two or three hundred had appeared out of nowhere and were closing in on the location of the Dread Pirate. His forces were starting to pull back and out of the complex to come to his aid, but it would be close. If Knox and his people pushed them now, it might be enough to force a retreat.

"Charge after the enemy!" Knox yelled, repeating himself enough times to get the movement going forward as the remaining undead were cut down, some as they fled.

Outside the gate, Knox could see a massive force of Ahtora slinging ice and water at a lone Captain Dread, who for his part withstood the assault with his black mist swirling about him. But the battle was over as far as Knox was concerned, the remaining undead were being cut down as they fled, and several pirates had raised their hands in surrender as Luminar's forces flowed out of the wall and into their ranks.

A small force made it back to Captain Dread, but something was happening, a black mist reaching out and enveloping all of Dread's forces. Then, just as fast as the battle had turned, a flash of darkness later and they stood in the field of battle alone. Even the undead that lay in pieces had gone. Where had he learned such a powerful spell as to retreat from the field of battle with all his forces?

Before he could understand how he'd done it, he felt him reappear at the very edge of his senses, fleeing back in the direction of their port. The day had been won, but the war was far from over.

CHAPTER 26
AFTERMATH

THE DEAD NUMBERED in the dozens and Knox was furious at the fact, but powerless to do anything about it. He spoke with Sarah shortly after the battle ended and learned that the Ahtora were already on the march when she'd found their forces halfway here, saying they answered the call of their king to aid in a conflict of Dark versus Light. Who their king was or how he knew they were under attack, Knox didn't learn.

The Ahtora turned and left as soon as their scouts confirmed the enemy force was in full retreat. Knox had very little chance to even speak with them or thank them for their timely arrival. Instead, he shook hands with Atar and thanked him personally before they left, though very little words were said on his part.

Knox was left to wonder after how they'd been so fortunate and what to do now that they knew their enemy had control of the forces of the undead, and at a scale that Knox didn't think was possible. The first thing he did was hunt down Frederick to ask him about the Path and how someone could manage such a feat.

"From what I've unlocked in the talent trees and my abilities, I haven't a clue how he'd be able to summon forth a massive army of the undead like that, it just doesn't seem possible," Frederick said, confirming what he'd hoped not to hear.

"Then perhaps this powerful technique was something being used outside the system," Knox said, his thoughts pouring into his words. "Mic had mentioned that more powerful beings might be able to resist the influence of the system, if for only a period of time. That might be what we are seeing here and if so, he's tremendously more powerful than I gave him credit."

"I will discuss with the other necromancers, but I fear you may be right, he is a necromancer but doesn't walk the path," Frederick said, shaking his head as if he could hardly believe it.

Next Knox bid Frederick farewell and sought out his father, he had words for him that couldn't wait. But before he found his father, Dernal and Leo found Knox.

"I think it's time to bring the Adventurer's Guild into this," Leo said, and Dernal agreed with one of his trademark verbal expressions.

"Hhrmm."

"What good would that do, but entangle us with another force that might want a hand in Luminar's control?" Knox said, shaking his head all the while. "No, I don't think it would be wise."

"I owe a certain amount of allegiance to the Adventurer's Guild, as do you, it is time to inform them," Leo said. "I will go myself, if you will lend me a stone to keep back the stronger monsters? I'm sure they will be sympathetic to your cause and if we give them access to the training, they'll be forced to admit that they need Luminar reinforced against possible outside influences."

"Dernal?" Knox asked, wanting his closer friend's opinion on the matter.

"It might be the only way forward," Dernal said, siding with Leo. "There is every chance that this first attack was meant to judge our strength and in that, we failed. They took the gate and without outside help we might have fallen this day. It is better that we involve the Adventurer's Guild now, than they come later in force against us as well. Besides, we cannot count on these Ahtora every time, can we?"

"You might be able to, but my point still stands," Leo said. "I know of the Ahtora people, my own people have involvements with them, they are an honorable race that follows the tenets of light and good. The fact that they sent forces before we asked for them tells me they've got their fingers on the pulse of Luminar and wish its safety to be maintained. They are a mysterious people though and their motivations for such remain unclear."

"I agree," Knox said, after some careful thought. He'd already played with the idea of sending Murdoch to the Guild Charterhouse, but Leo would probably be an even better bet. "I've had some dealings with them, and they think that I am an A Ranker, so perhaps that will help in discussions. Just do me a favor."

"What is it?" Leo asked.

"Be careful, the darkness out there is a tangible threat, and I don't want to lose anyone else to it," Knox said. "Be careful."

"I'll accompany him," Dernal said, but before Knox could protest, he pushed through. "I'll keep him healed and together we can deal with monsters instead of just avoiding them. I'll even take Caleb, free you up a bit from worry about him."

"What path did Caleb choose?" Knox asked, having seen him fight a little in the battle he had a good guess but he wanted to hear it for certain.

"Necromancer, Death Knight branch," Dernal said, and Knox nodded, it was as he thought.

He didn't fight like Hank, with shield and sword, instead he'd abandoned his shield and used a massive two-handed sword. However, his armored replacement arm worked well enough like a shield that Knox was surprised when he'd witnessed him fight. It had truly been a sight to behold, all the hundreds of people walking powerful paths and fighting against the undead.

But he couldn't forget those who had, despite being powerful, had fallen to magic, tooth, and claw. Knox said his goodbyes to

Dernal and Leo, bidding them farewell and good luck on their mission.

It looked like he'd need to take Henry back from the group he'd joined, assuming Henry wasn't among the dead. He hadn't had a chance to look through the names yet, truth be told he was avoiding it as doing so made it all too real. Before he could slow down and do that, he needed to find his father and... speak with him.

He found Askar celebrating with several other villagers, holding two glasses and drinking deeply one after the other. Knox had dealt with a drunk Askar many times over, so this didn't stop him from walking right up to him and putting a hand on his shoulder.

"What's that?" Askar said, turning to face the man who'd interrupted his merriment. "Oh, well boy, what do you want?"

"I need to say something," Knox began feeling his throat going dry. Was he really about to say what he was going to say, why did he need to do this? His thoughts whirled and finally solidified in what he wanted to say. "Thank you."

"Thank me?" Askar said, looking as shocked as Knox felt giving the message.

"You stood up and fought against overwhelming odds when you could just have easily fought in the back. Thank you for rallying the forces around yourself, you saved lives," Knox said, his mouth still dry. But having delivered what he wanted to say, he turned to leave.

A clink of two glasses followed by a hand on Knox's shoulder had him turning back around. The others pretended to be busy drinking, but Askar had a serious look on his face, the kind he rarely had except when angry.

"I've... well, I can't say really, but I've got to," Askar said, his words as mumbled and uncertain as Knox felt inside his gut. "That is to say, you fought well too, boy. No. You're a man, you're finally a man and you fought well."

Knox looked his father in the eyes and despite all the anger he felt towards the man, he was changing, if in only small ways, and he could understand that. They exchanged awkward looks for another few seconds, before Askar turned and coughed. Knox smiled at the back of Askar's head and left the Dinner Hall where drinks were being poured for everyone, he still had business to attend to and it couldn't wait.

The drinks everyone was enjoying were a recent invention by Mr. Tome, who'd created a machine that helped along the process of brewing a type of ale from plants found within the growing grounds of the complex. It had been a welcomed change to only having water, clean and clear as it was, variety was the spice of life.

The list of the dead weighed heavily on Knox as he looked over the names. Each one was someone he'd met or knew, some more than others. And among the dead was Brandon, the one that had introduced them to the dungeon and because of that the Ahtora people that had been such an aid this day. Henry wasn't on the list and after going over it, he sought out the older man to inform him that work was still yet to be done.

He found Henry, then Terrim, Beth, Murdoch, and Frederick all drinking away their troubles and he had them gather together, Knox retrieving a drink of his own.

"Dernal is gone again. Henry, I need you back on the team," Knox said. Turning to Frederick he added, "Are you able to come with us, I know you've spent a lot of your time doing your own thing, but we need as many as I can get right now."

Henry just nodded as if he knew as much already.

Frederick on the other hand looked a bit conflicted. "It's just I've kind of been a part of a group that focuses on completing quests and hunts, I'm sure they won't mind if I'm gone for a bit, but what'd you have in mind?"

"I want to go into the labyrinth and not come out until we've taken down another Guardian," Knox said. Seeing the look on his friends' faces he added, "There are only two left, we can do this and once I get the power I'll be able to stand up against Captain Dread, preventing anything like this from happening again."

"What if after all our work, the power from the Emblem thing isn't enough?" Terrim asked, eyeing Knox with a curious expression.

"It has to," Knox said, and he meant it. "This is the only path forward that I can see. Plus, we're getting more essence inside the labyrinth that outside of it, there is no other option that I can see working."

"That doesn't mean it will work," Murdoch said, adding to the discontent that Terrim had started. "We didn't do half bad against him today. I think as long as we continue to improve and repair the defenses on the wall, we have a good chance of surviving the next attack."

"The next attack?" Beth said, raising her eyebrows high on her head. "You think they'll attack so soon after running away with their tails between their legs?"

Knox shook his head. None of this was helping, they needed to get into the labyrinth and start training. "They almost had us, we weren't strong enough. As many groups as we can get into the Labyrinth, we need to do it. We need to be stronger if we hope to hold Luminar."

"What if we didn't have to hold Luminar," Terrim said, shrugging when Knox glared in his direction. "I mean what would happen if we just left, you too Knox, would the Titan Engine stop working, or would it be fine even if it were pirates feeding it cores?"

"Hey there's a point," Murdoch said, nodding. "What if we abandon the city and seek refuge someplace else. Winter is nearly over and now would be the time."

Knox couldn't believe what he was hearing, his lip began to bleed from where he was biting it too hard. Just as he was about to speak another voice joined the conversation.

"There is too much potential for power, learning, and the light of knowledge to allow this place to fall into the hands of someone like Captain Dread. His name alone speaks of a man who wouldn't share his discoveries with the world, much less people that don't follow him. No," Henry said, his voice stern, "it would not do to abandon this beacon of light and knowledge so easily. I stand with Knox; we should train and train as much as possible to avoid failing as we did this day."

Knox shared a look with Henry, smiling ever so slightly. "Thank you," he said, taking his eyes off Henry he swept the group. "If you will stand with me, I will see to it that we are better prepared next time. I promise."

Murdoch stood and took a long swig of his drink. "Let's do this!" He declared and a cheer rose up. "To Death! To Death! To Death!" Until the entire room was cheering the same call to action, the one Knox wasn't exactly keen on, but he understood the meaning behind it. Dedication to the point of death, that was the kind of dedication he needed from them now, so he chanted along with them.

Murdoch spread the word and groups were formed based on their strength and proved combat abilities. The labyrinth was going to be busy and stay that way until the overall level of power in Luminar was raised significantly.

Knox was preparing supplies and goods for an extended period of time in the labyrinth when Sarah appeared in his doorway.

"Sarah," Knox said, greeting her happily. "Thank you again for what you did today."

Sarah shook her head. "I did basically nothing and my friends died while I was away. Did you hear that Angie is injured? I shouldn't have gone; you shouldn't have picked me." She began to cry, and Knox turned in time to catch her in his arms.

Many had been injured, but the healers were working over-time to get them back on their feet, so Knox hadn't even looked at the list that had been prepared of the injured and the extent on their injuries. Squeezing Sarah tightly, he placed his head alongside hers, a gesture she misunderstood. She turned her head and kissed him, Knox let it happen, even enjoying the moment, mistakenly initiated or not.

"I'm sorry," Knox finally said when Sarah released him, but she just shook her head.

"It isn't your fault and Angie will be fine, her leg wasn't that bad," Sarah said, her eyes red from crying. "I just want life to be normal again. No more hunting monsters, no more pirates attacking us, no more darkness making us sick. I just want it all to go away."

"I know, I know," Knox said, pulling her back into a hug and patting her back. The stress of it all had nearly overwhelmed him at times, so he could understand what she was going through to a certain extent. What he couldn't understand was her desire to have everything go back to normal.

Despite all that had happened, Knox was still thrilled that he'd become an Adventurer, and he wouldn't have changed that. He was less thrilled about the becoming a Titan Born and having to pick a Path to walk, but it was as Mic said all those months ago. Despite the limitations Paths seemed to put on you, all was possible under the Titan System. So, all the powerful techniques he'd learned and those abilities he now learned, were all coming from the same place.

Then it hit him, perhaps this Captain Dread had figured out Mic's meaning that all power could be accessed in the system. Maybe, instead of resisting the paths like Knox had assumed he must be doing, he was fully integrated and just learning more than even Knox knew about how to push those abilities to their max. It stood to a certain amount of reason that if he could raise a single dead, that with practice he might be able to form an ability that allowed for raising several at a time.

What did this change though? Knox thought. In the end, he still needed to get stronger if he wanted to face off against such a powerful opponent. And to get stronger, he needed to defeat Guardians.

"Thank you, Sarah," Knox said, kissing her on the cheek this time. "I've got to go now but be careful. I know you don't like all the changes that have happened, but we can't avoid our destiny. Accept what you can and move forward."

Sarah just looked at Knox with raised eyebrows, a hand going up to the cheek he'd kissed as he walked from the room, large pack in tow.

CHAPTER 27
INTO THE LABYRINTH

THE CHALLENGE of monsters in this tier of the labyrinth was something to behold. Instead of being a single type of monster, there were mechanical plants, yes plants, that wrapped around unsuspecting limbs. Then there was a diverse amount of other monsters from rabbits with horns, to wolves as big as horses and everywhere in between. Currently they found themselves locked in battle with several foxes.

Knox weaved through the fight, cutting and destroying critical parts of the creatures as he went. He didn't need to use any magic, hardly any of them had any need to use abilities, until the plants got involved. The animals that this tier had fighting them were weak when compared to the undead pirates they'd faced, however the sudden pulling of arms and legs was enough to throw anyone off during a fight.

One such strand of thin mechanical looking wire, that somehow moved and had sharp cutting leaves on it, wrapped around his leg without him realizing. It pulled and Knox was taken off his feet. Turning he smashed his axe down on the stone floor, normally not a good idea for just any axe, but his axe was reinforced by powerful magic runes, so it would be fine.

The wire severed and Knox stopped moving away from the

group. He turned and used his teleporting step ability to put himself right back in the fight, catching a fox as it dove for Beth's back. Dog appeared a second later, catching another fox and tearing it to spare parts. The fight wore on for another solid minute before all the foxes were taken care of. They were unusually fast; about the only thing they had going for them really.

"That wasn't so bad," Terrim said, he had a hand on his back, likely in pain from having to stoop so low time and time again. The foxes were small and didn't stand more than a pace off the ground.

"Keep your eyes peeled for secret doors," Knox said, directing his comment to Beth, who nodded in turn. "I'm looking but I feel like it's gotten harder to detect with my sense, the magic essence around this level of the labyrinth is so thick."

"Incoming," Murdoch said, swishing his thin blade in an arc and pointing it toward four incoming bulky creatures. Bears, Knox realized with a groan, and big ones at that. Perhaps this floor will be a challenge after all.

Holding out his hand, Knox channeled the magic he'd learned, the force of light and power swirling about him as he cast his spells. Chains shot up around the bears, followed closely by tentacles of shadow and stars. They seemed at odds with each other, but they worked together to slow the targets to a near standstill while the team unleashed hell on the bears.

Heavy metal plates of armor covered the bulky bears so much so that even Beth's enhanced arrows couldn't piece their hide nor could Murdoch's sword or throwing knives do much. Terrim slammed his shield into the lead one, shattering its chains and knocking it back several feet. The armor on these monsters was going to make this battle interesting. Knox moved into place, shield up and ready.

"Shoot the ground beneath them, you can make it harder for them to walk if not damaging them directly!" Knox shouted orders to Beth and Murdoch, just as Frederick stepped forward— Knox had convinced him to go for at least the first few days of their adventure before letting him return—spirits swirled around him, ready to strike out.

With a raise of his hands green ghost like chains rose up and entangled the closest one, draining it of life. Next he let loose Plague Bolt after Plague Bolt, sometimes shooting more than one at a time, channeling through the spirits around him. The bear was pulverized within seconds, but shedding much of its broken armor it lunged forward, snapping the ghostly chains.

Knox moved to intercept the attack, but he was too slow and not needed, he realized with a grin. Frederick's entire form went see through white and he struck out, grabbing the bear with his bare hands and throwing it into the mess of other chained bears. Then, a moment later he shrank back, breathing hard. He'd clearly just done about everything he could and giving it all he had.

"Rest up," Knox said, as two of the three remaining bears broke free of the snares. "Break the ground!" Knox called and arrows slammed into the rocky ground, exploding a moment later. Knox added to the effect by slamming his foot down and activating Radiant Ground over the now large section of rubble.

The bears were mechanically made or creature somehow using gears and all manner of odd techniques, so when they missed their footing, they fell hard, unable to adjust fast enough to the uneven ground. Terrim and Knox tore into the two fallen bears, breaking and sundering armor after countless blows. Murdoch tried to stab one in the eye, but whatever controlled them wasn't located in the head on these particular creations.

The final bear showed some smarts and ran around the broken ground, to come face to face with Murdoch just as Terrim and Knox finished off the last two. Murdoch, sword held before him, swished it to the side, parrying a blow from the bear and tried his best to speak to it.

"You know, bear, you could be a very helpful companion," Murdoch said, the bear didn't slow its attack, swiping paw after paw at his head.

"I don't think he's interested in anything but the dance you two are doing," Knox said, standing and watching the fight play out. Murdoch was faster and even with his thin blade, strong enough and skilled enough to turn away blows from the bear. If only he could do any damage to it, he might be able to win. Instead he tried to talk to it, which proved to be interesting at best.

The bear began to slow its attacks the more Murdoch spoke, until finally stopping all together and regarding the man with a head tilted to the side. It fell back to all four and nuzzled Murdoch on the leg, not lashing out with tooth or claw.

"You didn't," Beth said, laughing. "Did you just tame a metal bear?"

"Should have tried that and replaced Dog," Terrim said, getting a flat look from Dog for the comment, almost as if he understood and didn't like what he heard.

Beth leaned down over Dog, the giant wolf, and pretended to cover his ears. "Don't say such naughty things. All I need is Dog, he does just fine in a fight," Beth said, then looking around and back to the bear she added, "Though a metal bear wouldn't be the worst second companion. I was going to go for a bird for scouting purposes, but..."

"The charm won't hold forever," Murdoch said, he kept glancing over to the bear that on all four stood nearly as tall as Murdoch. "What should we do with it?"

"Maintain it the best you can, let's keep hunting," Knox said. "I'll keep an eye on it and take it out before it can disembowel you."

"Great," Murdoch said through clenched teeth and a fake smile. "I'm so ready to take that chance."

They continued fighting, encountering stronger and weaker metallic monsters than the bears, but still the mechanical bear Murdoch charmed remained loyal to him. It was towards the end of the day, deep within the labyrinth, that they decided to camp out after clearing a particularly difficult group of cats. Thin cuts were slowly being healed by Henry's gentle Celestial aura, but they stung.

Big Dog, Beth's idea for the bear's name, sat beside Murdoch breathing awkwardly into his face. It was funny for several reasons, but most importantly was the breathing didn't seem necessary, the Big Dog only doing it when he was next to Murdoch. They set up camp, and still, Big Dog hadn't turned back to attack Murdoch, whether that was because Murdoch continued to talk to him or what, no one really knew.

"Looks like Terrim and I will be keeping watch in shifts," Knox said, drawing a look from the other three.

"Because of Big Dog," Beth said, understanding crossing her face before the others. "He's afraid it'll turn in the middle of the night, and we won't be able to put it down."

"He's probably right," Murdoch said, side eyeing the bear that continued to just stare at him, breathing hard. "Damn thing is scary as hell, but I'm growing used to his presence."

"I'll take first watch and wake you if I get tired," Knox said, knowing full well he would stay up the entire night and be fine in the morning. He could stay awake without sleep for another week before he'd even begin to feel the effects of needing to rest his eyes. Even then, he rarely fell into a full sleep.

The room they set up camp in had been filled with bunnies with horns on their heads, an oddity that Knox felt like he'd seen elsewhere before. But the biggest thing this room had going for it was the lack of mechanical vegetation that might sneak up on them while they slept. It was enough to offer a measure of comfort, as Knox watched the bear lying beside Murdoch, as if asleep.

Knox didn't plan on leaving this newest level of the labyrinth until they'd conquered another Guardian, which he hoped wouldn't take more than a day or two more. It might be wishful thinking on his part but having just had a conflict and problem occur outside with the pirates, he figured another day or two they might be able to expect some peace.

The very thought of course made him wonder if that was folly, but he had to find a way to grow more powerful and this labyrinth had been presented to him as a way to accomplish such a task.

Power.

In the end it always came down to being more Powerful.

"I need to grow more powerful," Knox mumbled the words to himself, not expecting an answering response, but getting one all the same.

"It won't be power that wins the day," Henry said from where he lay on the ground. Everyone else remained quiet so Knox assumed they must have drifted to sleep already. He'd been in deep thought for nearly twenty minutes, not long enough for Henry to fall asleep apparently.

"It's the only path forward I see," Knox said, keeping his voice low so as to not wake any others.

"And when you have all this power, you will be able to defeat any enemies you encounter?" Henry asked, sitting up in his bed, leaning on his elbows.

"That's the idea," Knox said. "I know it isn't foolproof, but it's the best idea that I can come up with. No matter how clever we are when dealing with that Dread Pirate, there will always be someone stronger. So, power and the accumulation of it is the best course of action."

"Always someone stronger," Henry repeated Knox's words, looking up at him with eyes filled with years of wisdom. "Think about your own words. If there will always be someone stronger, then why is getting stronger the answer?"

"Because I need to be able to protect those I care about, and power will help me do that," Knox said, feeling like he was talking in circles.

"Perhaps trust is the answer," Henry said, laying back down and rolling over.

"Trust?" Knox asked, but Henry had already fallen into a deep sleep, breathing steadily.

What did the old man know about anything, Knox wondered. *What good was trust when your foe could turn your fallen into soldiers for his undead army? I can trust that he will act according to his desires, using his immense power to shove people around as he sees fit.*

Knox shook his head and tried to understand what Henry meant. Trust? Was he saying he should trust in someone else to be able to stand up against their problems? Not likely. Perhaps he should trust himself enough to deal with the threats instead of seeking power as his answer? Perhaps.

Then it hit him like a force taking him right in the face. Trust your party, trust those around you who are also growing more powerful, trust in yourself to make the right decisions. Whether or not that is what Henry meant, Knox felt invigorated thinking about it. But the same issues arose despite who he relied on and trusted. When coming against an unstoppable force, he needed to make himself an immovable object. That was done by the acquisition of power, nothing else could substitute it and he knew it.

The bear never faltered from its lazy snores and when sufficient time had elapsed, Knox woke everyone for breakfast. The bear rose and wondered off to chase bunnies that had begun to respawn, Murdoch watching after him with a curious expression on his face. Big Dog, as Beth called it, was currently eating one of the mechanical bunnies while three others tried to attack its massive, armored plates, making not even a dent on him.

"What are the chances that the bear stays charmed?" Knox asked Beth who just shrugged.

"I don't know how Murdoch's powers work, but I am more than a little surprised they worked on a bear, a metal bear at that," Beth said, finishing off her breakfast as she stood.

"Wonder if it can leave the labyrinth," Terrim said, eyeing the bear with more than a little curiosity. "I'd love to see a dozen or more of them fighting on our side against those pirates."

"We all would," Knox said, smiling up to his tall friend. "Could you imagine the havoc they'd do to their frontline?"

"Murdoch," Knox called out to his friend, and he walked over to see what he wanted. "Keep talking to the bear, I'd love to get him out of the labyrinth and see if we can copy his design. Imagine an army of heavily armored bears. Shoot, they are big enough that even Terrim could ride one into battle."

"I'll try," Murdoch said, clearly not as excited by the prospects as the rest of them. "Here Mr. Bear or uh, Big Dog." The bear looked up from eating his metal feast, took the time to kill the other bunnies attacking it and then walked over to Murdoch. As he had before, he just kind of looked at him and breathed heavily.

"He really likes you," Knox said, barely containing a smile. "Keep him under control, that's an order."

"Right," Murdoch said, rolling his eyes. "Should be easy enough. You are my bear now and you are a good bear, so keep killing stuff for us, but uh not us, okay?"

The bear nodded and Knox's jaw fell open. Had the bear just understood what Murdoch asked of it? "I think it might be smarter than we are giving it credit," Knox said.

"You understand me?" Murdoch asked. Again, the bear nodded. "Are you going to kill us when we least expect it?" The bear shook his head back and forth, seemingly to say 'no'. "Well now that is settled. Knox come here please."

Knox walked over and Murdoch whispered in his ear. "This thing is creeping me out, can't we just kill it?" A low growl escaped the bear's lips and Knox looked at it with a raised eyebrow.

"I don't think he likes that idea," Knox said, chuckling and slapping Murdoch on the back. "Just keep him happy and I think he will be alright. Isn't that right, Big Dog?"

The bear nodded and let its mechanical tongue loll out the side of its mouth as it breathed hard toward Murdoch.

They encountered a new part of the labyrinth midway through the second day. A secret passageway, found by Beth, opened up into massive hallways without any rooms between them. It was much more maze like and after only two turns, each one to the right, Knox decided that perhaps this area would be better explored with some rope or way to mark where they've been.

Luckily Henry had brought some chalk with him and they went back to mark the way they'd come, only to find several more passage ways open to them than had not been there before. After only ten minutes of marking the way and trying to find the way back, they were thoroughly lost.

"Any chance you can sense a secret door to get us out of here?" Knox asked Beth, but she just shrugged.

"Not a clue, but I'll keep my eyes open," Beth said after a momentary pause.

They encountered the first trap two minutes later, a pit opened up before them and nearly caught Big Dog in its spiked bottom. Luckily for him, his heavy footsteps triggered the trap before actually stepping on the false floor. But what was most disconcerting was that Knox hadn't sensed the trap at all, neither had Beth.

"We need to slow it way down and scan for traps, get the poles out," Knox said, and they pulled free the two remaining poles they had, putting them together so that they could trigger traps from a distance.

They did just that, tapping the poles ahead of them while Knox tried his hardest to see traps before they appeared. The problem had to do with how much rich essence and magic covered the entire place, much more than normally filled the labyrinth. So much so that Knox was sure that they must be approaching the Guardian, otherwise why else have such a richly infused area?

Big Dog walked in front of them all, unworried about traps after being hit by two fireballs and not caring. Murdoch stood behind Terrim and Knox as they walked with shields ready, and Beth, Dog, and Henry took the back.

It was because of this line up and Beth's keen eyes that she saw the trap only just as it triggered.

"Watch out!" She cried, a sudden movement of stone behind Knox caught his attention and he turned just in time to see Murdoch nearly squashed by a stone wall. Instead he jumped forward and missed being crushed by a pace or two.

Just like that they were cut off from half of their group. Knox slammed his fist against the stone, but he couldn't even sense anything on the other side, so thickly infused the stone was with magic. So much so that he wondered if he should try to take a sample for study, but no, he had to focus on the problem at hand.

"What now?" Knox said, looking to his friends with a good measure of anxiety and fear. "Shit, this is so bad."

"They'll make for the exit, and we should do the same," Murdoch said. "There has to be a way out of here, we just need to push forward."

"Let me see if I can find the trigger for the trap, maybe the door will go back up?" Knox said, searching desperately for any sign of a switch or a push panel. He found nothing and after five excruciating minutes had to admit that he wasn't going to be opening the stone wall up.

"We should push forward," Terrim agreed with Murdoch and even Big Dog seemed to be nodding his head. Knox on the other hand wasn't sure. What if they were trapped inside the area with no way out and they were meant to solve a puzzle or something? There was no telling what would be expected of them or if they'd make it out in a single piece.

"Let's go," Knox finally said, his sense not helping him find anything and his patience worn thin. "We will find them and a way out of here."

CHAPTER 28
GUARDIAN OF LIFE

IT WAS EASIER to *say* that they'd find their way out, than it was to actually find a way out. Because they were separated from Beth, their best bet at finding traps, and Knox knew that she didn't have any poles to check for traps, it was slow going. He used his sense as best he could, but the poles and Big Dog found more traps than he did, much less any secret doors or ways out of this particularly annoying part of the labyrinth.

After hours of wandering and dealing with traps, Knox began to recognize a pattern. For each three pathways they found with only two options, left or right, there was then another three that would have three paths to choose from. What that meant or how he could use it to his advantage, he wasn't sure, but he decided that just going right over and over again wasn't helping, so he decided that he'd go left, right, left, straight, straight, in a bid to get deeper into the labyrinth and perhaps face off against whatever Guardian laid in wait for them.

The gambit paid off, not so much in finding the Guardian, but in getting them into another section of the labyrinth. Finally, the endless trap hallways gave way to bigger rooms with mechanical monsters awaiting them, the same wildlife types they'd been fighting all of the day before, but these ones seemed to glow with a golden light similar to Henry when he cast Celestial spells.

Facing off against a pack of seven wolves, about half the size of Big Dog but still a deadly threat for someone like Henry and Beth all by their lonesome, Knox could only hope that they were ahead of them now and that clearing the way would make it easier for them if they happened into the same place as them.

But there was no telling, so Knox just focused on the problem at hand, killing wolves. He lunged forward, slamming his shield into a wolf just as it went for Murdoch's leg. His axe came down with powerful light infusing the strike and took the wolf's head off its shoulders as easy as pie.

"Good hit!" Murdoch said, lunging forward himself and striking a wolf in the center where its core functions must be, as it slumped forward unmoving.

"Same to you!" Knox called back, just as Terrim slammed his shield into three wolves, throwing them backward.

He wasn't done yet. The giant of a man stepped forward, shield to the side, and slammed his mighty axe down on the first wolf, ending it. His translucent shield shimmered in the low light, but there was no magic to absorb, so it acted only as a physical shield. That didn't stop him from using it to slam the head of another wolf, just as Knox cast Arcane Pulse on another smaller group.

Focusing on his own bunch of three wolves, Knox tied them up with Lustrous Chains and Ethereal Stepped into their midst, axe slashing and smashing with speed that they couldn't hope to match. This wasn't a fight for him, it was a massacre.

Big Dog hadn't been idle the entire time either, slamming wolf after wolf with its mighty maw, killing them just as fast as they appeared. The stream of wolves cut off after two dozen or so and the fight was won.

Knox couldn't help but think that Henry and Beth were going to have a hard time about it, when he heard explosions ahead and a scream. Rushing forward there was a fork in the path, he took the left, following the sounds that continued to pour in.

After what felt like thousands of steps later, they came upon three figures facing off against two or three dozen mechanical wolves.

Beth was bloody, Henry had summoned his Celestial Guardian and it was likely the only thing keeping them alive for now. It swung and killed a wolf every few seconds, but it was already flickering and fading as Henry strained to keep his Celestial here longer than its set time. The Celestial vanished suddenly and the wolves howled.

"Charge!" Terrim yelled, jumping into the air and slamming down hard beside a bloodied Beth, her Dog at her side but barely able to stand.

Knox was right behind him, Ethereal Stepping into the midst of the wolves his Mystic Armor taking hits immediately as he swiped and killed with reckless abandon. He was seeing red and not relying on his sense, instead he took as many hits as he gave, but each one was a killing blow while the wolves were barely grazing his flesh.

"I can heal that," Henry could be heard saying and Beth grunted just as Knox fought his way into the center.

"You alright?" Knox asked, relief washing over him at seeing Beth in a single piece, damage done notwithstanding.

"Thought I'd finally reached that 'To Death' part you all are always going on about, this labyrinth is a shitty place to split the party."

Knox grinned to hear a touch of humor in her voice. "To Death then," Knox said. "Let's make these wolves pay."

"No," Beth said, pulling out a long dagger Knox hadn't seen her use before. "Let me finish these asshats off. They caught me off guard before, but now that I've got my footing, I'll eat them alive."

Around the same time Beth was saying that, Big Dog, the mechanical bear crashed into a dozen wolves and began to rip them apart, one by one. He took significant damage, but Murdoch fought beside him, saving the bear on several occasions.

Beth watched for a few long seconds before rushing into battle herself. She moved swiftly, maybe even faster than Murdoch could manage now, cutting and dodging with a grace that was almost magical. Knox let himself watch, completely fascinated by the strength of his party and ferocity that they were showing.

Henry had sweat beading down his forehead, but he continued to chant, throwing out helpful spells and heals as the fight progressed. Standing there, Knox thought he was close to understanding something, but he couldn't really put his finger on it. Whatever it was, he knew something for certain, he trusted his teammates and their power.

The fights continued for another eleven rooms before they found the Guardian's chambers. It gave its little speech and Knox stepped up to face it. The room was much the same as the other, but this one had real trees, grace, and a small little pond inside. Half-submerged by the water and looking more tree like than humanoid was the Guardian of Life.

It had eight arms total, stood a pace or two taller than Terrim and had two massive tree trunk thick legs. Of course, it was made of the same mechanical parts as the rest of the labyrinth, but it had a golden glow to it that spoke of power. But in the end it was just another challenge that Knox had to defeat in order to claim his ultimate prize.

"Whenever you're ready," the Guardian said, its voice was mellow, and it spoke more like a gentle grandmother than a Guardian of Life. "I've been waiting for this day for several years and now that it is here, I am glad to see someone like you with the mantle of light. Inquisitive, intellectual, and truly curious. Perhaps you'll even figure out why this labyrinth was created before you finish the challenges?"

Knox had thought about that, but he'd just assumed it was, as Mic hypothesized, a training ground for new Titan Born. Was there more to it or was the Guardian just trying to distract him? "It was created to store a powerful artifact and be a means to train new potential Titan Born," Knox said, gazing into the golden set of six eyes on the towering head of the monster before him.

The Guardian of Life was vaguely humanoid overall, but all the features were overdone and clad in bark-like armor, including the head, which bore a helmet that rose above the top of its head on all sides, ending in a kind of crown. Of course, it didn't help that it had so many arms and massively thick legs to boot.

"True, but I often wondered if there was more to it than that," the Guardian spoke, stretching its arms. "But no matter. Oh look, one of mine has chosen to ally themselves with you, how wholesome. I'll allow it."

The Guardian's gaze fell on Big Dog and the giant bear shrunk back until he said he'd allow it, then it stood tall and suddenly Knox wasn't so sure it was a charm effect the bear was under. No, he was pretty sure the bear had just decided to join their team for the hell of it, how they'd managed to be so lucky he wasn't sure, but they'd take what they could get.

"Let's get this over with," Knox said, raising his shield and readying his axe. If this thing wanted to be like a tree, then he'd chop it down like he had so many before it.

The battle started in earnest, several hands slamming into his shield but others waved about casting some spell or another. Vines of wire and metal shot out of the ground and began to tangle Knox up. Before he could be completely entangled, he cast Ethereal Step followed by Solar Wings.

Flying out of reach of the Guardian's attacks, Knox maintained the spell while he cast Luminous Surge. The light slammed into the Guardian but seemed to do very little damage.

"Light and Life are more similar than they are different," the Guardian said. "You will find fighting me to be a challenge beyond any you've faced before."

"Quit talking," Knox yelled, casting Arcane Pulse just as his wings faded and he fell to the ground. He landed with one knee down and one palm to soften his fall. Focusing on his target he cast Astral Projection to throw off his attacker. Vines shot out and engulfed his Astral Projection, a copy of himself while the real one used Ethereal Steps to put himself behind his target.

The first real blow came then, his axe shining with light, slammed into the back of the Guardian and threw it to the ground, it hit with a mighty thump.

But Knox wasn't finished, he cast Void Grasp followed by Reality Ripple to slow his opponent. Striking one after another he did significant damage to his opponent before he was able to get back up. But as calm as ever, it spoke as it stood, sounding calmer than Knox felt.

"Very good attack," it said. "You have all but worn out my back armor, but what will you do against eight blades coming at you at once?"

Suddenly, long slender blades, reminiscent of blades of grass, appeared in the Guardian's hands, all eight of them. The attack came with speed that didn't match the slow and calm way the Guardian spoke. Knox had to rely completely on his sense to dodge the incoming slashes.

Back, down, left, down, up, right, move, move, move!

It was hard to do much more than dodge, but Knox felt the Guardian slow after several swift seconds of attacking and he took his chance to end the barrage. Slamming his foot down he activated Radiant Ground then casting Radiant Rush, giving himself a speed boost. Those two combined were enough to give him an edge and he cut with his axe as hard as he could, slicing an arm free from the Guardian.

One down, seven to go.

Vines of wire and sharp metal wrapped around Knox's left leg and pulled, sending him flying through the air. The pain in his leg was intense, but he managed to keep from screaming as he rolled into a kneeling position, weapons at the ready.

Blood dripping down his leg, he stood and prepared a spell. His hands shot out as fast as lightning and an arc of arcane energy shot out toward the boss. Knox left no time to chance, instantly teleporting forward after his attack, closing half the distance. He would strike a moment after his magic attack, it had to work.

Arms went up to guard against the magic attack, the blow smashing into the tree-like humanoid with a crash. Arriving a moment later, Knox took two of the Guardian's outstretched arms, leaving him with only five. Back and forth they fought for ground, throwing light and spells back and forth. It was a drawn out battle, but the moment that Knox got one of his arms it was a losing one for the Guardian.

The fight ended with Knox's axe cutting a clean line through the Guardian's head.

CHAPTER 29
DANGER

KNOX COLLECTED the emblem and led his team to the way out. The exit opened up to safety, but Knox sent out a warning for any other teams that attempt this tier, as it had been increasingly difficult and dangerous with the maze section likely being enough to take care of most parties.

When he finally laid down to rest, Knox's dreams were interrupted by a familiar voice.

"I need your help," Mah'kus said, keeping his eyes away from Knox, but still he had the sense that he was being watched.

"Help with what?" Knox asked, wondering why Aetex wasn't here delivering this message.

"Aetex is in danger, I can say little else without interfering, but I feel where he is," Mah'kus said, looking up for just a moment toward Knox and it was like something hitting him with a force of several angry owlbears. Suddenly, Knox was awake and sweat beaded down his forehead in streams. The same exact type of pastry as he'd encountered before sat in his lap. It had been called a donut, if Knox was remembering right.

Blinking, feeling confused and frustrated, Knox ate his donut.

The moment he'd finished the pastry, he felt something odd at the edge of his sense, but after a second it went away and Knox pushed it from his mind to focus on more important tasks. By the time he reached the dedicated workshop, he'd all but forgotten the request Mah'kus had made, it filtered from him as most dreams do given enough time.

That left Knox to do some catch up work for the runic formations he needed to apply to the various arms and armor laid out before him. He started with a sword, using his equipment to inscribe formations of sturdiness, then sharpness, and finally one he'd picked up that allowed the weapon to slice an inch or two off the blade, saving the edge from damage and giving the wielder the ability to cut past non magical armor.

With that blade handled he went on to a focus rod that would be used by casters to narrow in their power and give their spells a bigger punch. For this he required a power source other than the caster, so he took out a Monster Core and affixed it to one end. Then inscribing pathways of positive flow, he ignited the entire rod with power. Once that was out of the way, it was all a matter of adding the right formations to speed the return of spells and empower them by allowing a slight rush of extra energy into each casting.

This particular runic formation had been difficult and worked only every other attempt Knox made, but luck was with him this time and he successfully created a focus rod. If he could take the knowledge he'd gained about transferring and focusing power, then apply it on the fly with his Radiant Glyph spell, the effects he could imagine would be explosive at best, deadly to more than just his opponent at worst.

Still the thoughts intrigued him enough that he kept several pages dedicated to how he could go about trying it. First he'd need to work on extending his Radiant Glyph spell, since the formation was long enough that the spell would fail before getting it all written out in the air. Next he'd need to overcome the pathways issues and find out a way to control flows of power outside an object, perhaps essence air infusion? Just a theory, but he was getting closer to an attempt that he felt might be successful.

That combined with the power he would get from the emblem, Knox imagined himself standing before the Dread Pirate and completely obliterating him. The feeling left him though as he thought he heard his name being called out, followed by a weird pulsing sensation in his head. He quickly located the pulsing as something coming from his sense, so he focused and sure enough that blip at the edge of his sense was back and it seemed angry at him, pulsing over and over again.

"Alright, alright," Knox said, acknowledging the pulsing caused it to stop and he was able to take a deep breath.

He had to go check out the blip, something distant in his memory told him it was important and he couldn't remember why... until suddenly the dream came back just for a moment before trying to leave his mind once more.

"No, damnit, stay in my head. I've got to save Aetex, but why? Where even is he?" Knox rattled off questions as he wrestled with his mind for the memories that wanted to escape him.

The pulsing began in earnest and suddenly Knox saw the connection between the pulsing and Aetex. He was feeling where he needed to go, or at least where an ancient deity thought he should go. As much as he wanted to trust this Mah'kus character, he didn't know him or his true motivations. He had sent Aetex to him, saving his life more than once, surely that meant he ought to give him some leeway in that regard.

Knox had to discuss the matter with Mic, and sit on the throne to see if it helped focus his sense or not. The pulsing stopped when he made up his mind that he would at least talk about it with Mic, then if it felt right, he'd go and try to help Aetex from whatever danger he might or might not be stuck in.

He was suddenly reminded of his first meeting with Aetex, how he'd been captured along with a few other powerful Adventurers. What had Captain Dread done to capture so many powerful Adventurers without him having to even watch over them after. Knox could think of only one thing that would give this Dread so much control over different types of magic and that had to be Runic Knowledge. Captain Dread had access to a vast array of Runic knowledge, Knox would bet his life on it.

This put Knox in a difficult position. If he were to do anything for Aetex, what are the chances he won't just end up in the same predicament as Aetex? The man was much stronger than Knox, that much was true. But Knox didn't have to go alone either, perhaps he could bring his party. But no, that would just put them into the same risk and danger potential he feared for himself.

Plus, there was the need to finish the last Guardian and get the final emblem piece. Perhaps if he did that first he'd be strong enough to deal with whatever Aetex faced? That was if Aetex made it that long, there was no telling what threat he was in or how urgent it must be that Knox go save him. A feeling settled over him and he knew that it was urgent.

"I've got a problem," Knox said. "Move off the chair and let me see something."

"As you wish," Mic said.

Knox sat and pulled up the display of the area that was currently covered in the Titan System. It had grown substantially, and it was clear that the Guild Charterhouse and the Mire's Gloom Dungeon had to be within its grasp now. He even noticed several blips, though they got smaller the further away from the Titan Engine they were, making it difficult to get a real count. He could tell that the pirates had much more in way of population to throw at Luminar, so why hadn't they during their previous attack?

It also looked like a healthy population had returned to the Mire's Gloom Dungeon. Many hundred little dots moved around here and there. Knox looked for a group of two or three roaming toward either location, but he found only larger groups roaming about, none of them close to Luminar. That was, until a group of three appeared almost out of nowhere half a day's journey away from the base, as if they were coming out of stealth. Knox marked the group for investigation and went back to looking over the map.

A large purple dot that he'd been all but ignoring until it began to pulse as well, appeared on the map. It was to the east, but not so far as to be in pirate lands and there was something else. As Knox focused the map shifted and a network of tunnels beneath the ground showed themselves, inside one of these tunnels was the dot that Knox knew to be Aetex.

He was surrounded by at least a hundred little blips that Knox knew to be monsters, they had a different color and look to them over normal humanoid dots. It was more a feeling than a look and hard to explain when connecting right into the system. Moreover, Knox just knew it to be true, some type of monster had taken Aetex capture, and monsters weren't known for keeping around food for long.

"I fear I need to leave for a day or two," Knox said as he stood. "Get me several days of supplies put together for two people and tell me you can see this blip here." Knox gestured to the general location it had been on the map.

"Ah yes, I can see it now," Mic said, sitting back in the command chair. "You are going into the tunnels? Be careful, I sense strong monsters that still lurk below."

"I assumed as much, I wish there was anyone strong enough to come with me, like Dernal or Leo, but I've got to do this on my own. I can't risk bringing my group and then having to protect them. I need to be able to cut loose and use all my power." Knox wanted to keep speaking, keep convincing himself this was the right move, but it was hard as he truly didn't know if it was a wise decision.

"I will put Luminar on high alert," Mic said. "Are you sure you don't want to take some golems with you? I can think of three powerful enough to be less of a liability."

"Right," Knox said, snapping his fingers. He'd take a black orb to keep stronger monsters back and take the three pirates as his backup. He'd grown accustomed to them, but it wouldn't be the end of his world if they lost a few parts. He was sure he'd be able to get them repaired if anything should happen.

Knox left at a run, reporting to the wall sentry to gather a force of two or three parties ready to fight, then beelined it for the three he'd seen on the map. His suspicion was confirmed the moment his sense washed over three familiar presences.

Dernal, Leo, and John.

"Wondered how long I could hide all three of us. When did you notice our approach, been a while you think?" John asked, seemingly more frustrated at his ability than excited to see Knox.

John laughed suddenly. "Come here you lug," he said, taking Knox into a tight manly hug. "We searched quite a bit for you, how the hell you end up way out here? They've told me bits and pieces, but Dernal seems to think it's a story you ought to tell."

Knox gave him the short version as they walked back toward the complex and the safety of its walls. John was hooked on every word, nodding his head at the mention of the Titan Engine.

"You should see people at the ole Gloom, it's like their world has ended. They can't use most of what they've learned for years and can't figure out how to access this training mode that the quests say is needed to progress." Leaning in, John cupped his hand to say, "But I got that information thanks to you." Then, standing with his back straight and lowering his hand, he said, "I am walking the Path of the Rogue, focusing on the Shadow Walker branch. My ability to stealth others was a big surprise, I just played around with how stealth, the ability not the general state of my being, worked and it worked."

"That last bit makes little sense," Knox said, frustrated that he hadn't figured out how to modify his own abilities and spells past shoving a little more mana into them. Although, if his idea for a Glyph focus came to be, he'd be able to take a big punch out of something and that counted for a lot.

"Where are you going?" Dernal asked. Though Knox hadn't done anything to prep, not taking a backpack or anything, somehow Dernal sensed his intentions.

"Someplace unsafe, you guys want to come?" Knox said, then launched into explaining Aetex being in danger and what Mah'kus was or at least what he appeared to be. Leo had the most questions and Knox filled him in as best he could. John was interested in the donut and wanted Knox to describe it better, which he tried but John wasn't convinced that it could taste as good as Knox said it did.

"I can only speak for myself," Leo said. "But I would like to accompany you on this quest given by the gods themselves. It seems only right that we should aid those who have aided you thus far."

"Hhrmm," Dernal said, looking to John.

"Well don't look at me like that, I wanted to see this cool new city our friend Knox has set up, can I do that before I commit to a quest off into the unknown?" John asked, looking flatly at Dernal who continued to silently stare at him. "Of course, I'll help," John blurted out and stuck his chin out toward Dernal.

"Good, let's run the rest of the way there, I don't know how much time we have," Knox said, and they were off toward Luminar.

Knox got several packs extra put together and within the hour they were ready to depart, a party of seven.

"Don't see whatcha need us for?" Borris complained, his hand messing with something under a flap of fragment.

"Stop that," Knox said, realizing what was happening. Borris just smiled and removed one of his four hands.

"You are the strongest among the golems, I need you," Knox said, assuring himself as much as them.

"Fascinating," John said, reaching out and touching Vlad in the face. Vlad looked toward Knox as if to say, 'really?' but Knox just shrugged.

"Get back," Vlad growled, and John jumped back lithely.

"We would prefer to stay, but we will do as you command," Edgar said, bowing his head slightly.

"Good, grab these packs and try to keep up as best you can,"

Knox said, they were going to take the distance at a run and try to make it to Aetex by first light the next morning. The black orb that thrummed with power inside one of the bags he'd given the golems would ensure only weak monsters got in their way, making the going that much easier.

Prepped in every sense of the word, and after giving John a suit of leather armor that would be several times stronger than what he was using, they were off. The air was cool, but not cold, and as they ran into the dark, Knox let his sense take over. Feeling the ground beneath his feet, the crunch of leaves where his foot fell, the sway of the branches, the growl of predators wise enough to stay out of their path, and so much more came to him as he ran.

Keeping his mind on the tunnels he'd seen on the Command Chair, Knox informed the group to look for any cracks in the ground or places where they might gain access below. The ground shakes had continued throughout the winter, but none so terrible as the ones that had released the large amount of black goo monsters. It made him wonder if the tunnels would be filled with those same black goo things as had come from below the ground or if they were safe from the darkness for now.

It wasn't until the first light of the morning came upon them and they neared the location where Knox's sense told him he'd find Aetex, that something happened. The ground began to shake, and massive cracks appeared in the ground, but no black ooze appeared. Instead, many hundreds of tiny red spiders came crawling to the surface.

"Gross," John said, making a face at the spiders. "Why did it have to be spiders? I hate spiders."

Leo stepped forward and with a wave of his hand he incinerated the lot of them. Fire swept out of his outstretched arm in a way Knox had never seen him use it before. Normally he worked best when fire sources were already present, but those limitations didn't seem to apply to system learned abilities and spells.

Of course, Knox knew better than that. The weeks and

months of training that allowed him to use his own magic so casually spoke to the process needed to learn how to manipulate the magic and internal powers. It was all more complex than just calling on the spell, no, it involved doing several steps all at once. Like you would with certain instruments, controlling your breathing, what you are pressing, and the movement of your tongue as one example. Another that came to mind was stringed instruments or traveling bards that sung a song, played a lute while controlling the pattern of strumming, what notes for which fingers and more all at once.

It was a casual thing for them to do once they'd mastered their trade, but at first it seems near impossible to achieve. The same could be applied to learning spells and skills or abilities as the system called them. It took a certain amount of time to get familiar enough with them that you could do it with very little thought. Leo had shown he had truly spent the time inside the time dilation wisely, learning the ins and outs of his spells.

"Going down?" Edgar asked, looking over the edge of the large crack in the ground and turning back to Knox.

"Let's do it," Knox said, stepping forward and activating Solar Wings, he had just enough space to lower himself into the crack. It went down some hundred paces, narrowing the entire time, Knox barely made it to the bottom. His wings provided enough light for him to see the thirty paces high and round tunnel he'd entered through the crack. His sense told him what direction to go, just as everyone else began to fall down all around him. Knox stepped aside as one by one he was joined by his party members. His wings faded and they were plunged into darkness.

CHAPTER 30
RESCUE

LEO CREATED a ball of fire that floated over them, providing limited light in a circle around their feet. Knox reached out with his sense and could faintly feel Aetex at its max distance. He was weak and covered in something.

"I've got a read on Aetex, stay ready," Knox said. "I don't sense anything else with him but that doesn't mean we are alone."

Everyone took up combat positions, pulling out weapons and focuses before following Knox's lead forward. From what he could see the tunnel was made of dirt, like something an animal would burrow out, but whatever had done it hadn't been around for some time. Knox knew this mostly in part to the many hundreds of tiny spiders and webbing that covered the outer edge of the tunnels as well as draping down and brushing against them as they walked.

"Spiders," John spat the words, squishing on under his boot. "I hate spiders."

"We know," Leo said, his fireball still floating above him in an impressive show of power and concentration.

Something moved ahead, just out of sight and Knox's sense latched onto it for the moment or two it was able to be detected.

"Spiders," Knox called out just as several new somethings appeared at the edge of the light.

"We know," John said, too busy smashing smaller spiders to notice the three massive ones that appeared before them.

"Focus up," Dernal said, nudging John, who groaned and made a 'ugh' noise when he saw the giant spiders circling them.

"I'm going to need a bigger boot," John said, twirling his daggers as he faced off against a spider in the back.

"Hit them hard, we are stronger," Knox said, scanning them with his sense now that they weren't stealthed. He'd wager they were D Ranked Monsters by their auras, but more disturbing was what his sense picked up for the barest of moments near Aetex. Another spider, a large one with an aura as powerful as Aetex.

One problem at a time, Knox told himself as he readied his spells.

The first spider lunged, followed by three more nearly at the same time. Dernal slammed one back with Arcane Pulse and Knox followed suit with Luminous Surge, the bright light showing them a sea of different sized spiders between them and Aetex.

"Shit!" John shouted, his eyes going wide. "Did you guys see all of them? Bring the fire, Leo, burn them down!"

Leo didn't need to be told twice. Fire filled the corridor and one of the spiders fell within moments, the other smaller ones around burning and dying just as fast.

Knox slammed down his foot and provided them with able light as the ground itself began to glow and damage the spiders. With this new light it was easy to see that they were outnumbered many to one, but the four spiders that had come near to them seemed to be the strongest, so he kept his focus on them for now.

A spider came in close and Knox caught it on his shield, legs came over the top of his shield and for a moment he could understand why John disliked spiders so much. Cutting with his axe he gave the spider something to think about, the other legs withdrew at the same moment.

Back and forth they fought, killing any smaller spiders that dared cross their path as they battled against the four strongest spiders. Eventually the last one fell to blade and magic, leaving them a path forward. The spiders seemed to sense they were no match for them, moving to the side as they came, but closing around them and staying at the edge of Leo's fire ball.

The path forward ignited with an eerie green glow as they entered a vast chamber filled with hundreds of cocooned things attached to the outer walls. Long stoney pillars emanated the green glow and they just about filled the massive room, providing ample light to see by. It wasn't until they'd made it to the center of the room that Knox realized that what he'd taken for massive curved stone pillars were in fact something else completely.

The spider legs flexed and the room rumbled from it. A spider the size of a small manor house was dug into the dirt and stone, only its face and legs in the room, the rest of its massive body either in the dirt or some other section of the room.

"We've made a mistake," Knox said, pulling power into himself and readying a spell. "A big, big mistake."

"No," John said, his eyes following the legs until he saw the massive face with three sets of fangs feeding into a massive maw of darkness. Smaller legs sprouted out from the massive legs, more like hairs than actual legs, but they carried one of the hundreds of cocooned figures to the maw. They watched in horror as it began to suck not only the life from it, but its very essence. Knox had a clear view with his sense and eyes to see the process.

"Where is your friend, we need to be quick," Dernal said, his eyes flicking from side to side.

Knox pointed at a figure about twenty paces up, a massive cocoon that emanated power. "He's weak, but I can still sense his massive pool of power, if we can get him free, he will be able to fight with us."

"This isn't a fight we want," Dernal said. "Get him and we go as fast as we can out of here."

Knox nodded. "Attack while I retrieve him. It should draw its attention enough for me to get him."

Dernal looked at him for a long second before nodding that he would attack the spider that was clearly a B Rank or higher, besides that, it was large enough to eat them all whole.

But that wasn't how it fed, Knox realized as he snuck closer to the maw and where Aetex lay. The spider flicked a massive arm towards Knox, making the room shake and catching Knox nearly off guard with the speed it had moved. However, his sense was powerful, and he Ethereal Stepped out of the way just in time. Appearing only a couple paces from the far wall, Knox began to climb.

It was a nasty sticky mess, but the rocks behind it all was enough for him to grip to and make it higher. Eventually, and several moments after they finally began to attack the legs, Knox reached Aetex.

"You alright?" he asked as he pulled off the threads of white from the massive man's face.

He didn't answer and his face was several dangerous shades paler than Knox had ever seen. Using a boot knife, he cut the rest of the strands as the very room around him began to shake and crumble.

Knox fell to the ground, Aetex with him, as the closest leg swiped the entire wall clean, squashing several of its own cocooned meals.

"Get up, snap out of it!" Knox yelled at the massive man, but though his eyes were open, he remained motionless. Putting a hand under his arm, he lifted him easily, C Ranked attributes more than enough to handle his weight.

Reaching Dernal, just as Leo unleashed a massive dragon of flame at the spider and John just straight up disappeared. "I've got him," Knox said, looking around for an exit but not seeing it any longer.

"It's blocked the exit, we've got to kill it or dig our way out,"

Dernal said, he seemed resigned to their fate, but Knox knew he still had some fight left in him.

"Heal him as best you can, I'll handle this spider," Knox said, his hand going to one of his suppression rings, but he stopped himself, it wasn't time for that just yet.

"Bring the pain!" Knox yelled, snapping the three pirate golems out of their shocked stupor. They looked to him, the exit that was no longer there, and back to Knox.

"Right," Edgar said, fire beginning to form above him. "Fight or die, I choose fight."

"More like fight and still die," Vlad said, but he rushed forward a moment later, slamming into one of the legs with impressive force, each of his punches breaking into the spider's leg and coming out with glowing green ichor.

Meanwhile, Borris began to throw out ice lances that stabbed through another leg. The spider had its hands full, but Knox knew attacking the legs would be a frivolous task, he needed to bring the pain to the brain. Rushing forward, he motioned for the golems to follow and trusted they would.

He reached the point on the wall where thirty paces up the mouth of the spider hissed and spat green ichor. Using Ethereal Step he brought himself close enough to strike out as he began to fall back. His axe cut one of the fangs right off, it sprayed more green and Knox began to fall. He cast Solar Wings and swooped in for more action.

Fire, stone, and Vlad rushed in front of him, slamming into the face. They'd gotten the hint after all. Vlad was no match for the speed of fangs or the power they displayed, he was thrown back and hit hard on the stone ground. The elemental attacks did a bit better, scorching one fang and bloodying another. Through the smoke and fire, Knox appeared, axe raised to strike.

At some point he'd lost his shield, so he held onto his axe with two hands and dove it hard into the spider's face. It wasn't enough, the blow barely penetrated its carapace, but it did hit an eye, ruining one of about a hundred of the black beady things.

"Be careful!" Came a booming voice below, Aetex was awake once more. "It has a paralyzing venom." Knox dodged another fang and cut another dozen eyes apart before his wings failed him and he went flying down toward the ground. He planned this and was about to land when a massive form caught him.

Aetex, looking pale but pleased with himself, gave Knox a knowing look. "Be careful young one," Aetex said. "We've got what it takes to beat this foe, but it will take all of us working together." With that Aetex set Knox on the ground, then the both of them dodged to either side to miss being struck by a leg.

Knox could see how they could do damage to such a massive foe, but to defeat it seemed unlikely. Pushing the unhelpful thoughts from his mind, Knox set about trying to figure out how to kill such a monster. They had access to the head, that meant something, most monsters needed a head to survive, so it should be the focus.

Aetex must have worked out as much as well, because he was currently a glowing mass of power flying right for the head at incredible speeds. But even with how fast he was, the legs blurred with equal speed, slamming into him and throwing up major debris as he crashed into the wall. If not for Knox's sense he'd be in real trouble, which meant that his party members would be completely outclassed.

Looking around, he saw that to be the case. John was disappearing and reappearing as fast as he could, but still he was bloody and had taken a major beating from a leg or two. Dernal had summoned forth his own Celestial to fight against the spider, and its shields were the only thing keeping Dernal from being crushed currently.

Leo on the other hand seemed to be doing pretty good, he was wreathed in fire and flame, shooting out and scorching any leg that dared get close to him. The golems were fairing a little better, Boris had lost two arms, Vlad had a major dent in his chest, and Edgar was missing his jaw.

How far had he gotten exactly on focusing his power through

the glyphs? Not far enough, but it should pack a powerful punch if he could get them set up right in front of the spider's face. That was the real issue then, how the hell was he meant to get that close and set off his attack?

"Aetex," Knox called out and the man appeared at his side several moments later, looking rough but still way better than he had when he was cocooned.

"You've got a plan?" Aetex said, sweat clearly dripping down his forehead as he watched the devastating fight play out.

"Part of one," Knox said, he cut off to dodge, pushing Aetex just out of the way as well. "I have a runic formation that should amplify anything I throw at it several times, but it'll take a while to get up and there is no guarantee that it won't blast us such as bad."

"Risky plan with a small chance of success?" Aetex asked, nodding to his own question. "I'm ready to make it happen. You rally our forces, and I will see about punching its face to give you time. Strike in exactly one minute," Aetex said, the air booming around him as he called his aura closer to him and he shot off into the air.

The room was lit with so many lights from several different paths, that it was slightly disorienting, but Knox managed to find the golems first, giving them the message, then he spoke with Dernal who promise to rally John and Leo at the right time. With only ten seconds to spare, Knox began to run for the boss's face. He'd have to fly up and find a place to hold on, unless...

He activated Solar Wings, but let his mind go back to the time he'd spent learning it. He imagined the part of the ability, or spell in this instance, that controlled the length of time and mana cost. If he focused on that and infused more mana so he could get additional time. Since mana wasn't his most major concern right now, he'd never truly run very low so far, he figured he'd be alright.

The wings flared around him with yellow light and he was lifting off the ground and into place just in time. Aetex appeared before him and started punching the spider right in the face. All of its fangs blurred as they tried to capture its prey once more. It was a losing fight, Aetex took his first scratch after only seconds and Knox knew he needed to hurry. Aetex slowed but kept fighting.

Knox focused on the task at hand and let his mind go over the Radiant Glyph learning that he'd done with the fake Titan Gowlen. He knew what it would take for him to extend the Glyphs but it was going to be painful while already using a taxing spell. It involved superior focus and of course, more mana. His head swam a little as he flushed a large amount of mana into the start of the spell and kept it flowing in as he began to write.

Line after desperate line, he wrote and he failed. But because of the nature of inscribing runes with Radiant Glyph, he was able to erase his mistakes and correct them with time and care. Aetex went flying past him and Knox's sense screamed at him to move, but he remained.

A leg came crashing for him, but suddenly Aetex was back, holding the leg in place with impossible strength. Fire, ice, and stone came hurdling through the air at the spider as the others joined the fight.

You can do this! Knox thought furiously. His focus remained intact and finally he finished the final line. The runes blazed in front of him, like a shield against the force of the spider, but Knox knew the truth. It would be fragile and break upon contact, so he needed to act fast.

"Throw everything you have at it!" Knox screamed above the din of battle. He'd said as much to them all before starting his plan, but it never hurt to be thorough.

Knox could feel the force of the attacks coming behind him as he readied his own. His head burned and for the first time he knew what it was like to go below ten percent of his mana, it hurt like hell. But he pumped every last bit of his power and force of will into the next Luminous Surge, knowing its power would be multiplied severalfold.

The attack unleashed just as several others screamed past him and hit the Radiant Glyph. Power swelled and pulsed outward, throwing Knox back just as his wings faded from long use. He was falling but he kept his eyes on target, not wanting to miss it. The spells rolled together into something massive and deadly, then it shot out in all directions. Shit, this is what he was worried about.

He had no more mana left for now, so putting up a ward was out of the question. He just had to weather whatever was coming. Deep and rhythmic channeling cut through the din of battle. Dernal was chanting and a barrier was appearing around him and the others. Knox rushed over just in time for it to solidify as the wave of energy crashed into it.

A shattering sound followed by pain was Knox's entire world for several long, dark seconds.

The disorientation and darkness lasted only a moment, a force pushed out from all directions and debris went flying as Aetex did some ability to free them from the rubble. The room still had a faint green glow to it, but it was dimming fast, which could only mean one thing. Checking his status, he found that he had indeed received a massive dump of essence. Just like that, they'd slain the monstrous spider.

"We did it," Knox said, looking around the cavern to see that most of the wall the spider had been in was sagging down. "Any chance someone wants to look for its Monster Core?"

"Do not fear," Aetex said, standing upright despite several injuries and a torn outfit. "I will retrieve the precious item and deliver it to you. But first," Aetex turned and held a hand outward, helping Knox to stand again, "thank you for saving me."

With that, Aetex was off, flying toward the fallen spider and into it with a sickening squelching noise.

"Your friend is gross," John said, dusting himself off as Dernal laid down a heal on him. He was bloody in most places and looked like he'd taken the worst of it. "But I wouldn't mind collecting my share of such a powerful Monster's Core."

"The golems didn't make it to the shield," Knox said, realizing the fact at the same time he paid attention to his sense long enough to get a lock on them. Like his other senses, if he didn't focus it was a wonder what he could miss.

He made his way over to the first pile of rubble that promised to have Borris underneath it if his sense was any good at telling them apart, which it was most days. Sure enough, as he cleared away a large rock and several piles of dirt, he found Borris. It took another few minutes to get him completely free, he had only a single arm left but luckily both legs, so he could walk.

"That hurt and I can't even feel that much," Borris said, putting a hand to his head as if he had a migraine. The other two golems, Vlad and Edgar were in better shape, despite many dents and rips in their armor.

Aetex appeared shortly afterward with a Monster Core the size of Knox's palm. "Something so small from a monster so big?" Knox asked, feeling for the massive amount of essence inside. It was there alright, pulsing with untapped power.

"It was set to the base of the area where the head connects to the body, if it hadn't been so far back it would have been destroyed. Your attack really did a number to that spider, good thing I weakened it from our prior battle," Aetex said.

Knox wasn't sure if he was bragging or being serious. Had the spider been weaker than it could have been? If so, Knox had to be one of the luckiest people in the Wyrd.

"Let's get back, and in the meanwhile, you can fill me in on why you were out hunting giant spiders," Knox said, and he wasn't sure if it was his imagination or the low lighting, but it appeared that Aetex blushed slightly on hearing his words.

CHAPTER 31
GUARDIAN OF DEATH

"YOU WERE INVESTIGATING THE GROUND SHAKES?" Knox asked, clarifying what he'd just heard from Aetex.

"That's right," Aetex said, his color was returning, and he looked much better after Dernal healed him a bit more. "Part of my mission is to anticipate threats, which I can't do if I don't know what I'm up against. I found an infestation of spiders and thought perhaps one of them were the cause of the shakes, perhaps displacing enough ground to cause the tunnels below to collapse. But I'm not certain that monster could have done more than a few localized ground shakes."

"Then what is causing them, something to do with the darkness most likely?" Knox asked, it made sense to him to lump them together as dark ooze had come up from the ground so something about the event was tied together.

"I'm more unsure now than when I started investigating it. For now, I think the tunnels, whatever their prior use, will be free of giant spiders for a time. Perhaps we ought to explore and see where the tunnels lead?" Aetex posed the last bit as a question and Knox shook his head.

"No," Knox said. "We've got more important matters to attend to, speaking of which, would you be okay to go into the labyrinth with me to clear out the last tier so I can face the final Guardian?"

"I can't see why not," Aetex said, slapping Knox on the back in what was likely meant to be a friendly gesture, but nearly took him off his feet.

With Aetex on his team he'd be able to take out any mobs with ease. If only he could help with the Guardian, but that wasn't a thought Knox kept for long. He'd faced off against five of them so far and each one was a challenge he overcame, this last fight would be no different.

"Give me a day to prep and I'll send word," Knox said, Aetex nodding.

They'd arrived back and Knox was going on his way to get cleaned up.

The party consisted of Terrim, Aetex, Beth, and Dernal, with both Frederick and Murdoch claiming to be too busy and Henry not needed because Dernal was stepping in.

The final tier had roaming mobs of blackened skeletons that shot powerful blasts of energy and wielded long blades that cut through armor with ease. They were still visibly mechanical, but they'd been darkened by Death essence to the point that you could barely tell.

This being the first time Knox had Dernal semi-alone as Aetex led the charge into the labyrinth, killing off monsters just as fast as they appeared, Knox turned to engage the man in conversation.

"How'd the trip to the Guild Charterhouse go?" Knox asked, keeping his voice low but even.

"They are a bit of a mess right now, missing several top Adventurer's Guild members but they heard my message and agreed to send someone out to speak with you. Not sure what I expected them to do, but Leo was insistent that we report every-thing," Dernal leaned in a little closer. "Though I didn't let slip about the new dungeon, perhaps we can go check that out before it gets all regulated."

"Leo didn't say anything either?" Knox asked, surprised as

Leo seemed pretty 'to the book' when it came to Adventurer Guild rules.

"I paid him the finder's fee and he let it go," Dernal said.

"Never would have taken Leo for someone who worried about coin," Knox said, mostly to himself but Dernal grunted and responded.

"He's got financial responsibilities the same as all of us," Dernal said.

They walked behind everyone, Dernal's black hair tied tight into a bun and his solemn face peering ever forward as if sensing something.

Knox let his own sense go out and wash over everything. He sensed Aetex going to battle just in front of them against a pair of swift death golems. One seemed to be about to strike him, but at the last moment Aetex flicked a finger at it and blew it apart. Further ahead there were a few traps, not that Knox was worried about them as the last two Aetex just walked right through without any harm. And even further a more intense aura that Knox knew to be a Guardian.

"That was fast," Knox commented. "Looks like we are at the Guardian already."

"I thought that might be what it was, seems pretty strong, you sure you've got this alone?" Dernal said, which got Knox to give it another look. Truly the aura was powerful, beyond any that he'd sensed in the Labyrinth before, and it was so filled with a sickly green aura that it about made Knox throw up when he narrowed in on it.

"I'll manage," Knox said, but that wasn't how he felt.

Aetex finished clearing the way to the Guardian but stopped short of attacking it.

"I think you are meant to challenge this fellow," Aetex said, his voice booming from only twenty paces away.

Knox stepped forward ready to hear the speech and the Guardian and take in the surroundings. It was a large cave with glowing purple mushrooms giving very little light to see by. The

Guardian was robed in some kind of cloak made of tiny bits of weaved metal, it didn't glimmer in the light and had a deep darkness around it, but Knox could sense the metal beneath it. The hood came up and covered a face that Knox couldn't make out and in its hands it held a blade as tall as Terrim.

No speech came, despite Knox stepping forward and even clearing his throat a few times, so he decided to address his foe first.

"I've come for the last piece of the emblem that you are appointed to guard," Knox said, but still the Guardian remained silent. Until finally after an entire two minutes of silence, a voice emanated forth, slow and painful.

"Challenge me at your own risk, for I am Death and I claim all in the end."

With that, his sword flashed and if not for his sense Knox would have been caught by the blow. Instead, he landed in a crouch some ten paces away after doing a short teleportation. He couldn't do that trick until he'd awaited the cooldown, so he needed to be paying attention if he wanted to avoid being cut into two. Jumping to the side, he dodged another blow. They were fast but also the wind-up was slow, meaning if Knox paid attention, it was easy to see where he was telegraphing the hits toward.

Keeping his sense and his eyes wide, he readied his axe for an attack. Dodging left, he gained ground, for the reach of the monster was great. Ducking low and to the left he put himself within range and swung. His blow hit the metallic weave of its cloak and bounced back as if hitting something solid.

That left him open to attack and the blade cut into his Mystic Armor, shattering it, but saving his actual armor from taking the hit. Rolling fast back to his feet, Knox groaned at the blunt force the blow had given him. His shoulder ached and he rolled it to try to loosen it back up.

But the monster wasn't waiting for him, queuing up another strike it swung for Knox's neck. Knox was ready, raising his shield just in time to catch the blow. However, his shield wasn't up to the task, it shattered from the blow and went flying in different directions. It stopped the blow and Knox was grateful of that small victory, but now he had no shield.

He looked to Terrim, thinking perhaps he'd borrow his magic absorbing shield, but he was far enough away that he wouldn't be able to easily grab it, nor did he know if that counted as accepting aid. Losing the emblem because he broke some rule would be ruin enough, so he decided he was on his own.

The Guardian reached back and readied another strike, but this one was odd. Knox was far enough away that he wouldn't be hit by it, so he relaxed a little and prepared to cast a spell. However, at the arc of the swing, a thin line of black energy shot off and struck Knox in the chest mid cast. The backlash from the spell and the pain in his chest were enough to drop him to a knee momentarily.

Still, the Guardian pressed its advantage, swinging once more and striking Knox just as he made it to his feet. He went flying backward, more of his Mystic Armor spell shattering as he hit the far wall. This opponent was strong, but Knox had just killed an impossible foe; what was one more?

Rolling to his feet just in time to see another attack coming, Knox shot out a Luminous Surge and the Guardian faltered, crying out in pain.

"A little light hurts, doesn't it?" Knox yelled, casting the spell again but with even more power than before. The Guardian screamed again, but continued to attack, stopping Knox from getting a third cast off. If it were possible, the attacks seemed to be coming faster and even the telegraphing seemed less noticeable when it only lasted half a second. Leaning fully into his sense, Knox danced around the blade, letting loose his spells in between dodging.

The fight continued on with neither side gaining any great upper hand over the other. Knox's spells were hurting it, but his physical strikes did nothing. Meanwhile, Knox had been forced to recast his armor spell as the final bits of it were blown away. That cost him precious seconds and he found himself back on his ass twenty paces away from the Guardian and spitting blood.

"Get beneath that cloak of his," Aetex said, leaning over but careful not to touch him, lest he be seen as helping.

"Oh yeah?" Knox asked, spitting more blood. "I'll try."

In fact he had tried once or twice to strike whatever lay beneath the robes, but the Guardian only proved to be more dangerous up close, the edges of the robe cutting just as easily as its sword. But he could try again if Aetex suspected it would help.

Knox smiled then, realizing that he was going to win this fight, even if it meant taking off a ring or two. The power that awaited him would all but make up for it, this much he was certain. Though he couldn't tap into the pieces of the emblem he had, he sensed vast power within each of them. He could only imagine the level gains he'd get from a completed and open emblem.

"Time to die, Death," Knox said, not expecting his taunt to get a response, but one came regardless.

"You mortals know nothing of Death's true power; I am but a drop in a vast ocean," the Guardian said, swishing its blade through the air and sending two lines of black toward Knox.

This is new, Knox had time to think as he moved just enough to avoid both hasty attacks. Not only was it new, but this was also the first time he'd seen the Guardian react out of anger, wasting an attack.

The attack wasn't wasted though, it hit the ground and sent up a billowing cloud of dust and debris. This in turn blinded Knox in all ways but one, his sense, which told him that the good ole Death golem was coming right for him, blade ready.

Knox waited, pretending that he could not see, while keeping a close watch on the incoming attack. In the last possible moment that Knox's speed would allow him to dodge, he spun to the side, releasing the spell he'd been mumbling to himself. Chains of light sprung up all around death just as the dust cleared, holding it in place. Having infused it with a touch more mana than normal, the chains were as tough as he'd ever cast them.

Even so several had already broke and the Guardian was getting free. Knox slipped forward, the giant Guardian thrashed about, but he was going to do it, he was going to get through its guard. Just as he slipped under a part of his cloak, it shifted and cut him bad across the face, but Knox fought through the pain.

He struck out with his axe, hitting something soft and crumbling it with a single strike, then followed up with a quick and dirty Luminous Surge. It lit the area up but held very little power to do damage. What Knox saw had him rolling out of there quick.

It was like thousands of spiders or small spider-like creatures made up a form under the cloak and he'd smashed through hundreds of them when he'd attacked, hurting even more with his spell. Whatever had been keeping them all together was failing now and the Guardian began to literally fall apart from the inside out. His cloak fell away with a heavy thump and a mass of something began to move toward Knox.

Holding his hand out before him and slamming his knee down, he activated Radiant Ground, then immediately began to cast a more powerful Luminous Surge. Power thrummed off him in waves as he unleashed his might. The remaining spider-like creatures didn't stand a chance without their cloak of protection. They went up in a puff of smoke and just as quickly as the battle had begun, it was over.

CHAPTER 32
POWER

"WELL FOUGHT," Aetex boomed above the voices of concern. Knox was breathing hard, injured, and ready to find the final emblem.

"Make way," Dernal said, pushing past the taller folk to get to Knox's side. "Wasn't sure how that battle was going to go, good job."

"Thanks," Knox said, but his eyes were searching the room for something. Heal after heal washed over him until he felt quite good again. He stood and walked over to the final emblem in a chest of gold and silver.

Reaching down he pulled open the lid and found the final piece within. It was a simple golden emblem that when all the parts were put together, resembled a cog wheel like he'd seen so many times around Luminar. He kneeled down on the ground and began placing the pieces one by one into place. It took mere seconds, but Knox's heart was beating furiously.

He'd known from the start that he was going to take the power himself, raise his level to as high as it would go, but now that he was here in the moment, he had doubts. Sure, his strength would be a vital part of defeating Captain Dread but being forced to fight alone against all these Guardians had taught him a lesson.

He didn't want to fight alone if he could help it. Perhaps he'd be able to do something better than just using up all the power for himself. Perhaps he would share it.

But first he needed to drink of the power and learn if he would even be able to take a sip of it, instead of completely consuming it at once. The parts of the emblem began to glow and suddenly it was whole as the last piece was put into place.

"Here goes nothing," Knox said, reaching down he touched it with his hand as well as his sense. It blazed with unknowable power and as he made physical contact with it, power raw and untamed shot through him.

Essence after point of essence filled him. He could feel the levels falling away as he reached higher and higher. Focusing his mind he tried to cut it off, but it was so addicting, the power so tantalizing. But no, he'd made up his mind that he needed to share the power and that is what he would do! His mind snapped back to reality and he saw he'd lifted his hand from the emblem.

He felt... different. Checking his level, he had to blink several times to make sure it wasn't his imagination. He'd reached level 43, going up nearly ten levels from where he'd been. He was technically a B Ranker now and had the attributes to match. His mind, his senses, and his special sense, all of them thrummed with new information that he hadn't had only moments before.

It was like he could sense the very flows of essence that made up the world around him. Was this truly how people at B Rank felt? They were powerful beyond imagining, yet here he was among their ranks. A part of his mind whispered that he could achieve A Rank or level 51 and higher, if he just used what energy was left.

His hand began to move back toward the emblem, but something stopped him. He imagined each Guardian fight and how much easier they'd have been if he had his group at his side with their own powers close to his own.

Strong or not, he wouldn't be able to do this alone. The

power would be shared, not horded. Turning to his team he smiled, seeing them with new eyes.

"I'm going to share this power," Knox said, his voice sounded off to his new ears, but he imagined he'd get used to it eventually. "If my guess is right, there is enough power in here to bring you all above level 31, or into the C Ranks."

Ignoring Dernal and Aetex, both of whom were strong enough on their own, Knox went up to Terrim. "I'll let you touch it for a second and we will see how much power that gives you. Resist the urge to take it all upon yourself, if we share this power, we will have powerful allies around us when the final battle comes."

"I'll try," Terrim said, looking more than a little apprehensive now that the emblem was being held in front of him.

Knox had a piece of fabric between his hand and the emblem, but a part of him was sure that now that he'd pushed back the emblem, he'd be able to control whether or not the power flowed into him. He even got the sense that he could add to it, taking away from either his own unused essence or from a monster core perhaps.

Terrim held out a single finger and touched the cog emblem.

His entire body went rigid and after only a half second Knox pulled it away and Terrim went to a knee, breathing hard. "Not there yet, once more," he said, standing but still breathing hard.

Knox obliged him and allowed him to touch it again. He saw the moment his aura shifted from D to C, the color being the key and pulled the emblem free. At the same time Terrim lifted his finger, showing that he was in more control than Knox had at first.

Clasping Terrim on the arm he matched his gaze and they nodded, understanding each other. Together they would fight against the darkness and they would prevail!

"Beth," Knox said offering the emblem, but she took a step back.

"Doesn't seem all that safe," she said, eyeing Terrim and likely wondering what kind of pain he'd suffered that dropped him to a knee.

"It's a rush," Terrim said, holding his hands before him. "Just remember not to try and take too much, because it is addicting and hurts if you have to pull away more than once."

"I guess," Beth said, stepping forward and trading a nervous glance at Dog, who growled in Knox's direction. It was clear to Knox that Dog had just told him that he better not hurt his person or he'd have words to say to him. Knox nodded to the wolf named Dog, hoping he wasn't about to have a chunk taken out of his backside.

"Take only what you need to hit level 31," Knox said, hoping the emblem had enough power to bring up Murdoch, Frederick, and Henry.

Beth reached out and touched the emblem. She shuddered immediately but stayed on her feet. After a second and a half, she pulled her finger free and looked up with tears in her eyes.

"I took a," she spoke in between deep breaths, "bit more than I needed, sorry."

"What level?" Knox asked, not angry per se but he really wanted the emblem to go as far as he could make it go to raise up as many as possible.

"Thirty-two," Beth said, glancing at the floor and petting Dog at the same time. "It was just so addicting to feel the power rushing into me that I couldn't cut it off in time."

The difference, at least for Knox, of one level from 31 to 32 was about twenty-thousand essence, so not a small amount at all. That was nothing compared to the amount Knox currently needed to achieve his next level, a sum of one hundred and eighty thousand essence. The requirements of leveling really increased the higher you got, something Knox had to remember when letting people take from the essence of the emblem.

"That isn't so bad," Knox said, covering the emblem in a bit of cloth that he was using as a barrier. "Aetex and Dernal, you are alright waiting until we've risen a few others to C Ranked before you give it a try?"

"I'm not interested," Aetex said, shaking his head in my direction. "I've my own path to advancement, thank you though."

"Same," Dernal said, thumbing to Aetex as he spoke. "What he said."

"Fine with me," Knox said, figuring there would be little left after he'd helped those he had planned already. His sense felt like it was working on overdrive now and he could make out that the emblem had lost over half the raw essence it held inside, much more than he expected to be honest. It might be enough that he could raise a few other hunting parties up to C rank, perhaps Sarah and her sister's party, they'd been doing good together since grouping.

Finishing up in the labyrinth, a door appeared that led them back to the exit, however something odd happened when they reached the first room where all the doors to the different tiers were located. A new door had appeared, normally Knox would take that to mean another tier to conquer was available, but that couldn't be the case as he'd taken care of all the guardians.

Going up to one of the maintenance golems that kept the place under guard, Knox pointed to the new door. "Keep everyone out of there until I get a chance to explore it." The golem nodded but said nothing.

"Seems like the journey into the labyrinth isn't yet finished," Aetex said, taking a step toward the portal. "Would you mind if I explored alone, I'll be sure to return by the day's end."

Knox considered it and remembered how single-handedly he'd dealt with the last tier and shrugged. "You'd be doing me a favor," Knox said. "Explore and report back what you find."

Knox found and empowered Murdoch, Frederick, Henry and three additional parties of five, making approximately a dozen or more C Ranked or Level 31 and above members of Luminar. It also helped that many of them were mid-twenties level wise, meaning the overall strength of Luminar was rising.

He'd sucked the emblem dry, but wore it on his chest, clipping it to his armor. It had the most advanced Runic Formations he'd ever seen, so it merited more study.

"This sense of magic and the world around you, you feel this all the time?" Beth asked, sitting beside Knox in the dinner hall.

"His is more powerful than ours," Terrim said, they'd already had this very same conversation so Knox let him tell it. "He has special Titan perks or whatever that allow him to use his sense at like ten times the power as ours."

It was true that at a certain point all Adventurers got a special feel for magical energies, but comparing Knox's sense to that whisper of feeling was foolish. It was so much more and at the same time, very similar, so perhaps not so foolish as Knox felt.

"I've always had the sense," Knox said, he hadn't told that to Terrim during their last conversation, so Terrim looked at him surprised. "Though mine is vastly different than the little hints of power you are feeling. But it is a useful ability, so practice with it and eventually you might be able to do as much as I do with it."

Knox wanted to be helpful and not discouraging, but Beth just snorted. "Not likely," she said, spooning food into her mouth.

"So how have you been?" Knox asked, he'd been around Beth for a good bit of the last two weeks but hadn't really had any significant conversations with her.

"Just surviving," Beth said, a weak smile thrown Knox's way.

"I know the feeling, things are just moving so fast and sometimes they feel out of my control," Knox said, leaning onto his friend.

"But through it all I have you," Beth said, looking up with more emotion than Knox expected to see.

"I'm glad you feel that way," Knox said, somewhat awkwardly. "Without all of you I'd not be able to face what is coming."

"You'd be fine without us," Beth said, teasingly, but Knox didn't let her words bother him. Instead, he smiled and squeezed her tighter.

"Together we will make it," Knox said, his words barely a whisper as he pondered over what would come in the next few months.

"So how are things with Sarah?" Beth asked, her voice coming across as casual as her eyes washed over the crowd searching for a particular person, not finding her she sighed.

"I'm not sure," Knox said honestly. "Last we talked she was a bit mad at me, but we've worked together since, so I don't know if that means I'm forgiven or if we are done for. Honestly, I've never been that great at understanding women."

"No?" Beth said, with as much shock and awe as she could put in her voice. "You? Really?"

"Stop it," Knox said, pushing her off him and making a show of being offended.

She reached back and held Knox's head in place just a hand's span away from her own, suddenly looking serious. "You are an idiot," she declared loudly and for everyone to hear. "When you've figured out what it is you want or who, and if I'm still available, that's a big *if* mind you, come find me and tell me how pretty I am." With that, she stood and left Knox to his own thoughts.

Knox wasn't so dense as to not know what to do next, but he hesitated going after her to tell her exactly that, but it wasn't Sarah or the relationship he had with her that stopped him that time, no it was something deeper. A fear grew inside him that he couldn't push out, he liked Beth a lot and didn't want to see her hurt.

What if he finally gave himself permission to be happy with her and he died, once more leaving her in pain and anguish. He couldn't do that after she'd already been through so much, suffered from all kinds of loss.

Not to mention the loss that she never spoke of, the one that led her to their village in the first place. He'd heard bits and pieces of the family she'd once had, when she was too drunk to keep her words from spilling out, but it had been such a rare occasion that no one really spoke of it. She had her secrets, same as everyone, and a right to keep those to herself if she wanted.

Knox just couldn't imagine being the source of that pain for her again. For he'd already caused her pain, the pain of loss when she'd first thought him lost to the wilderness and the life of an adventurer. Now that she had become the very thing that Knox had wanted all his life and they were in it together, Knox couldn't help but imagine them together, living a life as an adventuring party. But it was a dream that would have to exist without a certain romantic aspect.

Relationships were tricky things, trying to court Sarah had proven that. She was an ideal lady, beautiful, strong, and caring, but still he managed to mess things up with her, even despite not being in a direct party with her. How much worst would it be if they'd been stuck in a party together, relying on each other for life and limb.

It wasn't that he feared for his life in a situation like that, but a party needed to act without emotional prejudice no matter the situation so that whatever path they took, it led to victory. There in lied one of the biggest blocks Knox had when he imagined himself getting closer to Beth.

Beth was so strong, independent, beautiful, and more than anything else, she understood Knox in a way that few others did. She knew of his desires to come closer to his mother through learning and study. She understood his burning desire to be more than what he'd started out as. And most importantly, she accepted him despite his many flaws, not the least of which were his inability to accept the love and care of those close to him.

No his life wasn't perfect, nor was this situation they had going in Luminar, but Knox wasn't about to give up on either yet. He'd fight with all his might to defend his new home, and he'd do his best to discover the secrets that lay within. For there was more to all of this than met the eye and Knox was only scratching the surface of the knowledge that lay dormant here.

Aetex found Knox as he was leaving the dinner hall and spoke in a hushed tone but one filled with excitement. "I've discovered an impossibility."

Knox took him by the arm and walked out of the high traffic area to a alley of sorts between one large unused building and a residential smaller hut. "What'd you discover?" Knox asked.

"The final wing of the labyrinth holds a dungeon, one relatively new one, younger than any other I've sensed since arriving here," Aetex said. "I imagine it has been growing in power along with the system as such is the perfect tool to train these young would be adventurers. I cleared it already and can speak with certainty that the three paths within are well within the power of a party leveled 10 to 15 to be able to handle."

"Another dungeon?" Knox asked, more than a little confounded by the news. From all he'd heard dungeons were rare to the point of not finding another within a hundred miles of each other. But to find a young one so close to the Titan Engine, it was amazing yet also confusing. He'd have to take the news to Mic and see what he could remember.

"If you've cleared it and think it is an acceptable risk, then I'll speak with Murdoch and Mic about getting parties to clear it out regularly," Knox said. "We need the magic loot it will provide, weak or not than it might be from such a young dungeon."

"That's another thing," Aetex said, showing Knox a simple golden ring without any signs of runic formation on it, though his sense showed it to be covered with internal runic forms. "This ring was given to me in a chest on the first room of the first path. Put it on and look at this item I found."

Knox took the ring and slipped it on. He felt no different, but as he focused on a dagger that Aetex held out for him, a display of information appeared, not unlike the system information he could see about himself at will.

Shadowfang Dagger

Torn from the Fang of a Shadow Spider, this dagger, like the fang it's based off of, can be rendered invisible to the naked eye on command.

Alignment: Dark

Negative-Alignment: Light

Class Bonus: Necromancer, Rogue

Class Attribute Bonus: +5 Speed, +5 Endurance

Durability: 65/65

Knox dismissed the window with a wave of his hand and stared down at the ring on his hand. This item would be invaluable to his research and weapon construction. His mind tingled at the possibilities, perhaps if Knox could improve the ring he could get it to identify the runic formations within each item as well. Oh the possibilities.

"And you say this ring was given freely to all those that start the dungeon or do you think it was a first-time thing?" Knox asked, but Aetex just shrugged.

"Regardless, we have one now and I've seen you replicate items before, surely you can replicate this and provide us with more knowledge than could be expected," Aetex said, clearly excited by the idea as much as Knox.

"Let's go speak with Murdoch and Mic," Knox said, a plan forming in his head. He'd see what this dungeon had to offer and hopefully be able to replicate the rings effects.

They found Murdoch and Mic speaking in the command room, Mic on the chair directing repair work and other important tasks while listening to Murdoch give a report on supplies.

"I know that we are running short on those tart fruits everyone likes, but I needed to move energy to more potent food products if we want everyone to have the right amount of intake to keep them going strong. Even with your new bodies not needing as much food, with the rate of growing all of you have, the food is required," Mic said, ending whatever argument Murdoch had been having with him.

He had a point too, Knox mused. After his latest growth into the B Ranks, he'd had a terrible hunger as his body needed nutrients restored. After four bowls of stew, he'd begun to feel a small amount better, but he knew several more feasts were in store for him before he felt like a hundred percent again.

They informed Murdoch and Mic about the ring and Knox's plan to run groups through the dungeon for new loot and training. Then, showing Mic the ring, he asked the question he'd been holding back.

"Why is there a dungeon at the end of the labyrinth, better yet why is the labyrinth even here?" Knox asked, not waiting for a response he continued on. "I mean the labyrinth was clearly filled with monsters created by mechanical means, so a past Titan must have had a hand in creating it to guard the emblem, but why and how did a dungeon appear at the end of this labyrinth?"

"All wise questions," Mic said, smiling in the odd way that he could now that he'd adjusted his face. He even blinked at Knox several times just because he could. "I've remembered nothing new about the labyrinth or its creation. However, I concluded much the same as you, that it must be a creation of my prior master. I do have some news on the labyrinth since you conquered it."

"Which is?" Knox asked when he didn't immediately dive into whatever new information he'd discovered.

"There is a new control tab in the command chair that allows for manipulating the spawn rates of the labyrinth as well as moving essence around to either produce more raw materials or monsters," Mic said. "It would appear that we have full control over the labyrinth now. Though I can't speak to the dungeon, in fact the final wing of the labyrinth doesn't even show up on the schematics I've been given access to."

"Let me see that," Knox said, standing up to the command chair and waiting for Mic to move aside. He did so and Knox took a seat, mentally calling up information on the labyrinth.

As Mic had said, a schematic with several options and a view of the layout appeared. It was even more complex than he'd mentioned, with tabs to increase the average level of mobs and change their elemental alignment. It looked like each floor was operating on its lowest settings currently, which was good because the overall level of essence required for the labyrinth was a huge number. The Titan Engine had to maintain its area of influence as well as hundreds of other functions, which meant that it was also maintaining the labyrinth.

Knox almost looked for a way to shut it down to save essence, but he stopped himself when he realized what they were getting in return. Supplies, raw materials, and rare metals that hadn't even worked out what to do with yet. That was at least something they could adjust, Knox fingered a few options and made the rarer metal less likely to be found, instead increasing the iron that would be used to make steel more common.

Of course, he kept the blue iron as high as it would go, but even so it was rare enough to be useless for anything but weapons, armor being far to material heavy. Knox finished his work and stood, giving the chair back to Mic.

"None of that explains the dungeon, though if you look at the final wing of the labyrinth, you'll see the doorway that leads down, it just doesn't say anything about what lies beneath," Knox said, gesturing at the screen that was no longer visible to him.

"I've got an explanation," Aetex said, his hand running down the command chair and his eyes unfocused. What exactly he was doing Knox couldn't say, but he felt power pulsing all around him as he did it.

"What is it?" Knox asked.

"What do you know of the birth of dungeons?" Aetex asked, no one responded.

"Nothing really," Knox said, thinking about what he'd learned about dungeons in his times speaking with Dernal.

Truth be told, very little was known about the birth of dungeons, only that new ones would be found every several dozen years by adventurers exploring the less populated areas of the world, which as far as Knox knew was much of the world. Dernal had spoken very little about new dungeons in the years that Knox pumped him for every scrap of information, instead focusing on telling Knox all he knew about the dungeons he'd faced. Stories of monsters who could do this or that, Knox often thought he only did so to try and dissuade him from a life of adventuring, but all that information had been important to him in the end.

"They are born when enough essence collects in a singular place, then the system gives them purpose and direction. Or at least I've been told as much from my benefactor. So imagine the amount of essence required for a dungeon at the heart of the Titan Engine. I'd imagine it would take very little to jump start a dungeon so close to the system, but I know only what little has been revealed to me," Aetex said, his eyes distant as if he were speaking now to the mysterious Mah'kus. "Either way it isn't important to your current mission," his voice went from mysterious and thoughtful to stern in moments, "What is important now is that you strengthen yourself and those around you for the impending threats."

"I'll organize trips into the dungeon," Murdoch said, eyeing Aetex carefully as he spoke. "If it is as weak as you say, then we have plenty of groups that could steam roll it and collect these rings and other items."

"I want to be the first to go through," Knox said. "If there are more rings to be given out, I need to know. Until then see that this ring is given to our best crafter and shared among those that could benefit from seeing the details of an item," Knox said, handing the ring to Murdoch.

Knox left then, leaving Murdoch with orders to gather the group first thing in the morning for a dungeon run. He needed some rest, if not for his body, then his mind. So many thoughts and processes clouded his ability to think straight, but he needed clarity now more than ever.

CHAPTER 33
UNEXPECTED GREETINGS

THE DUNGEON RUN was short and sweet. He didn't get offered a ring at the start as Aetex had, which confirmed Knox's thought that it might be a 'first person into the dungeon' kind of bonus, but it was enough that they had the item, now Knox could unravel its secrets.

The dungeon consisted of much the same monsters they found outside the complex, Nolics, wolves, and even a few goblins in the final path. Each of the bosses were a step up challenge wise, but nothing for such a strong group as theirs. So the dungeon run ended after only a single day of clearing it out and Knox felt comfortable opening it up to all others of the city, seeing as they'd faced most of the monsters out in patrols already.

Knox was on his way back to the surface when a maintenance golem found him and relayed a message from Mic. "Incoming, six targets all within C and B Rank."

Shooting off down the corridors Knox made it to the surface within minutes, his team on his heels struggling to keep up. He reached Mic in the command chair, who stood and let him sit without a word.

Several targets with auras matching that of C and B Rank: three low Cs, two low Bs, and one high B. The Titan System was getting better at identifying the auras, giving the overlay a color to go with it and if Knox focused, he could get exact levels. However, these had no such levels no matter how hard he focused. A sign that they'd been able to keep from accepting the Titan System somehow.

This wasn't the case with the pirates they faced and they were coming from a very specific direction, Knox did not relax when he realized who they must be. A group from the Guild Charterhouse.

Knox went to find Dernal, Leo, and John, before heading to the Western gate to meet their newcomers. "As far as I can tell, they are all strong, stronger even than me, but they'll assume I'm an A Ranker, so don't shatter that illusion for them if you can," Knox said, climbing the stairs to stand atop the gate.

The newcomers were fast and already his sense told him they were approaching the deadman's zone that they'd created all around Luminar. Knox tried to see if any of the auras felt familiar but it was hard for him to remember those he'd encountered from so long ago, even days was enough to muddle his memory of auras, so weeks made it all but impossible for any aura to be recognized unless he'd seen them multiple times.

"Welcome them with open arms and make a show of not being hostile," Leo said, his mannerisms changing to all business. "They are wary of what they don't understand, but we've explained the basics to them. They know the world is changing and how they react here might set a precedent for all future reactions to the Titan System. Be open, but don't tell them everything all at once."

Knox had no plans of telling them anything he didn't have to, but Leo was wise, and he accepted the guidance his friend was offering. "I'll allow them inside but keep word of any dungeons to yourself. The last thing I want is some regulator trying to make his home in the middle of Luminar simply because a dungeon exists there."

"That is wise, for now," Leo said, nodding. "We should go out and meet them, a sign that they are welcome."

"Agreed," Knox said. They jumped from the top of the wall; all of their bodies well enhanced enough to suffer no injury from the jump. Soon the auras of the incoming Adventurers were unmistakable as they left the tree line and headed right for them at a slow walk now.

Knox could tell by the way their auras moved that each of them were skilled in masking their own aura. Unfortunately for them, Knox's sense was much more powerful than any they'd tried to hide from before, so he easily saw through their masking and into their true power within.

He recognized half of the group and let out a breath. Both Faelar Swiftnook and Master Thaddeus Loreweaver, two members of the Guild Charterhouse, were easily recognized. Behind them, were a group of three that were slightly more powerful than he remembered them being when he rescued them from the clutches of the pirates. Draven and two of his cousins, Calix and Vyren if he was remembering right.

Those five aside, he did not recognize the woman at the lead and the strongest among them. She looked young, but appearances were hard to gauge as Adventurers tended to remain looking young far into their lives and depending on how powerful they grew, natural aging would stop altogether. Knox guessed that this woman must have hit the age-slowing process when she had barely made it to adulthood, since she appeared no older than seventeen or eighteen.

She had long blonde hair, braided in the back with many small braids and the sides of her hair shaved to the skin. She wore armor that gleamed with enchantments far too complex and varied to be anything but a dungeon creation. Her weapon seemed to radiate light even in its scabbard, the sword a shining example of power infused Light. Knox wondered if she'd let him examine her arms and armor, but based on the scowl on her face, he doubted it.

They approached in silence, the only sound being Aetex calling out a greeting. "Hello there!" he said, then with a booming laugh added. "You've made good time I hope."

"We've arrived when we saw fit to arrive," the newcomer said, her voice sharp and not at all a match for her beautiful face. Then looking over the group, she nodded to both Leo and Dernal, saving a sneer for John.

John cleared his throat as if to speak, but Leo put a hand on his arm, stopping him. Whatever history these two had, Knox wished John would have cleared the air about it first, but he had to work with what he had.

"I'm Knox Trelling of Luminar," Knox said, bowing his head ever so slightly as he did so and unleashing a portion of his aura so that they could see it. He'd grown better at masking his own aura, despite the difficulty when accepting the system's way of doing it, he'd figured ways around it to help shield himself.

All of them took a step back, except for the lead woman who seemed to lean forward as Knox's aura was unleashed. "The reports were true, you are a rare find indeed," said the nameless woman. "My name is Eleanor Dawnbringer and I'm here to bring you into custody."

Her aura surged and Knox felt the workings of a spell beginning. Would she really just go and outright try to overpower him after showing her his red aura? This woman had brass for balls, and he had to do something to stop it before it devolved into a fight.

"Please," Knox said, and her surging aura calmed ever so slightly. "Allow me to show you around and let us speak civilly. If after we are finished you still wish to bring me into custody, I will go with you on my own accord. We are but a humble group of Adventurers looking to carve out a section of life for ourselves. We have enemies already and don't need to add more."

The last bit seemed to give Eleanor pause and she let go of the strands of magic she'd been pulling together. Not that Knox was particularly worried about it as he'd sensed it was nearly all Light essence infused magic, which meant he had a certain command over it. If she'd chained him with Light, he'd break and absorb it before she could blink. He was, after all, the Titan of Light now.

"I will see your," Eleanor paused and looked at the walls surrounding their settlement, seeming to choose her words carefully, "city and meet these so-called Adventurers. And perhaps you can start by explaining why this Titan System so badly wishes to overcome us all?"

"What do you mean?" Knox asked, knowing full well that being this close to the Titan Engine must be making resisting it nearly impossible. Knox was honestly surprised that the C Rankers could resist it at all. That was when he noticed each of them wearing a similar amulet that glowed with intense heat and power. It must be what they are using to fight off the effects of the system and by the looks and feel of them, they are operating at their limits.

"Your companions have already told us about the system and your role in it, so do not play dumb with me," she said, stepping forward in challenge as she spoke.

Knox felt everyone else take a step back, but he leaned forward, ready for any challenge she wished to offer. "The system is the way this world was always meant to be," Knox said, reciting what Mic had told him so long ago. "It is a restoring of the natural way of the world. Our ranks and techniques pale in comparison to the magic of the Titan System and the abilities unlocked when you pick a true path. But we can speak more about that inside the walls. Please come and see what we've made of Luminar."

"Very well," Dawnbringer said, bowing her head ever so slightly. "Lead the way, Knox of Luminar."

Knox gave the tour, inviting the potential enemies within their walls to learn a bit about them. Murdoch appeared, speaking as he did and seeming to comfort Dawnbringer by the looks of her —her shoulders lost a touch of the tension in them, and her scowl receded. Knox was almost positive that he'd used some of his path abilities on her, but if she suspected as much, it didn't show.

This enabled Knox to speak with some of the others, Eleanor now giving Murdoch her full attention.

"Where is Garrick Stonehelm?" Knox asked, remembering the name of the leader of the Guild Charterhouse, but also that he'd gone missing at some point.

"Still missing, Dawnbringer is his superior and she wasn't happy to hear about his disappearance and your involvement," Thaddeus said, his voice a low whisper but Dawnbringer moved her head ever so slightly toward them as they spoke, indicating to Knox that she could hear every word.

"I told you; he came back in with me, and I assumed he was going in for the night, I know nothing about his disappearance," Knox said, more for her benefit than Thaddeus's.

"I know, I know," Thaddeus said, putting a kind hand on his shoulder and leaning in a bit closer. A whisper barely audible to even Knox's ears, he caught what he said. "We come for your help as much as to see this city of yours. The earth shakes are getting worse, and a sickness is traveling throughout the land. All other A Rankers are busy dealing with threats to the kingdom, but perhaps you can deal with the threat."

"That's enough," Eleanor said, suddenly appearing before them with more stealth and speed than Knox would have given her credit. "We will see that matters are resolved, with or without his help."

Thaddeus nodded to her and kept his head bowed as he took several steps backwards. This gave Draven the opening he must have been waiting for, because he stepped up and as loud as someone speaking from five paces away said, "I do not come for this Adventurer Guild business. I brought myself and my cousins along to deliver a message."

"A message that can wait until he is safely in custody at the Charterhouse," Eleanor said, cutting off Draven and taking a threatening step towards him.

Draven for his credit, stood his ground and stared daggers at the Dawnbringer. "You speak for house Lumisar now, do you?"

This statement seemed to give even Dawnbringer pause, and she let out a loud sigh. "In this matter, even House nobility can wait, Lumisar or not."

"Very well, I will report as much when I return," Draven said, his words must have stung because Dawnbringer recoiled from them as if they did.

"Tour is over," Knox said, having enough of this Dawnbringer pushing people around. "Why do you resist the Titan System? I can give you a phrase that will help those who have been made a part of it to access the magical training. It is how this world is meant to be."

"Enough of that," Eleanor said, her words cutting like a blade. "We must leave soon; the magic that protects us from your vile system is at its max and I won't be forced under foreign control and done away with as you did Garrick."

"I did no such thing," Knox said, heat filling his words. He wanted to reach out and grab the amulets around their necks and pull it off. But he knew that wouldn't accomplish anything.

"We did not come to you in good faith to have you accuse Knox of such crimes," Leo said, he was clearly getting angry as well, something Knox rarely saw of the elderly man.

"You did as you were required by the bylaws of the guild," she said, barely glancing at Leo. "The same bylaws that we now use to arrest this man, who failed to do the same when he come across such a discovery."

"You are arresting me?" Knox asked, taking a deep breath and readying his magic.

"Do not fret her imprisonment," Draven said, stepping in

front of her. "House Lumisar has need of you and so you shall be free within the week, my sister is on her way with orders from our father to see to as much."

"You can't," Dawnbringer began to say, but Draven cut her off.

"I already have," he said, raising a ring to his lips and kissing it. It glowed with hidden runes and Knox wondered at what it did.

Pacified that he wasn't to remain a prisoner, Knox let his spells fall away and considered his next course of action. "I will spend three days in your care, Aetex will you attend me?" Knox asked.

Aetex nodded but said nothing. Something around his aura slipped though, and Dawnbringer's eyes went wide. Her words came out slower than before, her gaze never leaving Aetex.

"I would prefer that you come alone," she said.

Aetex just shook his head. "Where he goes, I will follow."

"Two of them," Draven said, then he started to laugh. "You've really stepped in it today, Eleanor, bearer of the Dawnslight. You know what, I think I'll see what this system has to offer, so many powerful adventurers in one place can't be a coincidence." With that, he pulled off his amulet and it went still, all the energy it was moving suddenly became dormant.

"Oh my," Draven said after a moment, then he began to swish a screen around in front of his vision that only he could see. "It appears I have a choice or two ahead of me. Do you mind if I stay here and learn of this system for a while, my cousin Calix can be trusted to deliver the message and receive my sister."

Knox was surprised by the sudden turn of events, but he clasped the man on the shoulder and said, "Welcome to the Titan System. Dernal, take him to Mic to begin his training and give him any resources he requires to help better inform his choice. We have those who have walked down all available paths who will be willing to speak with you before you make your choice."

"I thank you," Draven said, then left with Dernal while the Dawnbringer looked on with unmasked horror on her face.

The very idea of someone accepting the system seemed impossible to her, but Knox could understand someone who had spent their entire life believing and relying on things being one way, that a change would be monumentally hard for them. But he had faith that she'd come around, if only he could tell her the benefits of such a choice.

"Let's be off, then," Knox said, then turning to Aetex. "Go to Mic and gather a few days supplies then catch up."

"I can do that," Aetex said merrily. He understood, Knox hoped, that he wanted Mic to track them as well, but if not, he was sure Leo or John would get the message or idea of it across.

"Eleanor," John said, but the woman just looked the other way, looking rather childish in her display. "Can't we talk about it?"

"Nothing to talk about, come with me prisoner, and accept these shackles," Eleanor said, holding out glowing, light-infused shackles.

"That will be a hard no," Knox said, reaching out he pulled the essence from the shackles, it was Light, and he had the closest connection to it, so it came easy. The shackles' light diminished to nothing and the Dawnbringer furrowed her brow, pressing essence into it and bringing them back to life.

"You will submit or be made to," she said, with Aetex gone she appeared more confident than she had a moment before.

"I will break your toy if you offer them to me again," Knox said, infusing his voice with his power, it became louder than it had before with more vibration behind it. She recoiled ever so slightly and nodded.

"Fine, but you try to flee, and I will end you," she assured Knox, who just smiled in her direction.

"Three days," Knox said, looking her right in the eyes. "You get three days to ask me questions and hold me prisoner. Then I am leaving and if you come against my city again, it will be as an enemy."

"Understood," Eleanor said through clenched teeth.

CHAPTER 34
GUILD CHARTERHOUSE

Knox purposely didn't take an orb with him when he left, wanting to make sure that this group had to fight their way out of the Shadowfall Swamps. Even so, the trip took only a day at their speeds of running, far outpacing anything a horse could do in a day. There was the added benefit of incredible endurance as well, so even when they faced off against monsters, only C Ranked ones found their way to them, they were still fresh enough to do battle.

The Guild Charterhouse was much as Knox remembered it, a lonely looking cabin complex out in the middle of nowhere. Except that it was filled with forty or more auras inside, ranging from weak to high C Ranked. None matched the strength of the party that was returning, a fact that comforted Knox if only a little.

Aetex had caught up with them ages ago, but remained quiet and aloof as they traveled. Dawnbringer seemed to have that effect on her own party, all of them not daring to have any type of conversation, despite how many times Knox tried to start one.

"Master Dawnbringer," a voice called out as they neared the door. She turned her head and acknowledged a Rogue-like figure that came out of stealth. "The room is prepared; shall we escort the prisoner?"

"Yes," she said, then turning to Knox. "If you'd be so kind as to follow him to a room prepared for you. We will be there shortly with questions. Your friend can wait outside."

"I will wait inside," Aetex said, not a question but a statement of fact.

Eleanor pressed the bridge of her nose and took a deep breath. "Very well," she said, opening her arm as if inviting him in. "Would you please? Not like I could stop you." She muttered the last few words and Knox wondered something.

She'd obviously sensed Aetex's aura and the power coming off it, but hadn't she done the same for Knox? Why wasn't she more afraid of him than she was of Aetex? Questions that Knox didn't have the answer to rolled through his head as he was led into the Charterhouse and up to the same room that he'd spent the night in before. This time though, it was filled with runic scripts all meant to hamper his power in some way or another.

It was good work and would keep his power contained in the room, that was if he left the runic formations intact. He could see clearly where they were marked and how to disturb them. Just to show he wasn't one to be messed with, he used Radiant Glyph to cut a small section in the activation sequence, effectively hamstringing the formations by cutting the flow of power to almost nothing.

There were more runic formations, in fact the entire building was filled with them, but he left them alone. Knox was more worried about what questions they had for him and if they truly thought they'd be able to keep him captive. He needed their support and their help, otherwise he'd not have agreed to any of this. But if doing this could somehow clear his name and get even some of the guild members in his good graces, then he'd count it as a win.

Sitting there, he almost didn't feel the distinct lack of

anything that appeared behind him, like a void in his sense so deep it might as well have been a flag getting his attention.

"Hello?" Knox asked, as he turned to regard the newcomer.

"Hello there," Garrick Stonehelm said, a blank expression on his normally animated face. "Thank you for taking down the wards so that I might easily find you. I come from the lady of darkness to reap your soul. Will you fight me?"

His voice had lost all the life in it and came out flat, almost bored sounding. It was enough that it sent shivers up Knox's spine as he listened to the dead man's words. For he must be dead inside, because Knox sensed nothing of him other than the void of pure darkness.

"I'm sorry," Knox said, wishing that he could save the man somehow, but knowing that whatever he was now, was beyond such measures. "I'll try and make it quick."

With that, Knox pulled free his axe and swung for its neck.

His opponent, all burly and still wearing the same armor he'd seen on him the day they'd met, raised his hand almost casually and caught the blow, black ichor leaking from the gash it left on his palm. Knox didn't relent though; he knew that darkness had taken this man and only his light might be enough to snuff it out.

Raising his hands, he cast Luminous Surge and Garrick screamed out in pain, his voice coming two-fold, one as a human and another a monster that seemed to reverberate through Knox.

"Your little light isn't enough to deal with my kind, just wait!" Garrick hissed the words and suddenly he disappeared. Knox followed the void in his sense to the outside. Looking out the window he saw the man once known as Garrick standing beside a familiar girl, she smiled up at Knox and waved before both of them flickered and disappeared.

Whatever was going on wasn't over. As Knox thought the words, a darkness enveloped the building, effectively blocking his view of the outside world.

For several long seconds it was silent, then outside the wall were several screams of pain and anguish. Then heavy footsteps as the lock on the door, his little prison, were thrown and Dawn-bringer appeared.

"What have you done!" She screamed the words pulling free a powerfully glowing sword and leveling it as Knox's throat.

Knox moved like lightning, hooking his axe over the blade and thrusting it down, then placing the edge of his axe on her throat. Leaning forward he whispered in her ear, her entire frame suddenly still as a quiet night.

"I'm not your enemy and I have not done anything. The darkness is coming for us, and we won't stand a chance unless we fight together," Knox whispered the words, carefully removing his axe blade and using Ethereal Step to back away from her without giving her a chance to strike. Then returning his voice to its normal volume he said, "Do you have an armory here?"

"Of course," Eleanor said, her hand going to her neck and coming back red. Knox had drawn blood even being as careful as he had been. "I have your word this isn't you or your companion?"

"You have my word," Knox said without hesitation. "I'd swear to it using the runic language if I knew it well enough to do so, but you have to trust me, or we are all dead."

Whatever the darkness was planning Knox had to believe that it was more powerful here than it had been closer to Luminar. With that added strength, Knox wasn't sure he or Aetex would be enough to deal with it.

Knox followed Eleanor out of the room where over three dozen Adventurers stood looking a mix of terrified and annoyed. Knox noted that the strongest among them seemed annoyed more than scared. They would learn fear soon enough if things were going to happen as Knox imagined they would. Garrick alone had seemed strong enough to face off directly against Knox, who knows what other allies they have on their side now.

"Anyone not already armed, get to the armory and arm your-selves," Dawnbringer said, and people moved to find weapons for themselves. "You should go to the armory as well," she said gesturing to Aetex and Knox. "That axe is made for chopping wood and despite the enchantments you've placed on it, it isn't the best option here for battle. Come with me," she finally said when Knox didn't move at first.

She led him to a backroom, going through a door in the back of the armory where no others had gone to yet. It involved her speaking many runic phrases that Knox only barely heard and unlocking a powerfully large metal door. Whatever was in here they'd kept it guarded well. This led to an area that was shielded from the inside and as soon as they entered, Knox felt the powerful auras of the weapons and armor inside. He gave a quick look, his eyes hovering over it all and noting a strange suit of armor that his eyes seemed to pass right over, but he was too interested in everything else in the room to notice.

"We've got a few A Ranked weapons, and normally I'd never allow such legendary weapons to be touched by hands such as yours, but you are likely the best option we have to get out of this alive. I threw my most powerful magic against that black barrier surrounding us and it did nothing."

Knox looked her in the eyes and then looked over the weapons, wishing he'd brought the ring to tell him more about each one. Instead, he read the runes and asked aloud when that wasn't enough information. He looked over several swords, spears, but none of that would be comfortable in his hands. He was a woodcutter, and he had his mother's axe to aid him, what did he have of any of these... then he saw it. An axe made for battle with a design that wasn't dissimilar to the bronze color of the Titan Complex.

Picking it up he tested the weight and found it balanced even better than his own axe. "What can you tell me about this?" he asked as Aetex found a pair of golden gauntlets with gems set into the knuckles. He put on the gloves and snapped his fingers, but nothing happened. Aetex shrugged and kept the gauntlets on.

"Little is known about that axe, but it's an old weapon from centuries past. To date, no one has been able to wield it or identify the runes giving it any abilities. Try instead this sword here," Eleanor said, reaching for a blood red sword, but Knox held out a hand before gripping the axe with two.

He could just barely sense the deep set and powerful runic formations on the axe, though he couldn't make out what they did other than they involved light essence.

"Does it have a name?" Knox asked, the axe began to shine brightly in his grip, whatever magic it contained beginning to activate.

"No name, no one has ever been able to wield it, not even the A Ranker that found it. This is insane, we only got the relic because no one else wanted it and Garrick had a soft spot for axes, plus it was found in the Shadowfall Swamps. But now you are here, and it comes to life. You tell me, what is its name?" she asked, her voice filled with reverence and surprise.

Knox reached out with his sense and felt the weapon, tried to understand its purpose, its potential. As he felt through the threads of power within it, he almost had the sense of a name at the furthest reaches of his mind, but no matter how hard he focused nothing came. "I don't know, but I feel a kinship to it," Knox said, fingering the axe in his hands and giving it an experimental swing.

A ray of light followed after it and he knew without a doubt that this weapon had once been wielded by a Titan of Light. There was just a certain power to it that felt familiar in a way that words couldn't describe. He hated to set aside his mother's weapon, but right now he needed the weapon of a Titan, and this was it. Putting a hand on his own axe, he kept it in place, unwilling to give it up despite now being armed with a more powerful weapon.

"I see you've found a kinship in the Gauntlets of Kith," Eleanor said, seeing Aetex still wearing the gauntlets of gold and gems.

"It is fascinating," Aetex said, doing another test punch—the force of which knocked several ancient swords to the ground. "These will fit me well for a time."

"Take any armor you can find, but do not touch that accursed set," Eleanor said, pointing to a glass case that held nothing but a manakin shape meant to hold armor.

"There is no armor there," Knox said, that got her attention and she looked again. He tried to remember if there had been anything there when they entered but Knox had been so distracted that he'd only given everything a cursory glance.

"We are in trouble," she said, going pale in the face. "Arm yourselves and be ready, for whatever has taken that armor will return to try and destroy us for keeping it captive."

"Tell me what that armor was," Aetex said, suddenly serious.

"A relic found deep in the ground, it was as black as night and all that wore it succumbed to a darkness that only death could release them, but the last time it was worn, it took an A Ranker to take the C Ranker inside down. That was a hundred years ago, and we've dared not move it since, so it stayed here under guard and lock and key. A lock that I only released so I could arm you with the best we have. Curses to whatever is happening here!"

"Keep calm and we will do all we can to make sure everyone makes it out alive," Knox said, turning to try and find some armor better than his own. As he looked, a scream cut through the armory from the front room. His own armor would have to do.

CHAPTER 35
FIGHT THEN FLIGHT

Aetex and Knox moved as fast as the wind, Eleanor right behind them as they made it to the main room. Light from the fireplace in the middle seemed to flicker and half die out as something swept through the room, relieving men and women of their heads as it went. A dozen were dead before Knox could react, slicing out with his new weapon and cutting the black inky monster in half.

"What happened here?" Eleanor demanded, her sword out and glowing as fiercely as the fire in the center of the room.

"Tom opened the door and the blackness came in," said the rogue-like figure that had escorted Knox to his room. "Tom was... that *thing* was Tom. The darkness overtook him and he became that thing!"

The man was clearly disturbed and his rantings were only making things worse. Eleanor put a hand on his shoulder to calm him, a light seeming to pour out of her.

"I've got an idea of how you can all help," Knox said, a sudden plan forming in his mind. "Accept the system and say the phrase to enter the training. It takes mere seconds and you'll have weeks to learn and prepare!"

"That's not a half bad idea," Aetex said, smashing his fists together suddenly and rushing forward to smash a shadow that was entering the room and going for Eleanor. "But we should hurry if that's the plan, for the darkness will not waver or wait for us."

Eleanor wasn't a fan of the idea that much Knox could see on her face, but as another shadow jumped for her and she seemed unable to fight back against it, she conceded. "This System will provide powerful attacks against the darkness?" she asked, biting her lip.

"Yes, as long as you choose the right path," Knox said, wishing he could offer her the path of the Light as he followed. But any Path infused with her preference toward Light attacks would be helpful and more powerful than whatever she could bring to bear right now.

"I'll do as you say, but that doesn't mean I trust you or this Titan System as you call it," she said, then with her voice faltering she said in a low whisper that only Knox's enhanced ears could hear. "I don't want to die, not yet."

"You won't," Knox assured her, slamming his foot down a moment later. Cracks of light spreading out from his Radiant Stomp and warding off another shadow trying to unnaturally bend its way into the room.

Eleanor Dawnbringer grabbed hold of an amulet around her neck and pulled, snapping it off. She sighed as if pressure were being released and somehow, Knox could feel she was touching the Titan System. The others in the hall, most of them at least, did the same, littering the ground with dozens of amulets.

"We've got to keep them safe while they train," Knox said to Aetex, then going to Eleanor, he gave her the phrase to join the training system after she picked a path. "Chooose swiftly and say those words to get access to your abilities."

Knox readied himself against the shadow, Aetex at his side. The first shadows that came were easily dispatched, but with each one they pushed back, something more real and solid came through. Until they were fighting against half a dozen very real dark specters with sharp claw and tooth.

Zeroing in on the closest and biggest, Knox let loose a Luminous Surge, cutting it into two pieces. Aetex followed up punching two of them into oblivion in the moment where Knox recovered. The other three rushed into the gaps, one grabbing hold of someone spacing out nearby as they trained. He screamed, but Aetex was there a moment later ripping it free and smashing it to bits. Meanwhile, the other two were mid attack against Knox.

He raised his new axe, a weapon made for war and disposing of enemies. The axe struck out taking them full in the chest and instead of them falling into pieces, they were absorbed into the axe. It suddenly gleamed a dark color, but a half second later shimmered a brilliant light color. And all the while, Knox felt a surge of extra essence enter him from the hilt of the axe. Had it just absorbed the monsters base essence? This axe was a keeper for sure!

Just as he finished his final targets, he turned in time to see more shadows appearing, not only from the two double doors open in the front, but from windows that had been opened from the outside. Ten, eleven, twelve, and more began to fill the upper staircase that overlooked the downstairs, while half a dozen more came through the main entrance. Still, the darkness outside persisted to the point of pitch blackness.

"I'm going to love this," Knox said, cracking his neck to the side and checking that Aetex was ready to fight.

"Shall we show them true power, not the kind that is hidden in the dark, but the power of light shining forth on a bright and sunny day?" Aetex said, his eyes never leaving the shadows on the upper floors as they squirmed and writhed against the suppressed light of the fireplace.

But the fireplace wasn't the only thing giving off light, somehow Knox, as he unleashed his grip on his aura and loosened himself for battle, began to give off light on the visual spectrum.

Holding on to that feeling he surged it even further and the dark specters, all tooth and claw, shied backward.

A snarl from behind him had Knox raising his axe, but no shadow awaited him, only the Dawnbringer and she was showing off where she must have gotten her name. Her sword had been pulled and gave off as much light as Knox's aura, further forcing back the shadows.

As Knox stood, weapon ready, he met her eyes, and they shared a look. She would fight to her last and she had experience using the Light Essence, so hopefully whatever she chose as her Path would supplement that. Watching her, Knox wondered what she'd picked when suddenly she rushed forward slashing with impossible speed and he knew then that she walked the Warrior Path.

But then a barrier of light flickered up around her as a shadow struck out, repelling the attack and suddenly Knox wasn't so sure which path she walked. That was until he remembered the Mystic Templar path that allowed for the use of magic and steel. She was walking a path as close to her original as possible, so perhaps it would be enough to give her an edge, despite losing her techniques.

Suddenly she held out her hand and released a beam of light. What ability or talent allowed her to do that, Knox wasn't sure, but she flung it out in such a raw way that it almost seemed like a type of elemental control, perhaps she chose the light element as the elemental focus for her branch of the talent tree?

There was no more time to ponder over things, as more shadows moved to surround her and Knox was needed. He cut through the first one, absorbing it and feeling a rush from the kill. Then turning he activated Solar Wings, causing more area of effect damage and forcing the shadows to flinch. Using his wings he smacked at the shadows, pushing them into Dawnbringer's reach and ending their short lives.

More fighters began to fall out of their stupor and join the battle. But with each one that joined, more shadows appeared and the Charterhouse began to fill with blood. One by one people fell, Aetex, Knox, and Dawnbringer unable to keep up with the sheer amount of foes. The entire space was overly cramped and several times Knox had to duck friendly fire.

Several passages he'd read about runic formations suddenly flashed through his mind and he thought, just maybe, that he might be able to dispel the aura of shadow surrounding them. "I have a plan," Knox yelled above the din of battle. "Keep them off me while I work, and I might be able to break the shadows."

Knox focused as he had before when he needed to write more than would be normally necessary using Radiant Glyph. Line after line he repeated it from memory, stringing together several formations to create the one he needed. If it worked it would explode outward and disturb other formations, which this darkness had to be for it to be so persistent and strong.

He just hoped he could finish in time. Body after body fell around him as they defended Knox with their very lives. Only Aetex, Eleanor, and Draven's cousins were having any success in the attacks. Everyone else seemed like they were getting one hit in for every three they received. Heals were being thrown around as fast as possible, but it was a losing battle. Over half of their force had fallen by the time Knox finished the runic formation.

For a precious second, then two, nothing happened, and Knox just about cried out in fury, but then a force began to build, and he knew it was working. After several more seconds of charging, the force exploded outward and Knox felt his own personal wards shutter and fail, along with his armor and weapons enchantments.

As Knox hit a knee, the lack of wards a surprising twist, but already his items were beginning to shudder back and working once more. What was more important was the lack of a black barrier covering the Charterhouse now.

"Run!" Came the general cry from the group and before Knox could stop them, they began to funnel out into the dim light of the evening.

"It isn't over!" Knox cried out, pushing his way forward to try and confront the void he felt in his sense still.

But men screamed and fell dead to the void before Knox could get into position. Aetex was faster, saving someone just as Garrick—now wreathed in shadows and red eyes—cut down with his sword.

"Foul beast," Aetex cried as he punched Garrick right in the face. The shadow man went stumbling backwards, letting out a distant echoing laugh as he did so.

"Hah, hah, hah," Garrick turned his head toward Knox and smiled wider than what should be normal, the edges of his mouth nearly touching his ears. When he spoke, his voice had an ethereal quality to it that was at odds with his normal baritone voice. "Darkness comes to claim all in her name. You will be the first to fall, her eyes see all."

"Shut up!" Eleanor screamed, brandishing her sword in front of Garrick. "My good friend, of all those who might fall to the darkness, why you?" Her words grew soft as she asked her question, but there remained an intensity to her words.

"Eleanor?" Garrick said in his normal baritone voice. But he shook his head immediately and balls of shadow began to form around his hands.

"Is he still in there?" Eleanor asked, stepping up beside Knox with her sword raised. "Can we save him?"

"I don't know," Knox said honestly. "I can try to drive off the darkness with my light, but he won't stand by and let us try to save him."

Aetex traded blows with Garrick, but it was clear neither side was trying very hard. Shadows by the dozens began to appear in the surrounding trees and Aetex spared a glance toward Knox. He nodded and Knox got the idea, he needed to step into the fight against Garrick so that Aetex could help with the multitudes of shadows appearing.

Knox looked over to Eleanor who gave him a nod and they stepped forward together to face the shadow Garrick.

Axe and blade crashed together and struck at Garrick, but he pushed back both attacks and suddenly through the shadows his armor became visible.

"He has on the relic!" Knox shouted and Garrick grinned.

His voice returned to its dark ethereal version as he spoke. "And with this tool of the darkness I will crush you!"

He let loose a wave of dark energy, but it splashed against the combined light of the two before him and they stood steady against him. His smile faded somewhat as Knox rushed forward, slamming his axe against the armored man's chest. The blow let out a cascade of light and Garrick went flying back some ten feet, landing in a heap.

Garrick made it to his feet in what seemed like moments, then rushing forward with his sword of the deepest darkness, he struck. Eleanor caught the blow, light swirling around her and slamming outward. She seemed to have some amount of control over the power of light she'd summoned, and lashed out with it, throwing back Garrick once more.

But he was powerful in that armor, much more powerful than he'd been before, even with the aid of the dark. Knox didn't wait for him to get ready, holding out his hand he shot forth a Luminous Surge. The light seemed to burn wherever it touched him and he hissed in pain as his armor ignited on fire for a short time. But Knox was done fooling around, he cast Lustrous Chains next, binding him into place, then used Aeon Gaze to search for vulnerabilities.

The armor covered only his chest and his neck and face were exposed, that was probably the most obvious Aeon Gaze he'd ever let off, but it had a fair point. It was time to hit Garrick in the face as hard as he could manage. Meanwhile, he wondered if there was a way to save the man from the shadow.

"Was the last person that wore the armor able to be saved?" Knox asked, seeing the shadows struggle against his chains, but eventually they'd give in to his power.

"No," Eleanor said, a single tear going down her face. "We

need to put him down, for his own good and the memory of his legacy."

"I understand," Knox said. He turned as if to strike despite being too far, then activated Ethereal Step, teleporting right in front of Garrick. His axe slammed against his neck and slid through like a hot knife through butter.

And just like that, Knox ended the attack of the shadows on the Guild Charterhouse.

Only a dozen survived, but Knox was worried only about two figures, the ones that had spoken of having a message for him, Calix and Vyren. He found Calix over the corpse of Vyren, mourning his cousin's death.

"Shit," Knox muttered under his breath, but kneeled beside the man anyway.

"He was too slow," Calix said, sharing a look with Knox. "Always just a little too slow."

"I'm sorry I couldn't help him," Knox said, and he truly wished he could have changed this particular outcome. "You have a message for me, I'd like it now."

Calix looked over with tears running down his face but wiped them away and cleared his throat. "Yes, I've a note for you from the High Magi of our house. I believe she wishes an audience, but the letter was sealed by her magics so there really isn't any way to say truly."

He handed over a yellowed sheet of parchment sealed by a wax seal of a moon and a phoenix, the seal of House Lumisar, and home to one of the biggest cities in the nation. Tearing it open, Knox looked around to see Aetex and Eleanor busy taking the dark armor away from Garrick's corpse, he read the letter.

. . .

Dearest Knox,

It is my hope that I would never have to send you this letter. I believed that Askar would do well to dissuade you from a life of Adventuring, as the experience left his own mouth sour. But word has reached my ears that you are not only an Adventurer, but in the midst of some great change in the area.

My name is Scarlet Blackwood, High Magi of the House of Lumisar and your mother. I've done all I can to protect you from your fate, but destiny has a way of disrupting even the best laid plans. Seek me out in Lumisar and I will tell you of your destiny.

Signed, Scarlet Blackwood

Knox's throat went dry, and he couldn't breathe very well. The world around him seemed to shake, yet he stood as still as he'd ever done before. A weight in his chest seemed to form and expand as he thought about what he'd just read. His mother... his mother was alive? And not only that, but she was also a powerful magic user for a royal house!

Then why had Knox grown up in relative poverty and away from his mother? What protection was she offering to him that meant he had to live with his father, a mostly drunk asshole who proved time and time again he only cared for himself?

His imagination expanded as he thought how his life might have been different if he were to have stayed with his mother. Would he have studied and yearned for the truth and discovery of things without the loss of his mother to drive him? The intense desire to cling to anything that was about her had driven and shaped his very being.

Now to find out she was alive and well in a distant land—it broke him to the core and Knox wasn't sure if he could trust anyone anymore. Who else could be lying to him, Dernal or perhaps Beth? Sure everyone had secrets that they refused to share with him, that was likely the case and Knox knew it.

But no, he couldn't let the darkness, thoughts or otherwise

win. He had a duty to learn and discover, with or without the motivation of his mother and her secret.

Even in this short letter, she'd kept secrets from him. Some notion of a destiny that he was set to follow, but he had his *own* destiny he followed. He'd brought about so much change to this world that his name would be remembered for years to come, even if he fell this day.

So why did it hurt so much to think about the betrayal? Why oh, why hadn't she been around for him, to comfort him, to ease the harshness of his father, to be that loving support mothers know how to be instinctually? He'd seen it with his friends' family members, he knew how a normal family ought to work.

The pain gave way to a numbness just as Aetex approached, looking concerned.

"You have received grave news?" Aetex asked, gesturing to the note. "Has someone you loved fallen in battle?"

Knox shook his head. "No," he said. "In fact, quite the opposite. My mother, who I'd been told died in childbirth, is alive and well."

"That is wonderful news," Aetex said, then seeing Knox's expression hardened he added, "Is it not?"

"She abandoned me and now sends word that she wants to meet with me," Knox said, shaking his head. "What am I supposed to think?"

Aetex looked down at Knox for several long seconds before answering. "It is difficult to know what path is the right one, but I feel that your mother must have done it for a reason, one important enough to keep it a secret from you. It is not always easy watching over those you are meant to protect and sometimes you make a misstep, no matter how hard you try to do what is right."

Knox watched Aetex's expression darken as he spoke and wondered at what failure this mighty warrior could have endured to bring forth such strong emotions. But he didn't know Aetex well enough to ask, nor did he feel like he wanted to ask while dealing with his own emotional turmoil.

"I can't go to her now," Knox finally said, and Calix nodded from a ways away.

"I'll tell her that it was delivered and that you will come at your earliest convenience. Is there any message you personally wish passed on?" Calix asked, leaving the side of his cousin for the first time since the battle ended.

"Tell her th—," Knox began to say but he stumbled on his words and stopped speaking. Then thinking better of it he just shook his head. "No message."

"Alright, well after we see about burying the dead, I will be off to deliver your message, tell Draven I've left and that Vyren has fallen."

Knox nodded. "I'll pass it on."

From there, they split off and began the hard work of putting everyone that had fallen to rest. Little talk happened during that time, but it was clear by the small amounts that were said, that the people didn't know where they'd be going next. It wasn't until Dawnbringer spoke up that Knox realized their intentions.

"We've accepted this new system," Eleanor said, getting everyone's attention with her booming voice. "And it bears with it great power. I feel that our best course forward is to abandon the Charterhouse for now and live among the city of Luminar, if you will have us." She turned and looked at Knox as she spoke.

"All are welcome, but I must warn you," Knox said, meeting her eye and then looking to the others. "It won't be easy there and it isn't without threats. But you will grow in power and be able to face any threats as long as you are willing to work hard and keep yourself improving."

Several heads nodded, but several did not, and Knox wondered how many out of the dozen and half survivors would come with them this day. But he needn't have worried, all of them fell into line behind Dawnbringer.

"I will go to the Mire's Gloom Dungeon town and share your passcode while gathering more to your cause, if you are open to reinforcement," Eleanor said, her eyes looking toward the dungeon town some day or two away.

"Do they have amulets guarding them from the system?" Knox asked, curious.

"Everyone should have one, they are cheap to make and were given after this zone was declared compromised. However, nearly half as many that normally come still came to the area to run the dungeon and grow in power. I believe I can bring a hundred or more souls to Luminar if given a week or two," Eleanor said, she seemed confident in what she was saying, but Knox had his doubts.

"If you can," Knox said. "I welcome any newcomers as long as they are willing to follow the rule of law that we put down. Luminar is a place of safety and security, and I won't have that disrupted just to grow the population."

"I understand and will endeavor to keep out the riffraff," Eleanor said, smiling for one of the first times since meeting her.

CHAPTER 36
PLANNING

THE GROUND SHOOK and another wave of darkened ooze came out to fight. Knox had nearly made it back with the half dozen that were going to go directly to Luminar with him, the rest accompanied Eleanor to the dungeon town. But the ground shakes were getting worse and Aetex had once more disappeared into the wild to face a 'great threat' or something like that.

Knox knew the man well enough to say he was likely doing something important, but leaving him alone with a majority of D Rankers, only two Cs were among them, he was forced to do most —if not all—the fighting against the ooze. Normally this wasn't an issue, he'd grown strong enough now to blast them away without much effort, but a few C Ranked Monsters had been infected and had taken out one of his charges already.

He was supposed to protect these people and already he'd lost one, there would be blood to pay when he caught up to this fast monster. It was a wolf of a kind, but thinner and quicker than any he'd encountered before.

Still it lasted no longer than the time it took Knox to focus his mind and strike out with a powerful Luminous Surge. Speed or not, it wasn't able to outrun his spell.

They arrived at the complex later that same night. Knox got

them settled into places to live and Murdoch promised to stop in on them.

"You agreed to how many more people?" Murdoch said, his eyes going wide.

"A hundred, perhaps more," Knox repeated. Murdoch remained unconvinced by the look he held.

"Am I hearing wrong, don't you think that is something you should run by me first?" Murdoch asked, then sighing he pinched at the bridge of his nose. "Okay, okay, this is salvageable if they are willing to sign the accords we've been putting together."

"Accords?" Knox asked, not understanding what he meant.

"Yes, a sort of 'this is your powers and responsibilities' document for everyone to sign. I've even got some people working on ways to make it magically binding, but its slow work."

"Don't do that," Knox said, shaking his head. "I won't stand for a magically binding contract, but a socially binding one is fine."

"You're the boss," Murdoch said raising his hands in defeat, though there was something else in his statement that Knox would have to unpack later. "So, I hear Aetex has left us once more to deal with some threat or another?"

"Yeah, but he assured me he wouldn't need saving this time," Knox said, smiling at the memory of his friend's reassurance.

The ground shook somewhere distant, but Knox felt it in his bones.

"Those damn ground shakes are getting ridiculous," Murdoch said, waving off a bug that tried to land on his face.

Now that the weather had turned from winter, bugs were back in full force and no amount of power could keep those annoying buggers from getting all over you. They were harmless, none of their bites able to pierce any of the Adventurers' skins at this point, but they were still highly annoying.

"We've got to be prepared for the pirate threat as well, any reports on scouts or movements of large forces since I was gone?" Knox asked.

"I'd have led with that if there were," Murdoch said, picking something out of his teeth as he watched the sunset.

"Doesn't hurt to be sure," Knox said. "Between the darkness and the pirates, I don't know what is going to kill us first."

"Pirates seem our more direct threat," Murdoch said, rubbing at the stubble on his chin.

Knox disagreed. "The darkness, and whoever is controlling it, put out a hit on my head," Knox said. "There really isn't any other way to describe how far it's gone to kill me. And so many have died because of it. I wish I had a target I could punch, but where is all the darkness, the ooze and the sickness, where is it all coming from?"

"What about those tunnels Dernal told me about, with the spiders?" Murdoch asked. "Maybe there are answers down there if you keep looking."

"Perhaps," Knox said, he'd had a similar thought, but the power of the monsters he'd faced down there weren't something just any party could take on and he didn't want to put his party in needless risk if it turned out to be nothing.

Suddenly, the air around them cracked and out of the sky a figure slammed down some twenty paces away, forming a small crater where he landed. Down on a knee and a fist to the ground with smoke billowing around him, Aetex appeared. He was injured, with several deep gashes all over his body and darkness, the black ooze, seeping from some of the wounds.

"They are coming," Aetex said, finding his feet and stumbling over to Knox. "At their current pace it'll take them two weeks to arrive, but they are bringing the darkness with them. The pirates are working with the dark."

And with that, Aetex fell at Knox's feet, stone-still.

"Get Dernal now," Knox told Murdoch as he kneeled over Aetex and prepared a Luminous Surge. The attack hit and Aetex grunted, showing a sign of life. Several more attacks and finally he felt the darkness leave Aetex completely.

Just in time, Dernal showed up and began to cast heals on

him, pulling shut his wounds and drawing his blood back within himself.

Aetex spent the next four days in recovery, but finally he came out of it and relayed to Knox what had happened. He'd faced off against a pirate lieutenant who had been empowered by the darkness but was separate—so he thought—from the rest of the pirates. When battling him, Captain Dread himself appeared and began to kick Aetex across the forest like he was nothing. Despite the new level of power Aetex had achieved, Captain Dread was somehow more powerful.

What was more, is he seemed to be able to call on ground shakes at command, infusing his undead horde with black ooze from the ground, making them stronger, faster, and more intelligent. Their numbers had swelled to a force of three thousand, if Aetex had gotten a good count of the undead and living among them. Over half he said were monsters risen to fight at Captain Dread's side and he had several hundred other Necromancers working with him. It was like all of the living pirates had chosen the path and were raising more and more into the army of the undead.

"What do we do against such odds?" Knox asked. He was in a meeting with Aetex, Murdoch, the elders, Dernal, and a select other few, including a recently arrived Eleanor Dawnbringer. She'd arrived with another hundred and fifty-two souls, all willing to sign and become a part of a city that would grow them in power year-round. When it was revealed that they were within travel distance of three dungeons, one of which was right here in the city, many tried to sign up friends or family that they promised would come and live here if they could get a message out.

"We fight," Murdoch said, looking across the table at Knox. "We have the walls, the siege weapons, and now the numbers to face off a threat several times our number. With this new influx of people, we number nearly six hundred, each of us able and willing to fight using the System gifted abilities. I for one will not turn tail and run when we have every chance of success."

"You have not fought the darkness," Eleanor said, her hand on the hilt of her sword. "If those undead as you call them are infused with the darkness and have the power of those shadows we fought, then we are doomed."

"No," Knox said, standing and hitting his fist on the table. "We will stand against the threat and prevail. I will kill Captain Dread myself and with him down, their numbers will not know what to do. Plus, we have plenty strong enough to fight against those necromancers he's raised up to fight at his side. If we target them, even with assassinations attempts, we could thin the herd of undead. I believe we can do this, who will stand with me?"

Everyone nodded but for a second or two no one spoke. Then finally, Eleanor stood and drew her sword, it gleamed in the dimly lit room and cast long shadows from its brightness. "I will stand beside you one last time," she said, her voice booming with power. "I trust that you will see me through to the other side, Titan Born."

Knox smiled and inclined his head. She'd learned that he was a Titan of Light recently and had been treating him with a bit more respect than she'd shown previously. Every nation and people had ideas of what Titans were, but most agreed that they were beings of incredible power to rival that of a god. And since there were few gods that Knox had ever heard of and more stories of Titans, Knox was in a situation where some of the newcomers were treating him with an insane amount of respect.

"I will lead you through the darkness and we will stand in the light," Knox said, leaning into the Titan Born thing. "To Death!" Knox added and everyone chanted it back.

"On to more practical matters, we need to start sending

groups to every dungeon we can to get more magical items," Murdoch said. "I believe we've done good organizing the weaker groups to clear the labyrinth and its dungeon, but the other two need to be occupied."

"I can go to the Mire's Gloom Dungeon with several groups that are able to do full clears," Eleanor offered, and Knox nodded to her in acceptance.

"Do that, but only take a week, there is no telling if the pirates will increase their pace. As for the other dungeon, I think I will go with a few groups and see if we can full clear it as well, again we will shoot for taking only a week, that way we have time to prepare additional fortifications before the attack," Knox said. "Mic, can you reinforce the walls or make them harder to climb?"

"I'm working on a way to electrify sections of the wall on command, I believe undead or not when muscles spasm, bodies will fall," Mic said.

Knox nodded, good, good, this was going to work. He just needed to execute their plans and prepare everyone by pushing them to their limits over the next week and seeing what kind of improvements they could make.

The meeting broke up after that and they went on their ways, each with several tasks to complete. Knox for instance needed to visit the Titan Engine as it had been several levels since he'd upgraded his abilities and talent tree.

Getting to the Titan Engine took him minutes, despite not needing to actually be in the room anymore, Knox came to be alone, so when he found Mic had joined him he was slightly annoyed.

"What Mic?" Knox asked, shooting him a look.

"Nothing master," Mic said. "I've come to make adjustments to the Titan Engine to allow for electrifying the outer fence, but if you need the room I can wait."

"Give me a few seconds," Knox said, reaching out he touched the Titan Engine, and his mind was moved through time and space to stand before the Titan Gowlen, or at least his visage.

He ended up training three new abilities. For his Titan Born path he got Arcane Revelation which allowed him to copy a spell he saw with a reduced effect for a short period of time after witnessing such a spell. Next was Nexus Shift, that acted like his Ethereal Step, teleporting him a short distance except that it left behind an explosion of light. Lastly, he learned a single new Mystic ability, Dimensional Shift, allowing him to swap locations with a friend or foe, basically another type of teleportation.

-Personal Status-
  -Name: Knox-
  -Level: 44-
  -Essence To Next Level: 105,764/223,900-
  -Health: Excellent Tier 9-
  -Mana: Excellent Tier 9-
  -Stamina: Excellent Tier 9-
  -Mind: 180-
  -Body: 180-
  -Spirit: 180-

CHAPTER 37
CLEARING DUNGEONS

KNOX HAD DERNAL, Terrim, John, and Leo all set up and ready to run the water dungeon. He'd picked a composition that he hoped would be beneficial for all those involved, since key members were unable to come for various reasons. Beth for instance knew someone who'd come from the dungeon town, an old acquaintance and she'd promised to run a dungeon with him.

The others had varying levels of excuses that Knox listened to but didn't take to heart. He had enough choices for dungeon mates that he'd felt pretty good about how the group looked at the end. Caleb was back, having followed Eleanor from the dungeon town, but Knox hadn't had the displeasure of talking to him yet.

The Ahtora met with Knox before they entered the dungeon, and he had their assurances that if the force of darkness returned, they would stand with Knox to fight it. There was a certain amount of comfort hearing the words, but Knox knew that they'd still be vastly outnumbered. It would rely on him taking out Captain Dread and ending his threat for good.

The dungeon itself was an easy affair up to a certain point. They'd cleared out the first few paths without much effort and now stood looking down a new path, second to the last one in the dungeon.

"Think this one will offer any more of a challenge?" John asked; he'd been instrumental in finding several traps, hidden doors, and even a secret passageway that led to them getting more loot. So far, Knox hadn't gotten anything worth mentioning, but the others had new weapons or armor that they were happy about. This was good, as they would need whatever powerful magical items they could get their hands on if they were going to defeat those damned pirates.

If it weren't for the undead nature of the pirates and the huge force of undead monsters they'd gathered, Knox was sure that they'd be a match for them. It seemed unfair that one such path had a way of really outstripping the others via brute force of undead. There had to be a catch to it all, but if there was, Knox and the other necromancers couldn't see it.

They'd gotten better, Frederick most of all, summoning now half a dozen undead themselves instead of the normal one at a time. But they didn't last long and the more they rose the higher the cost to maintain them. This Captain Dread must have a massive amount of mana to draw on to keep an army together. With all the necromancers that Knox had access to, they'd have a small army of maybe a hundred undead monsters ready to fight when the time came, but that meant collecting corpses and keeping them fresh, not an easy task.

"I think we ought to hurry this up and get our rewards for a full clear," Knox said, patting John on the back in a friendly gesture.

The entire path was filled with more fish people, these ones throwing lightning of all things, but they were dispatched with only a small amount of effort. The final boss of the path was a giant fish man that seemed to grow stronger when hit by magic, so they were forced to beat it down the old fashion way, which was a lengthy process. But in the end, Knox got a curious trinket that he identified with his ring. His ring was a copy of the original, seven had been created so far, going to various others that needed them. Eventually, he wanted everyone to have one, but the metal and magical requirements were steep.

Glimmer Glass
   When breathed on it will reveal secrets within a fifty pace section from where the wielder stands.
   Durability: 25/25

It was a small, palm-sized piece of translucent crystal with a faint inner blue glow. With a mirror-like surface, it was surprisingly warm to the touch. The shard was incased in a leather pouch with runic formations on it that all had to do with containment. Knox slipped the crystal out and breathed on it.

A faint pull on his sense had him turning around where he noticed a faint outline of a door on the far wall.

"John," Knox said, getting the rogue's attention.

"What's that?" John asked coming over to where Knox stood in front of the outline of the door.

"Check this area for a hidden door," Knox said, smiling to himself.

"I did a quick check, but I'll give it another go," John said, running his hands along the wall until, with a small sighing noise, he turned to Knox. "How'd you know?"

"My new trinket shows secrets, I guess it means secret doors and whatnot," Knox said, grinning broadly.

John got the door open, and they came upon a new chest, this one a golden color whereas the previous boss chest had been bigger but silver.

"Shall we see what loot waits for us inside?" Leo asked, standing beside the chest and thrumming his fingers on its lid. Everyone nodded, except for Dernal who gave his usual 'Hhrmm' grunting noise.

Leo pulled out a staff of ancient wood that contained a bright red crystal on the top and gave off a strong aura of power. Knox held out his hand to look at it, he'd been doing as much each time to give everyone an idea of what the items were before someone chose them. Leo handed it over, but he never took his eyes off the staff.

Crimson Pyre Staff
  +10 Attunement, +10 Resonance
  Inferno's Whisper: Call down a pillar of fire to devastate your foe and anyone within ten paces of them. Once per day you may activate this innate staff spell without any cost. For a High cost of Mana you may cast this spell while channeling through the staff. Additionally, the use of Inferno's Whisper grants the caster immunity to fire for the remainder of the day.
  Durability: 125/125

It was a length of elegantly carved wood made from dark, polished wood that felt warm to the touch. Standing as tall as Leo, the staff was adorned with intricate carvings of flames and runic formations up the length. Atop the staff sat a large, deep red gem that pulsated with an inner light, as if a fire was burning within it.

The weapon was magnificent, and Knox could think of several elemental casters who could benefit from it, but the gleam in Leo's eyes told him that it would go to him before any others.

"I'll sell you my old staff so that it may be added to the armory, but I want that now," Leo said after hearing the description of the staff.

"Deal," Knox said, handing over the new staff to Leo.

With that taken care of the next natural step for them was to check out the final path of the dungeon. They'd made good enough time that they were only two days into the dive, so the final one, even if difficult, should be done before the deadline.

They made camp and relaxed around the fire while letting their strength return to full.

Standing outside of the final Path, they stepped forward and felt a familiar spinning in their head that denoted a themed dungeon path. Whatever lay ahead, Knox was excited to see a more powerful themed adventure than what they'd faced all those months ago.

The ground moved or wait... no, they were in a boat of some kind, and it was moving along with the water. Knox looked around and saw that he was on a boat maybe twenty paces long and six paces across. Benches had been installed inside and that was where he currently sat along with the rest of his group.

More people, with dark, weather-worn skin and long coats worked the boat, moving one massive sail and several smaller ones. At the end of the boat was a single man with a dark black beard and a missing eye, his hand was on some sort of steering oar attached to the back. He stood an impressive head taller than Knox and had a muscled build that matched Terrim's own.

"Aye, you land lovers sure about this?" said a scrawny man with ragged clothing on, the overcoat he wore being the most well taken care of garment he had, and it was marked with holes and tears.

Knox, having done a few of these themed dungeons before with this very group, minus Terrim who stood in for Caleb, knew exactly what to do, just go with it. "Oh I'm sure we're sure," Knox said, nodding to the group.

Terrim looked rather confused but the rest of the party nodded along amiably.

"But perhaps you can remind us, what exactly are we doing out here?" Knox asked, hoping he wouldn't ruin the storyline by not playing along. But he needn't have worried, the old timer smiled and sat beside them.

He began his tale, and they listened in rapt concentration.

"Years ago, the most feared pirate, Captain Blackheart, plundered the Seven Seas. His greatest find was the Siren's Pearl, a gem of unparalleled beauty said to be blessed by the sirens themselves. It was believed that whoever possessed the Pearl could command the seas. But the Pearl was cursed. Soon after taking it, Blackheart's ship, The Leviathan, met a terrible fate, vanishing in a storm near the Shattered Isles, a place dreaded by sailors for its treacherous reefs and the haunting songs of the sirens.

Legends say the Pearl still rests within the wreckage of The Leviathan, deep in the heart of the Isles. Many have tried to claim it, lured by its promise of power, but none have returned. The sea around the Isles is treacherous, filled with perilous currents, hidden reefs, and the alluring call of the sirens, leading unwary sailors to their doom.

Your mission is to dive into the ruins of The Leviathan, retrieve the Siren's Pearl, and bring it back. But beware, the curse of the Pearl is no mere sailors' tale. It's said that the sirens themselves guard the Pearl, and they won't part with it easily."

Knox bit his lip; it sounded like they'd be fighting Sirens and possibly be going underwater. He checked his pouch, and he had his coin, as well as knowing that each of the team had a breathing coin of their own, so if such a dive into the water were necessary then they'd be ready.

"How close will you get us?" Leo asked, standing to look over the side of the boat and into the distance.

"We will take you right up to the shattered isles, this boat is swift and small enough to make the trip as promised, but you'll be on your own until you lite the beacon. But only light it if you've found your prize, or you'll find the captain losing his temper with you and then you might as well be sleeping with the fishes," the old sailor said.

"Sounds easy enough," John said, flipping his dagger in his hand and slipping it away and out of sight the next moment. Knox noticed that he played with his daggers a lot when he was nervous. John hadn't been keen on the idea of water or breathing out of a coin, but he had come, so there was that.

No other group would be strong enough to get this far in this particular dungeon, so Knox was excited to see what it had to offer when they completed it.

"Take to the bow and keep a keen eye for rocks, call out any you see so that we can go around them," the old sailor said, taking to the side of the boat and grabbing one of many oars set there. He and the rest of the crew lowered the sails and began to row the boat.

Knox and his companions went to the front of the ship and kept their eyes out for rocks. There was a string of islands in the distance, but they had sheer cliffs and crashing waves as their most noticeable feature. He wanted nothing to do with that mess, but it appeared to be where they were headed, so he kept his eyes on the water and hoped they'd at least make it to the part of the dungeon with monsters before they died.

They avoided rocks here and there, but the captain seemed to know where they were already, moving to avoid them even as they were called out. The old sailor was passing out little balls of wax and Knox called over to him.

"What's with the wax?" Knox asked, just as a hauntingly beautiful song began to play out in the distant shore.

It was so enrapturing that Knox immediately looked away from the rocks he was meant to watch and scanned the shoreline to see the cause of such music. In a small section of the islands where it was more beach and less cliff, were a dozen or so naked women. Knox blinked several times, they were far enough away that he shouldn't even be able to see them in much detail, but it was suddenly as if his eyes had the ability to zoom in.

He could see them sitting in the soft rolling beach waves, gentle and soothing as they foamed up below their breasts. He felt himself leaning over the edge, wanting nothing more than to swim out to them and hear their sweet music. A rough hand pulled him back just as he went to dive off the boat.

Dernal, looking more flustered than Knox had ever seen him, held down both Terrim and Knox by their collars and was yelling something at them but all they could hear was the music, sweet, lovely music.

With a shake of his head, Dernal reached out and plucked something from the old sailor that looked down on them with a grin. He stuffed whatever it was into Knox's ears and suddenly the world went quiet, and he was able to think straight.

Dernal shook his head, saying something that Knox guessed was 'young boys' or something close to that, but he couldn't hear anything through the wax, just make guesses by his lips. The music was gone, as well as the desire to jump overboard and join the naked women or the sirens as Knox realized they must be.

Looking over the side, the space where the sirens had been was just gone, replaced by a sheer cliff that would absolutely have broken their boat into a million pieces. They'd affected his sight and hearing so easily, manipulating his desires and leaving him confused at best.

But Knox was strong-willed and soon he stood beside Terrim, pointing out rocks as they grew ever closer to a rocky beach area. It wouldn't be so safe, but it was the safest looking docking location they'd seen so far. Knox just hoped it wasn't a trap of some kind.

"Here is where you get off," said the old sailor as the boat neared the shore. It was still a swim away, but not one that should be hard for five strong Adventurers. John paled but Dernal put a reassuring hand on his back, then pushed him into the water.

Knox went next, figuring he'd do well to have some cold water dashed over him, the sirens still played on repeat in his mind, though their temptations were purely physical now, not the mental call of destruction so much as the physical call from their beauty.

The cold water rushed up to meet him and he gasped, nearly letting water into his mouth. Ahead of him, almost to the shore, John swam with a speed that surprised even Knox.

Once they made it to the shore, Dernal took out his earwax, so the rest did the same.

"Won't be able to hear much with these, keep them close just in case," Dernal commanded. "Get a fire going, we need to dry off before continuing."

It was prudent and Knox knew they had the time to kill so he didn't argue, letting Dernal take the space of group leader didn't bother him, in fact it took a bit of the pressure off his own shoulders.

The beach they'd landed on was covered in trees and rocks, but more rocks than trees. The trees were unlike any he'd seen before, with no leaves except on the top, and a thin trunk that looked like overlapping dragon scales. At the base of one such tree was a rock-like green ball. Knox picked it up and Leo nudged him.

"You know what that is?" Leo said, taking it from Knox and pulling free a dagger from his belt. "It's a coconut."

He cut into a thick shell that fell off to reveal a hard hairy looking smaller brown sphere. The 'coconut' as Leo called it split apart as he bashed it with the hilt of his dagger and milky fluid splashed out. Leo took a deep drink from one half before offering it to Knox.

"I'm okay," Knox said, pulling free his water canteen and taking a drink. He wasn't about to drink some strange liquid from a huge looking nut in the middle of a dungeon.

"Suit yourself," Dernal said, taking the coconut from Leo and drinking the rest.

"Hey, what about me?" John asked, taking care to add a mock face of sadness then anger.

"There are plenty of nut waters around for you to pick from,"

Knox said, gesturing to several more that looked freshly fallen from the tree.

"Focus up," Dernal said. "According to the old man we need to search these islands for a wrecked ship. I'd wager it'll be in some cove or cave, so let's split the party and cover more ground."

No one looked happy about the idea of splitting the party, but it was necessary. Knox, John, and Terrim went in one group and Leo and Dernal in the other group. Once they were finally dry, down to the last pair of stockings, they set out in opposite directions.

Knox and his group went deeper into the island's dense vegetation, cutting and earning each step as they fought back the overgrowth. Dernal and his group were just walking along the beach, as it curved in the direction they wanted to go eventually. Knox thought that perhaps that might be the way to go next time as a bush came back to smack him after Terrim moved it for himself.

Their search turned up precious little and as the day waned on, they returned to the meeting area to find the others already back with a fire going.

"We found a cave and the inside is filled with crab monsters, we think that might be the right way but we won't be able to tell until we clear them out," Leo said, handing over some type of cooked crustation over. Knox took a bite and enjoyed the salty flavor.

After they'd finished resting and ate their fill, they were off toward the cave that the other group found. It was on the coast, an area opened up into a massive cave opening that might just fit an entire ship, but Knox wasn't sure as he'd only ever seen ships in depictions in books, but he knew some could be pretty big.

A natural light, soft and blue, shone forth from within and the clack of something could be heard echoing inside. His eyes focusing, Knox made out several crabs the size of a man, with claws that could crunch someone in half if they wanted. His sense told him they were strong, but not a threat they couldn't handle.

Even with their numbers, Knox was sure they'd be able to take care of them if they came all at once.

Looking to Terrim, who shrugged, Knox stepped forward and into battle.

It lasted barely five minutes before all the crabs had fallen and they were victorious. They'd put up a decent fight, denting Knox's shield as well as chipping away at Terrim's crystalline shield, but Leo's fire magic cooked them almost as fast as they could appear.

The fight had all taken place right at the mouth of the cave, where the low light wouldn't inhibit their ability to see correctly, so there was no guarantee that they'd taken care of all the crabs. Knox's sense felt something ahead, but it wasn't crab-like.

Settling into a crouch they entered the cave, waiting for their eyes to adjust. It took only moments before the full truth of the cave became apparent to them.

A massive ship sat on the rocks within, half submerged in water and looking like it might wash away into pieces any moment. All sorts of greenery grew on and around it, but the oddest was the glowing blue mushrooms. They gave off enough light to see by and there was movement on the deck of the ship. Several humanoid figures with sea creatures of every kind attached to them or rather apart of them, were moving about.

One such humanoid figure had a shark head and another a star fish for a face. All around there were dozens of such figures, modified by different types of sea creatures. And in the midst of it all, Knox felt a powerful aura unlike any he'd sensed, short of the emblem that he recovered inside the labyrinth. That must be the pearl.

"The pearl is on one of the lower decks, perhaps underwater, but we've got a dozen or so sea monster people in our way. Plans?" Knox asked, ready to hear from someone else what the best way through would be.

"Straightforward approach," Dernal said, taking over.

"Nothing fancy, just get in, kill the monsters, and grab the loot, easy as that."

"They are stronger than the crabs, but I still think we'll be able to handle them," Knox said, nodding. "Good plan, let's kill them."

They reached the side of the ship and fought off three sea-raised pirates—up close you could tell that they were once pirates or sailors of some kind. When they got close, killing one after another, Knox noted the eyes of each of the sea monster men without fail, a brilliant blue.

Shark face came in fast, biting for Knox's neck, but his shield went up and caught the blow. His axe bit deep and ended the monster before he could even pull away. These fights weren't much of a challenge, but they were moving slow and being careful, so that had to count for something.

Getting onto the ship, the very boards seemed to creak and give underfoot, but they managed to make it to a drier part just as four more sea men came out to fight. Again they were challenging, but not anything to write home about. Each step they took put them closer and closer to the pearl that lay beneath the decks.

The floorboards creaked under their weight as they went deeper into the bows of the ship. There was a clicking sound below, but Knox sensed nothing but the Pearl, its overpowering aura masking anything else that might be around it.

Knox understood how these dungeons worked, even themed ones. They'd face some kind of greater threat, they had to, up to this point everything had been hard but not as hard as Knox expected. Was it his view of the challenge that needed to change or were they just being suckered into a false sense of peace?

Regardless of which would end up being true, Knox saw their next challenger as they made it into a wide room that was likely a captain's quarters at one point. On the back wall was a chest that lay open, and the aura of the pearl shone forth. Beside it with a tentacle hand touching it, was none other than the boss of this encounter. Knox knew as much because suddenly, his sense could tell that much of the aura he felt before was around this single combatant, and not the pearl exclusively.

"Be careful, that one is strong with a capital S," Knox said, getting in position to Terrim's right.

A soft almost whispered voice spoke next and Knox could feel power in each word. "I am the captain and the rightful owner of the pearl, leave now if you wish to live."

"Leo," Knox said.

"Yeah?" Leo asked, not taking his eyes off the target.

Knox smiled. "Light him up."

Leo returned the smile with one of his own. "With pleasure."

Fire erupted all around the captain and his screams filled the room. A moment later, an iridescent light shone through the fire and the captain stepped out, looking only a little less for wear. Knox hit him with Lustrous Chains to lock him in place as the party surged forward to attack.

Terrim got there first, slamming his shield into the tentacle face of the captain, drawing a grunt from him. Next John appeared behind him, slashing and cutting off several of his tentacle arms. Dernal was next, chanting a spell of some kind behind them all. A wave of warmth passed over them and suddenly Knox felt like he could fight all the harder.

Slashing his battle axe forward, he aimed to take the captain's head in one swipe. Instead, the man ducked the blow and stabbed out with a sword, shattering a section of his Mystic Armor in the process.

Knox staggered back, but the captain wasn't given a chance for a counter blow, instead he was forced back by the combined might of their party.

They beat down the boss, minute by minute, but they weren't killing him fast enough. Something triggered between the boss and the pearl and suddenly light poured out, throwing all of them back.

He was bathed in light and his wounds began to close. Then a thought occurred to Knox, turning to the others as they quickly made it back to their feet he said, "Let's destroy the pearl and I bet he goes down."

"Don't we need that for the completing of the dungeon?" Terrim said, looking perplexed.

"Boy has a point," Dernal grumbled.

"Which one?" Leo said. "Clearly, we won't make it out of here if we can't defeat this pirate and despite our best efforts, we aren't putting a dent in him. We need another way and I think destroying the pearl is our best chance."

"I'll go with that," John said, dodging a moment later as a tentacle from the boss monster shot out for him, bathed in white iridescent light.

"Fine," Dernal said. "Knox, you take care of the pearl, and we will hit him with all we have."

Knox nodded and suddenly the room was a buzz of movement. Dernal summoned forth his Celestial Guardian, and it almost looked like they would turn the tide of battle.

Knox ignored the fight to focus on his task, first he stepped through teleporting to where the pearl was being held, some five paces from the captain's back. Then he began to build his power up for a strong magical attack. Power swam around him, and he unleashed a Luminous Surge down into the chest.

Nothing happened.

Well, not nothing, if anything the flow of power from the pearl to the captain seemed to get larger and more powerful. Cursing himself for a fool, Knox got his axe out, Scarlet. She'd be better able to smash down on an object as the head was heavier and meant for that kind of work.

He reared back to deliver a blow and his hit connected! He heard a faint cracking noise and the captain screamed. Hurrying to finish the job Knox went to do it again, but tentacles grabbed hold of his arms and began to pull him away. John appeared from seemingly nowhere and cut down hard with his daggers.

Knox was free once more and rushed forward slamming his axe down on the pearl. A sudden whoosh of power followed as the pearl detonated, destroying the chest and filling Knox will bloody holes. His mystic armor had done nothing to stop the pieces of magical rock, and his armor caught only half of them.

In pain and bleeding out, Knox smiled. They'd done it, the captain lay dead and burning some few feet away.

"Time for loot?" John asked, leaning down over Knox who nodded and laughed at the rogue's straightforward attention.

"Let me heal him first," Dernal grumbled, beginning his chanting.

Knox felt the fuzziness in his head stop and suddenly he was back to 100%, feeling full of life. Getting to his feet, he picked up pieces of the pearl off the ground.

"Gather this up and we will give it to the sailors," Knox commanded. John groaned at ignoring the five golden chests not far away but helped.

Looting followed, they all got useful items that helped in protecting them from magic in one way or another, except for Knox.

He got a small pearl trinket that could be clipped to his armor.

Pearl Broach
  +10 Resonance
  Inner Light: One time use, this Pearl Broach will aid you in increasing your natural magical output by five times. This can only be used for any offensive or defensive spell, utility spells do not benefit as greatly.
  Durability: 20/20

It had magnifying effects that Knox could think of a million uses for, but he'd have to save it for an emergency, as his spells already hit harder than most normal mobs could handle. The item itself was a golden disc with raised runic letters around the edges and a single pearl lodged in the middle, thrumming with a portion of the magic Knox had sensed from the artifact they were meant to collect. This was good, as Knox would need something that packed a punch in the upcoming battles.

The biggest drawback that Knox could see was the fact that it could only be used once. Most items they'd been getting with greater effects had been a once per day thing, but this was by far the most powerful item he'd ever gotten from a dungeon before. Five times the power of his strongest cast of Luminous Surge might be the very thing that could end Captain Dread before his reign of terror overtook them.

Happy with their loot and eager to get back, Knox and his party returned and sent up a signal to the sailors. They came within an hour, and they delivered the remains of the artifact. The sailors grumbled but on the end of the boat a doorway opened up and they took it, leaving the dungeon path.

CHAPTER 38
EMISSARY

ALL THE PREPARATIONS that could be made had been made. They were four days from the arrival of the pirate army, but a group had broken off of the main body and would be arriving this very day, within hours if their speed continued at its current pace.

It was a small party, with only four dots on the giant display map of the commander's chair, but they'd shown themselves to be able to hide before, so they stayed on high alert. The Ahtora hadn't arrived yet, so if this did turn out to be an attack, it would be over before help had a chance to arrive. But anything short of Captain Dread himself coming on ahead, would likely signify not much of a true threat.

After all, it was the hordes of undead that they truly worried about. The command chair didn't show the undead, or rather it didn't *always* show the undead. The size of the group attack would fluctuate from five hundred strong to thousands. Mic guessed that it had to do with the process they were doing to keep the corpses fresh and battle ready, perhaps bringing them to life as needed instead of constantly.

This bit of information didn't help Knox sleep at night, in fact it worried him even more. They had the ability to throw thousands at Luminar and Captain Dread had proved his ability to raise even the most injured of undead. But Knox had a plan for that, he'd be taking a strike team into the heart of the enemy and killing Captain Dread before he got a chance to bring a second wave of undead back to fight.

It wasn't a plan everyone was onboard with, but it was all he had at the moment. There would be better minds than his going over strategies and ways to defeat the impossible odds, but Knox knew what truly needed to be done, Captain Dread needed to die.

Imagine Knox's surprise when four Pirates appeared waving a white flag outside their gate. Knox took with him Murdoch, Aetex, and Dernal, to go out and meet with them, eager to hear what message these pirates had to give.

The sky was unusually sunny this day, making it that much easier to keep an eye on the approaching pirates, but Knox had told Mic to stay on high alert, he didn't trust them at all.

"Hail to the master of this city," came a very relaxed, almost humored, voice. "My name is Gad and I speak for Captain Dread as his emissary. Will you hear my words?" Gad asked, eyeing each of them in turn as their hands settled on their weapons.

Knox stepped forward and met Gad's steely grey eyes. "I'll hear your words, but if you have a mind toward treachery, be warned that I won't keep you as prisoners."

Gad wore a light brown tunic with a black coat with a high collar over it. The jacket seemed far too thick and heavy for the weather, but he didn't appear to be bothered by it. He had a scar going down his cheek all the way down to his neck, one of only a few blemishes on an otherwise handsome face. He had deep brown hair that sat lightly atop his head, brushed back and tied into a knot.

"I've come with a proposition from Captain Dread that will help you avoid bloodshed," Gad said, when no one stopped him he continued. "You can save lives by submitting to him. But he doesn't ask for something for nothing, no, Captain Dread is generous. He will allow you to act as his 2nd in command in charge of ruling over the city. In addition, he will ensure that none of your citizens will be harmed or harassed by his sailors."

"You see, we are a peaceful lot of sailors who seek only the private trade and barter of the ocean. The time has come for us to go back out into the great waters and trade with other nations. You would be doing us a great honor in holding your fair city in his name, perhaps even checking in with our holdings on the coast while the majority of our trade ships are out. What say you to this proposal?"

"What assurances do we have that you'd honor a deal such as this and not take hostile actions once you've gotten inside the city?" Murdoch asked, Knox could feel power in his words. He was using one or more of his abilities to try and fish out the truth.

"There would be no need to conquer that which has surrendered. Furthermore, Captain Dread truly wants only one of you dead, the rest will be fine," Gad said, raising his eyebrows at Murdoch and reaching up to touch his own lips. "I mean to say..."

Caught in a lie, Knox smiled at him as he stuttered a few more words half formed. "You see that," Knox said, pointing at the man and putting his other hand on the head of his battle axe. "They will lie, cheat, and steal their way to a victory. We can't trust a word they say, and we are wasting our time here. In fact, you probably knew this was a waste of time, didn't you?"

"I don't know what you mean?" Gad asked, clearly hiding something.

"We need to get back," Knox said, reaching out with his sense toward the city he felt the intruders at the same time a cry of alarm went up.

Gad pulled free his sword and struck out at Murdoch. But Murdoch was a duelist before he was anything else and he'd anticipated the movement. With one clean movement he put his blade through the eye of Gad and stopped him with a single strike. The other pirates fled, but Knox was already running on his way back to the city and couldn't be bothered to care. They'd retrieve Gad's body later, if the pirates didn't, but he had to get back as soon as possible.

The sound of fighting came from the command center, a crowd was already gathering outside, but Knox used all the teleports he had at his disposal to get himself inside before the crowd.

Mic was down and in pieces, several other golems had lost parts too, but Edgar was finishing off a rogue pirate as Knox appeared in the room. Several bodies of dead villagers lay strewn about the room, cut or dismembered as much as the golems.

"Mic is hurt bad, Borris is dead, and Vlad lost both his arms," Edgar said, practically spitting the words, his anger boiling up.

"Grab Borris's core and help me find Mic's, we can save them if we hurry," Knox said, then thinking twice about it he added, "Did you get them all?"

"No, I didn't, one escaped," Edgar said, kicking at two more bodies on the ground in black roguish attire. "They were interrogating Mic when we arrived, and we stopped them. I don't know what he told them, but we do feel a semblance of pain when damaged, so he might have cracked."

They spoke as they walked toward the workshop where the golems awaited. They had hundreds active at this point, but no more new ones had been activated in weeks. Instead, the remaining golems were being studied so that Knox could replicate the designs as well as the maintenance golems—they could modify just fine but creating an entirely new golem wasn't within their capabilities.

They got to the place and Knox went to work. The cores of both Borris and Mic were still functional, so he could save them he knew. Working alongside several maintenance drones, Knox installed the cores and spoke the activation runes.

"I told them much," Mic said, his voice sounding slightly off in his new form. It didn't have any of the upgrades or changes, but it was definitely Mic.

Mic went over all that he'd told them, about how the command chair could see them coming, how the Titan Engine controlled the spread of the system and how eventually it would reach over all lands and water. He told them their troop numbers, including golems, then even went on to tell them how if the command chair was taken it could be used to command the golems to attack the citizens within Luminar.

"What's that now?" Knox asked, stopping him mid explanation. "Golems would attack citizens if told to do so from the command chair?"

"Yes," Mic said, lowering his head as if in shame or disappointment, Knox couldn't tell which. "It involved more than I told them, but essentially to sit on the command chair would enable them to exert control over Luminar. No golem would dare attack you, Titan of Light, but all else could be identified as enemies, they just aren't built with the ability to tell where allegiances lie."

"Then we know their plan, they'll make a push for this room, and we must defend it to the last, to death!" Knox declared, his emotions setting off.

Knox stood over the bodies of the fallen, four had died, three golems were damaged beyond repair, but Borris and Mic had made it. He knew everyone expected him to say something inspirational in this time of great sorrow, but all he could think about was how this wouldn't be the end. More would die and he'd have more weight on his shoulders from the burden.

Knox said words about each of the fallen, keeping it short and to the point. He spoke of their need to pull together now and not apart, how death was a common thing among them and they would prevail. His words felt hollow and thin, but he said them and got nods from the crowd.

It was a sad day, but worse days lay ahead, so Knox kept his chin up and his power ready to strike out against those that would do his people harm.

"I've got an urgent mission to attend to," Aetex told Knox, catching him off guard.

"Right now?" Knox asked, confused by the sudden change.

"It's important, I will try and be back before the battle," Aetex said, shooting off into the sky before Knox could say another word.

CHAPTER 39
THE LAST BATTLE

"I'M NOT sure that really matters right now," Knox said, looking over to Mic who had already begun to restore himself to his former glory of blinking eyes and movable mouth.

"The portal behind the command chair has been getting energy touches from somewhere else," Mic said, as if repeating himself would make Knox more willing to care when he was staring down an army of undead and necromancers.

"And we have more pressing matters," Knox said, turning to leave and return to the meeting about the defense of the city that he was so rudely taken from by the request of Mic.

"The only other place that could do that would be another Titan Complex," Mic said and suddenly the words hit Knox, who stopped and turned.

"I thought we were the only one left," Knox said, he'd read about Ramses of course, but the system didn't rule here so obviously he'd failed in some way.

"I assumed as much as well," Mic said. "But this isn't likely to be as good of news as you might think. I have a vague remembrance of my last master being more than a little wary toward the other Titans, even going so far as to move the Titan Complex with a powerful relocation spell before he died."

"That's a lot to remember, anything else you are holding out on me?" Knox asked, turning and giving Mic his full attention.

"Nothing pertinent to our current conflict," Mic said, his artificial face tweaking up in a smile.

"So, what happens if the power keeps reaching for us or whatever it was you said?" Knox asked, putting his hand on the command chair he checked, as he did every hour now, on the distance of the pirate army. They were a day's walk at most away, and Knox assumed that their scouts and rogue-ish types were already here someplace.

"The gateway was meant to be a form of travel between the various points set up by Titans, so in theory, it could open and whatever is awaiting us on the other side would come through. But what baffles me is how they are finding us," Mic said, playing at scratching his head.

"Why?" Knox asked.

"They'd need an anchor of power, something to help them know where to point. If they had some strong magical item that resonated with the same light frequency as Luminar, they could do it, but without it or something similarly powerful that they could track, it just makes no sense. The odds of them randomly finding us are millions to one."

Knox sighed and removed his hand from the command chair. "Monitor the situation and have more combat golems stationed inside the command center. Speaking of which, where are Edgar, Borris, and Vlad?" Knox asked. The three were supposed to be guarding Mic at all times, but once again they appeared to have gotten pulled away.

"I sent them away to help with a small matter, but they will return shortly," Mic promised, then he began shooing Knox away. "You've got a meeting to attend, and I'm done with you now."

"Sure, sure, fine, I'm going," Knox said. "Oh, and don't send them away again, or I'll take up your guarding duties myself and I'm needed elsewhere."

Mic just nodded and continued to shoo Knox out of the

command room and back to where he'd been. Glancing back Knox saw the most disturbing little smile on the golem's face, but what it might mean, he didn't know.

"What about the ones that want to leave now?" one of the Elder's asked, his focus on Murdoch so he didn't see Knox enter the tent where they'd been doing their military planning.

"Then they should have left days ago," Knox said, his latest check confirming that the pirates were too close now for them to safely let anyone flee.

A small band of three parties took all the children several days ago to stay in the dungeon town. It was far enough away that the pirates shouldn't waste their time, and if they did, they'd find more than just the parties he had sent to keep them safe, several hundred Adventurers had remained in the dungeon town, and they'd fight to protect them. Either way, it was safer there than it would be here, so the children not old enough to pick a path yet had been taken as well as some of the older folk that didn't want to fight.

It wasn't that they couldn't fight, Henry was a perfect example of someone who was up there in years and still able to make a great impact. Henry stood in the meeting some few places down from where the other elder had spoken, and he nodded his head in greeting to Knox as he entered.

"Who wants to leave?" Knox asked when no one was immediately forthcoming with the information.

"It doesn't matter," Murdoch said, waving to Knox discreetly. "The time for that has come and gone. While we can't force everyone to fight, we can make it clear that their lives are on the line as well as the lives of those that they love."

Knox nodded back to Murdoch and cleared his throat.

"Where did we land on sabotage groups; do we try it or is it too risky?"

"We've got the numbers to make an impact," Murdoch said. "But I fear only John has the skill to pull something off without being detected. We voted that it would be too deadly a cost to send out troops to try and slow them down or poison them."

"Understandable," Knox said. "Then did we discuss the party formations and best placements for when they overwhelm us at the wall?"

"We did and if you're hungry I can explain some it to you while we eat, I think we've covered all that needs to be covered, so meeting is adjourned," Murdoch said, showing that he'd taken into the role of leader quite well.

Everyone began to leave, some coming and talking to Knox for a bit, but Knox kept his responses terse and short. His nerves were on edge, and he couldn't do much to hide it. An army far greater in numbers than them marched on their location and he had to figure out how to protect them.

"Your father is causing more than his fair share of problems," Murdoch said as they walked.

Knox looked across the open complex hoping that he might see his father and confront him directly, but he didn't see him.

"What did he do now?" Knox asked, letting out a long-exaggerated sigh.

The ground beneath his feet was soft and more than a little muddy. They'd gotten rain over the last few days and the clouds, dark and ominous, still hung low in the sky.

"He's scared and he's started to drink again," Murdoch said, and Knox knew what that meant.

"What's he been saying?" Knox asked.

Murdoch shared a look with Knox, and he could tell he didn't want to say, but he spoke regardless a moment later. "Raising questions about your leadership and that of the council and even me." He said the last bit as if shocked someone might not trust his leadership. It made Knox smile despite the tone of the conversation.

"He's afraid and wants to leave," Knox said. "I understand his fear, but just when I think he's changing, he goes and does something like this. Do you know where he is? I'll speak with him."

"In his hut, he's all dried out after the golem's helped him home last night. There have been instructions given that he is not to be served any more alcoholic drinks until after the conflict. People are scared Knox, and I'm scared too. We don't need someone bringing up our fears when we're already struggling to face them ourselves."

"Let's do a raincheck on that meal," Knox said. "I'll deal with my father and get him to shut up, or he can take his chances on the road."

"Don't do that," Murdoch said, shaking his head. "He is afraid, he needs reassurance, and it would come best from you. Build him up, don't break him down further."

Knox looked at Murdoch and couldn't help but smile. He'd grown so much since taking the true role of a leader and it was really shining through right now. He was right, of course, Knox needed to help and not make things worse. With that in mind, he bid farewell to his friend and went looking for his father.

The conversation with his father went about as well as expected. He was afraid and it showed, but Knox did his best to be reassuring and not judgmental. But with the battle coming so soon he hardly had the time to spend helping his father. It was enough then that his father agreed he'd help fight and keep his thoughts to himself.

The battle was upon them, the enemy forces gathering outside the walls and undead massing in the front of the eastern gate, but none came within bow range yet. Knox stood at the head of his forces, the Ahtora stood within the walls, with only a few actually standing on the walls, ready to strike out.

There was a different feel in the air over last time. This would be the final battle, the final conflict. This much Knox was sure. There would be no fleeing from this battle, Knox would see to it that Captain Dread saw his final day today.

There was a strange heaviness in the air that came along with all the waiting. Battle would soon follow and the rush of it would take him up, ridding him of any feelings of anxiety, but until then his mind swirled with possibilities. Was it possible that they'd be overrun, would they perhaps not have enough defenses in place to deal with such an assault? So many questions bogged down his mind, but he cleared them with one simple thought. He'd kill Captain Dread this day and save lives.

A horn was blown, and dark figures emerged from the distant tree line at a run. Several undead, swift, and deadly, ran for the wall, but not nearly enough to do anything serious.

"Hold," Knox said, holding up an arm to forestall any attacks. He'd let the walls take care of these ones; they'd been electrified by Mic so they should do well against flesh.

Onward they came, running at a slow pace but much faster than Knox thought should be possible for reanimated corpses. The moons shone forth, filling the clearing with light, but even so, as the undead arrived they seemed to be covered in darkness that grew thicker as they ran. Halfway to the gate and walls they simply disappeared in a fog of darkness.

It wasn't terribly hard for Knox to track them with his sense, but everyone else would have trouble seeing them and aiming shots. Reaching out his hand just as they approached the wall, Knox fired off a powerful Luminous Surge and the darkness blew back, revealing the undead just as they began to climb up the wall.

Several sharp sounds later and they were on the ground writhing in muscle induced pain. Whether or not undead could feel pain remained a mystery to Knox, but the shock had done enough to bring them down and keep them there.

"Fire," Knox called out before the darkness could return and shade them from sight. Two dozen arrows loosed and ended the first wave of undead. This had been just a testing probe, and more was soon to follow, Knox knew.

The waiting was the worst part.

An hour went by with seemingly no attack. Knox kept his sense probing. Every once and a while he'd use his trinket to try and look for hidden objects, or in this case rogues, trying to breach the wall. It was during one of these moments that he caught sight of an outlined figure approaching the wall.

Instead of immediately attacking it, as far as he could tell there was only one, he watched it. The wall proved to be the more able defender though, because the man cried out in pain the moment he touched the wall, letting go of a rope he'd somehow affixed higher up on the wall. There would be no sneaking over this wall today, not while they had the power to keep the charge on it.

That was the thing though, Mic informed Knox that the wall would last until sunrise, then it would need time to recharge, or they'd need to empty the vault of Monster Cores to keep it running. He'd emptied the vault in preparation of using them if it became necessary, but he hoped it wouldn't.

More waiting followed, Knox was almost wondering if Captain Dread knew they'd be able to outlast the charge on the wall when more horns were blown and a second wave of undead began their march. This time it was equal to the amount that had assaulted them before, and they had wooden ladders with them. They were going to try and take the wall, but Knox was ready for them.

"Stand ready!" Knox called and the demand went up to all lengths of the wall.

There would be a moment in all the chaos to follow that would allow Knox to find Captain Dread and when that moment came, he had to be ready. Until then, he had a force of defenders to lead.

"Release!" Knox called out and the air was darkened further by the whistle of arrows. Undead fell by the dozens, but where one fell, two more were there to take their place. Over and over again they loosed arrows, intent on thinning the ranks, but Titans be damned, they had so many undead.

Shadows began to build up around the approaching undead and Knox was unsure he had the power to push back so much of it, so instead, he just ordered the volleys to continue. They brought down less than before, but still, undead fell and more surged up to fight.

They made it to the wall and began putting ladders up, but they immediately caught fire as the wall continuously pumped damaging power into it. A few undead still tried to make it up, but they were quickly dealt with. It was a bloodbath, undead piling up on other undead as they rained down arrows on them.

Movement in the back of the ranks caught Knox's attention and suddenly a chill went down his spine. Captain Dread had somehow snuck up with the undead, another force just behind him lying in shadows. He began to chant, and power swirled around him.

Before Knox could start to cast his own spell, a wave of dark energy shot forward and the doors, so thick and secure, blew inward allowing a flood of undead in. Just like that, Luminar lost their advantage of the walls.

"Turn and fight!" Knox shouted as he Ethereal Stepped to the stairwell leading down to the gate.

He slashed out with his powerful battle axe, cleaving two

undead in two as he went. Turning, he hit a third with the shaft of his axe, braining it hard enough to bring it down.

The Ahtora fought on an entirely different level than most, shooting out with magic and spears, leveling the incoming charge. Knox fought all around them, never once did he almost get hit, so accurate were their shots.

Back and forth the fight went, until finally the waves of undead seemed to stop and Knox heard chanting outside the wall again.

Not this time, he thought as he used his various teleporting abilities to close the gap and rush the pirate captain.

It worked, he appeared just beside the pirate, having switched spots with one of his necromancers standing nearby. He really shouldn't be this out of place, but he needed to put an end to Captain Dread and this was the way to do it.

His axe swung low and smashed into a dark barrier surrounding Captain Dread. The captain's chanting grew to a fever pitch and ended, his spell cast. Tendrils of darkness rose up and began to bring back the undead that had fallen, some even being stitched together from parts of others.

Not again!

Knox swung his axe again; this time it began to glow with a lethal white light and smashed into the barrier with such force that Knox staggered back as it shattered.

Raising his hand, he let loose a powerful Luminous Surge, taking the captain off his feet. It wouldn't be enough though, and Knox knew it. Reaching down, he ripped free his first binding ring, his body felt like fire the moment it came off, but he was all the stronger for it.

Swiping to his left, he took the head off a necromancer approaching him and then turning right he took another in the gut.

He was a whirlwind of power and force, cutting and striking out with his spells until finally he stood before Captain Dread.

"You'll never defeat me," Captain Dread said, then sighing he began to monologue. "You know why I'm destined to win. I've always had…"

His words were cut off as Knox ripped off another ring, throwing himself up beyond A Rank. His body hurt so bad, and he could feel his essence being channeled away into oblivion.

Pulling out his trinket, the one-time use item, he channeled his magic through it and struck out with a Luminous Surge right into Captain Dread's face.

The entire night sky lit up from the force and power of the light that Knox channeled through himself. So powerful and mighty was his strike that he felt hundreds of undead, necromancers, and more hidden figures die before his strike. But through it all, he still sensed the captain. His attack cut off, his trinket falling to pieces, and he fell to the ground, overwhelmed by the sheer power he'd wielded.

Moving as fast as he could, he put his rings back on and saw that he'd only lost two levels.

Had he done it? He didn't know and his sense was so frazzled by everything going on around him that he couldn't check until he made it to his feet. In front of him, standing with his hands out and most of his flesh burnt away, was Captain Dread.

He looked more undead than alive, with black goo dripping from every wound that covered his body.

"No," Knox said, his words barely above a whisper. He'd given it all he had, used his most powerful attack and trinket, and it hadn't been enough. What was this Captain Dread made of?

But it wasn't all for naught, Knox realized as he hefted his axe up to strike out once more. He'd killed hundreds of undead and obliterated a number of Dread's necromancers. Besides all that, the force of power coming off of Captain Dread was less than half that it was before.

Regardless, he'd put himself out of place and now found himself surrounded. He had plenty of power left in him to fight against these encroaching enemies, but standing there all alone, he wondered if he'd make it out alive.

Then a cry went up behind him and he turned just in time to see a group fighting to reach his position. Terrim at the lead, smashing and cutting. Beth shooting arrows while her Dog ripped apart anything that came near. Murdoch, slashing throats and killing undead one swish of his sword at a time. Then came Frederick, Dernal, John, Leo, and surprisingly, his father. Each of them fought with vigor and strength, but the numbers they faced seemed insurmountable.

So, Knox turned and made a path. His Luminous Surge wasn't nearly as powerful as it had been a moment before, but it cut down undead all the same. He fought tooth and nail until he came to fight with his friends.

"Let's go!" Terrim called out, beginning to retreat now that they'd reached Knox.

"We've got to end this," Knox called back over the din of battle. "Push forward and together we will put an end to Captain Dread!"

Terrim nodded once and then took up a battle cry that was all too familiar to them by now.

"To death!" he called out and it was answered by the rest. "To death!"

And so, they did walk into the maw of death together. Each strike bringing them closer to their goal, each wound they took making them realize how foolhardy such a goal remained to be, but still they continued forward.

Knox cast spells as fast as he could to keep them from being overwhelmed and Leo did the same. His fire shot out like a whip against a superior foe, keeping them at bay so that they could advance.

Askar was the first to fall behind, followed shortly by Frederick. They didn't die, but separated as they were, Knox didn't know how long they'd last. That was when spirits, dozens of them, appeared around Frederick. His mother, his father, his siblings all armored up and with weapons began to fight back the darkness around them. They'd come to defend their kin and it would take more than a few undead to beat them back.

Knox couldn't spare another glance, but he said a silent prayer to the Titans or gods that existed that they'd be alright.

Mid chant, Leo took a sword to the throat from a random undead that broke through their line and fell still. Dernal stopped to try and heal him, but Knox could feel that the worst had already happened.

"He's gone," Knox said, pulling Dernal away.

"He's not gone till I say he is!" Dernal screamed the words. Reaching down he chanted a few phrases and his Celestial Guardian appeared, fighting beside them.

"I can return him, stand aside, but be warned, you will lose your connection with me as it'll take much of what I am to do this," the Celestial Guardian said, his words so deep and vibrating.

"Do it!" Dernal snarled the words, his own powers healing the wound on his neck and spine, but still Knox couldn't feel anything from Leo and the battle was getting worse all around them.

The giant Celestial Guardian poofed into a spray of golden light and it rushed into Leo. With his sense, Knox could feel something being pulled back into Leo, whether it was his spirit or his life force, he couldn't tell, but suddenly Leo sat up and blinked.

"You alright?" Knox asked, Leo only nodded and got to his feet. He began casting immediately, fire coming to cover him from head to toe but not burning him. His staff surged with power as he unleashed its ability.

A blast of fire cleared out all the way to Captain Dread and they ran forward as soon as it dissipated to come face to face with their opponent.

"He's weaker than he was, but he is still strong, so be careful," Knox called out to his companions as they all readied their strongest attacks.

Captain Dread pulled free a sword and jumped into the air toward Knox. Axe ready, he took the blow right on the shaft of his weapon and turned it aside. He felt a flash of energy behind him and suddenly he felt refreshed.

Fire lanced at the pirate, and he took a step back, but whatever was keeping him going wasn't going to be stopped by fire. Knox let off another Luminous Surge, followed by a Radiant Stomp, light lancing all around. Then spell after spell he tried to tie up the pirate, but he seemed to shrug off everything they threw at him.

Back and forth they fought for what felt like hours, though in fact it was in the realm of seconds or perhaps a minute. Until finally, before Knox was done, he had to try one more powerful attack.

"Buy me some time," Knox shouted as he began to weave together a runic formation to end this fight. Using Radiant Glyph he began his work.

He watched as Terrim came forward, slamming his shield into Dread's face, and Beth and Murdoch cutting into him as he did so. Fire intercepted a shadow bolt headed for Knox's head and Dernal kept them all fresh with heals.

Second after painful second, they fought and began to lose as Knox prepared his final spell.

Pain lanced up his back as someone took a lucky stab but moments later it was healed. Dernal was working overtime throwing heals left and right.

Finally, the spell finished, and Knox called out for everyone to get clear. Casting his Luminous Surge into the formation he felt it begin to work. Knox threw all the power he could into the spell formation, and it began to bubble over, light spilling here and there.

With a powerful bang the spell went off and it struck the Dread Pirate's shield, shattering it on contact. He started to say something, but the power overwhelmed him before his words came out.

And just like that, Captain Dread fell dead.

Instead of turning the tide of the battle as Knox had hoped, the undead seemed to fight with a renewed frenzy. They retreated in the chaos back toward the walls, the Ahtora coming out to aid them in their retreat. By the time they got back into the walls, the entire complex was swarming with undead, and people were dying left and right.

"Why aren't they unanimating?" Knox asked no one in particular.

"That black goo is keeping them going," Dernal said, and sure enough when Knox looked, he saw that each undead had some of that black goo on it.

The only good news that Knox could tell from the turn of the tides was that even the pirates were being attacked by the undead now, with only a small portion of undead still fighting to defend the few necromancers left.

Chaos ruled the day and fighting turned bloody.

Knox and his forces were pushed back all the way to the center of the complex, where Mic controlled the golems from the command chair.

"What are we going to do?" Beth asked, she'd run out of arrows and now fought with long daggers.

"Keep fighting," Knox said, though he knew that it was hopeless. There were just too many undead and the black goo was rising up any that fell to fight as well.

"Portals activating," Mic said as Knox entered the command room to see swirling blue lights behind the command chair. "We have incoming!"

CHAPTER 40
NEW ARRIVALS

THE GROUND SHOOK and the battle seemed to pause as everyone took a breath and looked at the open portal. Who or what could they expect, and how would they fight off another opponent when they were already neck deep in a battle with an unstoppable foe?

"Can we do anything to close it?" Knox asked as he ran up to Mic and put his hand on the command chair.

"It's too late, the power incoming is too great to hold off any longer, whatever is coming, it's here," Mic said.

From inside the portal Knox could sense an immensely powerful being emerging. What stumbled out did not carry any of that look of power, but his sense confirmed the skeletally thin man who emerged was the one who wielded it.

"Uh, excuse me, but do you have anything to eat? I'm afraid I'm a bit starving," the man said, before collapsing in a heap outside the portal.

"Friend or foe?" Knox asked Mic, but he just shook his head as he stared down at the man.

"That power," Mic finally said, looking to Knox with wide eyes. "This man is a Titan."

"Dernal," Knox called, and the squat man appeared mere seconds later. "Heal that man if you can, he might be the key to us getting out of this in one piece."

The ground shook more violently than ever before and suddenly Knox was more worried that the walls around them might collapse.

Dernal did his work, bringing the Titan back to consciousness.

"So thirsty," the man croaked, Dernal gave him some water, pulling out a cracker from someplace he handed that over as well.

The man devoured it and a touch of his color seemed to return. "Sorry about that," he said, standing up. "Allow me to introduce myself. I am-"

"You're Ramses, aren't you?" Knox asked, cutting off the man before he could introduce himself.

"Ah yes, well I have a few more titles than just my namesake, but I suppose it'll do for now," Ramses said.

He looked old, but not because of wrinkles or dusty skin, there was a weight about him, and his eyes spoke of untold centuries lived. He wore simple, black tattered robes, with more holes than not. His eyes were a shimmering blue color and they seemed to burn with power.

Knox felt a kinship to him without knowing why. There was a pull that seemed to come out of nowhere and suddenly he knew he was truly in the presence of another Titan. He could feel the length of his power and how far it outstripped his own.

"Are you here to help?" Knox asked, turning as an undead made it through the wall of defenders. He slashed down with his axe and killed it before it could get much further.

"Oh," Ramses said, seeming surprised by the sudden appearance of the undead. "How unfortune my timing seems to be. I'm actually here to ask help of you, but I can see you've got an infection here that needs rooting out. Take my hand and together we will wipe this evil free of your land."

Ramses stood, albeit slowly, and reached out his hand.

Without knowing why, Knox trusted the man and took his hand. His power surged in a way he'd never felt before and suddenly he felt Ramses taking hold of his power and directing it.

A flash of blue and white light later, undead were dropping all around. Walking hand in hand, everywhere they went the darkness was eradicated and the undead fell to rest, monster and man alike.

It took a solid hour before the army was turned away and the complex freed, but it was a simple matter for Ramses, or at least Knox felt that way as he was connected to him.

Releasing their connection when the remaining pirates fled, only a few undead left to flee with them, Knox fell to his knees in exhaustion.

"I can barely move," Knox said, through shuddered breathes.

"Oh," Ramses said, looking far healthier than he had only an hour before. "I borrowed a touch of your power at the end there, you're young so you'll recover. I, on the other hand, was pretty near death. So, tell me, how long have you been Titan Born and where did my Grimoire get to?"

"Your journal?" Knox asked, knowing what he meant somehow. "It's safe. How did you send it to me all those months ago?"

"Months?" Ramses asked, looking confused. "Oh right, time is so funny. I just sent it ahead of me to the closest Titan, my spell must have gone a bit sideways and sent it to the past. Oh well. I'm sure you wouldn't mind returning it to me. Now that I'm back in civilized lands, I can begin preparations for my grand return. I wonder if any of those old coots are still alive, doubtful, but perhaps I can hold it over their ancestors."

"Thank you," Knox said, ignoring much of the new man's ramblings.

They'd done it, they'd faced off against the impossible and come out ahead. Knox looked around to find his friends, ready to celebrate and mourn those who'd fallen. But the ground shook again and the wall cracked under the force of the shaking.

"Well, that's not good," Ramses said. "You live on a very unstable place, you know that?"

"Can you stop the ground shakes?" Knox asked, wondering at what powers this Titan Born might hold.

Ramses just shrugged. "My element is water. I'm adept at channeling healing and stemming the tides. If it were a mountain of water coming to crush us, then I could be of help. But the ground isn't my prevue."

Calls went up from the wall, the few that remained up there, and Knox turned to join them, using his teleporting spells to get there quickly. To his surprise, Ramses appeared right next to him a moment later.

"Fabulous control of dimensional displacement," he remarked, then appeared on Knox's other side. "However, I think with a bit of study you could do much better."

"I'm busy right now," Knox said, feeling a tiny bit of annoyance build up at the aloof Ramses.

Frederick ran up to Knox and pointed out into the deadman's zone they'd created. It was littered with bodies, but massive cracks had appeared, and figures were emerging. A new host of figures, all wearing black armor or cloaks, and each of them thrumming with untold power.

They were being surrounded by an army of darkness.

"What do we do now?" Frederick asked, panic in his voice.

"Prepare for battle," Knox said, then looking to Ramses he asked, "Do you have anything that will help?"

Ramses looked out at the quickly growing host of dark figures and blinked rapidly before fainting at Knox's feet.

"Looks like we will have to figure this out ourselves," Knox said, cracking his neck to the side.

"To death!" Came a cry from behind him as Terrim made his way up the wall. The survivors chanted the same and for what felt like the hundredth time, they prepared for battle.

Aetex slammed down before the army of darkness and looked

over his shoulder to Knox, giving him a thumbs up. At least they had Aetex on their side again. This battle was going to be one for the history books, win or lose, Knox was ready to give it his all.

The End of Book 2 of the Path of the Titans.

LEAVE A REVIEW

Thank you for reading. Please leave a review!

If you really liked the book, please consider reaching out and telling me what you enjoyed about it at, Timothy.mcgowen1@ gmail.com.

Join my Facebook group and discuss the books at: https://www. facebook.com/groups/234653175151521/

Join my Patreon at: https://www.patreon.com/ TimothyMcGowen

ABOUT THE AUTHOR

 Timothy McGowen, a Kansas-based author, cherishes the joys of family life with his wife and two daughters. His journey in the literary world began in grade school, and it's a passion that continues to flourish. Inspired by the imaginative realms of Terry Brooks and Brandon Sanderson, Timothy endeavors to follow in their footsteps, crafting stories that resonate with fantasy and adventure enthusiasts.

Prior to dedicating himself to the art of storytelling, Timothy honed his skills as a Software Developer, an experience that not only enriched his technical knowledge but also subtly influences his narrative style. This unique blend of technology and creativity is evident in his work, where he seamlessly integrates elements of Fantasy with splashes of Sci-Fi and the innovative concepts of LitRPG/Gamelit.

Timothy's passion for both reading and writing books is the lifeblood of his creative journey. For those who share this enthusiasm, he warmly invites you to join his newsletter. Stay updated with the latest news and embark on an exciting journey with each new book release.

His debut novel Haven Chronicles: Eldritch Knight has sold over a thousand copies of both ebook and audible so far. He writes Fantasy that contains a splash of scifi and Litrpg/Gamelit stories. Consider signing up for my newsletter for news on book releases as they become available.

LITRPG GROUP

Check out this group if you want to gather together and hear about new great LitRPG books.

(https://www.facebook.com/groups/LitRPGGroup/)

LEARN MORE ABOUT LITRPG/GAMELIT GENRE

To learn more about LitRPG & GameLit, talk to authors-myself included-, and just have an awesome time by joining some LitRPG/Gamelit groups.

Here is another LitRPG group you can join if you are looking for the next great read!

Facebook.com/groups/LitRPG.books

List of LitRPG/Gamelit Facebook Groups:

- https://www.facebook.com/groups/ LitRPGReleases/
- https://www.facebook.com/groups/litrpgforum/
- https://www.facebook.com/groups/litrpglegends/
- https://www.facebook.com/groups/LitRPGsociety/
- https://www.facebook.com/groups/AleronKong/

www.ingramcontent.com/pod-product-compliance
Lightning Source LLC
Chambersburg PA
CBHW031029030726
47497CB00004B/1064